CAPTIVE

BOOKS BY IRIS JOHANSEN
(IN ORDER OF PUBLICATION)

EVE DUNCAN SERIES
The Face of Deception
*The Killing Game**
The Search
Body of Lies
*Blind Alley**
*Countdown**
Stalemate
Quicksand
*Blood Game**
*Eight Days to Live**
Chasing the Night
Eve
Quinn
Bonnie
Sleep No More
Taking Eve+
Hunting Eve+
Silencing Eve+*
Shadow Play+
Hide Away+
Night and Day
*Mind Game**
Shattered Mirror
Dark Tribute
Smokescreen
*The Persuasion**
The Bullet
*A Face to Die For^*
*Starring Jane MacGuire
+Featuring Margaret Douglas
^Featuring Riley Smith

CATHERINE LING SERIES
Chasing the Night
What Doesn't Kill You
Live to See Tomorrow
Your Next Breath

KENDRA MICHAELS SERIES
(written with Roy Johansen)
"With Open Eyes" (short story)
Close Your Eyes
Sight Unseen
The Naked Eye
Night Watch
Look Behind You
Double Blind
Hindsight
Blink of an Eye
Killer View (Roy Johansen)

STANDALONES
The Ugly Duckling
Long After Midnight
And Then You Die
Final Target
No One to Trust
Dead Aim
Fatal Tide
Firestorm
On the Run
Killer Dreams
Pandora's Daughter
Silent Thunder (Iris & Roy Johansen)
Dark Summer
Deadlock
Storm Cycle (Iris & Roy Johansen)
Shadow Zone (Iris & Roy Johansen)
The Perfect Witness
No Easy Target (featuring Margaret Douglas)
Vendetta
Chaos (featuring Margaret Douglas)
High Stakes

For a complete list of books by Iris Johansen, as well as previews of upcoming books and information about the author, visit IrisJohansen.com.

CAPTIVE

IRIS JOHANSEN

GRAND CENTRAL
PUBLISHING

New York Boston

Grand Central Publishing
Hachette Book Group
1290 Avenue of the Americas, New York, NY 10104
grandcentralpublishing.com
twitter.com/grandcentralpub

First Edition: September 2022

Grand Central Publishing is a division of Hachette Book Group, Inc. The Grand Central Publishing name and logo is a trademark of Hachette Book Group, Inc.

The publisher is not responsible for websites (or their content) that are not owned by the publisher.

The Hachette Speakers Bureau provides a wide range of authors for speaking events. To find out more, go to www.hachettespeakersbureau.com or call (866) 376-6591.

Library of Congress Cataloging-in-Publication Data
Names: Johansen, Iris, author.
Title: Captive / Iris Johansen.
Description: First edition. | New York : Grand Central Publishing, 2022. |
    Series: Eve Duncan
Identifiers: LCCN 2022019473 | ISBN 9781538726297 (hardcover) |
    ISBN 9781538726594 (large print) | ISBN 9781538726327 (ebook)
Subjects: LCGFT: Spy fiction. | Thrillers (Fiction)
Classification: LCC PS3560.O275 C37 2022 | DDC 813/.54--dc23/eng
    /20220426
LC record available at https://lccn.loc.gov/2022019473

ISBNs: 978-1-5387-2629-7 (hardcover), 978-1-5387-2659-4 (large print),
978-1-5387-2632-7 (ebook), 978-1-5387-2631-0 (Canadian trade paperback)

Printed in Canada

MRQ-T

10 9 8 7 6 5 4 3 2 1

CAPTIVE

CHAPTER

1

MACDUFF'S RUN
SCOTLAND

W here is she?" MacDuff asked impatiently. "I told you that she wasn't to leave the castle without an escort, Fergus. Yet this is the third time this month that Jane Mac-Guire has slipped away from you."

"It was the fog," Fergus said quickly. "It was heavy this morning and the guards didn't see her go out the gates. She didn't stop to eat breakfast. She probably just took her sketchbook and went up to the hills to do some sketching."

"And no maids or guards saw fit to question why it's almost noon and no one has seen her yet?" MacDuff asked caustically. "I made a promise, and I don't like the thought of breaking it. Do you understand?"

"Of course, my lord," Fergus said. "I take full responsibility. Everyone was on alert, and I should have double-checked that Ms. MacGuire realized we didn't want to interfere with her personal freedom." He gestured to the courtyard that was still almost totally lost in fog. "Only watch for possible accidents."

He added gravely, "I didn't believe I had the right to speak to her in those terms. Perhaps it would be better if you explained that to her?"

"Or perhaps I should place a call to Seth Caleb and let you explain to him why you didn't take better care of her?" His voice was low and silky. "Yes, that might be a better way to handle it."

"No, it wouldn't." They still couldn't see Jane, but MacDuff could recognize her voice somewhere on the other side of the fountain. "Stop trying to intimidate him, MacDuff. We both know it's my fault." She was crossing the courtyard toward the steps. She was wearing a brown leather jacket over taupe suede pants and carrying a sketch portfolio over her shoulder. She smiled at Fergus as she climbed the steps toward them. "Sorry, Fergus. I thought I'd be back an hour before this. I got...involved. When I woke and saw the fog, I knew I wasn't going to want company."

"That's quite all right," Fergus smiled back at her. "But I'd appreciate seeing what involved you if I was going to suffer for it. Will you show it to me?"

She nodded. "Tomorrow. But you weren't going to suffer. MacDuff was bluffing."

"Don't be too sure," MacDuff said dryly. "I wasn't going to be the one to take the brunt of Caleb's irritation when he found out you'd disappeared for half the day." He gestured for Fergus to leave. "But she's right, it's her fault, so we'll let her handle Caleb." He turned back to Jane. "Since you're the only one who appears to be able to do it. You didn't have breakfast? Would you care for tea and biscuits?"

She nodded. "I'm starved." She followed him into the library. "And I really am sorry I caused a ruckus. I've just been surrounded by people ever since I got here, and I needed some alone time."

"I might be persuaded to forgive you," MacDuff said as he gestured to a seat on the couch. "As long as I get a glimpse of that sketch before you show it to Fergus. I refuse to be in second place. It must have been a masterstroke of inspiration that sent you out into the fog." He buzzed for the housekeeper. "Was it worth it?"

"It was for me." She leaned back on the cushions. "But I don't know if it will be worthwhile to anyone else. We all have our own values."

"Well, there's evidently an entire art world that embraces your values," MacDuff said. "I had to take out a loan to pay for that landscape I bought at your last gallery exhibit."

"Bullshit." Jane grinned. "Poor MacDuff. Remember, I was the one who went with you to the Royal Bank of Scotland when you deposited that family treasure. I believe you can afford to buy a few of my humble offerings."

"Perhaps." He watched her take the cup of tea the housekeeper served her. "But keeping it to a few is the problem. Every time you come for a visit you paint several 'offerings' that I want to buy." He made a face. "And sometimes you won't let me buy them. Not fair, Jane."

"Very fair," Jane said. "I've always loved MacDuff's Run. I have a right to keep the ones that I have a particular fondness for."

"And MacDuff's Run has always loved you," MacDuff said. "Did I tell you that Caleb tried to buy the portrait of Fiona again before he flew out after dropping you here? He never gives up."

"Why should that surprise you? It's always been difficult for

Caleb to keep from taking whatever he wants. It's just been a matter of selection." Jane took a sip of her tea. "He's Seth Caleb and even MI6 comes knocking on his door when he lets them know he's available."

"Do I detect a little bitterness?" MacDuff's gaze narrowed on her face. "Was there some reason he brought you here rather than taking you to his house near Sky Island?"

"No bitterness. He felt safer about leaving me here with you." She smiled crookedly. "Because he knew he'd have someone to blame if anything happened to me. As evidenced by your totally unreasonable response to poor Fergus today."

MacDuff frowned. "Fergus should have known where you were. I gave him his orders when you walked through that door this time."

"As dictated by you and Caleb." She nibbled on a bun. "I told you, I didn't want to have company today. I've put up with having your very efficient employees trailing me around since I got here. I'll try to keep doing it until it's time for me to leave. But don't push it, MacDuff. I always enjoy being here with you, but I won't feel like a prisoner."

"Tell that to Caleb," MacDuff said bluntly. "You know that he has enemies galore who would like nothing better than to bring you down. Caleb has a target on his back whenever he's given an assignment. He's a unique weapon, and if they can't get to him, you'll do fine. It's happened before, it could happen again."

"I can take care of myself. What with Joe, Eve, and Caleb, I'm very well trained. You know that, MacDuff."

"Then why did he send you to me?"

"Could it be because you're an earl, you're a war hero, and you have Parliament at your beck and call? Those are pretty impressive credentials." She grinned. "And I let him send me because I was feeling guilty. I'd asked him not to accept any assignments while Eve and Joe were going to be tied up with keeping their son, Michael, safe. They trust Caleb and their lives had become awkward, even dangerous, and they were really grateful to have him there as a safeguard." She lifted her shoulders in a half shrug. "But now that they're heading back to their lake cottage in Atlanta, there's no reason for Caleb to refuse any more assignments. So, I told him I needed to work and to go away and not bother me."

"And he immediately obeyed you?" He shook his head. "I don't think so. The last time I saw you together he couldn't let you out of his sight." He was studying her face. "And you were thinking about marriage. What happened?"

"Life got in the way," she said. "We had to delay quite a few things. But so did the entire world. We'll get around to it."

"Will you?" MacDuff asked. "That doesn't sound like you."

"Maybe I've changed."

"Not that much. You've always been stubborn as a mule once you've made up your mind. And I tried, but I couldn't change your mind about Caleb. All that passion..." MacDuff smiled. "He almost had you hypnotized. I believe I'll have to study the situation. There has to be a reason. What did he do to you?"

"Nothing." She finished her tea and set the cup in the saucer. "Caleb is almost perfect. I couldn't be happier with our arrangement. Stop probing, MacDuff."

"It's my nature." His eyes were twinkling. "And you calling Caleb almost perfect really annoys me. I prefer to be the only person given that designation. Particularly since I don't like the tendency he has to order me around when everyone knows I'm far superior."

"I can see the problem," she said gravely. "But you'll have to take it up with Caleb."

"Sometimes that's difficult. Where did MI6 send him this time?"

"Somewhere near the Congo I believe. I really don't know. He doesn't discuss his business unless it directly concerns me."

"Until then you just sit and wait meekly for him to come back to you?"

"No, it depends how much it concerns me." Her lips were twitching. "I might go after him. After all, one doesn't let a man that close to perfection just wander off. There aren't that many around."

MacDuff flinched. "Wicked."

She chuckled. "You deserved it. Any other questions?"

He nodded at her leather art portfolio. "When am I going to get to see the new sketch?"

"Now." She unfastened the latch and pulled out her sketchbook. "But you might not even like it. It's different from what I usually do. It just seemed...right. I looked out at the fog in the courtyard this morning and something seemed to be waiting for me there..."

MacDuff's brows lifted. "Something?"

She shrugged. "*She* was waiting for me."

"Interesting." He added as he opened the sketchbook, "And familiar..." His expression remained impassive as he studied the black-and-white sketch of the little girl sitting on the bank of a creek. Her curly hair was tousled, and her face was full of wonder and excitement. "Charming. How old?"

"Six. Seven," Jane said. "How do I know? It's not as if

I've ever seen her before. I was settling myself down by the creek and idly starting to sketch the trees when her face just appeared on the pad. The sketch was pure imagination. Which isn't at all unusual as far as I'm concerned. Sometimes it just happens." She frowned. "Though she looked familiar to me, too. I thought I might have seen her here at the Run. Do you recognize her? Does she live in the village?"

"Not as far as I know. I'll ask Fergus," he added absently as he studied the sketch. "Very familiar...maybe if I study it a little longer." He suddenly looked up at her. "And I do like the sketch. Will you let me buy it?"

"What?" She gazed at him incredulously. "Just because she looks familiar?"

"Why not?" He smiled recklessly. "You can't have any special attachment for it since it literally appeared out of the fog for you. I won't cheat you. You'll get your usual fee and I'll get a genuine MacGuire." He winked. "That was created on my property and might even be the child of one of my employees."

She stared at him uncertainly. "Or might not. If she is, it would only be a reason for me to offer the sketch to her parents. It would mean something to them."

He made a face. "Are you making this a bidding war? With anyone else I could have relied on pure selfishness. You've always been a great disappointment to me."

"Money isn't everything. Stop pretending that you think it is." She was studying the sketch again. "She's very young, and maybe her parents are also young. They might not have an opportunity to get a painting of her at this age again." She brushed her index finger over the child's cheek. "I believe I'll call the sketch the *Mist Child*. She looks like she was touched by the mist, and it's still clinging to her hair. She's so...alive."

He sighed. "And I've lost out on buying the sketch unless I can prove she's only your imagination and not one of my employees' progeny?"

"I'd consider it," Jane said. "But I've spent too many years watching Eve try to bring children home to their parents with her reconstructions to treat that search with anything but respect." She smiled. "I'd welcome the kid being my imagination. That can be magical to an artist, too. So why don't you ask Fergus, and you might get lucky." She took the camera out of her art bag, shot a few photos of the sketch, and texted them to MacDuff. "But you'll have to show him the photos. I'm taking the sketch upstairs to my room to work on a little more. Okay?"

"Okay," he said. "As if I have a choice. I don't blame you for not wanting to let her go. After I talk to Fergus, I'll call you and let you know if you're going to be rich or philanthropic." He gave a last look at the sketch. "She does look like the mist is clinging to her..."

Jane put the sketchbook in her case. "It has potential. Maybe I'll decide to finish it." She headed for the arched doorway. "It isn't often that a subject appears out of the blue to an artist with such precise detail. It's like being given a gift."

"Not precise detail," he said. "It's a black-and-white sketch. Lack of color always has limits. The eyes are dark, but so is that riot of curly hair the kid has. Is that how you saw it?"

"Maybe." She grinned back at him. "Or maybe not. I wasn't seeing much. I was only getting down whatever I could, as fast as I could, while I still had the fever. I'll take a look at it later. Or perhaps you can ask Fergus if he's seen the kid around the village."

"I'll do that." He tilted his head. "Because it doesn't seem quite right to me."

"Now you're an art critic?"

"I know what I like." He was looking down at his photo. "And that usually satisfies me. So does this sketch. There's just something a little . . . off." He waved her out of the library. "Go finish the sketch. I'll see you at lunch. Maybe one of us will come up with an answer before that."

"Yes, my lord," she said solemnly. "Whatever you say. But I should remind you that I usually rely on my own answers when it comes to either my work or my personal affairs."

"That doesn't mean they're always correct," MacDuff said with a catlike smile. "I might trust your vision about your work. But what about Seth Caleb? There aren't many people who'd argue that he's not a threat."

"Except me," she said coolly. "And threat or not, we both know there's no one you'd rather have in your corner than Caleb if the going got rough. So drop it, MacDuff. See you at lunch." She closed the door behind her and headed for the grand staircase.

———◆———

She wasn't really annoyed with MacDuff, Jane thought resignedly. They'd known each other far too long. Most of the time the barbed interplay between him and Caleb even amused her. MacDuff was everything a laird should be with his tall, well-muscled body and the intelligence that shone out of those keen gray-blue eyes. But that intelligence could be deliberately obstructive when he decided to exert the half-mischievous, half-mocking side of his character. Or perhaps it was just that she'd been aware from the moment she'd opened her eyes this morning that she hadn't seen or spoken to Caleb for the last two weeks, and it hurt more than usual. He'd told her that might be the case before he'd left, and it wasn't as if she wasn't accustomed to the demands MI6 and other agencies and world organizations periodically made on Caleb. Because he was totally unique, they called on him when there was a dictator to erase, a rogue government that needed taking down, a brilliant scientist to be extracted, or any other complicated situation that no one else could handle. And it wasn't as if he even accepted every assignment. As she'd told MacDuff, just recently he'd spent months with Jane guarding her family. He and Jane both had their own careers, and she was being unfair to ask any more of him. All he asked of her when he was on one of those damn assignments was that she let him make arrangements so that he'd know she was safe. Like this stay at MacDuff's Run, where she had MacDuff and his guards keeping a constant eye on her, she thought ruefully. But she hadn't kept that promise to Caleb today; from the moment she'd opened her eyes this morning she'd felt lonely and on edge and wanted desperately to see Caleb, touch him, be with him. It had been an emotion that she couldn't deny, so she'd played truant and gone out into the fog to try to forget everything but her own work. An action that had gotten poor Fergus in trouble, she thought guiltily. She'd have to make it up to him. Though it wasn't as if she couldn't take care of herself. She'd been raised by Joe Quinn, and her adopted father was not only a detective but a former Navy SEAL, and he had taught her well. She'd even taken her pistol with her this morning for additional protection.

And she was making excuses, she realized. Caleb had asked a favor and she'd made a promise. She didn't know why she'd been impatient enough to break that promise today. It was immature, not like her, and yet that impatience had been growing steadily for the last week she'd been here.

Forget it. She'd just be sure that it wouldn't happen again. Though she knew that she'd have to confess to him that she'd broken her word. Honesty was essential in their relationship. There were already too many hazards to overcome without risking another one.

Hazard. She felt a chill. Why had that word occurred to her? There had been no real threat to her today. She had felt perfectly safe. And certainly, she had not been worried about Caleb. The entire world knew what a badass he was.

But that didn't mean that he couldn't be touched. That might be why she had woken this morning with that sense of panic.

Steady. Only imagination. She started up the steps. She'd go upstairs to her room and finish her sketch. Then she'd go down for lunch and talk with MacDuff and perhaps Fergus. By that time, she'd be calm, and this foolish case of nerves would have vanished.

And maybe in a day or two she'd hear from Caleb, and he'd tell her when he'd be coming back...

SAVGARD AIRPORT
CONGO

Caleb's phone was ringing.

Gavin Jennings.

He'd better take it. "You got my message about Zeller? Just

get the hell out of there. I can't talk now. I'm going to check out the airport. I'll get back to you when I reach Rome."

"*If* you reach Rome," Jennings said sourly. "If you even get out of that hellhole before they cut your bloody head off like they did Zeller's. We all have to get the hell out of here. And you can't use the airport. I've heard it's been compromised. They have to know about you, dammit."

"I figured that out," Caleb said dryly. "I found Zeller's body and it wasn't pretty. They had a good time with him before they beheaded him. He would have told them anything they wanted to know." He paused. "But I was hoping that you'd just get out when I notified you. There was a chance that Zeller wouldn't have told Hugh Bohdan about anyone but me. You and Pasternak were part of his basic MI6 team. You were like brothers. He would have tried to save you."

"You don't know what you're talking about," Jennings said roughly. "All three of us had our orders to keep you alive until you took down General Rozkor. After you accomplished your mission naturally Zeller would have wanted to protect you."

"You're thinking of him only as a professional," Caleb said. "But I knew from the moment I met him that I'd have to probe deeper. It was clear people and relationships meant too much to Zeller. When a man is suffering torture, his motivation has to go beyond any mission or paycheck. He would have been loyal to me, devoted to his job, but he would have died for either of you. I was hoping you'd get out of Savgard airspace before Bohdan tied Zeller to you."

"Well, I didn't," Jennings said curtly. "I had to do my job. Just like you did yours. I noticed you took out Bohdan's four bodyguards outside the warehouse even before you eliminated the general. Nice job. Though it doesn't make up for what happened to Zeller."

"Stop talking and start moving. I told you to get out of the country."

"Pasternak and I are on the run. I just wanted to warn you not to head for the airport. The whole town is in an uproar. We'll pick you up and take you over the border."

"Too late," Caleb said impatiently. "No one is supposed to know I have anything to do with eliminating the general. I'm not going to be seen with you. I'll avoid the airport and get myself over the border."

"You know Bohdan has you on his hit list," Jennings said. "The crazy bastard will have everyone from his own men to Isis searching for you."

"Then I suggest you get your director at MI6 to send you far away to some deserted island so that they won't find you until I get rid of Bohdan. As soon as I reach Rome, I'll notify your chief I told you to go undercover."

"Yeah, sure." Jennings paused. "You mean it?"

"I mean it," he said flatly. "You won't hear from me after I hang up, but that might not help with Bohdan. He was the general's second in command, and he was lusting to take over the entire business. Now that I've eliminated his competition, he'll think he has to prove himself all over again. He'll be on the hunt, and he'll track you down because you'll be one of his only leads to me. The stakes on this job were too enormous. Bohdan bragged that no one could take down the general as long as he was in charge of his mercenaries. You know he was damn good at that. Any threat and they ended up like Zeller. That's why he has to make an example of me." His lips twisted. "So if Zeller also told him about you, then you'll be on his list, too. He'll be going after you. If you're stupid enough to stick around and try to obey orders and do your duty to save me, you'll be disappointed. Just get out of here. I don't need you. You'll be in my way." He paused. "Take care of yourself."

"We will. Who needs you? I'll report back to the director that you completed your mission when I get back to London."

"Send him a text from that desert island I mentioned. Good luck, Jennings." He cut the connection and took off through the woods in the opposite direction from the airport. It would take him about thirty minutes to reach Kelly's cabin, where he could steal a vehicle that he could use to get to the border. Unless the borders had already been closed, then he'd find another way. There was always another route if one failed. But it might be close, and he had to be very sure to cover his bases. Bohdan was the crazy bastard Jennings had called him, and he knew that the hunt would already be on. He'd prefer not to be cornered here where Bohdan had a virtual army to call on. Better to set up the conflict on his own turf.

But first make sure both his valuable assets and that turf were absolutely protected.

He reached for his phone and quickly dialed.

"Speak of the devil," MacDuff said when he answered the call. "I was just talking about you earlier today with Jane. But it's really not too interesting having discussions about you with her. She persists in defending you whether or not she really believes you're innocent of all the things we've all heard about you. Perhaps she feels sorry for you? What do you think?"

"I think that emotion doesn't enter into our relationship, and you're trying to find a way to annoy me," Caleb said. "How is she?"

"Well, she started a new sketch that I'm trying to buy from

her. It's extraordinary. Different...Why don't you ask her yourself how she is?"

"I will. I just wanted to make sure that you hadn't bored her so badly she'd decided to run back to London."

"She's never bored here. She *belongs* here."

"That's what you've kept telling her since you first met her, when you showed her that portrait of Fiona. She does love it at MacDuff's Run, but she belongs where she wants to belong. And it's always been with Eve and Joe. Not with me, not with you. So stop pushing her, MacDuff. I don't want her bolting on you."

MacDuff was silent. "Bolting? Is that why you called me?" He paused. "I wonder why. Is there something wrong?"

"Possibly. Not at the moment, but I thought it wouldn't hurt to check if there are any signs of disturbance on the horizon."

MacDuff muttered a curse. "And warn me that you didn't want Jane to go on the run? What the hell are you up to, Caleb?"

"Letting you take care of Jane when I should be the one to do it," Caleb said roughly. "It's safer for her if I don't go anywhere near her for the time being. Though I was hoping that I'd have this problem completely eliminated before it would have a chance of touching her."

"What problem?" MacDuff asked. "And, dammit, she'll *know* about it. We both know that Jane has instincts that are super sharp. Why is it safer for her?"

Caleb paused. "Because MI6 convinced me that I should rid the world of General Niko Rozkor before he could give the orders to have his mercenaries butcher the opposition party in Savgard who have been trying to boot him out of power. He couldn't be touched by the courts or local government. They were all on his payroll."

"I've heard of the bastard. And you did it?"

"Yes, how could I resist? It was a challenge. I have a dislike for butchers. He'd set himself up as dictator and has already had Bohdan, his second in command, start drafting the young boys in the village to serve in his army. I agreed with MI6 that it was time to put a stop to it."

"But you still think they'll be coming after you?"

"Probably. Bohdan is a narcissistic bastard and I made him look bad. I didn't have the chance to take him out at the same time I went after the general. But he's not stupid, and I don't want to take any chances that he might find out about Jane and zero in on her instead. I'll get MI6 to keep an eye on your property and she should be perfectly safe there with you, but it wouldn't hurt if you arranged for additional security."

"Of course," MacDuff said curtly. "I won't let anything happen to her. But if you're calling on MI6, you're more worried than I thought." He paused. "And I can't believe you're leaving this entirely in my hands."

"I didn't say that. I only said it was better if I wasn't seen anywhere near her. I don't want anyone to believe she has any importance to me."

"Then you definitely shouldn't be seen with her," MacDuff said sourly. "You're fairly transparent."

"Am I? That's not the usual impression I give. Perhaps only to old and perceptive friends. I have to hang up now. Goodbye, MacDuff."

"What do you want me to tell Jane?"

"Nothing. I'll talk to her myself. I'm just in a bit of a hurry right now."

"I can imagine," he said flatly. "Are you going to tell her the truth?"

"Of course." His voice was slightly mocking. "I always tell her the truth. No matter how difficult. I learned a long time ago that would be the only way I have any chance of keeping her. There are too many people like you ready to give her advice about sending me on my way."

"Wise people."

"Undoubtedly. And someday she might agree, but I'll fight it as long as I can." He cut the connection.

CHAPTER

2

SAVGARD JUNGLE
CONGO

Caleb ducked behind the tall buttress roots of a lombi tree, where he removed his phone battery and pocketed it. He'd been assured that the MI6-issued phone was untraceable when not in use, but you couldn't be too careful when dealing with a well-funded butcher like Bohdan.

He felt vibrations beneath his feet and heard a low rumble from the east. Dammit. Heavy military equipment on the nearby jungle roads, no doubt, marshaled for one reason: to find and capture him. The armies had mobilized faster than he'd expected.

He was certain there were already dozens of troops swarming through the trees, and hundreds more would be arriving within minutes. No time to waste.

He crouched low and bolted through the foliage, knowing that the dense vegetation could harbor poisonous snakes and monitor lizards. At least it would offer some cover against the sentries.

He cocked his head. Was that a helicopter in the distance? He listened. Not just one, but *two* copters. Bohdan wasn't playing around.

Caleb felt something slither by his ankle. Probably a snake. Keep moving.

He traveled over a mile without seeing Bohdan's men, but then he heard voices on the other side of a low ridge. Caleb dropped low and crawled toward the ridge's rim on his stomach. He reached for his binoculars but quickly realized there was no need. An entire unit of seventy to eighty men was less than a hundred yards away, spread evenly in a line search formation. They were surprisingly well trained, he thought, and equipped with the latest weaponry and uniforms. Bohdan had obviously invested heavily in his army.

Bad luck.

He needed to punch a hole in that search line, but how?

He turned and looked back. The hillside behind jutted out in three places that would cause the line to part at least momentarily. Maybe he could exploit that...

Caleb scrambled down the hillside and leaped into a clump of large cane plants. He peered through the thick stems at the approaching troops. Their automatic weapons were drawn, and they jabbed their gun barrels into every clump of vegetation they passed.

As predicted, the line parted as it neared him. A hawk-faced older soldier jabbed his automatic rifle through the large leaves.

Caleb ducked. A near-miss.

Another jab. Caleb spun around to avoid the gun barrel as it landed inches from his chest. Before the soldier could draw the gun back, Caleb lunged forward, gripped the man's right forearm, and pulled him into the clump of plants. The soldier opened his mouth to scream, but Caleb drew his knife and slashed the man's throat.

He clasped his hand over the soldier's mouth. It was over in under a minute.

Caleb looked through the cane plants to see that the line had re-formed at the bottom of the ridge. So far, no one missed their fallen comrade.

But it was still a long way to the border.

———◆———

Helicopter pilot Gaius Diehl dropped below the tree line as he flew across a clearing. His gunner, Glen Bowers, had sworn he saw something at the bottom of the hill.

Bowers pointed. "There!"

Diehl slowed and banked around for a better look. There was a blood-soaked soldier sprawled in the clearing.

"He's one of ours," Bowers said. "Looks like he's dead."

"I'll radio it in."

While Diehl radioed for instructions, Bowers squinted at the wounded man. "Wait. He's alive!"

"Are you sure?"

"Yes. He just moved."

Diehl updated Central Command and looked back toward his partner. Since coming home from Iraq and accepting their jobs with Bohdan's army, their assignments had mostly been about escorting drug shipments through the jungle. They'd never been tasked to track someone before.

Bohdan himself came on the radio with the order: "Bring him in. But watch the jungle. The bastard might be trying for an ambush."

"Roger."

Diehl swung wide and descended to the clearing. Bowers leveled his mounted gun toward the jungle.

The soldier rolled over as the helicopter's rotors kicked up a tornado of fine dirt. The uniform was even bloodier in back, Diehl thought.

He touched down just twenty feet from the soldier, and Bowers leaped from the open hatch. He ran toward the wounded soldier, who looked up and managed a faint nod. With support from Bowers, the man stood and limped back toward the helicopter hatch.

As they readied themselves to climb aboard, Bowers suddenly tensed. "Stop. Something's not right." The wounded soldier whirled, raised his gun and fired eight quick shots into Bowers's chest.

RAT-AT-AT-AT-AT-AT-AT!

———◆———

Caleb leaped aboard the helicopter and leveled his gun at the pilot. "Don't move."

The pilot stared at him in shock. "You're not one of ours."

Caleb gestured down to the too-tight bloodstained uniform. "I assume this would fit better if I was."

The pilot craned his neck to see his dead partner on the ground outside. He looked back up with anger and sadness. "You killed a great man. Bowers was my friend."

"If he was a great man, he wouldn't be working for a monster like Bohdan. And neither would you."

The pilot crossed his arms in front of him. "I'm not taking you anywhere. You'll just have to kill me too."

Caleb nodded and looked over the instrument panel. "I've

never flown an Mi-26 helicopter before, but it can't be that different than a Mi-24. Can it?"

The pilot didn't respond.

"You stopped for wounded. I don't really want to kill you. Take your gun out of the holster, toss it onto the floor, and get out." Caleb raised his gun. "Unless you're really wedded to the idea of me blowing your brains out."

The pilot hesitated and then tossed his sidearm onto the floor and stepped toward the hatch. He turned toward Caleb. "Bohdan will find you, wherever you go. You know that, don't you?"

"Let me worry about Bohdan. You'll have enough problems when he finds out that I took the helicopter from you."

The pilot left the helicopter.

Caleb slid into the cockpit and took off. As he increased altitude, he could see the hundreds of soldiers now searching for him in and around the jungle.

The pilot had been right about one thing: Bohdan would never stop looking for him. It would never be over until that son of a bitch was dead.

But that wouldn't happen today, Caleb thought with regret. Soon.

He pulled the flight stick and headed west toward the border.

———◆———

ROYAL PALACE
COUDARA AIRPORT
CONGO

"You fool." Bohdan whirled on George Chiswick in a fury. "Did you actually let this Seth Caleb leave the country? What good are you? I told you that I wanted to make an example of him. Fear is the only thing that's keeping the troops in line right now. I won't have someone else stepping up and pushing me aside when I'm this close to taking over the entire country."

"No one would do that," Chiswick said quickly. "They're all afraid of you. I've sent a troop to Savgard Airport and one to the border. I'm sure we'll locate him soon."

"How? We didn't even know the bastard was in the country before he managed to get close enough to the general to take him down. Who the hell is he?"

"We found out a few details from Zeller before we killed him. Caleb was a special agent from MI6. Very special. They only send him on assignments that require a certain skill and expertise. He moves in like a ghost, stalks the prey, and then takes him down. Then he's gone again. He never misses and has a good many other talents that are unusual. I'm afraid we wouldn't have known even that much if Zeller hadn't been identified as MI6 by one of our men. We were able to catch him and force him to reveal Caleb's mission." He added apologetically, "I would have learned more, but you were so furious with Zeller that you wanted him dead. I didn't have time for any other questions. I do know he was working with Agents Jennings and Pasternak. I'll access my contacts and find out more for you."

"See that you do." He scowled. "Caleb's like a ghost? I'll make a ghost out of him all right. I can't wait to bring him back and show everyone how I treat a son of a bitch who has the nerve to get in my way."

"One more question," Chiswick said. "What do I do with Diehl, the helicopter pilot? He's a good man and valuable to you."

"What do you think you should do? He let Caleb escape. Kill the asshole." He turned on his heel. "Now get busy. Find Caleb. I want to know everything about him."

———◆———

MACDUFF'S RUN
9:40 P.M.

"Dammit, why are you being so quiet, MacDuff?" Jane leaned back in her dining chair, her gaze narrowed on him. "Is something wrong?" She made a face. "Besides the fact that I was so rude to Fergus and won't sell you that sketch. I've already apologized to him, and I may still let you have the blasted sketch. It was just that she looked so familiar to me that it...bothered me. Did you ask Fergus if he recognized any children in the village who looked like that kid in my mystery sketch?"

"Of course I did." MacDuff took a sip of his wine. "Do you think I'd give up anything I wanted so easily? He didn't recognize the child in the photo, so I had him go down to the village this afternoon to talk to his neighbors and the vicar." He sighed. "I'm afraid that mystery child must be a true figment of your imagination, because no one has claimed her. Can you blame me for being depressed? I truly wanted to have a reason to make you give up that sketch to me."

Jane threw back her head and laughed. "Bullshit. You're being a little too dramatic, aren't you? I was just guessing, but now I really want to know why you're being so moody." Her smile ebbed. "Talk to me. Am I being an annoyance you don't want to deal with?"

"If you were, I'd toss you in the sea," he said lightly. "We've

25

never been shy about expressing our true feelings to each other. You know you're always welcome here. Aren't I allowed to have an occasional period of introspection?"

She was silent, studying him. "Yes, but not when I'm not sure what sparked it. I accepted your hospitality not only because we've been friends for years, but because it seemed to make Caleb feel better that I do it. Yet both of those reasons could have ramifications all the way down the line. Though I haven't seen any signs of that yet."

"But you're always on the lookout for trouble." MacDuff shook his head. "What a suspicious woman you are, Jane. Did it ever occur to you how much more peaceful your life would be if Caleb wasn't always hovering in the background?"

"No." She smiled. "But I do realize how infinitely dull it would be."

He shrugged. "Hopeless."

"No, you have no idea how much hope I have." Her gaze was on his face again. "However, I don't believe you're going to tell me why you're so 'introspective.' I suspect it has something to do with Caleb since he appears to have the almost effortless ability to upset you. It's probably because you enjoy sparring with each other, and sometimes he scores."

"Rarely. Or it could be that besides being my friend, I regard you as a member of my family I must protect at all costs." He paused. "Caleb does amuse me, but I also recognize him as a possible threat to you."

"Bullshit." Her gaze narrowed thoughtfully on his face. "That all sounded very Laird of the castle, but I don't think that's why you're being moody." She shrugged. "But I'll find out eventually."

"Because Caleb tells you everything?" he asked caustically.

"You guessed it." She tilted her head. "Or was it a guess?"

"Stop trying to read me." He was suddenly smiling. "If you do, as a reward I'll give you a gift. Everything I told you about Fergus and the villagers was true, but I didn't give up about your *Mist Child*. I put some thought into it and came up with a possible reason why we both thought she looked so familiar." He got to his feet and held out his hand to her. "Want to come and see what I deduced?"

"How can I resist, Sherlock?" She took his hand and jumped to her feet. "You're my host and it's only polite to let you distract me since you're being so secretive."

"Secretive?" His eyes twinkled as he pulled her out of the dining room and down the main hall. "No such thing. That's entirely your imagination. I'm sharing with you now, aren't I?" He was pulling her through the main corridor. "And you're going to be very chagrinned that I was the one who put two and two together before you figured it out for yourself." He turned a corner as he reached the grand gallery. "After all, you're the artist." He turned on the lights in the gallery and threw out his hand in a grandiose gesture toward the far wall. "Though I admit that it was a little difficult to make the connection, you can't deny that your little lost waif does bear a resemblance to our Fiona."

"What?" Jane was staring in bewilderment at the portrait of MacDuff's forebear. "Fiona? I know she's one of your favorite ancestresses, but you're really reaching. Despite the fact that the portrait was painted hundreds of years ago, Fiona was a grown woman when it was done, not a child of six or seven. Where do you see the resemblance?"

MacDuff shrugged. "Her smile. The way she holds her head. Yes, the child's hair is dark and not red like Fiona's, but the expression has the same liveliness. All I can say is that I was glancing at the photo and all of a sudden, I found myself strolling down here to look at Fiona's portrait."

"Because you have a fixation with her," Jane said flatly. "How long have you been trying to convince me that she looks like me and that must mean I'm part of the MacDuff clan? You even tried to get me to have a DNA test when you knew it probably wouldn't be conclusive. Give it up. For goodness' sake, different continents! I believe in choice, and I couldn't be happier that Eve and Joe chose to adopt me." She tried to make her tone kinder. "I know I'm supposed to be flattered, but I'd much rather be your friend than one of those portraits on this wall. It would smother me."

He chuckled. "Why don't you tell me what you really think?"

"Well, you deserve it. You never listen to me."

"Because I believe I'm right and you're wrong. Someday I'll convince you. And I'm not the only one who won't listen. You've refused to hear anything about Fiona or her story since that day I tried to convince you that the two of you were related. You didn't want to believe anything that would disturb the way you felt about your adopted parents."

"Nothing could," Jane said. "And I didn't want to encourage you when I wasn't interested."

"But you're not usually so stubborn about at least listening. You're an artist and that's very close to storytelling. Fiona had a very interesting story that should intrigue you." He continued, "For instance, did you know that our family had no idea whatever about what happened to Fiona? She disappeared from the glen one summer day and was never heard from again. An accident? A dire murder? An enemy of our house who kidnapped her to punish the clan? All the men in the glen

28

searched for weeks trying to find some sign of her. They found nothing." He narrowed his gaze on her face. "And that did intrigue you. See? You should have listened to me before."

"No, I shouldn't. It's a sad story and naturally I was interested. But it has nothing to do with me."

"I've always thought it did. It just seemed too fortuitous for a woman with Fiona's face to appear here at the Run centuries later. You can't blame me for wanting to explore the possibilities." His smile faded. "I guess this may not be the right time to begin." He glanced once more at the portrait of Fiona. "But take a glance at the sketch of the child when you get back to your room. I think it does look a little like Fiona. It's not just because I can't stand not being right about you."

"I wouldn't put it past you. Though it doesn't really matter, does it?"

"In a way it might." He turned away with a shrug. "It reminded me how much I value all the art in this gallery, and with you running around the property, it might not be a bad idea to get a few more guards to protect that, too." He strode out of the gallery as he tossed back over his shoulder, "You demonstrated to me this morning that Fergus has more than enough to do."

Then he was gone, leaving her to stare after him, puzzled. It wasn't like MacDuff to be that abrupt. But then he'd been a little strange all through dinner and the conversation after it. She'd thought everything was normal after she'd left to go up to her room, but perhaps not. She was definitely uneasy. She'd have to go over the conversation and make certain nothing was wrong. MacDuff's Run. MacDuff's distinctly prickly attitude tonight toward Caleb. A few slightly off-key remarks he'd made. Take each element apart and put it back together and it might tell an entirely different story than the one she'd just heard from MacDuff...

———◆———

MACDUFF'S RUN
2:40 A.M.

Jane's phone was ringing...

It didn't wake her. She hadn't been sleeping anyway.

She rolled over in bed, reached over and checked the ID. Caleb. That shocked her. She was immediately uneasy. Usually if she got a call from Caleb when he was on a mission, the ID was blocked. She quickly answered it. "Caleb? What's happening?"

"You're awake and that means I might be in trouble," Caleb said dryly. "Should I have called you earlier?"

"Probably," Jane said. "And I don't know if you're in trouble or not. I suspect it, because MacDuff has been on edge and suddenly decided he needed more guards for his gallery. You wouldn't know anything about that?"

"I might have mentioned it. But I hoped MacDuff would be more subtle."

"He might have been, if he hadn't been absorbed in whatever else you probably discussed. How much trouble are you in?"

"Nothing I can't handle."

"I know that." Her hand clenched on the phone. "Everyone knows that there's nothing you can't handle. It's not only in your DNA, every law enforcement service on the planet has it written in your dossier. That's why they keep calling. I only want to know what you're handling at the moment."

"At the moment, I've finished up an assignment and I'm in Paris." He added roughly, "And what I'm handling is that things aren't going the way I want them to at this particular instant. You're too far away and I want to touch you so much I'm aching. Are you well?"

"Of course. Didn't MacDuff tell you? I'm sure he has, because I'm quite certain that was the briefest part of your discussion." She added curtly, "You checked if I was safe, then told MacDuff why he had to get more guards to make sure MacDuff's Run stayed that way. Right?"

He was silent. "Right," he finally said. "And then I took care of a few details of my own, like getting out of the country. While I gave MacDuff the opportunity to do what I'd asked of him." He added ruefully, "And waited until I could talk to you privately because I knew you'd see right through anything MacDuff told you when he was trying to protect your delicate feelings."

"And you knew I had no delicate feelings to protect," she said ironically. "You were quite right. I only wanted to know the truth so that I could take action if I needed to." She braced herself. "I never ask about the assignments you take because I'd only worry, and no one knows better than I do how good you are at what you do. However, I believe I have to ask this time. You were worried about MacDuff's Run. That strikes close to home. You wouldn't have brought me here if you hadn't thought it was safe. Do I need to leave here? Is MacDuff or any of his employees or villagers going to be in danger because I'm here?"

"No, I only called as a precaution, Jane. None of them are in actual danger as far as I know. The only one who has a bull's-eye painted on his back is me. And since I have no intention of coming back to the Run anytime soon, everyone else should be safe. Both MI6 and MacDuff's men are going to be there to make certain it stays that way."

"And that's supposed to make me feel better?" Jane tried to keep her voice steady. "Not until I know every detail of what's going on. Particularly, that damn bull's-eye. Give me the entire story, Caleb."

She listened carefully, only asking a clarifying question every now and then until he stopped speaking. "Yes, I can see how they'd be a little irritated with you," she said finally. "And I can see how you couldn't resist going after that general and Bohdan. Not only a challenge, but you got a chance to save all those boys being terrorized and forced to be child soldiers by Bohdan."

"Not yet," Caleb said. "Stop making me out to be a hero. I didn't know about the child army recruitment until I got to the Congo. MI6 thought if I got rid of the general in charge that Bohdan's power would dissipate. That's not going to happen. Then Zeller broke under questioning and I had no choice even if I wanted to go after Bohdan. I figure I only got half the job done before I had to go on the run."

She tensed. "So you have to go back?"

"Not necessarily, I'll have to see what can be done."

"But I won't be able to see you, be with you?"

Silence. "Not a good idea. Not for a little while."

She drew a deep breath. "Okay, then let me get this straight. You obviously don't believe the personal danger to me is very great, but you're not willing to take the slightest chance that Bohdan or one of his men might decide that I'm worth using to draw you into a trap. Which means you're leaving me here surrounded by MacDuff's guards and going after the bastard on your own. Is that correct?"

"You know it is," he said wryly. "You have no problem reading me. And it's the most efficient and safest way to handle it, Jane."

"Maybe. I'm sure MI6 and MacDuff and you are in complete agreement about treating me like one of those big-eyed Russian nesting dolls you stack whichever way you want, leaving me out of any decisions. How dare you? I think it *sucks*, Caleb."

"Yes, it does. I knew you'd react like this. I can't help it. I won't risk it. I didn't expect this assignment to involve you in any way. It was just going to be in and out. But it didn't turn out that way." He added, "And you could tell me not to take any more assignments if you think I'm not being fair. I'd listen to you."

"How can I do that?" she asked fiercely. "You're the Hunter. Joe has been a detective for years and Eve would never tell him that he shouldn't take any risk he has to take."

"We both know that the missions I tend to accept are a bit more intense than the usual assignment. It's not quite the same thing."

"Maybe not. But I accepted that I wouldn't be living an ordinary life with you. It was my choice. I won't back down because I'm scared some asshole might target you. I'll just find a way to get around it. You're stuck with me, dammit."

He chuckled. "Whatever you say. Whew, thank God." He added lightly, "I was getting a little uneasy. I recall that you were very adamant about marriage vows being in our near future, but you haven't mentioned it lately."

"I decided that I'd give you a chance to get used to the idea. Everyone knows what a lousy childhood and upbringing you had. Family has always been important to me. I've never wanted you to think marriage and family would be just another burden."

"I believe I could suffer through it. I was beginning to think I was being jilted."

She was silent a moment. "Funny you should mention that wedding. MacDuff asked me about it, too."

"What did you say?"

"That sometimes things change. And that the whole world seems to have changed lately."

"And is that how you feel?"

"Perhaps." She added, "Like I said, sometimes."

Caleb muttered a curse. "Well, then we'll have to have a more in-depth discussion. Because I'm not willing to have anything changed where you're concerned. If you feel any-thing between us needs to be adjusted, come to me and I'll take care of it." He paused. "And I'm angry as hell this Bohdan mess has come up right now. Because I've been thinking lately that there may be something not quite right with you, and I have to find out what's wrong."

"Don't be ridiculous," Jane said curtly. "I'm not the one who's on the run from a mercenary who wants to behead me. I might not be happy about it, but you've explained the problem and now I'll go along with what you've decided is best to protect MacDuff and his people here." She hesitated. "But if the situation changes, let me know right away. I've loved this place since the day I came here years ago to research Cira and the ancestral line of the MacDuff family. MacDuff and his people have always been good to me. I won't stay one more minute if it means I put anyone here in danger. Will you promise me that?"

"You know I will."

"And I want you to call me whenever you get a chance and let me know that no one has managed to separate your head from your body. I've always kind of liked them as a matched set."

"Then I'll be sure to accommodate you. Maybe you have your share of delicate feelings after all. Or it might just be that artistic temperament." He added softly, "I promise I'll finish this up as quickly as I can. Everything is going to be fine."

"I know that." Jane cleared her throat. "But maybe after you get through with saving the Congo, we might go visit Eve and Joe at the lake cottage for a week or two. I'll check with Eve, but I don't believe anyone there has chopped off anyone's head in a long time. That sounds pretty good to me."

"Anywhere you want to go. I'll contact Bezos and see if there are any seats left on the next rocket."

"No, the lake cottage is fine. In the meantime, take care of yourself. I *won't* lose you, Caleb."

"Lose me? No, you won't. Not ever. I'll touch base with you whenever I have news." He cut the connection.

CHAPTER

3

J ane sat there for a moment, staring down at her phone.

Lose me? No, you won't. Not ever.

A few words that meant so much.

Caleb was so confident, so certain that no one could touch him . . . She should be confident, too. She'd been with him long enough to see how competent he could be. But she'd never be that confident until she was allowed into that dark world in which he moved, and that rarely happened these days. He was being as overprotective as MacDuff where she was concerned. Being with him was always exciting, the discussions fascinating and amusing, the sex fantastic, but lately she'd been aware that it was like being taken to the circus and never allowed near the lion cages.

She was being ridiculous. Lion cages? It's not as if she wanted to trail after Caleb on one of those damn missions. She just wanted to make certain that she was a part of his life no matter where he was. Just as Eve was a part of Joe's. It was no coincidence that she'd compared Joe's career and Caleb's

37

missions. Eve had her own career but if there was danger she and Joe would always be together, because they were family.

And perhaps that was what Jane was missing most, that sense of ultimate togetherness that could never be replaced by anything less powerful. She had never really had that with Caleb.

Though sex came pretty damn close, she thought wryly. It was what had held them together before she realized that what she felt for Caleb was far beyond anything she'd felt for anyone else. And that realization was still there and so strong that all this fretting and worrying made no sense unless she was going to do something about it. She turned on the bedside light, got to her feet, and moved over to her sketchbook on the desk across the room. She flipped open the book to the last sketch she'd made of Caleb at the fountain in the courtyard before she'd walked him back to the helicopter.

Bold dark eyes, the faint indention in his chin, the way his lips curved with just a suggestion of mockery and sexuality...Totally fascinating and yet with perhaps a hint of stormy vulnerability that he would never admit even to her.

She walked over to the window and stood there with the moonlight playing over the sketch. Her index finger gently traced that faint indentation in his chin. Then she looked out at the sea crashing against the shore beyond the castle towers.

He'd brought her here to this beautiful place to be safe and then gone off to save another wild part of the planet.

But who was going to save him if something went wrong? Her hand clenched on the sketch. Then she moved away and put the sketch back into her case. There was nothing to do tonight, but she had to consider what was in the future.

She turned out the light and got into bed. Go to sleep.

Think about that imaginary little *Mist Child* she'd sketched, not about Caleb who had never really been a child at all. It hurt too much to remember the pain he'd never talk about. Nor the cynicism that he used as a guardrail. But this couldn't go on. Except for sex they'd been growing further and further apart during the last six months. Even Caleb had been aware that she'd been on edge before he'd left her here at MacDuff's Run.

Caleb was right, they were going to have to have that in-depth discussion he'd spoken about...

Or she might lose him.

———◆———

THE GALLERY
MACDUFF'S RUN
NEXT DAY

"What are you doing in here?" MacDuff asked curiously. "Fergus told me that you've been in here with Fiona for most of the morning. I must be more persuasive than I thought."

Jane turned away from the portrait of Fiona to see him leaning against the doorjamb of the gallery. "You're always persuasive, MacDuff. Between diplomacy and your economic ventures, we're all lost in admiration of the great Lord MacDuff." She made a face. "Not that you've managed to talk me into anything. It just occurred to me that I might have some time to spare while I'm here and I could spend it amusing myself by trying to solve your Fiona mystery. It was an intriguing story, and I can't believe that no one has ever discovered what happened to Fiona. There's no way that I'm any relation to her, but maybe you'll stop nagging me if I can find out something that will satisfy your curiosity."

"It might be a possibility." He crossed his arms across his chest. "But since you came here, you've spent all your time outside on the grounds sketching. Why did you decide to change your routine?"

She shrugged and then said bluntly, "Circumstances, Mac-Duff. And why did you decide to bring in extra guards to watch over the gallery? I'm tired of this bullshit. It seemed the time to make the move."

MacDuff tensed and then relaxed. "I gather Caleb called you last night? He said he would and tell you everything."

"And he did. I wouldn't have accepted anything else. I was particularly impressed by the tales of the beheadings." She shivered. "Caleb seems to think my presence here won't be a threat to your people, but I want you to know that if you have any doubts, I'll leave at once."

"Don't be ridiculous," he said roughly. "You're my good friend. I've arranged for enough extra guards to make this an armed camp." He smiled crookedly. "And I'll enjoy holding it over Caleb's head that I was the one who could keep you safe. That will be particularly satisfying."

"I'm sure it will," Jane said. "But Caleb will probably be too busy to let it bother him. He'll be going after Bohdan. The mission isn't quite finished."

"And you'll be worried." MacDuff paused. "I don't have to tell you that no one is more able to take care of himself than Caleb. He's . . . remarkable."

"No, you don't have to tell me." And right now, she couldn't talk any more about what might wait for Caleb when he returned to that monster Bohdan. "I've seen what he can do." Her gaze went back to the painting of Fiona on the wall. "But evidently I'm not going to be able to do anything about it, any more than I can help Fergus or any of your men here at the Run." Her voice held a tinge of bitterness. "According to both Caleb and you, I'm not equipped for anything more demanding than sitting here and waiting in case, God forbid, someone has to rescue me. And because I've been put in a position where you or your men could be hurt if they'd have to do that, I'll play your game."

He gave a low whistle. "You're very pissed off, and now I'm being thrown in with Caleb. I think I resent that, Jane."

"Tough. That's because you're behaving like Caleb, and you should know better." She added through set teeth, "We've been so close through the years. I first came here to trace Cira, the founder of your family, when she fled here from Herculaneum. I helped you find your family treasure and deliver it to the Bank of Scotland. You were there when Eve and Joe were married. There were so many other times we've been there for each other. You know damn well I can take care of myself."

"Sometimes logic doesn't enter into it," MacDuff said. "And I can almost sympathize with Caleb in this moment. Unfortunately, you've had an even more colorful history with him than with me. I hope you were equally venomous to him last night. It would only be fair."

"He knew I wasn't pleased."

MacDuff shook his head. "But he's your lover, and you were afraid that it might be the last time you heard from him." He sighed. "So you stored it up and attacked me."

She stared at him in frustration. Damn, he was smart. "I didn't mean... It wasn't like that. It was just that neither of you will let me—" She broke off as she saw him smile. "I didn't realize it. I'm sorry. I'll find a way to make it up to you."

"I'm sure you will," MacDuff said gently. "You always do. As I said, sometimes logic doesn't enter into it."

"Well, I can start with Fiona." She took a step closer to the portrait. "That's why I've decided not to make my presence here any more difficult than I have to for all of you. I'll stay inside the castle for the most part instead of moving freely around the grounds."

His brows rose. "No more *Mist Child*?"

"If I choose, I can finish the painting here inside the castle." She smiled. "Or I can give the sketch to you for being so kind as to shelter me. But, as I said, I'll be spending most of my time with your Fiona until I solve her puzzle. It will give me something to do if I need the distraction." She glanced over her shoulder at him. "I'll want to know more about her. Do you have any family literature about Fiona? If there's such a mystery, there must have been some kind of historical data to document it."

"There are a few books about her." He made a face. "Actually, I have to admit that I haven't been entirely honest about Fiona. I guess it's time I cleared up the small discrepancies I might have made regarding her history. Come along to the library and we'll talk and I'll give the books to you. You may know more about her than you think. I'm sure I've mentioned her now and then. Fiona made her mark on this place. It was one of the reasons I could detect a resemblance between the two of you." He smiled. "I'll even give you a cup of tea while I tell you all that I personally know about her. She's one of my favorite ancestresses, and I've been studying her in-depth since I thought I discovered the connection with you."

"Which didn't exist," Jane said firmly.

"We'll see." His eyes were twinkling. "But now I'm at last getting to lure you into my parlor." He waved his hand toward the hall. "Or in this case, my library. That's true progress after all this time."

———

"Only two books?" Jane gazed down at the two slim volumes on her lap that MacDuff had handed her. "You weren't exaggerating. I thought she'd get a bit more attention from your august family."

"August family?" MacDuff repeated. "You have to remember that the MacDuffs had fallen into hard times before Fiona appeared on the scene." He paused. "Which happened about 1852."

Jane was frowning. "No, that can't be correct. The time span wouldn't be right. I remember when you showed me her portrait that I was impressed by the story you told me about her marrying a MacGuire and having five children. You said two of them moved out of her house in the Lowlands to go to America in 1872."

"You have an excellent memory." His eyes were twinkling. "There's only one problem with it."

"What's that?"

"It was a lie." He chuckled when she opened her lips. "That slight discrepancy I mentioned. I thought I reeled off that false family history with amazing detail."

"You *lied* to me? Why would you do that, dammit?"

"I had to have time to search for my family's treasure. I was poor as a church mouse back then, remember?" He shrugged.

"I hadn't found it yet, and I was worried that the castle grounds would be swamped by fortune hunters. The treasure was *mine*; you knew that."

"Of course. I helped you search for it later. But why on earth lie to me about it?"

"I thought that if I could make you believe you had ties to the Run, you'd not only want to keep any fortune hunters from pouncing but might want to stay yourself." He grimaced. "All you wanted to do, though, was go back to your Eve and Joe and forget all about the Run. I could have let you go." He added quietly, "But I couldn't do that, because it wasn't only the treasure that was mine. I was head of the family, Earl of Cranought, the laird. After I saw the portrait, I knew you were mine, too. Part of my family, my kin, and I had to have time to convince you that you belonged here." He shook his head and sighed. "But you're extremely stubborn, Jane. It's taken years and you're still fighting it."

"*I'm* stubborn, MacDuff? You tried to manipulate me."

"Nonsense. I never did anything that I thought was against your best interests. I helped you whenever I could, didn't I? We became good friends."

She couldn't deny it. "There was still something shady about you lying to me."

"It had to be done. It was for the good of MacDuff's Run." He added simply, "The good of our family."

And that was the end-all of every argument as far as MacDuff was concerned, she thought. "Your family, not mine. Back off, MacDuff."

"Our family," he repeated. "Stop fighting it."

"Can't do it. The fight goes on." She reached out and affectionately squeezed his arm. "These days you're rich as Midas and have villages and distant relatives all over the property. You don't need me around. Give it up, MacDuff."

"I'll think about it." Then he smiled. "Nah, I'm a Scot. It's not in my genes."

"You're impossible. I refuse to discuss it." She was carefully turning the stiff pages of the diary. "And there's practically nothing of interest in this journal. No other paintings or portraits like the one in the gallery. Just a few lists and what looks like diagrams." She turned another page. "And this old faded green ribbon that looks like it's going to fall apart."

"I'm surprised it hasn't." MacDuff handed her a cup of tea. "I found the journal and diary buried in a trunk in the attic in the house of Fiona's father, Jamie MacDuff, when I went exploring for the connection with you. They were in pretty sad shape. Yet as soon as I could tell what they were, I set about getting them restored. I wasn't about to let them be lost."

She frowned, puzzled. "And what are they?"

"The ribbon belonged to Fiona. She won it during the athletic games that were held here at the Run. It was sort of our version of the Scottish Olympics, and all the young people participated. Jamie MacDuff was a second son who was something of a black sheep. He was a drunkard and a gambler and seldom visited the Run except when he hit up his brother, Colin, for loans. He owned a house on the border and let his daughter run wild in the Highlands. But she was still allowed to participate in the games here and often won prizes. Those notes and diagrams were because she spent time researching the terrain when there was a race to be won. Take a look, they're in great detail. She evidently liked to win."

"Don't we all," she murmured. She was looking at the sheets again. "Very precise."

"And the reason there were no portraits or sketches was that Jamie didn't have any painted of Fiona until she was grown. He'd sowed all his wild oats and blown what money he had left. Then he decided it was time to use Fiona to become more respectable, so he had her portrait painted and began looking for a match for her. Preferably one that would give him the power he'd always envied his brother, Colin, having." He shrugged. "That's the portrait in the gallery. It's an excellent painting."

"Providing you want to sell a young, vibrant woman to the highest bidder," Jane said grimly. "It's no wonder the artist didn't sign that painting. He must have had a conscience."

"Or he wasn't well enough known to have his identity mean anything important to the patron. Maybe Jamie was too poor to be able to afford anyone but a rank beginner," MacDuff said. "I like your reasoning better. It's probably not historically accurate, though."

She looked down at the book again. "But I bet she must have been a good deal happier when she wrote in this book than when she was posing for that portrait."

"I don't know . . . I think she looks very bold and excited in the painting. Kind of . . . adventurous. Maybe she was looking forward to becoming the head of her own household."

She made a rude sound. "You said that she took part in all those fantastic Scottish games as a young girl. You showed me how hard she worked at winning them. She even drew the rocks and creeks on the property. I doubt if she'd think that being some rich man's glorified housekeeper would thrill her."

"You're speaking from your own viewpoint."

Jane looked down at the diary on her lap. "No, I believe

46

I'm speaking from hers. Did her father find that rich match for Fiona?"

MacDuff nodded. "Alastair Graeme. He was a man in his fifties, no title and not considered to be honorable by any means. He hadn't been a border reiver for years, but he was very, very rich."

"Reiver?" She was searching her mind for the meaning. Then it came to her. "They were raiders along the Anglo-Scottish border from the thirteenth century to the sixteenth century. So, this Graeme was a thief?"

"His family had been raiders for centuries. The practice had almost ended by the time Graeme inherited. But evidently, he was very accomplished and had a good many enemies. Practically no friends or respectable connections. And that could be why he might have taken Jamie MacDuff up on his offer of an arranged marriage with Fiona. The MacDuffs did have a certain status even then."

"Friendless? That might also have put Fiona in a bad position. Besides being forced to marry a husband twice her age."

"But she wasn't forced to marry him. She was betrothed, but she disappeared a week before the actual vows."

"Aha." Jane grinned. "Now, that was the Fiona who won that ribbon. Good for her."

"Don't be so happy about it," he said quietly. "If she did decide to skip out on Alastair, her father would have been furious. I told you he was a son of a bitch. He wouldn't have tolerated the humiliation. There are all kinds of ways to rid yourself of a disobedient daughter. Perhaps throw her down a deep well? Poison? She might have even been buried in the dungeon at Jamie's castle. At any rate, he would have hunted her down. She might not have survived."

Jane's smile vanished. "Or she might have. We don't know, do we? I'll just have to learn more about her." She looked down at the second journal MacDuff had given her. "What's in this one?"

"I don't know. Less than the first one. No memories to ponder over. Addresses, a few names, something that looks like a trunk. Markings that I've never been able to decipher. See if you can."

"I will." She finished her tea. "And then I'll see if I can find out anything more about what she was doing with that damn reiver." She glanced around the library. "You have hundreds of books in here. You said that you found these two books in the attic at Jamie MacDuff's residence. What about his libraries? Were there any other journals besides these books?"

"No, but she was evidently a great reader." He shook his head. "Jamie's library was purely for show. Fancy covers and not much content. Family history says he was no scholar and never picked up a book. He probably didn't even know what he had. Jamie preferred hunting and the card tables. I sent a clerk to look the stock over, but he said none of the books in Jamie's library belonged to Fiona. But evidently, she was a great reader because she told her tutor that she loved Shakespeare and Dickens and poetry."

"Then where are her books?"

He shrugged. "I have no idea. All I could find were those two in the attic." He frowned. "Wait. There are supposed to be a few other items belonging to her in a few of the lower storage rooms at the old stable across from the court-yard. We haven't used that stable for horses since I had the new one built across the lake. But there's never enough storage on the property so I haven't gotten around to having the storage rooms cleaned out. Probably nothing of importance is there, or someone would have brought them to the castle when they were searching for her when she disappeared. As I said, I haven't had time to go through them yet, but feel free to do it yourself." He added, "Though remember that stable and the lower storage rooms are connected directly to the boat dock down on the shore. I should send someone with you."

She made a face. "Another guard? Maybe I'll wait until later." She got to her feet. "I think I'll go back to the gallery and take another look at the portrait. You saw something that I didn't, and I want to know which one of us was right."

"Good idea. Because I always like to be proved correct. I believe I might have a good chance this time."

"What? Don't be cocky, MacDuff."

"Perish the thought." He grinned. "It's just that I could never understand why you weren't impressed whenever you saw the portrait. You were an artist yourself and you must have been able to appreciate the workmanship. But you appeared to ignore it. And then I thought that perhaps it was because Fiona looked so much like you, and you were struggling not to acknowledge it out of loyalty to Eve and Joe. It could be either one, but maybe you'll be able to tell me after you get another look at her today."

"Or maybe I merely got sick and tired of both you and Caleb being so intrigued by her, when you had an entire gallery of fantastic paintings that were probably just as remarkable."

"Not to either of us. As you know, I had my own reason, and Caleb saw only you when he looked at that portrait of Fiona. You should have been flattered in either case." He waved his hand. "Go on. I have a few calls to make so I'll finish my tea and let you have a little time to yourself with Fiona. I'll join you shortly."

She stopped at the door to look back at him. "Calls? Caleb?"

"Among others. Any objection? He'll want to know if I was able to arrange for additional guards for the Run. It's not as if we're talking about you behind your back. You've made it clear that you don't want that happening."

"I don't really mind the two of you talking about me. It doesn't matter. In the end, it will be my decision. Caleb realizes that I won't tolerate any interference unless I approve. Just as long as you promise to let me know what else is happening, and if there's any danger to Caleb. Can I trust you? Will you do that?"

"Of course I'll do that."

"Good." The library door was closing behind her. "Then by all means, make your calls."

"Have you arranged for the additional guards?" was the first question Caleb asked when MacDuff reached him. "You'll have six or seven MI6 specialists showing up on your doorstep later today. Check their IDs and show them around the property. They should be efficient enough even for you, MacDuff."

"I prefer my own men. I arranged to bring in some of my old buddies from the Royal Marines," MacDuff said testily.

"Of course you did," Caleb murmured. "Because they regard you with fawning worship and admiration. Everyone knows about the chestful of medals you earned in combat. It's not only in Scotland that you're a damn folk hero."

"How can I deny it? I won't bother. But the Scots always

had the intelligence to appreciate one of their favorite sons, and the marines were always there when I needed them." He added, "Like now. They'll be here by noon and Fergus says he's arranged for them before when we've had difficulties with politicians and media showing up on the property unexpectedly."

"I'm not worried about politicians or media," Caleb said. "Can they shoot, and will they do it?"

"They're marines," MacDuff repeated. "Everything has been done that should be done. And if you're worried about Jane, she's already informed me that she isn't going to be wandering all over the property. She's decided that she'll be working inside the main castle and in the gallery." He added, "Though I'm not sure if that's bad or good. It's not her usual routine, as you know."

"Yes, I do know." Caleb's voice was clipped. "And I'm not any more certain than you were. She wasn't...herself when I talked to her last night."

"It might have had something to do with the beheadings," MacDuff said sarcastically. "It probably made a difference. Being truthful could be a real downer if you're having to describe blood and gore."

"Be quiet, MacDuff. I'm doing the best I can."

"How good is that? I believe I'm supposed to temper anything I talk about with you when I relay information. Have you heard anything about Bohdan from MI6?"

"Other than I have a fat bounty on my head? Not a thing. Well, except that the Congo is in complete chaos. But I've contacted Gamba Mandia myself. He's head of the Bohdan opposition, and they've said that they'll be ready to take over ruling the country if I can remove Bohdan from the equation."

He added dryly, "Such a small thing. But I'm certain Bohdan will be willing to meet-and-greet with me since I'm exceptionally high on his list."

"What are you going to do?"

"I've brought my information specialist, Dimak Palik, in from Greece, and he's gathering all the info he can about Bohdan and his men. Along with any chatter about anyone connected to me from Bohdan's camp. I'm expecting a callback from him any minute." He paused. "So far there's not been any talk about MacDuff's Run or Jane or you. But that doesn't mean someone won't stumble onto something."

"You and Jane have been very discreet about your relationship. I can count on one hand the number of people who know about you."

"We've never tried to hide it. I usually manage to keep an eye on Jane even when I'm not with her. And I always go to her gallery openings. It's just that we're private people."

"I've noticed," MacDuff said. "And you probably prefer that no one be around to get in your way."

"I'd never interfere with her friends or family. You're a fool if you think I'd ever want to damage her in that way."

"Because you've gone through that particular hell yourself?" Caleb was silent. "Maybe not. But there are all kinds of other ways you could damage her. For some reason she believes that she wants you. Or perhaps she just wants to save you from yourself."

"That's possible. Do you expect me to deny it? But I've given up fighting her about it. She's a bit sensitive right now and I'd appreciate it if you'd do the same." His voice lowered silkily. "I'd be most displeased."

"Tough," MacDuff said. "I'll keep you informed how things

are doing here at the Run. But I promised Jane I'd let her know if you were in any danger. That includes any report from your information guru."

"Of course. I've told you that I'm honest with Jane," Caleb said, then added, "and I'm grateful for your help, MacDuff."

"As long as it's limited to the areas that you specifically designate? Sorry, that won't happen. You take what you get." MacDuff broke the connection.

CHAPTER

4

THE GALLERY
MACDUFF'S RUN
1:45 P.M.

Okay. Give Fiona every chance, Jane thought, bracing herself as she walked down the long hallway. It would really annoy her if MacDuff was right about her being intentionally blind regarding the blasted portrait. She turned all the lights on as soon as she entered the gallery. Then she put the two volumes MacDuff had given her together with her sketch pad on the velvet chair against the wall.

Only then did she turn and directly face the portrait of Fiona MacDuff.

Just look at her for a moment. Jane usually avoided it because of the resemblance MacDuff always called to her attention. The long auburn hair, the hazel eyes, the features that even Jane could see were similar to her own.

But MacDuff had said she wasn't being fair. So she tried to see what he did in Fiona. What had he said? *Bold and excited...* Yes, she could see the faint flush on Fiona's cheeks, the way her eyes shone out from the canvas. *A bit adventurous...* Jane could see that also in the lift of her chin, the faint curve of her lips.

She hated to admit it, but MacDuff had probably been right.

Okay, maybe I've been unfair to you, Fiona. But I don't want you to think that I believe anything else MacDuff said. No offense. But I'm my own person and I like it that way. From what he just told me about you, I believe you might be able to understand that. Personally, I think your father sounds like an asshole. I'm sorry you had to deal with him. MacDuff thinks that the cards were stacked against you because you were a woman in a man's world. I hope that's not true. Just because I don't want to be related to you doesn't mean I don't want what's best for you.

Of course, whatever had happened to her had occurred back in the late eighteen hundreds and there was nothing that Jane could do about it. That was as infuriating as everything else that was happening around her right now.

She wondered if Jamie MacDuff had been as much a son of a bitch as Jane was suspecting. "Because I really don't like the idea of him getting away with anything," she whispered.

"Don't tell me you're communing with my Fiona?" MacDuff was chuckling as he strolled into the gallery. "I approve. I told you that you'd have a chance of getting along if you took off the blinders."

"Nonsense." Jane turned away from the portrait. "Communing? I was just examining the brushstrokes. They're quite amazing. You don't know anything about the artist? Not even if it was a man or a woman?"

He shook his head. "Jamie never told any of the family anything about the artist. I guess they just assumed the artist was male. It would give the portrait more status in their eyes, and Jamie was all into status during that period of his life."

"You mean when he wasn't throwing his closest kin down

the nearest well?" she asked dryly. "And there are women artists who could achieve this quality of brushstrokes."

MacDuff nodded. "I didn't mean to imply you couldn't have done it. I know you could. I've seen you do much more detailed work. I'm just trying to give you the correct perspective."

"I'm getting very annoyed with that perspective." She gazed back at the portrait. "It's a wonder that she was able to win any of those prizes or ribbons when she was being smothered by all that machismo bullshit."

"Maybe she regarded it as a challenge." MacDuff's lips indented in a faint smile. "I know someone who would react like that. But you're being very defensive of Fiona. Am I to assume that you agree I've been right about her?"

"Not entirely. I do agree that I've probably been unfair in my assessment of her." She made a face. "How could I help it when everyone has been pushing her at me? She appears to be an extraordinary woman, and I intend to learn much more about her. But there's no reason why I should believe she's any relation to me. I'm still more than content to be Jane MacGuire with parents like Joe and Eve instead of having any connection with a bastard like Jamie MacDuff." She stared him in the eye. "Understood?"

"Certainly." He grinned. "I've gotten this far. I wouldn't dare push my luck. It's much smarter to let you make any other discoveries on your own. Do you have any other questions?"

"Not about Fiona." She was gathering her books from the chair. "Did you get hold of Caleb?"

"Yes, he's well, and he's contacted Dimak Palik—an information specialist—to track down Bohdan. He was supposed to hear from him later today. I told him that you'd want a report if he heard anything."

She nodded. "I know Palik. He's always done a good job for Caleb. He'll probably be able to find him if anyone can." She gave a half grin. "Of course, I've seen Caleb himself hunt down prey that no one else could find." She shivered as she remembered the first time she had seen Caleb in hunter mode. She had told him she needed answers from a killer stalking them in the forest and she'd been shocked at the ferocity of his smile and the sheer electricity that illuminated his entire body as he'd turned and left her. But it had been nothing compared with the moment when he'd returned later carrying an unconscious victim on his back and tossed the man at her feet. It had been savage and frightening and it had taken her a long time to begin to understand the forces that drove Caleb. And longer still to realize that she couldn't live without him. "I'm just glad he has help this time."

MacDuff frowned, his gaze on her expression. "And I can imagine what you probably went through with him. He shouldn't have taken you with him."

"I didn't think so, either, at the time. It scared the hell out of me. But I got over it. Caleb has never tried to hide anything from me that he thought I could take." She shrugged. "And I'm glad. He's had to carry too many secrets over the years." She tilted her head. "He didn't tell you anything else?"

MacDuff shook his head. "I would have told you." He glanced at the books she was carrying. "What are you doing this afternoon? Getting to know Fiona?"

"Perhaps later." She was heading toward the door. "Right now I'm going to go upstairs and place a Skype call to Eve. All this talk about Fiona and everything she probably went through has made me want to tell Eve how much I love her and the rest of my family." She glanced back at him and deliberately winked. "And that I know how lucky I am to belong to them and not to the MacDuff clan."

———◆———

Dimak Palik called Caleb thirty minutes after he'd hung up from MacDuff. "Bohdan has left the Congo and headed for Rome. Word is that he was searching for a couple of MI6 agents that his men told him were meeting with their chief. You wouldn't know anything about that, would you?"

"I know that I told Jennings not to go to that meeting," Caleb said grimly. "I told them to hide out and screw the report until I could take out Bohdan. Do you know if the bastard has his hands on them yet?"

"I know that there was an unidentified body found in the Tiber River last night. It was pretty well chopped up, but I'll check to see if it was one of your MI6."

"Not mine," Caleb said. "I wanted to go in alone. But the MI6 chief wanted insurance and sent a team. It's almost sure to be Jennings in that river."

"I could have told them to let you do it your way," Palik said quietly. "Next time I'm available for references. Why did you even agree to do the job?"

"I don't like the idea of bullies, and I didn't see why an entire country on the edge of starvation should have to kowtow to Bohdan and his General Rozkor." He shrugged. "And I hadn't done anything for MI6 for a long time while I was occupied with doing that favor for Jane's brother and her parents."

"Ah, the wonderful Jane MacGuire," Palik said. "Say no more. How is she?"

"The same. Safe, I think. She's at MacDuff's Run and well

protected. There's a good chance that Bohdan won't even know that she has any connection with me."

"You *think*?" Silence. "You never just think when it comes to Jane MacGuire. You know or you find out. Or you have me find out. Which is it?"

"You'll have one of your men keep an eye on MacDuff's Run. A very good man. If there's even a hint of a threat there, I'm to know about it."

"I hear you," Palik said. "But I'm surprised you're not going yourself. Is there something I should know?"

"Maybe that I'm Bohdan's prime target and don't want to lead any of his goons to Jane if they manage to track me?" Caleb asked caustically.

"I've never seen anyone who could track you," Palik said. "I couldn't do it, and I've known your moves for a long time."

"There's always the exception to prove the rule. That exception isn't going to have ramifications for Jane."

"I can see where you're going," Palik said. "What are you doing in Paris?"

"I won't stay there. A bull's-eye needs to keep moving. Bohdan will be on the hunt for me." He chuckled. "Just as I'll be hunting for him. I have to take him down before he zeros in on anyone I care about. It's going to be an interesting game. And I have you to pave the way for me, Palik."

"I'm actually relieved that you're leaving part of it to us. I'm always worried when you get restless. You have a tendency toward recklessness. You may be able to get away with that crap, but I'd just as soon take it slow and easy." He sighed. "And I know damn well that you're not going to be able to resist checking on any agent I send to MacDuff's Run. No matter how high a recommendation I give him."

"Maybe I will. It depends if you're able to locate Bohdan for me before he gets too close to Jane. I've no objection to putting an end to our contract right away. I'd prefer it."

"So would I," Palik said. "But it's rare when I'm able to indulge myself when I'm working for you. I'll check on that man they pulled out of the Tiber and verify if he's MI6, and I'll text you the credentials on my own excellent agent I'll send to watch your Jane."

"And locate Bohdan," Caleb reminded him.

"That goes without saying. Where will you be?"

"Perhaps in Paris. Or move down to Lisbon. Though I might join you in Rome if you can find a clue to lead me to Bohdan."

"Don't count on it. You're right, Bohdan may be coming after you. Did I tell you how chopped up that agent was when they pulled him out of the Tiber? Bohdan might have tortured him for information before he threw him in the river. Even if he didn't, it might take a while to get an autopsy report. Either way, do me a favor, don't get too restless." He ended the call.

Don't get too restless.

Palik's words echoed in his mind as Caleb pressed DISCONNECT. Palik knew him too damn well, he thought impatiently. They had been working together for a number of years and he could almost read Caleb's thoughts. He *was* restless, and he couldn't make a move on Bohdan yet. Even if he was able to locate him in Rome, it wouldn't be the most efficient way to rid the world of the son of a bitch. He had to arrange to have Gamba Mandia, head of the Congo opposition party, alerted to what he was doing so that the country wouldn't slip into chaos.

Don't get too restless.

Too late for that, he thought recklessly. Why not rent a helicopter, check out MacDuff's Run, and make certain that everything was the way he wanted it to be? He could be back by tomorrow and he'd feel better about MacDuff's preparations. For all he knew, one of Bohdan's men could already be there on the property. Wasn't it his duty to be certain that wasn't true?

Bullshit. He was making excuses.

But he'd be careful and not even go near Jane.

He'd just know she was there, near him, and safe . . .

That would be enough.

———

MACDUFF'S RUN
3:40 P.M.

Eve was wearing her blue chambray work shirt and her hair was tied back away from her face when she appeared on the Skype screen. "Jane?" She frowned. "Is everything all right?"

"Everything is fine," Jane said. "I just haven't talked to you since you arrived back at the lake cottage, and I thought I'd check in. Is Michael back in school?"

"For the time being." She shook her head. "But he's going to New Orleans with Cara next week. She has a concert and she's going to let Michael help backstage. He's over the moon. So much for giving him a normal American lifestyle after all the time he's spent in Scotland and London."

"It won't hurt him a bit. You know he adores Cara. I was always the practical sister. Cara wasn't only a star, she had her own magic." Jane chuckled. "And besides, you look like you're going to need time to yourself anyway. I recognize that blue work shirt. How far are you behind on the reconstructions?"

"Too far. I should own stock in FedEx. There was a backlog from half the forensic police departments around the country waiting for me when we pulled up to the cottage. Everything that we did when we were overseas had worth and I'd do it again, but these victims need me, too." She added brusquely, "But I'll catch up, and I told Michael we'll take a family vacation to Colorado and go up to the cabin in the mountains we bought before we left. It's beautiful scenery and Michael loves to look at the stars." She paused. "Still, there's no place more beautiful than MacDuff's Run. Are you enjoying your stay there? How is MacDuff?"

"As usual."

After a moment: "And Caleb?"

"As usual."

"Uh-oh. I don't like that." Eve dropped down into her office chair. "That's not good enough. There's never anything 'usual' about Caleb. Joe and I were very grateful when he volunteered to watch over Michael while we were tied up in Azerbaijan. We couldn't feel any safer than having you and Caleb to protect him." Her gaze searched Jane's face. "So what the hell is wrong? Don't give me that 'usual' bull. Everyone knows that MI6 uses Caleb whenever he'll let them. Joe said that even the intelligence chief is intimidated by him." She added wryly, "Which is dangerous in itself. You can never tell when they might find him inconvenient to have around. Particularly if they know about that family trait that makes most of them uncomfortable. Do they?"

"Of course, they do," Jane said impatiently. "It's not something that he could keep hidden even if he wanted to. Not working with MI6. They accept it. Why shouldn't they? It's just a physical skill that has run through Caleb's family for generations that allows them to be able to control the blood flow of anyone close to them. Hospitals even call on Caleb when they have patients that are having problems."

"But that's not why MI6 values him," Eve said quietly. "It's because they realize that his blood skill can kill as well as heal. Joe says they call him the Hunter." She held up her hand. "Don't say anything. Caleb has helped us too many times for us to condemn anything that he's done. If he's a hunter, then we know it's the bad guys he's hunting. I just wanted to be sure that he's not in any trouble."

"Caleb is never in trouble," Jane said. "He always comes out on top."

Eve just looked at her.

"It's the truth," Jane said. "But it doesn't stop me from worrying. It's one of those times." Eve was still looking at her. "Svangar. It's a township near the Congo. I won't be able to see him for a while and I miss him." She grinned. "And that's all I'm going to say. Now you've squeezed it all out of me just like you did when I was a teenager. All you had to do was take one look at me."

"Because I know you."

"Yes, you do. No one could know me better." She chuckled. "In fact, I had a discussion with MacDuff about you and Joe and Fiona just today. And I made it clear to him for the zillionth time that I belong with you guys. Maybe I got through to him this time."

"Or maybe you didn't," Eve said. "MacDuff's family is important to him, too. I've told you that I don't mind sharing."

"But I do. I've always known you were special. Stop trying to get rid of me."

"Not a chance," she shot back. "Look, I can't blame MacDuff for being persistent. You have a history with him from the time you showed up at the castle because you'd been having dreams about Cira, his ancestress, who came from Herculaneum and later established the MacDuff family. I was worried about you, too, since they started when you were only a teenager."

"I stopped having the dreams. They eventually went away. It was probably something I read or saw on TV."

"That's what Joe and I told you, but you seemed driven. We were glad when they went away. But they left that relationship with MacDuff behind. You've been friends for a long time."

"And I'm grateful. I love it here, even when he and Caleb persist in sparring off each other. I just want him to stop trying to adopt me."

Eve laughed. "I believe you can handle MacDuff. So now tell me what unusual thing Caleb has done that made you run to tell me how usual he's being."

"A kind of difficult job with MI6." Jane shrugged. "I told you, nothing that he's in the least worried about."

"Except where it concerns you," Eve said. "Then he does worry. Like a tiger on the prowl."

"He's not prowling now, which must mean I'm safe here at MacDuff's Run." She smiled. "I just felt the need to talk to you. Maybe I've been bored this week and felt a little lost."

"Now, that's really unusual. I'll have to think about why you'd feel like that. You haven't been lost since the day I saw you bossing around all the other slum kids on the streets when you were ten," Eve said. "You're the one who could always take care of me. Want to come and help me with about fifteen of these reconstructions I have on my list?"

"Are you kidding? You're the world-famous forensic sculptor.

You know you wouldn't let me touch them. I'll pass." She had to stop this right now before Eve actually started to worry about her. "But I would like you to tell me everything Michael is doing and how much you and Joe are enjoying the lake. Then I'll tell you all about Fiona and what a bastard of a father she had. And you can tell me how lucky I am that you let me come home with you that day. Is it a deal?"

Jane shook her head and her smile vanished when she pressed the DISCONNECT button on the Skype screen thirty minutes later. She'd definitely messed that up, she thought ruefully. She should have known that Eve would have been able to see right through any attempt Jane could fabricate to hide any disturbance. They'd been too close over the years, and she'd never been able to mask the passion and emotion of her relationship with Caleb from her. It didn't help that Eve always wanted the very best for her and had a tendency to try to solve all the problems of the universe plaguing her family. Jane would just have to call her back in a day or two and smooth it over.

But talking to Eve had made her feel better as it always did. She'd even discussed Fiona and for once she hadn't experienced any feeling of antagonism connected to MacDuff's ancestress. Which had even brought a strange sense of relief.

She picked up one of the Fiona journals she'd thrown down on the nightstand when she'd come into the bedroom. It was the book with the strange characters that MacDuff had not been able to identify. Well, as she'd told Eve, there was no way on earth she could help her with those reconstructions she had to do. Why not see if she could make heads or tails of Fiona's puzzle? It would be nice if she had something to at least talk about with Eve the next time she called her back. She crossed to the window seat and sat down. It wasn't foggy today and the courtyard was bright and beautiful. She saw MacDuff talking to a number of men by the fountain. His own employees from the village, or MI6? It had to be one or the other. She supposed it should make her feel safer, but somehow it didn't. She was only grateful that it might mean no one would be hurt by her being here at the Run. Along with experiencing a deep frustration that she couldn't do more herself to take charge of her own life.

Her gaze wandered to the large stable on the far side of the courtyard. Pristinely clean, and the storage rooms would probably be equally well kept. She'd known that no horses were kept in that old stable now. Perhaps she should go and take a look at Fiona's belongings there and see if she had left any secrets...

Forget about it. She had no desire to go down to the courtyard and stumble over any of MacDuff's sentries and have to be polite. She deliberately turned away from the fountain and opened Fiona's journal. Start at the beginning and see what occurred to her as she turned the pages. Those dark marks that looked like dashes were odd. Maybe if she started to copy them into her sketchbook, they'd become more her own, and she'd be able to work with them...

She started to work...

BELL HELICOPTER

SOMEWHERE NORTH OF CALAIS, FRANCE

Palik called Caleb at just before midnight. "Nice night for a jaunt across the channel. Enjoying yourself?"

"Not particularly. But there better be a good reason why you're inquiring. I don't recall discussing these plans with you. I can't say I like the idea of you keeping such a close eye on me, Palik."

"Just doing my job," Palik said flippantly. "The autopsy report is in on the guy they fished out of the Tiber River. It was your MI6 friend, Jennings. Extensive torture, as suspected." He paused. "How much did he know about you?"

"Not enough to make the effort worthwhile for Bohdan. I try not to become too chummy with other agents. It can be dangerous for them."

"Like Jennings?"

"Exactly. That's another reason why it's better if I work alone."

"Then Bohdan won't be able to track you."

"I didn't say that. There are always ways, if I'm not careful. Agents talk to each other. Or someone at the MI6 home office could have loose lips."

"You wouldn't tolerate that and they know it. And I don't believe any of the agents from MI6 are going to do any talking."

"Then you'd be wrong. The guy they just fished out of the Tiber River probably told them everything he knew. We just have to hope that wasn't much. Any word on Bohdan's location?"

"Nothing definite. He owns several drug houses and meth labs throughout Europe. He might be checking on them. But we think he might be heading for Naples. There are rumors he owns a brothel there that he uses to house and train kids he imports from his contacts in the Congo. We're checking on it."

"Makes sense. He was partners with the general in several brothels in Central Africa before I removed his senior partner from the equation. Is that all?"

"One other item. I've assigned Sean Rodland to MacDuff's Run. You remember Rodland. You're the one who sent him to me."

"I remember him. He's probably better than anyone else you have."

"That crazy Irishman is hell on wheels, and he's been with me for almost two years now. No one could be more loyal to you. He'll be arriving there tomorrow morning. You'll be pleased with him."

"We'll see," Caleb said. "Anything else?"

"Not from me." He added sourly, "Unless you'd like me to send a man out to the Run tonight to monitor what you're doing out there."

"That won't be necessary. I know MacDuff's property like the back of my hand. Jane has always liked the Run and it seemed a safe enough place to leave her occasionally." Caleb added mockingly, "Though I appreciate your interest. But we both know what I'm doing is no one's business but mine."

"It's my business," Palik said testily. "You pay my salary, and I don't want to lose a valuable source of income. I'm just telling you that Rodland will take good care of Jane and you don't have to go trekking across those hills tonight."

"I'm touched by your concern. But I have to make certain that the entire area is still safe since Bohdan got to Jennings. Back off, Palik."

Palik muttered a curse. "I'm backing off. Don't you think it took a lot for me to confront you on this? I just realized you're being reckless and it wouldn't hurt to opt out and let one of my people do the job. Which blows my professionalism to hell."

"Or increases it enormously. It depends on how you look at it. Not everyone would find it annoying."

"When will you arrive at MacDuff's Run?"

"Another hour. But it will be at least another two hours after that before I'll finish going over the property." He suddenly chuckled. "I have to be careful. I don't want to have one of MacDuff's marines shoot a hole in me. I wouldn't want to seriously damage your source of income."

"Very funny," Palik said. "But I'm not in the mood to be amused. I had to go down to the coroner's office to get that report and I saw what Bohdan did to that agent. I didn't like it. Because I think Bohdan enjoyed the hell out of it. Not that I give a damn about you. But I like Jane, and it makes me sick to think of Bohdan hurting her like that. So make sure whatever you do tonight doesn't target her."

Caleb's hand tightened on the phone. He couldn't speak for a moment. "There's no way on earth I'd let it happen," he said hoarsely. "Not if I have to bring down all Bohdan's forces in the Congo. Look, I'm going to do everything right. All I'll do is check out the property and then get out. I'm not even going to see Jane tonight. Stop worrying about her and get me a line on Bohdan. I can't tell you how badly I want him."

"You'll have him," Palik said grimly. "But I gave you Rodland, too. I told him that Jane wasn't to be out of his sight. Make use of him." He ended the call.

CHAPTER

5

It was raining...

Jane rolled over in bed as she saw a flash of lightning streak across the night sky outside her window.

Thunder...

And something else...

She could *feel* it.

She sat up and swung her legs to the floor. Then she was out of bed and crossing the room toward the window.

More lightning... She could see the rain driving across the stones of the courtyard below her.

And shadows...

She stiffened as she gazed down at the stable across the courtyard.

Shadows?

Her heart was beating fast as she leaned forward, her gaze narrowed on the building.

Shadows.

Oh, yes, definitely something else.

She whirled away from the window, grabbed her jacket from the chair, and ran out of the bedroom.

She flew down the staircase, unlocked the front door, tossed the jacket over her head to protect her from the rain, and then was running across the courtyard toward the stable.

Thunder. Rain. Lightning.

And the door of the stable that flew open as she reached it!

"Crazy woman." Caleb jerked her inside, slammed the stable door shut, and locked it. "What are you doing running around in the storm? What good does it do for me to tell MacDuff to get you more protection when you decide to stroll around here in the middle of the night."

"Shut up." She tossed her leather jacket aside and went into his arms. "You were *here*. I knew you were here. I could *feel* you. And I'm not crazy. I could see the shadows."

"And that's not crazy?"

"Of course not. I only had to catch a glimpse of you as you entered the stable. I know that smooth gait, the way your body moves. Are you telling me that you wouldn't be able to do the same?"

"I might have trouble with shadows."

"Liar. You opened the door and were waiting for me."

"I was trying not to." His arms closed around her, and he buried his lips in her throat. "I wanted to be cool and collected so that I could tell you what an idiot you are." His voice was thick. "And impress you that you shouldn't do this ever again. And then I saw those damn bare feet splashing across the courtyard." He picked her up and carried her to a vacant stall near the back of the stables. "Why the hell couldn't you have put shoes on?"

"I didn't know I hadn't." She wriggled her bare toes. "I remembered the jacket. I was in a hurry to get to you."

He took off his shirt and was wiping her damp feet with it. "Well, you're here. I suppose I'll have to confess that yes, I'd know you in the shadows, or the mountains, or in the depths of the ocean." He gently rubbed the top of her foot. "Anywhere. Anytime. But I'd just as soon not test it in the next week or so."

"That started out to be very nice, but it didn't end up that way." She tucked her feet beneath her. "I believe you'd better tell me why you're here."

"I wanted to check out MacDuff's arrangements to make sure they're everything I'd want them to be."

"And are they?"

He nodded. "Absolutely no slip-ups. This vacant stable was the last item on my list. It leads down to the boat dock by the shore. If they're okay, you couldn't be more safe."

"Wonderful. I'm so glad that you approve."

Caleb tensed. "Do I detect sarcasm?"

"How clever of you to recognize it." She smiled. "A little sarcasm. Perhaps I'm just sick of you telling me what to do."

"I believe you know I'm just trying to keep you secure. Have I done anything else to displease you? What can I do to make up for it?"

"Let me think... Only one thing occurs to me at the moment. I'm tired of being without you. But you're the one who came visiting me, aren't you?" She got to her feet, pulled her nightgown over her head, and threw it on the floor. "Now do something about it."

"Oh, shit." He was on his feet. His hands moving over her breasts. "I told Palik I was going to do everything right, that I wasn't even going to see you."

"Then he's an idiot if he believed you. I don't remember

him being that stupid." She kissed him. "And right now, I think it's up to me. I'm very angry with Bohdan for causing us all this trouble. I have no intention of letting him cheat us of anything more of what we have together. Not for a minute."

"Well, if you're in charge, I'm obviously lost." He was suddenly smiling as he took a step back. "Tell me what you want."

Electricity. Fire. Caleb...

"I want you out of those clothes." Her voice was shaking. "I want you inside me."

"Any minute now." He was already undressing. "Come here..."

Then his hands were cradling her buttocks, lifting her as her thighs slid around his hips.

Then he sank deep!

She cried out and her nails dug into his shoulders.

"More?" he murmured.

"Yes." She was clenching, breathing hard, bringing him closer, still closer. "No, I want to give to you. Let me..." She brought him down to the floor and then he was on top of her. His teeth tugging at her nipples.

Madness.

Heat.

Deep.

Deeper.

Fire.

She was gasping, moaning, shaking.

"Caleb..."

"Easy."

There was nothing easy about it. Something was happening

and she didn't realize what it was. She just knew she couldn't let him go. Not yet. There was something waiting for them.

But then it was gone. Or was it? She couldn't tell. Because her entire body seemed to be exploding with need again.

It was too intense. This time when the explosion came, she was vaguely aware there were tears running down her cheeks.

"Jane?" Caleb was looking down at her. "Okay?"

She drew a deep breath. "Fine. It was..." She didn't know what she'd been about to say. There weren't any words. "You were very...accommodating."

"I'm glad that I pleased you." He chuckled. "You scared me for a minute. The last thing I'd want is to disappoint you when I've obviously been doing that far too much lately." His smile faded. "And I believe we'd better have that talk I spoke about now."

"I suppose that means I have to put on my clothes again." She reached for her nightgown. "And I don't know if I want to have that talk now. I'd rather talk about the two of us and what we are together. Maybe I'd like to tell you about Fiona and the talk I had about her with Eve today." She paused. "And perhaps I'd like to talk about leaving here and going away somewhere I could help you take down Bohdan."

"No!"

"I thought that would be your reaction." She was putting on her gown. "I'll give you time to think about it. But you should know that's what I've been doing. I have my own work and it's not as if I intend to go after monsters like Bohdan. But this is different. You've said you believe Bohdan may target me? Then I should be there to help. There should be some way that I can be with you. Don't you see?"

"I see that we should talk about it later."

"It's not only me. He could hurt MacDuff or any of his people. And I'd be responsible." She moistened her lips. "He could hurt *you*. I don't think I could bear that. I *won't* bear it. I'd have to do something about it."

"Listen to me." His hands grasped her shoulders. "I'm the only one responsible for anything that happens to me. We both know that I've lived with that knowledge since the day that I was born. My loving parents drilled it into me that I was a bad seed after they found out that I'd inherited the family blood talent. They kicked me out to live with my uncle when I was fourteen, and they were probably right to do it. Some people are meant to be the protectors and others are meant to be the hunters. You're definitely not a hunter, so stop trying to go down that road." His hand was on her cheek. "Okay?"

"No. You're talking bullshit. I've told you what I think about the way your parents treated you. It's a wonder that you turned out as well as you have." She swallowed. "I'll let it go for the moment." She met his eyes. "But not for long, Caleb. This is bothering me. I'm going to have to take care of it."

His lips tightened. "Then I'd better make certain to do it myself before you get the chance." He shrugged. "And I don't have much time to go into it with you right now. I want to be out of here in the next hour. I still have the boat dock to check out."

"Are you kicking me out?"

"No way." He pulled her back down to him. "I'm very good with time conservation. And Lord knows I need to distract you. Though we both know that's not going to last long." He pretended to think about it. "Okay, but you gave me a list of the subjects you wanted to talk about . . . Fiona . . . Eve . . . what else? Anything but Bohdan." He pushed the nightgown off her shoulders. "Fiona. Tell me about Fiona. Why did you decide to talk to Eve about Fiona?"

He was still naked, and he was smiling down at her. He was totally sensual. The brush of gray at his temples, the faint indentation in his chin, those fascinating dark eyes glittering with humor and intensity. She could feel her body stirring again. "It's not going to work, you know," she whispered.

"Only if you want it to." He brushed his lips over her upper breasts. "And it's okay with me whatever you choose. I can feel something...isn't quite right. Talk to me. Tell me how I can fix it. That will be good, too."

She suddenly chuckled. "But not *as* good. And you'll do anything to keep me from mentioning Bohdan again."

"What can I say? I never told you I didn't like my own way. I'm just a poor, lustful philistine."

"You're more than that." She cuddled closer to him. "I have great taste and I chose you. Don't insult me. Though I may throw that philistine description back at you later. And I have absolutely nothing against lust." She nestled her head on his shoulder. "But maybe I will tell you a little about Eve and Fiona because that's what I've been doing to keep myself busy. As a matter of fact, I've been going through the storage rooms downstairs and looking for info about Fiona. And I just wanted to talk to Eve about her. Eve because she'll always be my family, Fiona because I'm not sure she ever really had one. I guess I didn't want to think about what you were doing with Bohdan." She added, "And MacDuff has been regaling me with his family mystery stories and that didn't help. Did you know what an asshole her father was? He came from a background of border reivers, but that didn't mean he didn't use it as an excuse to..."

———◆———

Caleb was fully dressed and bending over her when she woke a little later. "I have to leave you." He brushed her hair back from her face. "But I can't go until I see that you're back inside the castle." He kissed her long, hard. "So will you get the hell out of here?"

It was over.

She smothered the pain. Accept it and go on.

"I'm thinking about it." She looked up at him. "I suppose I will. MacDuff would probably be very pissed off at you if he found out you hadn't trusted him and came here to check up on his arrangements." She shook her head. "And you were very obliging. It wasn't totally sex. That was important, too. You listened, you made me feel..." She suddenly pushed away from him and got to her feet. "You know how you made me feel," she said jerkily. "You're very good at it." She grabbed her jacket, went to the stable door, and threw up the lock. "It's still raining. I guess that's good. Less chance of anyone noticing me crossing back to the castle."

His brows rose, "*Now* you're worrying about it?"

"Only for your sake. I don't give a damn. You seem to have a plan. You always have a plan." She looked back at him. "Call me as soon as you've left the Run. It's okay, you can leave now, if you like."

"Thank you." He mockingly inclined his head. "I'm glad I have your permission."

"That doesn't even deserve a reply," she said. "I told you

what I wanted to do. I haven't changed my mind. We'll talk about it later." She suddenly said fiercely, "But not too long. I won't have it. I have to be there for you. We have to be together." She could feel her eyes sting. "You've never under-stood that that's the way it should be. You've got to learn that." Then she was turning and running out into the rain. "That's the way it has to be..."

"Jane!"

She could feel his gaze on her as she ran across the courtyard and then up the steps to the front door.

Then she was inside the hall and leaning against the door, her breath coming in short gasps.

Darkness. Lightning. Thunder.

She reset the door alarm and ran up the grand staircase to the second floor.

A moment later she was in her own room and walking over to the window.

The stable door was closed.

Of course it was. He'd only waited until he knew she was safe inside the castle. Now he was on his way down to the beach to make certain that boat area was safe.

She took off her leather jacket and stood there, gazing out the window.

Gone.

Those hours had come and then vanished like the lightning. Sex, intensity, excitement, and emotion swirling around them as it always did. Her breasts were taut and swollen and the need for him was still there. Yet so was the frustration and fear. He hadn't listened to her, and she should have made him listen. Her fists clenched at her sides. She had been too happy to see him after all the fear and worry that had gone before. She had let herself put off everything but what she felt for him.

Mistake. She just hoped it wouldn't prove a fatal one...

Don't even think it might. Just go on and find a way to get what she needed for both of them. But she knew she wasn't going to be able to sleep until he called her and told her he'd left the property. Keep busy! She threw her jacket down on the window seat and headed for the shower.

Forty-five minutes later she was out of the shower and drying her body with the towel. Her skin still felt warm and full and taut from being with Caleb. She gazed in the mirror while she was drying her hair and she could see the flush on her cheeks and the life that glowed from her face. All coming from Caleb and what she felt for him. It was almost magical...

Surely they could work through anything as long as they still had that magic.

Or could they? She inhaled sharply as a sudden thought occurred to her that shook her to her core. Her eyes widened as she stared at herself in the mirror. She stiffened with panic as she slowly lowered her hair dryer to the vanity.

Dear God in heaven...

———◆———

Caleb called Jane an hour later. "Everything checked out fine on the boat dock. I'm on my way back across the channel. I'll probably be heading for Naples to see if I can find Bohdan." He changed the subject and asked, "How are you?"

"Fine." She added, "How should I be? I couldn't be safer, could I? Between you and MacDuff I can hardly take a deep breath without asking permission." That sounded a little bitter and she tried to lighten her tone. "I'm glad the boat dock checked out. I realize you're only doing what you think best."

"Do you?" he asked slowly. "It didn't sound like that before you ran across the courtyard. I want this over, too, Jane. I'm working as hard as I can to clear it up."

"I know you are," she said wearily. "You just caught me at a bad time tonight. I'll bounce back." Lord, she hoped she was telling the truth. Right now she was so filled with confusion that she didn't know when she'd be able to straighten out her thinking. "Things just seem to be very difficult at the moment and I have to see what I can do to clear them up. Don't worry, I'll do it."

"Why would I worry about you?" Caleb asked hoarsely. "You persist in telling me you can take care of yourself." He paused. "But I suppose I should tell you that Palik is sending one of his men to the Run as your personal bodyguard. Even though there's no sign of Bohdan's men anywhere near the Run, it will be just another safeguard so that MacDuff's employees don't have to assume responsibility for your care. You seemed to be concerned about that."

"I told you about poor Fergus."

"Yes, you did. I have to warn you that Sean Rodland is one of Palik's best men and he probably won't let you out of his sight. But I promise he'll do anything you ask him to do. Is that okay with you?"

"Maybe. I'll have to see. If it's not, I'll send him on his way."

He said grimly, "Or you can send him to me, and I'll have a word with him. Then I guarantee you won't have any more problems."

"That's all I'd need," she sighed. "Another guard to hover

over me. And you acting like MacDuff does with Fergus. Palik usually doesn't interfere in your business."

"No, but he likes you. And he has a problem with Bohdan." He was silent for a moment. "As I do. And Palik's not entirely to blame for any of this. So forgive us both for taking extra care, even if you find it annoying. Is there anything I can do to make any of this better for you?"

"You're doing everything you can. We aren't even certain Bohdan knows I'm here. And I'm sure I'm not the only one being stalked by the bastard."

"At the moment it seems to me as if you are. You're at least the only innocent one being stalked." He muttered a curse. "And I don't like the fact that you've been sounding almost numb ever since you picked up my call. That's not like you."

"Numb? That's your imagination."

"Is it? I hope so. But you can be sure I'll be in touch. Good night, Jane."

"Good night." She stared at the phone for a moment after he ended the call. Then she got to her feet and moved over to the window to look down at the courtyard. There was a slight graying in the east. It was going to be dawn soon.

And Caleb had come very close when he'd guessed she was numb.

Even though she'd denied it, it hadn't surprised her that he'd read that response. It was what she'd felt and had tried desperately to keep him from seeing. So much had happened tonight . . .

But there was only one thing that seemed to be important in retrospect. It was the single moment when she had stood before that mirror a short time ago.

Shock.

Yes, she was still in shock.

But she had to get over it. She would sit here and watch the dawn and try to make plans. It shouldn't be that difficult. It was just a question of making up her mind and following through. But she might have to use every skill and asset at her command in order to do that. There was a chance she was going to be more vulnerable than she had ever been before.

Because as she'd spoken to Caleb it had occurred to her that she might have to go through this nightmare heading her way entirely alone...

———◆———

ROME

"Seth Caleb." Chiswick strode into Bohdan's office and threw down a report on his desk. "I told you I'd find him."

"It's taken you long enough. You've bungled this incredibly, Chiswick," Bohdan said sharply. "And you told me that you didn't get any information about him out of Jennings before you killed him."

"I didn't, but I located his partner, Ray Pasternak, and he was more than willing to tell me what I wanted to know after I showed him the photos of what we did to Jennings. He was pissed off anyway because his buddies were ordered to back up Caleb and ended up dead."

"Good. Stop bragging and tell me how quick I can get my hands on him. Where is the son of a bitch?" He was reaching for the report in front of him. "I'm going to—"

"The report's not exactly about Caleb," Chiswick said quickly. "Pasternak picked up some gossip from a Scotland

Yard detective about a murder case he was sent to work on a few years ago at the request of some posh earl who was a friend of Seth Caleb's."

"How good a friend?"

"Good enough. Lord MacDuff gave Caleb a call and told him that Jane MacGuire, a woman Caleb was involved with at the time, might be a suspect. He dropped everything and was driving up to MacDuff's estate in a matter of hours." He tapped his finger on the photograph. "You can see why. Jane MacGuire. I wouldn't kick her out of bed. Even if it turns out they're no longer an item, it would be a weapon, wouldn't it?"

"It might be. It wouldn't be for me. A woman is just a woman. How fast can we get hold of her?"

"I'm checking on it. She's an artist and lives in London. I've sent a man to track her down. In the meantime, I thought it wouldn't be a bad idea for me to take a trip to MacDuff's estate and see if I can find out what his connection is to Caleb. There's a chance you might be able to use him. Caleb might not give a damn about those other agents we've been taking down." He shrugged. "But he might pay attention if we hit him on a more personal level. MacDuff is supposed to be his friend. How do you think he'd react if we sent him MacDuff's head? It might be just the goad we need to draw him out."

"From what I've heard about Caleb he doesn't need much goading," Bohdan said dryly. "We just have to find the son of a bitch before he finds us." He looked down at the photo again. "Though there's something about breaking a woman that has an effect on some men. I've decided it has to do with the softness of their flesh and the way it reacts to pain. It could possibly bring up a sexual memory that confuses them."

His index finger moved across Jane's face in the photo almost caressingly. "I've done a little experimenting with some of the whores here and it was interesting. I felt nothing, but it appeared to bother some of the other clients."

But then Bohdan seldom felt anything, Chiswick thought. He was the coldest asshole on the face of the earth. He'd seen him torture one of his officers who had displeased him for three days in the square in the center of the city. He'd even offered a bonus to the man in the company who could come up with the most innovative way to inflict pain on the poor bastard. Chiswick couldn't understand it. Torture had always been a means to an end to him. You did it to get what you wanted and then you disposed of the victim and walked away. Anything else was a waste of time. But of course, he'd never let Bohdan know how he felt. In Bohdan's army there were no opinions except Bohdan's. It wasn't safe. "So do I go and see what I can find out in Scotland?"

"Try London first. The woman looks more promising."

And he probably wanted to do more experimenting, Chiswick thought cynically. "Whatever you say." He headed for the door. "I'll have answers for you by tomorrow."

<hr>

MACDUFF'S RUN
NEXT DAY

"I need you down here," MacDuff said impatiently. "Right now, Jane. Drop whatever you're doing and come and handle this package Caleb sent to make my life more difficult."

"What package?"

"Sean Rodland. Don't tell me he's a surprise to you, too."

"Not exactly. Caleb told me Palik was sending someone and that he was very efficient. But I can't believe that you'd need help to handle anyone. What's the problem?"

"I'm trying to decide whether to drown him or just throw him in the dungeon," he said silkily. "But if you don't come down and save him, I might call Caleb and tell him I'm going to send him gift-wrapped to Bohdan, and he can go after him."

"I'll be right down." She cut the connection and was out of her room and running down the stairs. What the hell had Caleb done to her? She didn't need problems with MacDuff after the sleepless night she'd just had.

MacDuff met her at the foot of the staircase. "That's what I appreciate, cooperation and someone to realize who is presiding over things here at the Run. Evidently, Rodland has no conception of my position in the scheme of things." He gestured to the man following him down the hall. "Sean Rodland. Jane MacGuire. Rodland was sent by Palik and strolled down here from the hills bold as brass to pay you a visit." His lips tightened. "Though I don't know how the hell he got on the property. I was about to ask him and tell him that no one sees you without going through me first. Perhaps you can explain it to him, Jane. You know what a reasonable, peaceful man I am."

"When you get your own way." She glanced at Rodland and then did a double take. He was possibly the most alive and intense individual she had ever seen. Lean and muscular, blue eyes, dark hair, cut close to keep from curling, and a lazy smile that was both warm and appealing. In spite of her irritation, she found herself smiling back. "You're Sean Rodland? What did you do to MacDuff? I won't have you being rude to him."

Rodland shook his head. "I wouldn't think of being rude to His Lordship, Ms. MacGuire." He had a decided Irish accent. "He must have misunderstood." He added solemnly, "But I had my orders, and I don't deviate. I thought it only fair to advise him so that he could make adjustments."

"*I* could make adjustments," MacDuff repeated. "Did you hear that? I was generously telling him what role I might be able to give him in protecting the Run, and he wasn't having any of it."

"I have my orders," Rodland repeated quietly. "Naturally I'll be glad to help out if it doesn't get in the way, but it can't interfere."

"Did it occur to you that I'm the one who gives the orders here?" MacDuff asked. "And no one makes a move without them. What would you do then?"

"Find a way," he said gently. "I'm very good at that. And I want you to know I'd do it with all courtesy, sir."

"What a relief," MacDuff said sarcastically. "I'd hate the idea that you'd be rude as well as—" He abruptly stopped in exasperation. Then he started to laugh. "I think I've decided on the dungeon, Jane."

"You might ask what his orders are first." Jane was gazing at Rodland appraisingly. She was beginning to get an idea. "And he wasn't really rude to you. Occasionally it's good for you to have someone who won't kowtow to you."

"I beg your pardon?" He turned back to Rodland. "So okay, what were your orders?"

"To take care of Jane MacGuire," Rodland replied. "Nothing must happen to her while she's on my watch." He smiled at Jane. "And it won't. I guarantee it. But I can't have my attention drawn anywhere else or I'll hear from Palik. He gave me strict orders that I was to obey no one but her." He made a face. "Which is most unusual for Palik. But he was on edge, and I owe him big time. I wasn't about to argue."

"Except with me," MacDuff said sourly. "And I evidently don't count if Seth Caleb is on the scene. I take it Palik's nerves were due to Caleb?"

"I wouldn't know, sir," Rodland said. "I suppose it could be considering that Caleb is a valuable client. But Palik doesn't confide in me."

"Or anyone else." He glanced at Jane. "Is this all right with you?"

"Or you'll toss him in the dungeon?"

"I'm thinking about it. It would be interesting to see if he'd manage to escape. I don't like the way he got past my guards. He's a little too sure of himself." His gaze narrowed on Rodland's face. "I don't believe I like it."

"You'd like it if he was taking orders from you. You always appreciate confidence," Jane said. "And I'm not in the mood for you to set any traps to punish him for doing what he was told. Let him alone, MacDuff."

"Because he's actually taking his orders from Caleb?"

She turned on Rodland. "Are you?"

He shook his head. "He took the time to give me an in-depth description of MacDuff's Run when I asked, but my orders actually came from Palik. Caleb was in a hurry to get on his way to Naples."

She gazed at him for a long minute. *Why not?* she thought recklessly. She could at least explore the possibility. He might be the key she'd been searching for during that sleepless night. She turned back to MacDuff. "Then he's working for me. I rather like the idea of someone actually doing what I tell them to do. It might be pleasant not to worry about having every male on the property keeping an eagle eye every time I step out the door."

He frowned. "That might still happen."

She pressed her index finger on his chest. "Then I might be the one to toss someone into your dungeon."

MacDuff suddenly grinned. "Now, I'd pay to see that." He turned on his heel. "I'll let you have your guard dog as long as he doesn't get in my way. The minute he does, he's out of here." He glanced over his shoulder at Rodland. "And if you make a mistake with Jane, you won't make another one. I'll see you at dinner, Jane. I hope you won't insist on inviting him to be your taste tester."

"You can never tell," she said, deadpan.

He shot her a resigned glance before he went out the door.

"How close was I to that dungeon?" Rodland asked.

"Not too close," Jane said. "He wanted to make a statement because things haven't been going his way lately." She shrugged. "But he doesn't bluff, so don't even think about that."

"I'll keep it in mind." He turned and looked at her. "So why did you decide to save my ass?"

"I told the truth: I like the idea of having someone to boss around if I find it necessary. I'm feeling a bit . . . smothered."

"I can understand that." He was studying her. "And?"

"You didn't back down to MacDuff. I can't say that for many people. He can be intimidating. And it occurred to me last night that I might need help to solve a particular problem. I remembered that Palik usually keeps men on his payroll who are trained to get things done. You impress me as being in that same category. Are you?"

"Perhaps. I don't like to be pigeonholed. I prefer to stand alone."

She shrugged. "Then I'll make my own judgments. I'll need you to answer a few questions. How did you get on the property without the guards intercepting you?"

"You might say it's one of my specialties. I spent almost a year in the mountains of Afghanistan being hunted before they finally took me down. After I received Caleb's basic instructions, it didn't take me long to look the estate over and get my bearings."

"How? Helicopter? Car? Boat?"

He didn't speak for a moment. Then he replied slowly, "Boat."

She frowned. "Then MacDuff will find it. We can probably scratch that off."

He shook his head. "I was careful and tucked it away very neatly some distance from the castle. He's welcome to try." He added, "What difference does it make?"

"I need to know what I have to work with."

"Now I have to ask a question. I'm curious about your 'problem.' Would it interfere with Palik's directive?"

"Not to begin with, but it might escalate." She met his eyes. "And it very well could cause him to have trouble with Caleb. He wouldn't like that."

Rodland gave a low whistle. "I can see that. I've not met many men that Palik wouldn't want to cross, but Seth Caleb is one of them." His eyes were suddenly gleaming with a hint of mischief. "What are you up to, Jane MacGuire?" he murmured. "I thought this job was going to prove boring. But now it's taking on aspects that might be intriguing."

"I'm giving you a chance to say no," she said bluntly. "I may need to use you, and if I do, it won't please MacDuff or Palik or Caleb."

"Then why should I do it?"

"Because if you don't, I'll call MacDuff and he'll find a way to make your life very uncomfortable here. And I'll let Palik know that I don't want you near me and won't permit you on the property to do what he sent you here to do."

"I can see that happening." He was studying her. "Yet I'm not sure you'd do it. I think it would have to be very important for you to go to those lengths."

Very perceptive, she thought. And as sharp as she'd first estimated. "It couldn't be more important to me."

"I believe you," he said slowly. "Does that mean I might have to kill someone?"

"Of course not," she said impatiently. "Don't be ridiculous."

"Just asking. I'd judge you to be very intense. What do you have in mind?"

"Only what you promised Palik you'd do. I've decided I need to leave MacDuff's Run for a few hours. You'll take me where I want to go. Do what I tell you. Keep me safe." She paused. "And don't talk to anyone about what you're doing."

"That last order is the one that could maybe get me seriously injured," Rodland said. "The others are strictly in line with Palik's directives. Would you care to tell me where I'm supposed to take you? I assume nowhere near Hugh Bohdan?"

"Nothing to do with Bohdan."

"And what would you really do if I said no? Besides get me thrown into MacDuff's dungeon."

"Find a way to go by myself. It would just be easier if MacDuff thinks you're with me." She took a step closer to him. "Either way, it's going to happen, Rodland. It *has* to happen."

He was silent a moment. Then he shrugged. "I guess I'd

better make certain it's done right. When and where are we going? You said it involves blowing this magnificent family home of MacDuff's for a time?"

She nodded. "But not right away. We'll spend the afternoon over at the courtyard stables and you can help me look through some storage rooms for a few of MacDuff's ancestral treasures. We'll let MacDuff's guards and stablemen see us working there." Her lips twisted. "And that will also give me a chance to keep an eye on you and decide whether or not I'm making a mistake in trusting you. I'm not usually this impulsive."

"That won't give you enough time," he said lightly. "I have hidden depths. Evidently so have you." He gestured toward the door. "But we can both make the attempt. It should prove interesting..."

CHAPTER

6

When do I get to be a food taster?" Rodland asked her as he handed Jane another volume to add to the ones they'd already put in the box at the foot of the steps. "I'm getting bored. I need a little pizzazz in my life. I'm sure MacDuff would prefer me to risk my life imbibing cyanide rather than go blind going through all these moldy books. I think I'm developing an allergy."

"Don't be disrespectful." She grinned. "MacDuff would be upset. I've told you the whole story about Fiona, and MacDuff's belief that someday he'll find some kind of proof that I'm one of his kin." She took the book and leafed through it. "Or at least find that Fiona wasn't thrown down a deep well by Papa dearest."

"The MacDuffs don't appear to be kind to their women. I don't blame you for not wanting to claim them. You're much better off sticking with me."

"You can hardly blame MacDuff for my being a prisoner here. He's doing everything he can to help keep me safe."

"Well, I refuse to blame Seth Caleb," he said dryly. "It's not nearly as safe."

"Then blame me. I've always been the captain of my fate. I make my own choices." She shrugged. "Or stay out of it. It's none of your business anyway."

"But it is, since I agreed to go along with you into the great beyond." He angled his head. "And I think I like you. Ordinarily I wouldn't tolerate any form of blackmail, and you came close." His eyes were gleaming slyly. "But I might forgive you if you tell me where the hell we're going."

"So you can decide whether you should change your mind?"

"No, I've already given my word. But I'd like to know if I need to make preparations. Particularly since MacDuff might decide I took a bribe from Bohdan and intend to kidnap you. Is that too much to ask?"

She slowly shook her head. "But I told you Bohdan has nothing to do with this." She hesitated and then said, "I want you to take me to Kilgoray, a small village about ten miles down the coast from here. There's something I want to do there, and it shouldn't take more than an hour. Then we'll be back on our way to MacDuff's Run." She added mockingly, "No villains waiting in the shadows. Just farmers and merchants and a friendly pub where I can park you while I go about my business."

"You never mentioned going off and leaving me. We should talk about that."

"I'll be within view the entire time," Jane said. "For heaven's sake, I told you, it's a small village. I've no intention of letting anything happen to me. If I thought there was any danger, I'd find another way to do this. You were only a convenience."

"And what does Kilgoray have that the village here at MacDuff's Run doesn't have?"

"Privacy." She raised her brows. "Satisfied?"

"Not at all. But I believe you're satisfied you're telling me the truth. That's enough for me until we get to this Kilgoray, and I can look it over myself. That pub doesn't sound too bad."

"Not too boring? I have an idea that might be a saving grace as far as you're concerned."

"Possible."

"More than possible. Why else do you work for Palik?"

His smile faded. "Because Seth Caleb sent me to him when I was wounded after he broke me out of a Taliban prison. He gave Palik orders to get me well because he wouldn't let the Taliban win by claiming they'd killed me. Palik did what he told him, and after I got out of the hospital, I found Palik a fairly good boss to work for . . . and he usually lets me run my own show."

"That would do it."

He added, "I thought you'd understand. Since you clearly aren't prone to going along with the status quo yourself. When are you going to let me sample the ale at that pub in Kilgoray?"

"Tomorrow evening. I want everyone here to become accustomed to the sight of us together. We'll work in the stable again tomorrow afternoon and then after dark we'll hit the boat dock and head for Kilgoray. As I said, we should be back here before dinner."

"So that's when I get to be the taste taster?"

"Why not?" she asked as she handed him another journal. "In the meantime, you'll have another day of searching for Fiona. Do you agree?"

He thought about it. "Except about taking a boat from the dock. You'll go down to the dock by yourself. Give me forty minutes and I'll fetch the boat I brought to the property and stashed in a cave in the cliffs. I'll pick you up on the other side of the castle. That will be much more efficient and less noticeable."

"I might like my way better."

"Too bad. Compromise."

"What if this is some kind of trick?" she asked warily.

"I could ask the same of you." He added, "You said Caleb told you I was being sent here. Do you trust him?"

"Yes."

"So do I. And I might have more reason than you. But if you want your way, we both have to compromise."

She studied him for an instant and then handed him the journal. "Okay. However, I'll be taking my Smith and Wesson as part of my compromise. If I get suspicious, I'll shoot you."

He laughed. "Seems fair." He reluctantly accepted the journal. "But I'd much rather forget about Fiona for a little while. I'm really not good with these journals. I'm totally brilliant with computers. You'd be amazed. You're sure we can't leave for Kilgoray a little early? This is beginning to be annoying."

"Apply yourself. If you find anything interesting MacDuff might even forgive you if he finds out about our trip to Kilgoray." She wrinkled her nose. "And maybe you can tell me what those dot-and-dash codes are that I keep running across."

"Codes?" He opened the book. "Weird. Your Fiona wrote in code?"

"Maybe. I can't figure it out. Neither could MacDuff." She looked at him suspiciously. "Why are you grinning?"

He was laughing out loud now as his gaze went through the pages in front of him. "Because I was thinking how much I'm going to enjoy explaining these 'codes' to our brilliant Earl of MacDuff's Run."

CAPTIVE

———◆———

MacDuff was frowning as he glanced up from the latest Fiona journal they'd found that afternoon. "Railway tracks? Not like any tracks I've seen. It looks more like dots and dashes."

"Because they're a bit primitive," Rodland replied. "Probably constructed back in Fiona's day. And for some reason I don't believe Fiona wanted anyone to know what she was drawing in those books." His shoulders lifted in a half shrug. "But I've seen even more primitive rail track construction when I was in the mountains between Kashmir and India. When I was a prisoner of the Taliban, the commander made a deal with the Kashmir government for them to use Taliban prisoners to do the labor on that stretch of rail from the jungles of the southern villages to the mountains." He made a face. "Using the cheapest materials, and half the time we had to clear the poisonous vipers out from between the spikes. Not a fun project. I was glad to see Seth Caleb when MI6 sent him with a team to raid the encampment and get us out of there." He turned to Jane. "Caleb didn't tell you about that?"

She shook her head. "Caleb seldom talks about anything he does for MI6 or any other organization. I suppose he believes it's safer for me." She changed the subject. "But why would you think that Fiona wouldn't want anyone to know about those railroad tracks?"

"Just a guess. All the other details in what she's drawn in

97

her diaries and journals appear to be clean and legible. It just seems unlikely that she'd do those tracks clumsily."

"And you could be wrong," MacDuff said.

Rodland grinned. "But that would make you right and I don't think I could bear the disappointment. Look at them closely and I'm sure you'll see what I saw."

"I suppose they could be tracks," Jane said reluctantly. "I'll go through her other books and compare them." She shook her head. "For Pete's sake, I'm an artist. It's humiliating that I couldn't identify those dashes as railroad tracks."

"That she didn't want you or anyone else to identify," Rodland said. "Don't feel bad. I've got a hunch Fiona was probably very clever. Maybe your friend MacDuff is right about the two of you having a close bond of some sort."

"Rodland," Jane said warningly.

"Just a thought." He smothered a smile as he immediately got to his feet. "But I'll leave you to have dinner and discuss it while I check out the courtyard and upper bedroom area."

"Why don't we invite him to dinner, Jane?" MacDuff mused. "Maybe he's not as objectionable as I first thought."

"No thanks," Rodland said. "Not unless it's to be your taste tester. You had the right idea to begin with. You mustn't raise my hopes now that you've convinced me to know my place in the laird's scheme of things." He winked at Jane. "Enjoy." He strolled out of the dining room.

"I could call him back," MacDuff said. "He seems to have a good work ethic. Fergus said the two of you appeared to be working very hard today. And then he came up with the rail ties. Perhaps you should pay more attention to his opinion."

"Since it agrees with your own?"

"Now that you mention it." MacDuff's smile was

mischievous. "Though he did temper it with a dig or two about my lack of discernment, too. But I can forgive him that since he obviously didn't want to make you look bad in contrast. Should I call him back?"

She thought about it before she shook her head. Not a good idea. She didn't want MacDuff to become too impressed by Rodland. She'd already found how sharp he could be. She'd prefer he fade into the background as far as MacDuff was concerned until she got what she wanted at Kilgoray. "He does work hard, but I've no desire to have to deal with the two of you at the dinner table. You're difficult enough. Besides, Caleb didn't send him here to entertain you."

"No." He lifted his wineglass to his lips. "I just thought you might want to hear Rodland reminisce about his heroic rescue at Caleb's hands. Since you said he never talks about his missions, I thought you might be feeling cheated."

"No, you didn't. You merely had a hunch you might have found a way to cause a little trouble."

"Ah, caught again." MacDuff laughed. "So you intend to continue to use Rodland as slave labor?"

"Certainly not. I don't believe in slave labor. But he did agree to work with me to find out what I could about Fiona. I'll have him help me go back through all of Fiona's journals and try to figure out why she was enamored with railroad tracks. There's one more storage unit at the stable that might tell us something. Perhaps another couple of days of research and we'll have answers."

"Or perhaps not." MacDuff looked suddenly thoughtful as he stared at her expression. "I've never seen you quite this on edge and driven. You're usually very cool. Look, I realize you have reason, but is there something I can do?"

So much for trying to act normal around MacDuff. He knew her too well. "No, I'm tired of worrying about Caleb. I'm being a bother to you and all your employees here at the Run. I feel guilty and I want it to stop." She held up her hand as he opened his lips to speak. "But it's nothing I can't handle. I'll just keep busy working on Fiona. It will at least give me something to do. Now can we sit down and have dinner?"

"I'm not allowed to offer comfort or discussion?"

She shook her head. "You're doing too much already. Just ignore me until everything miraculously straightens itself out or I get Caleb back. Okay?"

He sighed. "I imagine that means I can't indulge myself with attacking Caleb for the duration of your time with me?"

She nodded. "Absolutely not. Just ignore me."

"If you insist, but you're all that's made these weeks interesting." He was holding her chair for her. "As a reward I believe it's only fair that you consider selling me the *Mist Child*..."

———◆———

Railroad tracks...

Jane stopped just as she started to climb the staircase to her room after dinner. She'd believed she'd dismissed the thought of Rodland's guesswork about Fiona and the code that was no code. She should have known that it would stay with her. She hated what an idiot she'd been not to know what seemed obvious to Rodland. It was the second mistake she'd made about Fiona.

Railroad tracks.

That didn't mean she had to make any more mistakes. She whirled on the stairs and ran back down. Not when MacDuff had a library overflowing with ancient books about the property and all of Scotland itself. Fiona might even have been exposed to some of those books at one time or another. Or not. That didn't mean Jane couldn't explore and learn and find out if there was anything in them that could help her unveil a little of the mystery that was Fiona.

God knows, she doubted if she was going to be able to sleep tonight.

Not when she had no idea what was waiting for her tomorrow at Kilgoray.

"You were right to tell me to go after the woman," Chiswick said when Bohdan picked up the phone later that night. "I just spent an interesting few hours with Jane MacGuire's agent, Felicia Dillard, at her apartment in London. I couldn't get in touch with MacGuire herself." His voice was filled with satisfaction. "But it didn't really make a difference because I got what you wanted. Seth Caleb goes to all MacGuire's exhibits, and Dillard is sure that they're lovers. At the moment she's a guest at the estate of John Angus MacDuff, the Earl of MacDuff's Run. That was the friend of Caleb's who called him when he thought MacGuire was in trouble a couple years ago. So he might still be watching out for her." He added softly, "Or Caleb could possibly be there, too, and we might be able to gather both of them in."

"Or MacGuire could be MacDuff's mistress and Caleb might not give a damn about her any longer," Bohdan said sarcastically. "He probably got bored with her and gave her to MacDuff. Two years can be a lifetime. She might not be any use to us at all."

"That's not what her agent said," Chiswick replied. "I spent a long time questioning Felicia Dillard and she swore that Caleb was still MacGuire's lover." He chuckled. "I even used some of your special techniques to make certain she was telling the truth. I knew you'd be skeptical. I guarantee that she wouldn't have lied after what I put the bitch through."

"You're an amateur. You should have left her for me."

"You were in a hurry. You'll have MacGuire soon enough. I didn't want to bother keeping Dillard alive when there was no reason. I got the information and then took her for a ride on a yacht I rented to go up to bonnie Scotland and scout out MacDuff's Run. Unfortunately, if MacGuire survives, she'll have to get another agent."

"She won't survive."

"I didn't think so. That's why I didn't want to have to deal with Felicia. I'm on my way to check out MacDuff's Run, and exactly who is guarding it. If Caleb had anything to do with it, I imagine it's been upgraded by now. He probably pulled in MI6. I did a little initial probing and got info about the general setup of the estate. The number of people occupying the castle and the village. It depends on how many additional guards are there, if we're going to get lucky with Caleb as well as Jane MacGuire." He paused. "I believe we have a chance to reel them in. I know there's no way you want anyone to touch Caleb but you. But we both know how lethal he can be. If I get a chance, can I take him down?"

"Hell, no," he snarled. "Not unless you want me to cut your nuts off. He's *mine*. Stake out the place, get me the information, and I'll go in and take him down." But Chiswick might actually be close this time, he thought. He could feel the blood pumping through his veins as he considered it. It had been years since anyone had humiliated him the way Caleb had. He couldn't wait to pound that son of a bitch into the ground. "But I'm going to trust you on this, and you'd better not fail me. I'll be leaving Naples in a couple of days to join you. I'll call you when I'm near enough to rendezvous with you at MacDuff's Run." He concluded, "So get your ass in gear and do your job," then pressed DISCONNECT.

COURTYARD STABLE
NEXT DAY

"It's about time you got here." Jane's tone was caustic as Rodland came down the steps to the storage unit. "It's almost two in the afternoon. Where have you been? So much for devoting your entire time to guarding me even if it meant battling MacDuff."

"Stop complaining. MacDuff told me he was sending Fergus to watch over you." He dropped to his knees beside her. "Besides, it was entirely your fault. I ran into MacDuff on my way here this morning and he was actually fairly civil to me." He made a face. "Though he does have a puckish sense of humor and insisted that he show me the dungeon that he'd been threatening me with during our first encounter. When we got there, he bet me that I wouldn't have been able to get out of the damn place." He shrugged. "What could I do? I had to prove my worth, didn't I? He wouldn't have trusted you with me if I hadn't."

"So you let him lock you up?"

"It seemed the best thing to do." He grinned. "But I made sure that it would work for us."

She was frowning. "You got out of the dungeon?"

"His dungeon was a piece of cake after the prisons I'd occupied in Afghanistan. They didn't know how to build them right in the good old days. But I deliberately stalled for an hour or two to make MacDuff feel good about how hard I was finding it. Then I was duly humble when I supposedly discovered the way out of his precious hoosegow. Though I let him know how upset you were going to be because I'd wasted all that time and we'd probably both have to work late going through these diaries. That should give us a little extra time if Kilgoray takes longer than you think it will."

"It shouldn't. But you're right, it could help." She smiled. "I guess perhaps I'll forgive you for keeping MacDuff amused all morning." She added thoughtfully, "But don't be too sure that MacDuff was fooled. I've been in that dungeon, and he knows it's possible to get out. He might have known you were playing him. He's very sharp."

He nodded. "There was always that possibility. However, I think there's a decent chance that he was. If he wasn't, then he was in a mood to let me play a game that he also enjoyed. At any rate, even though I'd won the bet he took me back to the castle for a brandy and we parted on good terms. That's not bad." He asked curiously, "You were in that dungeon?"

She shrugged. "I couldn't resist. My father, Joe, is a detective and an expert in any number of restraint techniques from handcuffs to safes. He spent a summer when I was a teenager teaching me. It was great fun."

"And so was showing up MacDuff when you came here?"

"We were friends, he was glad that I'd been taught a skill. It wasn't a game between us. I wouldn't have tried to show him up. But never underestimate him."

"I won't. I'm glad you warned me." He gazed at the pile of volumes on the floor beside Jane. "You found more Fiona journals?"

She shook her head. "Historical books from MacDuff's library. I went over most of them in my room last night, but I wanted to compare the contents with entries from Fiona's diaries and journals. These are very good. They go back to the time of Cira and her arrival in a very savage Gaul from Herculaneum."

"Cira. I've heard you mention her before."

"It doesn't surprise me. Even after two thousand years she still seems to dominate the Highlands and the MacDuff family. She wasn't only colorful, but also the protectress. She's always fascinated me."

"Interesting. Maybe I'll glance through it."

"Careful. Cira's never light reading. But you might be amused by some of the stories about her legendary treasure troves. However, you'd probably do better to check the more modern allusions in this book." She made a face. "Those include any known references to railroads in the area at the time Fiona MacDuff was living near MacDuff's Run."

"It doesn't surprise me you'd latch onto those rail tracks. Did it sting a little?"

"Of course it did. Now I have to know all about them." She tilted her head. "And I'm getting there. The first railroads were built in England and Scotland between 1802 and 1826. From that time on it became the primary form of transportation in both areas. But I wasn't interested in general history, I wanted to know why Fiona would have been intrigued by them." She frowned thoughtfully. "And why she didn't want anyone to know that she was."

"Did you find out?"

"Not entirely. She won all those ribbons as a young girl, so we knew she was probably a sportswoman and not likely to be fascinated by the mechanics of a locomotive." She frowned. "Of course, she might have been thinking of escape since Jamie was trying to sell her down the river. But it might have been more complicated than that." She tapped her finger on a faded, vellum-covered book she was holding. "For instance, there was a railway service that operated from the Highlands to the coast that was used by both the farmers and lairds. It was past the time of the border reivers, but there was still an occasional robbery after the railroads were built. Actually, that particular railroad wasn't located too far from where Jamie raised Fiona before he decided to become more respectable and move closer to his brother, Colin, at MacDuff's Run. The builders got mega donations from both the rich landowners and some of the less-than-honest descendants of the reivers who ran the border before the law got tough on them. As a matter of fact, they called the railroad the Reiver after it was finished. But that didn't last long. They changed it to the Great Exeter Transport later. It turned out to be quite a luxurious production and extended from the upper Highlands to the forests below the border. It's still there, but now it's become more of a historical tourist attraction." She grinned. "I was so fascinated by the map that I spent most of last night going over it until I practically had it memorized. It was so convoluted I'll bet that the reivers had more to do with the construction than those rich landowners. They were probably up to no good."

"My, what a suspicious mind," he said. "It must come from the company you keep. Everyone knows what kind of reputation Seth Caleb has."

Jane's smile disappeared. "Do they? You obviously don't

know very much about him," she said curtly. "But you knew enough to let him save your life, didn't you? You thought he was good enough for that."

"Whoa." He held up his hand defensively. "Don't attack me. It was just a remark. If I'd wanted to insult Caleb, I would have done it to his face." He added wryly, "And taken the consequences. I never asked Palik what your relationship was to Caleb, but he dropped enough hints that I knew you were special. That's why I took the damn job. But I'm not going to pussyfoot around and pretend I don't know who and what Caleb is." He gave her a lopsided smile. "When I've made a study of him, and probably know his capabilities better than the director of MI6."

She tensed. "Perhaps you know a little too much. I'm sure Bohdan would pay well."

"No doubt. But you trust Seth Caleb and realize he would never be fool enough to risk you by sending in someone he'd have to clean up after. Think about it."

She was thinking about it. She relaxed a little. "Then you said the wrong thing."

"It happens." He shrugged. "But I also thought that since you were possibly dragging me into hot water, we should get to be a little more familiar so that you could trust me."

"For instance?"

"You could let me know what's happening at Kilgoray," he said coaxingly.

She shook her head.

"If you're going to meet a lover, I'm not about to tell Caleb. That's between the two of you. I'm supposed to keep you safe, not act as truant officer. But it would help to know more in case I need to execute my primary duty."

She shook her head again.

"Okay, I could only try." He added soberly, "But you need to know that even if I have to go at this blind, I'll do what has to be done and keep you safe for Caleb. So don't do anything stupid."

"I'm never stupid. I've been known to make occasional mistakes." She stared at him coolly. "And you told me flat out you were working for Palik and had hardly spoken to Caleb when I asked you."

"It's true. But it's still all about Caleb." He was suddenly smiling. "And because you're not stupid, you'd see right through anything I said and realize that he's the center. Though in this instance he obviously gave that designation to you."

"I could do without it. Why is it all about Caleb?" She was working it out. "You said he'd saved your life, but you were very casual about it. Then you took the job with Palik after you recovered..." Her gaze was fixed on his face. "So maybe you weren't that casual. Just how did he save your life?"

"By taking my place after the Taliban had tied me to a tree and were in the process of whipping me to death. He was outnumbered, but he sent some of his men to get me away and let them take him instead." He shrugged. "He escaped later that night, but they'd hurt him. I tried to thank him later, but he ignored me. He was impatient as hell. He said he didn't want to hear it. I heard later that he was always like that, but I couldn't let it go. It might not have meant much to him, but it did to me."

"So, you decided to stick around and find a way to pay him back." It was a statement. "You took the job with Palik."

"It was a good job. Palik is fair." He paused. "And everyone knows that Caleb is the Hunter and Palik works with him whenever he can. But I didn't think it would take this long. I was about ready to move on."

She shook her head. "You wouldn't have done that."

His brows rose. "Why not?"

"Because it's Seth Caleb. It's hard to move on from Caleb. He's...special. You knew that." Her lips indented at the corners. "I'm sure you have the wounds to prove it."

He nodded. "And I'm doing my best to keep you from having any of your own wounds to worry him. Kilgoray?"

"No wounds there that won't heal." Her voice softened. "But I want you to know that I'm grateful to you for wanting to save him from pain. A lot of people take from him and don't give back. They believe since they know about all those skills and how tough he is that he doesn't need any help at all." She met his eyes. "Like you did, but you were going to give it anyway."

"My choice."

"Everyone has choices. But you made the right one as far as I'm concerned."

"But you still won't talk about Kilgoray."

She ignored the comment. "I want you to pick me up at the boat dock as soon as darkness falls." She opened the historical book in front of her. "You'll like the pub. Jock, the bartender, is funny. Caleb and I spent an afternoon there a couple of months ago. I promise I won't keep you waiting there long." She waved her hand. "Now hush while I look at the photos and sketches of this Reiver train. Someone spent a long time on the decorations on these cars..."

CHAPTER

7

Y ou're right, pleasant little village." It was almost dark when Rodland tied off the motorboat at the pier. He jumped out and swung Jane onto the pier. "Emphasis on *little*." His gaze raked the stone buildings that lined the narrow streets. "Several shops, a tearoom." He smiled as he heard music issuing from a brightly lit building a few doors away. There was an outdoor patio with several tables and chairs beneath the tan-and-blue umbrellas. "And that must be my designated home away from home. Jock's pub?"

"That's right." She could feel her tension growing and she drew a deep breath. She turned to her left and headed for the bank of shops and offices down the street. "Have an ale on me. I'll see you soon. I'll watch the time. We have to get back to MacDuff's Run."

"Sure, I'll just be sitting here at one of Jock's outdoor tables." He dropped down in a chair. "Will you tell me which shop or building you'll be going into?"

"No." She looked back at him. "But I'll be close enough that

111

you'd be able to hear me from that chair if I called out to you. So don't follow me. If you do, I won't trust you again."

He was silent. "I'll give you an hour. Then I'll come and find you."

"It shouldn't take longer than that." She waved and turned right into the bank of shops.

She stopped and drew a deep breath as she glanced back at the pub. Rodland was sitting totally at ease, but his gaze was still fixed on where she'd disappeared. Forget about him. Think about Caleb. Concentrate on what she had to do and hope she could trust Rodland. If she couldn't, she'd worry about handling the fallout later. That might be the least of her worries.

She glanced away from Rodland and hurried down the next street and into the foyer of the sandstone building set back from the cobblestone street.

Get it over with.

She hadn't thought she'd be in a panic, but the panic was there...

———◆———

"You're early." Rodland straightened in his chair as he saw Jane coming toward him. "Fifty-five minutes."

Jane chuckled. "And were you about to jump up from your chair and start stalking if I didn't show up exactly on time?"

"Probably." His eyes were narrowed on her face. "I might have given you an extra five or ten minutes, but I'd have to keep my word to you. We had an agreement."

She was still smiling. "Which was really an agreement you had with Palik and Caleb. I was just an afterthought."

"It didn't turn out that way. You turned the tables on me. But I'm glad that it seems to have worked out well for you." He got to his feet and threw some money on the table. "Very well. You're...happy. Whoever it was must have satisfied you."

She nodded. "Absolutely." Her smile faded. "But you're wasting that additional five minutes I gave you. We have to get back to the Run. Let's get out of here." She turned and headed for the pier at a run. "I've no desire to have to explain to MacDuff what I was doing here with you."

"But once he saw your expression, he'd realize how happy I'd made you." His grin held a catlike hint of mischief. "Though that might keep him guessing. He might enjoy the idea that I'd made you forget about Seth Caleb for a little while. I've noticed there appears to be a certain antagonism in his attitude about Caleb on occasion."

"Their relationship is complicated." She jumped into the boat as he untied it. "They respect each other, but MacDuff likes to run things and there's no way Caleb will allow that to happen."

"Particularly anything to do with you." He snapped his fingers. "Fiona. Is it something to do with the family?"

"Heavens no," she said flatly. "Caleb understands how I feel and would never interfere with my family. And he's always had the same fascination with Fiona as MacDuff. It's probably just two alpha males wanting their own way. Most of the time they manage to get along." She was looking back at Kilgoray as he pulled away from the pier. "You should understand that concept."

"I've never tried to go head-to-head with Caleb. It's hard not to remember what he went through to keep me alive. It puts a damper on any aggressiveness I might be feeling."

"I can see how it might." The wind was caressing her cheeks and the moonlight was casting a shimmer on the sea. It was over! Everything seemed wonderfully alive in this moment. The relief was zinging through her. "Maybe you could work on it," she said lightly. "You already have an edge. Caleb told Palik he was to keep you alive."

"Very funny," he said sourly. "I'm not amused." He shot her a glance. "But you are. You wouldn't care to tell me why you're in such a good mood?"

She grinned. "It must be a feeling of accomplishment. I had something to do, and I did it. It's finished." She added, "Thank you."

"You're welcome. You'd be even more welcome if you assured me that we weren't going to make this journey again. You have to admit there's a certain amount of risk to a jaunt like this. Can you do that?"

"I don't see why not. As I said, it's finished. It's not as if I want to risk anything happening to me. It was just...necessary." She met his eyes. "I'm not going to demand anything like that again. The most dangerous thing I'll ask is that you help me with Fiona so that I can give MacDuff some answers in return for all he's doing for me." She shrugged. "And it's not as if this little trip caused any real trouble. We skimmed over there and now we're halfway back. Did you see anyone suspicious while you were waiting for me?"

He shook his head. "Did you?"

She grinned. "No. You keep trying, don't you?"

"Always," he said. "And just because we made it here doesn't mean we can be certain no one knew that we did it. Or that security wasn't breached while we've been gone. After we get back, I'll slip you into the castle and I'll do a trek around the property and the boat dock to be sure there aren't any signs that would make me uneasy. Sound good?"

"Of course it does. I told you that from now on I'm not taking any chances."

"Music to my ears." He smiled. "And tomorrow I'll start helping you with Fiona again." He pressed on the accelerator and the boat leaped forward as he caught sight of MacDuff's Run on the horizon. "And we'll forget about Kilgoray."

But Kilgoray was very much on her mind as they were climbing back up the curving steps through the dark stable to get to the courtyard twenty minutes later.

Jane's phone rang.

She inhaled sharply as she saw the number. "Caleb."

He shook his head. "Not the time. Ignore it."

"I don't ignore Caleb. Not ever." She'd reached the stall level and she leaned against the wall, her gaze on the brightly lit screen. "I'll take the call. Go ahead if you want to."

"That wasn't the plan."

"Then do what you want." She pressed the access. "Caleb?"

"I won't keep you long," Caleb said. "I think I just wanted to hear your voice. And I told you I'd be in touch. Is everything with you okay?"

"Why wouldn't it be? I have an army here keeping an eye on me. Are you in Naples?"

"Yes. But I don't know how long I'll be here. I'm getting impatient. Bohdan hasn't shown up yet. Palik is sure he will, but I might have to do something to stir the man into action."

"The last actions he took involved beheading and torture," Jane said. "Why can't you let MI6 do the stirring?"

"As I said, I'm impatient. I was uneasy about the way I left you. Everything is crazy now and I have to make it right. I want to get back to you." He cleared his throat. "You haven't said anything about Rodland. Is he working out for you?"

"I can't complain. Rodland is doing all right." She looked at Rodland standing by the stable door. "At least he's been doing what I tell him to do."

Rodland nodded mockingly and tipped his hand to his head.

Caleb was silent. Then he said suddenly, "He's with you now, isn't he? I can tell by your tone. Where are you?"

Damn. She had forgotten how sensitive Caleb always was to her every tone and expression. Standing here in the darkness she had felt safe. But she wouldn't lie to him.

"I'm in the courtyard stable. Rodland has been helping me go through the Fiona diaries and historical documents. We've almost finished with the storage units here."

"The stable," he repeated. "How helpful?"

Suddenly the darkness seemed terribly intimate as she remembered the last time she'd been in this stable with Caleb. Her breasts were swelling and her pulse was pounding in the hollow of her throat. "Helpful enough. He gets bored easily. But he did come up with an idea about the railroad tracks." She went on quickly, "But it's time I got back to the castle now. We only worked late because MacDuff wasted hours of our day with trying to trip Rodland up getting out of that ancient dungeon."

"It all sounds very...pleasant and amusing. But perhaps I should let you get back to the castle. I'm glad you're keeping busy." He was silent again. "Tell Rodland that he should spend more time taking care of you and less with MacDuff's games."

"You're the one who sent him. Do you want to tell him yourself?"

"Not now. I don't believe it's come to that yet. I'll keep an eye on the situation and call you soon. Good night, Jane." He cut the connection.

"Whew," Rodland said. "Am I in trouble?"

"Why should you be? All I did was tell him the truth."

"Not quite all the truth. Are you going to tell him about Kilgoray?"

"Eventually. Now isn't the time."

"I believe that's what I said. You took the call anyway."

"That was different. It would be like ignoring Caleb himself. I'd never do that." She made a face. "It's not possible. We have problems but we're way past lies or games. We just have to get past this patch to the other side."

"Really?" he asked curiously. "And what is on the other side?"

She smiled brilliantly. "I can't wait to see. Something wonderful and challenging and splendid. Because we'll make it that way."

Rodland's gaze was still on her face as he nodded slowly. "I believe you mean it. I'm relieved. You do care about him. I admit I didn't feel I could entirely accept that you weren't meeting a lover at Kilgoray. It was the logical conclusion. I wasn't sure how I was going to have to handle that complication."

Jane's jaw dropped. "You weren't going to handle it at all. I wouldn't have let you. Not your business."

"Wrong," he said quietly. "You became my business the minute I found out Caleb was moving heaven and earth to keep you safe. I owe him my life, and it's going to be hard as hell to clear that debt. So, this is payback. I just have to make sure that nothing gets in the way of me giving him what he needs."

"Not even if I'd choose to not go along?" she asked sarcastically.

"A complication." He smiled. "One I don't have to face now. You were very eloquent. Whatever you were doing at the village, it didn't have anything to do with any relationship that would hurt Seth Caleb."

"And what would you do if it had?"

"Anything I had to do," he said simply. "But why worry? I would have tried to work it out. And now it's not necessary. We can start fresh. So just consider me your good angel who's standing by to sweep all the demons from your path." He was suddenly beside her at the stable door. "Stay here while I take a look around the courtyard. I'll have you tucked back in the castle in another ten minutes."

She watched him move across the courtyard. *Good angel?* she thought in bewildered frustration. He was more like an Irish leprechaun, and the demons he'd spoken about fighting would have been in service to Caleb.

Well, what was wrong with that? Her annoyance was suddenly gone. Caleb was usually alone in his battles. She liked the idea of someone who cared enough about him to watch his back. As far as being guardian to her, she couldn't afford to reject that, either. Independence was all very well, but she would take all the help she could get.

Because everything had changed during that hour spent in Kilgoray . . .

———◆———

"Kilgoray," Bohdan repeated when Chiswick called him later that night. "What the hell does this Kilgoray have to do with anything? I thought you were monitoring that earl's property at MacDuff's Run. You told me that your team had sighted the woman at the castle earlier today."

"They did, and it was definitely Jane MacGuire. But somehow she managed to leave the property in a speedboat with one of MacDuff's men and was taken to a village down the coast."

"Why?" Bohdan swore viciously. "Did she meet with Caleb there? Did you follow her?"

"Of course I did. But by the time I got the message, she'd left the castle and all we could do was keep watch on her from the yacht. I told you how well MacDuff's property was guarded. We have to remain out of sight and maintain our distance or have MI6 agents on top of us. I knew that wasn't what you'd want to happen. They'd get in our way." He added quickly, "She only stayed a short time at the village and then they were on their way back to the castle. I'm about to take a team to Kilgoray and ask a few casual questions to see if Caleb has been seen there. He's not someone who is easy to forget."

"No, he's not," Bohdan said curtly. "And he'll be even more memorable once I get my hands on him. Don't blow this, Chiswick. If he's there in the village, find him. If he's not, comb the area, but try to be subtle, dammit. We don't want to tip our hands before we can get hold of him. Dealing directly with MI6 and the British aristocracy could be awkward."

Awkward? Chiswick almost had to laugh. No one was less subtle than the Bohdan he had come to know over the years. He thrived on brutality and power, and his position as second in command to the general had only exaggerated that arrogance. "Naturally, I'll do as you say. We also got photos of the man who was with the MacGuire woman. If Kilgoray doesn't pan out, maybe I can deliver him to you. He might be able to give us the information we need about Caleb."

"Perhaps. But you've convinced me Jane MacGuire almost certainly could. Which means I need to know everything about her. Phone, close relatives or friends. Anything I can use to make her come to heel. I want her scared and shivering whenever I come near her." He added with soft sarcasm, "And if you hadn't let her slip through your fingers tonight, I would have had her. I wouldn't have needed anything but a few hours and my own skill to make her give me Caleb. Remember that when you're searching Kilgoray for him."

"I'll remember. But we're getting closer all the time. Are you on your way?"

"I will be after I hang up. Get back to that village and find Caleb!"

———

Caleb called Palik when he was on his way to Palik's hotel. "Has Bohdan showed up in the city yet?"

"Not at the brothel. But I've heard he's been checking on his drug houses in Milan and Campania. And there was an explosion at a meth house near Maggiano Beach. Probably Bohdan was unhappy with their output. He usually saves the brothels for more personal entertainment. Other than that, he's been playing his visit here very low-key. He has to know that MI6 is after him for the Tiber murder, and he might be facing a war crimes accusation in the Congo. I think he's trying to keep his investments here in line until he can go back there and take over the general's position. Which means he's been principally occupied with trying to locate you." He paused. "Why? Restless?"

"I want it over."

"Jane MacGuire is safe. Did you check with Rodland?"

"She seems pleased enough with him."

"He's a good man," he said. "And he'll take care of her."

"So will MacDuff and his Royal Marines," Caleb said bitterly. "I've got the situation covered, haven't I?"

"Yes, you have."

"But it doesn't stop me from imagining Bohdan sitting on the doorstep waiting for a chance to pounce."

"And that means that we're not going to wait for that to happen? What are you planning?"

"I need him to come out in the open so that I can target *him*. I believe Bohdan has too many businesses to take care of. I think we should lighten his load."

"You don't think you're high enough on his kill list?"

"He's obviously thinking too much about hunting me. Let's give him something else to think about. I'm pulling into the parking lot of your hotel now. Gather all the info you have on Bohdan and meet me in the bar. Concentrate on his most expensive and profitable assets. We have choices to make."

———◆———

STORAGE ROOM
MACDUFF'S RUN
TWO DAYS LATER

"You're leaving me to check out all those diaries by myself," Rodland complained. "There's nothing of interest. I'm sure

Fiona was a fascinating young woman, but she definitely wasn't as well rounded as any modern-day lass. She visits the castle to see Uncle Colin, she goes to chapel, she helps nurse the ill in the village. But she never even says what she's thinking about any of it. She might as well be a mummy."

Jane took a drink of water from her bottle. "And you're bored."

"You could let me study those historical tomes about those trains that you've been devouring for the past few days. You've been totally absorbed. They'd be much more my cup of tea, too."

She shook her head. "Waste of effort. You already know all about trains. You went through hell building that crude one in Kashmir. And you're the one who told us that Fiona was drawing pictures of railroad tracks." She smiled. "I'm the one who needs to learn why she was doing it. Sorry she's not entertaining you. But I'm not giving them up." When he made a face, she chuckled. Oh, what the hell, he might make fun of her, but they'd become friends and it didn't matter. "But I'll share this one of the Reiver car with you." She handed him the book. "It has some of the later photos of the train as a whole, but there are also several shots of the car when they were first building it back in 1869. Look at the photos of the murals painted on its wall. They're exceptional. I particularly like the one of the lake in the Highlands." Her smile deepened. "Although that might be because I've seen it before. It's not too far from MacDuff's Run."

"Really?" He looked closer. "Remarkable."

She nodded, waiting a moment before adding, "Or it might be because I recognized the technique of the artist. Those brushstrokes are almost unmistakable."

Rodland glanced up at her. "And you're so excited you obviously want to tell someone about it. What did you find out, Jane?"

"I'm almost sure that the artist was the same one who painted the portrait of Fiona. I won't know definitely until I find a larger, more detailed photo of that picture. Or the picture itself."

"If it still exists," he said gently. "It's not likely. That was at the time of the American Civil War. A mural that old, from a railcar that might have been scrapped over a hundred years ago?"

"It wasn't," Jane said. "I called the railroad and talked to a clerk yesterday afternoon. It's no longer in use, but the car is considered an antique and is sitting sidelined in one of the company rail yards."

"Which one?"

"She couldn't tell me. Not one of the city yards."

"And the mural?"

She shook her head. "The clerk couldn't tell me any details about the present furnishings. I'll have to see for myself. But she went back into the company historical Rolodex and was able to pull out the name of the artist. It was painted by Farrell MacClaren. No other information."

He was studying her face. "But it could be enough?"

"Maybe. If I can find a connection between MacClaren and Fiona. The painting on the train was of a place in the hills near here. It's possible that while MacClaren was painting Fiona, they got to know each other. But how well?" She was trying to work it out. "The rail ties. She must have known he was working with the railroad, too. If she didn't want anyone to know he was communicating with her, there had to be a reason."

"He was her lover?"

"We don't even know how old he was. He could have been her father's age. Maybe he just wanted to help her escape from a bad marriage."

"I'll still vote for the lover. If he was older, he would have been more sympathetic to the older generation. He'd have been on her father's side. The secret messages speak of a young man out for adventure."

She had to smile. "I believe you're a romantic."

"I'm just Irish. Sometimes it's the same thing. And I deplore the fact that you're being so practical. It doesn't bode well for your relationship with Caleb. He's hard and practical enough for all of us combined. He needs a little softness in his life. I'll make you a deal. Go for the young lovers. And I'll help you track down this Farrell MacClaren and get you a dossier on him. I've told you how brilliant I am working with computers. I've learned a lot about gathering info of all kinds working for Palik. I'll man the telephones and computers and you'll have your information. Just don't make me read any more diaries."

"So now you're protecting Caleb's delicate feelings from me? I don't think he finds me too harsh."

"Friendship isn't only physical, it goes deeper."

"That's what your Irish soul tells you?"

"Is it a deal?"

"Okay, it's a deal. It's not as if I didn't want Fiona to have had a great love in her life. I was only remembering what MacDuff told me about how women could be punished back then if they didn't toe the line. She was as much Jamie's captive as if she was in prison." She shook her head. "I won't let you do all the research work. It might be better if I read the rest of her diaries and journals anyway. You might not catch nuances."

"I beg your pardon? I'm insulted."

"Besides, I wanted to take time to go to Jamie MacDuff's residence that was her actual home and look around there."

"Didn't MacDuff tell you the house has been vacant for decades? You don't expect to find anything?"

"Probably not. I just wanted to see where she lived."

"Sentiment?"

"Maybe." She wrinkled her nose as she saw his skeptical look. "Okay, I've been living with her one way or another for a long time. And lately she's become...close to me."

"I promise I won't tell MacDuff," he said, deadpan.

"I'm not going to count on it. I've found you have a devilish sense of humor. You blame it on being Irish, but I'd be an idiot if I didn't realize it originates in a much more fiery region."

"And when do you intend for us to take this trip? You do know I go with you."

"I wouldn't think of violating Palik's prime directive. We'll pick up two horses at the main stable tomorrow morning and ride up there."

"What about MacDuff?"

"What about him? The house is on the property."

"Horses?"

"You don't like horses?"

"I didn't say that. I appreciate them. However, in the past I haven't been around them enough for them to have the opportunity to appreciate me."

"I see." She couldn't keep her lips from twitching. "I'll be sure to choose you a horse that will be gentle and smart enough to understand what an honor it is to have your company." She picked up the diary he'd laid down to look at the Reiver history. "Now go make notes on

MacClaren and do your thing. Then give that book back to me. There are all kinds of diagrams and photos of everything connected to the Reiver Railway Company. I want to see if I can make any more sense of these Reiver train yards."

"What do you have in mind?" he asked warily. "You promised me no more field trips off the property."

"And I'll keep my word. I know the border is too far from here. Besides, I'd end up with MacDuff and his men trailing me along with you. I'll be content with going to visit Jamie MacDuff's house and saving the Reiver train for when Caleb takes down Bohdan. By that time, you'll be gone and won't have to bother with where I go."

"It's not too much of a bother." He smiled slyly. "I've begun to feel almost brotherly toward you. You're a little skittish, but I've managed to keep you under control."

"And if this book wasn't so fragile, I'd smash it on your arrogant head."

"Not at all a sisterly response." He opened the book. "And I thought we were getting along so well. But you'll forgive me when I hand you Farrell MacClaren on a platter."

"That's debatable. Do it, and I'll give you a decision...or a judgment." She was still trying not to smile. He was a thorough scamp but having him here had been a relief and distraction. She'd needed that distraction between worrying about Caleb and the ramifications of that trip to Kilgoray. Caleb hadn't called her since that night, and she'd wanted to strangle him. No, she didn't, she amended quickly. She just wanted him to safely end this nightmare and come back to her. She'd frantically dived into the study surrounding Fiona and tried to pretend to MacDuff and not let him see what she was feeling.

Working with Rodland had given her an excuse that had filled a multitude of purposes.

"Caleb is all right, you know." Rodland had not looked up from the book. "He's extraordinary and he knows what he wants. Evidently, he wants you. He'll never stop."

"I know that. Most of the time." She took a drink of her water. "Neither will I. You don't have to worry about your friend Caleb. I'll take care of him." She added wryly, "If I can push aside all the people in my way."

"That's good to know." He glanced up with the smallest smile. "I'll keep it in mind. Though you can't possibly be talking about me." He looked down again. "Now don't bother me. I've got calls to make."

———◆———

MAGGIANO LAKE
ITALY
11:50 P.M.

Palik slid down the side of the ditch to where Caleb was waiting. "I hope you know this is beneath my dignity. I have men who do this kind of thing for me these days. I should charge you extra."

"You will." Caleb lifted the infrared binoculars to his eyes again. "As soon as you're certain it will be enough for what you might be forced to go through for this little foray. You wouldn't want to undercharge me. That would be a disaster."

"I'm glad you understand." He gazed out over the water to the opposite bank. "Are you sure this is the target you want?"

"No, that's why I'm still here. For a meth lab it appears to be getting plenty of business. The warehouse is huge. It may be the right choice."

"It's the biggest Bohdan property in Italy and definitely the most profitable. He also sells out of the country to drug dealers in France. What else could you want."

"I want him to hurt. I want him to go back to the Congo and forget about me for a while until I can set a trap far from MacDuff's Run."

"This might not do it."

"Then I'll hit him again. Have you set everything up?"

"Except for the time and the final decision. You didn't seem to be in a hurry."

"Oh, I'm in a hurry. But the drug house in Campania is still in the running. I just want it to be the right choice. I might be able to make it, if you stop talking and let me concentrate."

Palik sighed and leaned back. "Either way, it might be my fault for not giving you what you need. Right? I'll pull this whiskey out of my pocket I brought to soothe me in case you were being difficult. Then I'll definitely shut up."

CHAPTER

8

I don't know if I approve of this." MacDuff was frowning as he approached Jane, who was mounting her horse outside the main stables. "It doesn't make sense. You're not going to find anything at Jamie's house." He glanced at Sean Rodland. "Did you encourage her? You both should stay at the castle."

"I just obey orders." Rodland swung onto the back of the chestnut. "And you're the one who told her you found those first books at Jamie MacDuff's house, sir. But I've looked over the route this morning and it's clear. I'll check the house interior before I let her enter. May I suggest you have a few of your men follow us? It would make you feel better. That way you wouldn't have to totally trust me. After all, I'm a stranger to you."

And crafty as hell, Jane thought, smothering a smile as she swung onto the bay stallion. But she doubted if MacDuff would fall for it.

He didn't. "You're definitely a strange one," he said. "Do you even know how to ride a horse?"

129

"Not well, but I tend to get along with both man and beast." He lowered his eyes as he leaned forward to pat the chestnut's neck. "Though I occasionally have problems with keeping ahead of women like Jane. But you'll understand, since you have the same cross to bear."

"I don't know what you mean. Jane and I get along splendidly." He turned to Jane. "You won't change your mind?"

"I have to see for myself if Fiona left anything else there besides those two books you found and restored. You weren't looking for anything to do with railroads or paintings at the time." She waved her hand around to indicate the beauty of the horses, the trees, and the brilliant blue of the sky above them. "Besides, I need to see something other than the four walls I've been looking at down in those storage rooms. It's only five or six miles from the castle. Rodland is right—if it will make you feel better, send someone to escort us." She made a face. "Only not too close on our heels. I'd feel like Princess Di under siege by paparazzi. And there's nothing royal about me, thank heavens."

"You never know," MacDuff murmured. "There are stories about the MacDuffs and Bonnie Prince Charlie." He started to laugh as she opened her lips to protest. "Okay, okay. But I'll send Fergus and a couple of the marines to follow you in one of the cars. You'll be back inside the castle gates by dark?"

"Whatever the laird decrees," she said. "Even when he's ridiculous. Bye, MacDuff." She nudged the horse and he trotted toward the road. "Come along, Rodland, I'm in the mood for a brisk run."

"Whatever you say. Maybe after this horse becomes used to me." He added in a low tone, "And we reach the curve in the road ahead so that MacDuff won't see me fall on my ass. It would seriously damage the balance of power we have between us."

She pulled in her horse and grinned at him. "And MacDuff would enjoy it far too much. We can't have that." She gazed critically at him. "You look good on that horse."

"Pure show. So you're going to spare me the humiliation?"

"I'm thinking about it," she said. "We appear to have reached the curve in the road." Then she nodded. "It would probably be traumatic to your horse to have you flying over her head. Maisie is supposed to be gentle and ladylike. Why don't you just get to know her on the road to Jamie's house? Then we'll see how you do on the ride back."

"It works for me. Her name is Maisie? I knew a bar girl in Dublin by that name." He grinned. "But she was neither gentle nor ladylike."

"It could have been a response to how you treated her," Jane said. "Give Maisie her due and you might survive until we get to Jamie's house."

"I treat all females with respect." He patted the mare again. "I've always found it safer. Women have too many weapons." His eyes twinkled. "And you never know when one will appear. Like you, Jane."

"I've never drawn a weapon on you."

"But you might have to get what you wanted," he said. "And I believe a weapon would have definitely been an option to protect Caleb. Yes?"

"Yes."

"But I feel perfectly safe because I'm no threat to you. I'm on your side all the way. Teach me how to get along with Maisie, and I'll forgive you for making me display a bit of weakness in front of MacDuff."

"But you didn't display it. He didn't see it."

"*I* saw it. And that means that I'll have to work like hell to correct it so that it won't become a true weakness."

"I can see that would be a terrible thing."

"It's the only way I've been able to survive," he said simply.

She realized that he meant it. "And how are you going to correct it? Become a rodeo rider?"

"Maybe." He smiled. "That might be amusing if I can stand the bumps and bruises. I'll have to think about it. I'll let you know when I'm ready to erase that moment of weakness from your memory."

"I can hardly wait," she said sincerely before she kicked her horse into a trot. "We've got to get moving or Fergus and the marines will be catching up with us. Jocko is my horse's name and he's a little more spirited than Maisie. Would you mind if I have a short run and leave you and Maisie to get to know each other?"

"By all means." He waved her away. "That appears to be the name of the game. Hopefully we'll catch up with you by the time you reach Jamie MacDuff's place."

But Jane had to wait over fifteen minutes until Rodland ambled up to the front entrance on Maisie.

"I was wondering if she threw you." Jane nodded at the Range Rover parked in the trees a short distance away. "Even Fergus and his men got here before you did." She glanced at Maisie. "But you seem to be doing okay together."

"We're getting there. It will just take a while for us to understand each other." He was looking at the stately mansion a short distance away. "Almost impressive. Evidently Jamie had more funds than I thought."

"Not enough for him. But I read where he opened his home twice a month for gambling soirees and invited all the neighbors to come." She got off her horse. "And he was amazingly fortunate at the tables. Not surprising since he was raised as a reiver and didn't have a sterling reputation." She frowned. "I don't know where to start."

"Start by keeping Maisie company for a short time while I go check out the interior." He dismounted. "As I promised MacDuff I'd do." He started down the path toward the ornate front door. "And considering how smart we think Fiona might be, if I were you I wouldn't look where you'd think she'd hide something."

"Amazing insight." Jane watched him disappear into the house. But in spite of her sarcasm, she was feeling a touch of excitement as she looked at the house. Such a formal residence for a girl who ran wild in the hills, who won races, and defied her father when he'd tried to sell her. She must have hated living here.

And Fiona would have studied the situation as she had the racecourses where she'd triumphed and found a way to hide her intentions for defeating Jamie. Would proof still be there?

Is it there, Fiona? It's been a long time. But your life had to have been a bit crazy and filled with panic back then. The ribbon you won? Surely you would have taken that ribbon if you could. Perhaps you left another trail for me . . .

———◆———

MAGGIANO LAKE
ITALY
2:40 P.M.

"You're certain it should be this one?" Palik asked when he picked up the phone.

133

"Do it," Caleb said.

"Then get out of there. I'll give the word."

"I'm staying here in the hills. I want to see the response."

"And I want you to get out of there alive."

"Do it," Caleb repeated.

Palik muttered a curse and then hung up.

Caleb lifted his binoculars again. He waited.

Not for long.

The prisms of the crown glass of the binoculars flamed brilliant red that turned into a puff of smoke as a roar echoed over the lake!

The earth beneath Caleb's boots shook and almost knocked him from his feet.

Done...

He settled down to wait.

JAMIE MACDUFF'S HOME

"You've got dirt on your face." Rodland handed Jane a bottle of water and a roll of paper towels that they'd found in the kitchen cabinet when they'd first arrived at Jamie's house over five hours ago. "I told you I'd search the attic. It was bound to be the area most left neglected by the cleaning crews MacDuff sent out."

"I was desperate." She opened the bottle of water and took a long drink. "I couldn't believe that we weren't finding anything in the other rooms. I was hoping since MacDuff found Fiona's two books there that I'd get lucky and discover some secret cache where she'd hidden something else."

"And what did you find?"

She made a face. "Dirt. Cobwebs. Various spiders of dubious, possibly frightening potential." She took another drink of water. "What did you find up in Jamie's master bedroom?"

"Period furniture. Nice carpets. Everything spick-and-span and looking as if it was cleaned every thirty days just as MacDuff decreed." He shook his head. "You couldn't expect anything else, Jane."

"But I could hope." She put the cap back on the water bottle. "And I can still hope. I won't give up."

"Of course you won't. What's next?"

"First, I find a bathroom and wash up a little. I wouldn't want to upset MacDuff's cleaners by soiling any furniture." She got to her feet. "And then I'll go downstairs to Jamie's library and take a look around."

"You said that he used it only for show and his gambling soirees. Fiona wouldn't have been permitted in that section of the house."

"But you told me not to look for anything in a place where I thought Fiona might hide it. I've exhausted everything else. I've decided to follow your advice."

"As a last resort?"

"I didn't say that." She grinned. "But she liked books and she wasn't supposed to be in Jamie's library. It might have been a temptation she couldn't resist. Want to come down and help me? If you do, I'll meet you in the library in ten minutes." She turned and ran down the steps.

He was in the library, going through books, when she entered the library ten minutes later. He looked up. "I had to put my money where my mouth was. But I'm warning you that it looks like these books have never been touched."

"Maybe they haven't. But if we see any that appear to have even a little wear, we should pay attention to them. It might mean that Fiona was thumbing her nose at Jamie."

He shrugged. "I'll do what I can. Where are you going to start?"

She gazed around the huge room. All the books appeared pristine. "I'm not certain . . ." She made a decision. "There are a few rows on transportation over there. I'll see if I can find anything on trains since Fiona clearly had an interest."

"Good luck."

She knew immediately that she'd need luck as she started to go through the books. They were all expensive, antique tomes, but they were stiff, and she had to be careful of the bindings. It wasn't until she reached the row on the second shelf that concerned the trains that she noticed anything different. In the middle of the third book—*The History of the Oystermouth Steam Railway*—she saw something peculiar. "What the hell . . ."

Rodland looked up. "What?"

Jane was carefully separating two pages that had been glued together in the center of the book. "Hush, I'm trying to concentrate and not cause these pages to fall apart. Old . . . so old."

Rodland was beside her. "Can I help?"

She shook her head. "It's a letter and there's no way I can remove it without damaging it. The ink is faded, and I can barely make it out. I'll have to take time and do it slowly, carefully."

"You can't make out any of the words?"

Jane was squinting but she shook her head. "I don't think I—" She broke off and suddenly smiled. "Except the signature. It's very bold." She met his eyes. "He signed it. *All my love, Farrell.*"

136

He chuckled. "I told you they were lovers. Farrell MacClaren. The artist who painted her portrait."

"We can't be sure they were lovers until I manage to read this letter."

"You're quibbling. Anything else?"

"I'm looking." She was carefully turning the pages. But she was nearly at the end of the book when she noticed a thickening on the inner back cover. She hurriedly flipped it and saw the inch-thick surface that was hiding the exterior cover. "That's too thick to be another letter." She gently worked the edge of the upper cover loose. "It's not sealed, it's a kind of envelope." She pulled the object slowly away from the back cover. "But it feels like a letter. Maybe I'm wrong..." Then the object came free and slid out into her hand.

"What on earth!" She stared blankly down at the slick colorful surface. "It looks like a cheap paperback book that was hidden inside Jamie's historical train book. Why would Fiona have done that?"

"You'll have to figure it out." Rodland was chuckling. "But maybe she had a sense of humor. Look at the title and the artwork on the cover."

Jane could see what was amusing him. *Daring Cowboy Bob Stops the Train Robbery*. And the artwork showed a dashing cowboy shooting at a train that looked like a dragon chugging down a railroad track. The art was excellent, and it reminded her of something... Then it came to her.

"It's a dime novel," she murmured. "I studied them in one of my art classes. They were popular in the U.S. from around 1860 until 1915. They were only about twenty-five thousand words and they all had colorful covers. They cost a nickel or a dime and were shaped to fit the pocket. Fiona wouldn't have had any trouble hiding this in the book. But why would she have wanted to?"

"If she was never in the U.S., someone must have sent it to her. I can't imagine it would have been imported here."

"You may be right." Jane was looking through the novel. "There are words and passages underlined."

"Someone who had a connection with the railway? My, my."

"Be quiet." She was smiling. "You're lucky I'm too happy about finding these Fiona treasures to properly put you in your place. Now let's go through the rest of this library and see if we can find anything else."

"I doubt if we will. She put two of her treasures in one single book. She probably wanted to be able to grab and run if she had to."

"Maybe. But we'll try anyway." She opened another book. "Hurry, I want to finish before dark. Get to work, Rodland."

———◆———

They finished going through the library before twilight, and Rodland was annoyingly correct about the search being a waste of time. Then they had to carefully, separately wrap the letter and the novel and replace them in the original book. Rodland found a burlap sack in the kitchen, and they wrapped the Oystermouth train book itself and slipped it into the sack. Rodland bowed and ceremoniously handed Jane the sack. "Not a very elegant clue. But may it be the first of many. At least it's a decent start."

"Actually, I've been thinking about it, and that dime novel might be very elegant in its way," she said slowly. "The reason my art teacher had us study them was that she said they were as important in their way as a work by Shakespeare."

"Cowboy Bob?"

"It didn't matter about the content. They were stories, and because they were cheap, they were available to everyone. Books were no longer only for the rich. Everyone wanted them. Not only for the stories, but for the colorful illustrations. It opened the world to artists as well as writers." She shook her head. "Who would have guessed it?"

"Not me. But it's interesting. Evidently Fiona thought so, too. I wonder why?"

"We'll find out." Jane tucked the sack carefully in her art case and fastened it. "But you'll have a good deal of work to give us a picture of MacClaren and his relationship with Fiona."

"I've already got the groundwork done on MacClaren. I just have to complete the connections."

"You could have told me. I can't see why the connections would—" Jane's phone was ringing and she pulled it out of her jacket.

"MacDuff?" Rodland asked. "It's getting dark, but I didn't think he'd be nagging so soon."

"No. Not MacDuff." And it wasn't Caleb, either. She was puzzled as she checked the ID. "Wilma Dillard. It's my agent Felicia's mother. This shouldn't take long." She punched the access. "Hello, Wilma. It's nice to hear from you. Are you trying to reach Felicia? I'm afraid I can't help you. I'm not in London."

"I know you aren't." Wilma Dillard's voice was shaking a little. "She told me when you left town. I'm sorry to bother you, Jane. I just didn't know what else to do. I don't know where she is."

Jane stiffened. "Something's wrong? What are you talking about? The two of you are so close. You must know where she is."

"I thought you might have an idea. The last I heard from her was a few days ago. We'd made plans to go out to dinner and then she was going to take me to a concert. I talked to her that morning and she told me she'd pick me up at seven." She paused. "She didn't show up. I called her, but her phone was turned off. At first, I thought it was just an electronic glitch. I don't know anything about those things." She was breathing hard. "So I called the gallery and asked her assistant, Penny, if she knew what had happened. Penny said she'd left with a well-dressed man around noon. She'd thought maybe she'd gone out to lunch. But she didn't come back even though she had an appointment for two with a client. When she couldn't reach her by phone, Penny had to take over the appointment."

"Weird," Jane said. "No one is more reliable than Felicia."

"Do you think I don't know that? She was a little crazy as a teenager, but once she found her way, no one was steadier. When you hired her to be your agent, she loved every minute of working with you. I was so proud of her. And she...loved me. She would never have stood me up without calling." Her voice broke. "And she's been gone for four days. I'm scared to death, Jane. Sometimes bad things happen out there."

No one knew that better than Jane. But she didn't want to panic Wilma. "It might be okay. Felicia didn't tell me if she was planning on visiting any of her other clients living out of the city. But we don't have an exclusive contract. Why don't you ask Penny to call them and—"

"I already did that," Wilma interrupted. "No one has spoken to her. I even called the hospitals. And yesterday I couldn't take it any longer and I phoned the police. They weren't worried, they thought she might have gone away on a long weekend with a boyfriend. I tried to tell them she was between boy-friends right now." She added bitterly, "I'm only a mother, what do I know? But they did one thing right, they got the gallery to give them the video camera photos of Felicia and the man she was with that day. The police said they'd check him out. I didn't recognize him."

"You probably wouldn't if he was a client."

"And what if he wasn't? I've got a bad feeling." Her voice was full of pain. "I don't know *anything*. You're my last hope. She said you and Seth Caleb know people with MI6 and Scotland Yard. They'd pay more attention to her being missing, wouldn't they? *Please*, don't pat me on the head and send me away. You cared about Felicia, too."

Past tense. A shiver ran through Jane. "I do care about her. She's my good friend. Look, send me the photo. I'll see what I can do." Her hand tightened on the phone. "I'll get back to you as soon as I can, Wilma. Look, don't stay there alone. Go visit Penny, or Felicia told me you have neighbors you spend a lot of time with. This doesn't have to be bad. Try not to worry." Lord, that sounded lame. "I won't stop until I have an answer."

"Thank you, Jane." Wilma was openly sobbing now. "I'm desperate. All I can do is pray. Like I said, I'm sorry I had to bother you."

"It's no bother, you're both my friends. I want to do this. Bye, Wilma." She cut the connection.

"Shit," she whispered.

"Trouble?" Rodland asked. "I heard a bit of it. How can I help?"

"My agent, Felicia, disappeared four days ago and her mother is going crazy. Her phone was disconnected. She no-showed a business appointment, and she wouldn't have done that. Wilma notified the police but they're not taking it seriously yet." She heard a ping. "That should be the photo of the man she was seen with at the gallery." She pulled up the photo. "Sleek, well dressed, not a very good shot of his face."

"May I?" He took her phone. "He's probably trying to avoid the cameras. He didn't do a very good job. There may be a way we can make it clearer." He typed in a number on her keypad and pressed TRANSMIT. "It shouldn't take long." He handed the phone back to her. "This really scared you. Why?"

"Besides the fact that she's disappeared off the face of the earth for the last few days? Because Felicia would never do anything to hurt her mother. And she wouldn't ignore a client appointment to go somewhere with a stranger."

"Good enough reasons for me." He took her elbow and nudged her toward the hall. "You promised to get her answers. Let's go back to the castle so we can discuss it with MacDuff right away."

"You're in a hurry." Her eyes narrowed on his face. "And it's not usual for you to be so eager to involve MacDuff. Tell me why."

"Did your agent, Felicia, know where you were going when you left London?"

"Yes, of course."

"Then you should know why I want you behind those castle gates with MacDuff and his little army." He pushed her toward the front door. "And I believe you know why you should be there."

"You think she's dead." She felt sick at the thought. "You

think one of Bohdan's men took her to find out where I was. Then he killed her when he no longer needed her."

He nodded. "When he got his information. I'm sorry. Bohdan would have only considered it efficient."

Jane closed her eyes for an instant. "Efficient? Felicia was so *good*."

"Jane." He had opened the front door. "I think we should hurry. He's evidently known where you are for the past few days. I don't know why he hasn't struck yet. Perhaps if he's had eyes on the Run, he'd know it wouldn't be an easy victory. MacDuff's men might have intimidated him. Or he could have been waiting for Caleb to show. Or maybe he's just sitting like a cat outside a mouse hole seeing if he could scoop you up."

"I'm *not* a mouse," she said through set teeth. She shook her head to clear it. "Let's go!"

She ran out into the darkness and down the formal path. Then she shouted at Fergus as she passed the Range Rover he and the marines were occupying. "We're going back to the castle. Move, Fergus! MacDuff might need you." She dove left into the trees where she'd tied the horses.

Rodland was already there and throwing her art case over the pommel. "You should have gone with Fergus."

"I'm fine. It's not as if we're even sure there's a threat yet. We're just on edge because of Felicia." She swung onto the stallion. "But you'll have to be a little more stern with Maisie. I'm not going to wait for you this time."

"I'll rise to the occasion." He was on Maisie's back and following Jane out of the forest onto the road. "Stop talking and get the hell out of here. Fergus is already halfway down to the gates. Caleb wouldn't like you to be in this situation. He'll have my ass."

"He thought there was a chance it might happen. That's why he arranged to get extra agents here at the property."

"He'll still blame me."

"No, he'll blame himself, and that's much worse."

"It depends on how you're looking at it."

"I can't worry about that now. There are few things more—"

Jane suddenly pulled her horse's reins and drew to a halt. "Stop!"

Rodland stopped alongside. "What?"

"Listen."

They sat in silence for a moment. In the distance, there was a high-pitched buzzing sound, like a swarm of bees.

Rodland nodded. "I hear it. Where's it coming from?"

Jane turned her head. "That's just it. The sound isn't coming from just one place. It's coming from . . . everywhere."

The buzzing grew louder.

Jane spun around. "They sound like—"

"Drones!" Rodland pointed behind her, where dozens of small drone helicopters roared over the hillside, silhouetted by the twilight sky.

The ground exploded in front of them!

"They're dropping bombs!" Jane tightened her grip on the reins as her horse, Jocko, grew agitated and started bucking.

Waves of fire leaped into the sky, illuminating the drones as they swooped down and dropped another round of explosive charges.

"Move!" Rodland said. "Now!"

Boom! Boom! Boom! Boom!

Jane and Rodland turned their horses and raced across the grassy field, desperately trying to outrun the wave of explosions roaring toward them.

"Faster!" Rodland shouted.

Boom! Boom! Boom!

Jane felt heat from the blasts on her back. She turned toward Rodland. "We have to get to the castle!"

"We'll never make it."

"We have to!"

Another swarm of drones appeared in front of them. Jane braced herself for more explosions, but the drones banked left and sped into the darkness.

"Oh, my God," Jane said. "They're headed for the castle and the main residences. We have to warn them!"

"Way ahead of you." Rodland's phone was in his hand. "But I can't get a signal. Those drones must be jamming us. We need to get clear of those things."

Jane tugged the reins. "First we need to get there and help those people."

"MacDuff already has a small army there, Jane."

"They're under attack because of me."

"Because of *Caleb*."

"Exactly!" She snapped the reins and took off toward the castle. "Same thing."

"Jane!"

But she wasn't listening. Rodland followed Jane as their horses galloped across the pasture, the animals' muscle memory enabling them to navigate every depression and jump every gully even in almost total darkness.

Boom. Boom. Boom. Boom.

The explosions were coming from up ahead.

At the castle, Jane realized. The second wave of drones had found their target.

Dammit.

They rode to the hilltop and saw that the residences and surrounding grounds were ablaze.

In a matter of minutes, this beautiful retreat had become a fiery hellscape.

Boom. Boom. Boom. Boom.

More bombs from the sky, destroying the once magnificent gardens. Another blast laid waste to the automotive garage and MacDuff's classic car collection.

The staff had emerged from their burning residences and were running across the grounds in a panic.

The buzzing sound returned. More drones, all around them.

RAT-AT-AT-AT-AT!

"Guns!" Jane shouted.

The latest drone wave was equipped with automatic rifles, firing at the already panicked staff. The gun drones swooped low and zeroed in on their targets.

RAT-AT-AT-AT!

Two mechanics went down, followed by a housekeeper. Blood spurted from their wounds.

Jane raced down on her horse, yelling to the others, "Take cover! Now!"

BLAM! BLAM! BLAM! BLAM!

Jane ducked, but she realized that the last series of gunshots had come from MacDuff's people, who had taken positions with their weapons and were firing upward at the still-shooting gun drones.

Rodland joined in the assault, leaning forward in his saddle and firing his handgun alongside them.

Jane heard a child's scream. She turned. God, no . . .

A housekeeper was running across the circular driveway, clutching a little girl against her chest. The girl was wailing, terrified of a low-flying gun drone pursuing them just a few feet behind.

Jane snapped her horse's reins and galloped toward them. As she passed a tall hedge, she grabbed a gardener's rake leaning against it. She turned back toward the drone.

RAT-AT-AT-AT-AT!

A trail of bullets followed the woman and her crying daughter.

Jane swung the rake upward and struck the drone. It wobbled, and she turned back for another swing.

WHAP!

This blow took it down, and it smashed onto the driveway.

"Get away from here," Jane called out to the woman. "Take cover!"

Jane rode back to join Rodland and the line of gunmen. "Where's MacDuff?"

"Pinned down at the castle," one of the marines replied. "We have a squad rendezvousing with him there right now."

Rodland exchanged gunshots with a drone that had descended just a few feet in front of them. It splinted apart and crashed. He turned back to Jane. "I have to get you out of here. Right now."

She shook her head. "Not until everyone else gets away."

"Look around you. MacDuff's people are on it."

Jane looked at one of the other residences, which she knew housed the head groundskeeper and his large family. The roof was on fire, and the blaze was descending to the rest of the house. She turned back to Rodland. "Come on. We have to make sure everyone made it out of there."

"Then we get you out of here," he said grimly.

"We'll see."

They rode around to the burning house, where the groundskeeper and his family huddled outside.

"Is everyone okay?" Jane called out.

The groundskeeper nodded and spoke in his thick brogue. "Fine. But if you have an extra gun, I'd like to take a few shots at those things."

"Just stay here and take care of your family," Rodland said.

BLAM! BLAM! POW! More gunshots rang out, and the family ducked behind a tractor.

Rodland turned. "Those didn't come from the air."

BLAM!

Blood spurted from Rodland's shoulder, and he slumped forward.

"Shit," Rodland grunted.

Blood on the front of his shirt. He pitched forward over Maisie's head and hit the ground!

"No!" Jane reined in her horse and jumped off him. She held the reins as she ran back to where Rodland lay crumpled on the ground.

Another bullet plowed into the tree next to her as she fell to her knees beside Rodland. His eyes were closed and his forehead bloody. Dead?

No, he was opening his eyes. "Get out—of—here," he said hoarsely. "You can't help me. Sniper..."

"Shut up." She was looking at the wound in his shoulder. "I think it's only a flesh wound. It's not bleeding much. But I don't like the way your head looks. And you're slurring."

"That's because I'm talking to ... three of you. Tell the other two of you to go away." He reached out and grabbed her hand. "No, all of you go away. That sniper will be on top of us soon.

He doesn't . . . want me. They'll have orders to grab you. And it might be dead or . . . alive."

"I'm not going without you." She propped him up. "Now stand up and get back on Maisie. You're strong. I'll steady you."

"She doesn't like me that much. She's not going to stand still."

"Just get halfway up." She had to use all her strength to get him even half mounted on the saddle. Then he fainted. It was just as well. She arranged his body facedown over the saddle and gave Maisie a sharp slap on the buttocks that sent her running down the road toward the castle.

She was praying Maisie wouldn't start bucking again as she dialed Fergus. "It's Jane. Stop going toward the gates. There's a sniper on this side. Rodland's been shot. He's on Maisie. Come back for him and take him to the village to be treated. But call MacDuff and warn him that there are snipers on the grounds. I don't know how many or where they are. We just ran into one here at the groundskeeper's house. The drones were only the first wave of attack."

"Are you all right, ma'am?"

"Fine. Just take care of Rodland." She cut the connection.

Then she mounted the stallion and, avoiding the road, took the route through the forest that led south. The sniper's bullet had come from the north, and she would have to be super careful because Rodland was right. The chances were that the sniper had been after her because Bohdan would figure that she could lead him to Caleb. That was what this nightmare was all about. Her friend had been killed, a wonderful castle that had survived centuries was in flames, and she had no idea how many people had died today. Bohdan didn't care what pain and suffering he caused if he got what he wanted. And what he wanted was Caleb's death. She could feel the anger start to burn within her at the thought.

Screw you, Bohdan. You're going to start losing. I'm tired of hiding. I'm not letting you take another thing from me. I'm keeping everything that's mine.

And the first thing you'll lose is that sniper you sent after me. First I track, then I take him out. How do you think he'll stack up against the SEAL training Joe gave me . . .

CHAPTER

9

MAGGIANO LAKE
ITALY

B ohdan didn't show," Caleb said tightly when he reached Palik. "Neither did any of his top mobsters. The entire valley is filled with his meth and drug hierarchy screaming and blaming each other, but no Bohdan. I thought sure that I'd be able to zero in on him here. Where the hell is he?"

"Maybe he had something better to do," Palik said. "Have you heard from MacDuff lately?"

Caleb tensed. "What's that supposed to mean?"

"It means I can't get in touch with Rodland or MacDuff, and I don't like it."

"*Shit!*" Caleb cut the connection and dialed MacDuff.
No answer.

But he breathed a sigh of relief when he saw that he was getting an incoming call from Jane. "Everything okay? I couldn't reach MacDuff."

"He's probably a little busy," Jane said shakily. "The last I saw was that he was trying to keep the Run from burning down.

And then of course there were the drones that were dropping explosives. That could have been a distraction."

"What the hell are you talking about?"

"I'm talking about Bohdan. Who else could it be? I only called you because I couldn't imagine that if you knew about the attack you wouldn't have been here. But it's pretty clear you didn't know."

"Are you all right? Where's Rodland?"

"He was wounded, and I sent Fergus to take him to the village."

"Rodland is supposed to be taking care of you."

"Isn't everyone?" she asked wearily. "It doesn't seem to be working out, does it? You'll pardon me if I bow out. Too many people are getting hurt and dying. I won't let it happen any longer. I'll call MacDuff after I hang up from you and find out what damage I've done to him. But after that I'm on my own."

"That's crazy," he said roughly. "Where are you?"

"At the moment, I'm still at MacDuff's Run. But you know what a huge property it is, and I can't promise I'll stay here."

"Are you trying to shut me out, too? You know I can't let you do that. I'm coming after you."

"And you might find me, but I'll try my best not to let you. Because you're the one I most need to keep away from. Bohdan will kill you if he uses me as bait. That's what we've been trying to avoid."

"No, it's not. And I don't care anymore. I won't have you out there by yourself. I have to be with you."

"You will be." Her voice was suddenly soft. "Always. But the stakes are suddenly much higher right now. I can't risk you, too. Goodbye, Caleb." She ended the call.

Caleb's hand clenched on the phone. "Son of a *bitch*." He dialed Palik. "I suppose you've heard what happened at the Run?"

"Yes, I got through. I don't know all the details. Rodland was still a little out of it. Something about drones and explosives. It probably took place about the same time you rigged your meth explosion. Bohdan must have found out about Jane and where she was located. He probably had his own attack plans ready to initiate." He added, "I believe you got your response. Jane?"

"Alive. Well. With a guilt trip that's going to cause me a hell of a lot of trouble." He added hoarsely, "And may get her killed. I'm heading for MacDuff's Run right away."

"Might be a mistake. He could be waiting for you."

"Then make certain that there are enough men up in those hills. Get me an army if you have to."

"If she'll go with you."

"She'll go with me."

"Such confidence."

"I've no choice. I've seen what Bohdan does to captives." He was already heading for his rental car, parked on the road. "I'll see you at the Run, Palik."

———◆———

BOHDAN'S YACHT
1:40 A.M.

"The drones worked." Chiswick climbed out of the speedboat on board the yacht. He strode toward where Bohdan was at the rail gazing out at the castle. "I told you that it was the best way to access that castle. Between MacDuff and MI6, the property couldn't be touched any other way. The explosions made it possible for us to send forces into the courtyard and attack their forces."

"Dead?" Bohdan asked. "How many dead?"

"We couldn't get a count. We had to withdraw after we set the gates on fire. Perhaps a dozen or so kills." He added quickly, "But that courtyard will never be the same and we lost only a few men in the attack."

"The woman?"

"I sent in the sniper as you said. I haven't had a report from him yet. It might take a bit longer. You said that you wanted her taken captive."

Bohdan whirled on him. Chiswick had never seen him this angry; he was blazing with rage. "That was before Caleb blew my meth house to hell," he said savagely. "He cost me a damn fortune. I want her *dead*. I want them all dead. I'll tear them all apart. He can't get away with this."

"We'll have to be a bit cautious because of the attack. MacDuff has a lot of political influence and can make trouble for us when we go back to the Congo."

"Don't tell me that." Bohdan's hands clenched on the railing. "Find a way I can get Caleb and his woman. Hunt them down. Or by God, I'll have my soldiers hunt *you* down. You're no good to me if you let Caleb disrespect me like this. Find me a safe house and then bring them to me." He turned back to watch the burning gates of MacDuff's Run. "Now get out of my sight. I don't want to hear from you until you tell me you've found Jane MacGuire."

CAPTIVE

The sniper had to be camped around the next bend, Jane thought. He had been out for most of the night following her trail. She could smell the smoke.

He was on foot. She had made sure of it. She had located his truck about midnight and slashed the tires. Now he was tired and pissed off and wasn't sure how many of MacDuff's people were hunting him. He might have caught sight of her when she'd been trailing along the creek. But that was okay— he wouldn't perceive her as a threat, because she was a woman. His shot had been aimed at Rodland. Either he had orders not to kill her or he had contempt for women as adversaries. Probably the latter. And she knew he was alone in the forest. She'd heard him talking on his phone when she'd managed to locate the duck blind where he'd set up to take his shots. His name was Nojer, and he'd sounded very apologetic when he'd told someone it wouldn't take much longer to get the job done. Was he talking to Bohdan?

Well, it was time to prove him wrong and get rid of the threat of having him on her heels.

Move silently.

Do exactly what Joe had taught her.

She had no rifle. She'd have to get close enough that her 9mm pistol would be able to do the job.

But Joe always said that it was the skill of the shooter not the weapon that mattered.

Head for the brush now. Circle the blind and then take aim . . .

Stay with me, Joe . . .

———◆———

MACDUFF'S RUN
1:25 P.M.

"My God." Caleb gazed at the smashed stones at the top rim of the courtyard fountain. "Those drones blew up your fountain, MacDuff? Can I replace it?"

"Not unless you can pull a few nine-hundred-year-old stones from a Roman quarry," MacDuff said. "But I can find a way to rebuild the top rim so that it won't be noticeable." His lips twisted bitterly. "And if it is, it will only add to the story of the Run. Maybe it needed a more modern approach to give it color and pizzazz."

"Bullshit. I'm sorry, MacDuff. Anything I can do, just call on me." His gaze moved to the courtyard gates, which were burned and blackened. "Would you like to tell me how that burned-out gate adds to the general pizzazz?"

"No, I'd like to tell you to shut up about it," MacDuff said. "I lost five men in the explosions that tore the courtyard apart. They can't be replaced, either." He turned on Caleb. "But this is my home, my heritage, and everything that has ever happened here has told its own story. I meant what I said: When I finish the repairs and make those bastards pay for what they did to my people, they'll tell their own story. It will only make MacDuff's history richer and more complete. Understand?"

"Absolutely. An interesting plan, and, as usual, totally your own. But I don't believe you'll be selfish enough to keep me from helping with that rebuild?" His lips tightened. "Jane is still out there."

"Do you think we haven't been looking for her?" MacDuff

asked. "We've been a little busy beating back those assholes who invaded the castle. I figured she was safer outside the gates than if we sent someone to bring her in. But as soon as I could spare the men, I ordered a unit to go out to find her."

"And you found that she'd disappeared," Caleb said. "You should have known that she'd opt out once she saw the castle burning. She warned me that she wouldn't stay if she thought she was causing trouble for you. Bohdan couldn't have been more trouble."

"We'll dispatch another unit," MacDuff said. "We don't think that Bohdan has managed to get any more men into the hills yet. We managed to beat him back this time. And if he hadn't arranged to shoot off those drones, he wouldn't have been able to inflict near the damage."

"Bohdan may be a sadistic beast, but he's a damn good soldier," Caleb said. "Give him a chance to recoup and he'll be back in the game. Let me go after him...before he goes after Jane."

MacDuff frowned. "And if I say no?"

"Then you'd better tell any men you order out on the property to stay out of my way. I'll be going to get her, and no one is going to stop me."

"Anything else?" MacDuff asked coldly.

"Palik will be here, and he'll furnish you with protection while you're doing your repairs. If you have any more urgent needs, call me." He stared him in the eye. "Don't be an ass. I owe you. Let me pay you."

MacDuff was silent a moment. "Yes, you do. And I don't see why I shouldn't collect." He turned away. "But you'd better go and get Rodland from the library. I can't be bothered to take care of him. He showed up early this morning and he's been stumbling around the place waiting for you to get here."

"I'm supposed to take care of him?"

"You sent him to Jane. He belongs to you." He turned and started to cross the courtyard. "And he belongs to Jane. He might be useful."

Caleb hesitated. Then he turned and went into the castle and down the hall to the library.

Rodland was sitting in an easy chair talking on the phone. He held up his finger as Caleb walked into the room, but he finished his call. "It's about time," he said. "I thought you'd be here before this. What kept you?"

"I was otherwise occupied in Italy." He added coldly, "You didn't do your job. You were supposed to take care of her. I ought to break your neck."

"You probably will before this is over, but a horse named Maisie and a sniper with a bad aim managed to give me sufficient punishment for the time being." He smiled crookedly. "I did the best I could considering my handicaps. I told her to leave me and not trust anyone since she was the target. Evidently, she took my advice because MacDuff told me she's been on the run."

"You should have told her I'd take care of her," Caleb said harshly.

"You weren't here," he said simply.

Caleb muttered a curse.

"And I don't know if it would have mattered. Jane tends to go down her own path," Rodland added. "She makes up her mind and sticks to it. She worries a lot about MacDuff and his people." He shook his head. "You probably wouldn't have had a chance from the minute she saw the fire burning the front gate."

"I would have had a chance. I could have *talked* to her."

"But you weren't—"

"Here," Caleb finished. "I believe you've made that clear."

"But if anyone could have convinced her, it would have been you," Rodland said quickly. "I've found she does listen."

"Thanks for your insight," Caleb said sarcastically. "You've gotten to know her in the last week. How well?"

"Well enough to help you find her," he said quietly. "She'll be defensive with you. But she has a different relationship with me. I'm no threat, only humor and friendship. And we have a common interest in what happened to Fiona. I've promised to help her find the end of her story. She needs that right now. There's been too much blood and anxiety and she's an artist. It could bring her back to you." He looked down at his phone. "I'm almost there . . ."

"You do know her," Caleb said slowly. "But she's more than a wonderful artist. Did she ever tell you about Joe Quinn and how he raised her?"

He shrugged. "She mentioned something about how he taught her about locks."

"More than that. He wanted to keep his little girl safe. That was fine with me. Joe and I were on the same page. Only I wanted to do it myself."

"You always want to do everything yourself," Rodland said. "Some people would consider it a cheat that you don't let them share the burden. You might rethink that philosophy."

Caleb stiffened. "Are you speaking for yourself?"

"No, I was willing to wait. I knew my turn would come. But don't try to leave me behind."

"You might not even be able to make it to the courtyard." His gaze raked Rodland's face. "You look banged up as hell. Palik said you probably have a concussion. Even if I decided to take you along, you wouldn't be of any help to me."

"I'd be of help. And I'll get stronger all the time." He smiled. "And you like to take care of people. Jane might not let you get away with it, but I will. And I'll do whatever you tell me to do. The only thing I'll ask is that you don't make me get on a horse in the next month. I'm saving that for my next challenge, maybe next year."

Caleb was silent. Then he nodded. "Then it's fortunate I was considering using a Range Rover." He turned on his heel. "I'll see you in the courtyard in twenty minutes. Be there."

———◆———

Caleb and Rodland had picked up a Range Rover from the garage and were only thirty minutes out of the blackened ruin of the front gates when they got a call from MacDuff.

"Change direction to the southern forest," MacDuff said as soon as Caleb picked up. "She said Nojer would be in a cave about twelve miles from the road. She told me she'd left a note."

Caleb went still. "She? Who?"

"Who do you think?" MacDuff said. "Jane. She said she was sorry for everything and hoped I'd forgive her. Then she started to rattle off directions. I told her that she should wait for you, but she said that wouldn't be a good idea. Then she was gone. Now go get her and bring her back."

"I will. Who's Nojer?"

"She didn't say." He ended the call.

"Jane?" Rodland repeated. "Nojer?"

"You heard him." Caleb drove off the road and turned south. "I don't know what the hell is happening. Except that she couldn't bother to wait for me." He stomped on the accelerator as he drove into the brush. "And that she was still alive ten minutes ago. I'll take that."

Rodland nodded. "Yeah. We'll take that."

———————◆———————

The first thing they saw was the smoke. It took another ten minutes after they reached the coordinates they'd been given before they located the cave.

But it was only a few minutes later before they found Nojer.

He was roped, gagged, and tied to a rock inside the cave. He was squirming and fighting the gag, and they didn't notice the blood until they were almost on top of him.

The note Jane had mentioned was beneath a smaller rock nearby.

MacDuff

This is Eric Nojer according to the documents I found on him. All I know about him is that he's the sniper who shot Rodland and was trying to track me. But I figured that was reason enough to shoot him so that he'd be out of commission. He was on the phone with someone, and I couldn't afford to have him behind me and bringing up reinforcements. I thought you might be able to get information from him about where to find Bohdan. I made sure he wouldn't bleed to death if you get to him in time.

Jane

Caleb handed the note to Rodland. "Shall we untie him and see how accurate Jane's aim was?" He was taking off the gag as he spoke. The moment he slipped it down, Nojer started to spew curse words. His eyes were glittering with fury. "She shot me! The bitch wasn't there one minute and the next I felt the bullet tear into my side. I'm going to *kill* her."

"I wouldn't try that." Caleb was examining the wound in Nojer's side. "It looks like she patched you up pretty well. She could have just let you bleed out. But Jane has problems with death except in the most extreme cases." He added with soft menace, "I have no such hesitancy. And if you decide to ignore my advice, I'll make certain that you'll die very soon and in great pain. Do you understand?"

"I'll do what I please," Nojer snarled. "Who do you think—" He stopped short as he met Caleb's eyes. "I guess I understand." He moistened his lips. "You're Caleb, aren't you? I've heard about you."

"But I've heard practically nothing about you, and Jane went to a great deal of trouble to keep you alive so that you could tell us about yourself and all your friends." Caleb smiled. "Which you will do. I won't have her disappointed."

"Bohdan would kill me."

"But then you'll have a choice to make. You do have a little time. Rodland is going to call MacDuff to have him send someone else to pick you up. Oops, but MacDuff is also angry with anyone who helped damage his castle. You seem to be in an uncomfortable position and nowhere to go." He turned away. "It might help if you could tell me in what direction Jane took off after she did her fine work on your rib cage."

"I don't remember." Nojer was breathing hard. "Don't leave me here alone."

"Which direction?"

He was silent. "North," he said grudgingly.

"Good." Caleb pulled the gag back up over Nojer's mouth. "You'll have company soon. I just don't want any of Bohdan's men to drop in and take you away from MacDuff. You may prove to be a valuable commodity."

Rodland started to dial MacDuff as he followed Caleb out of the cave. They'd reached their Range Rover by the time he finished talking. "Nojer could have been lying about the direction Jane took off in."

"He could have been, but I don't believe he was." Caleb got into the driver's seat. "I have a hunch."

"And you're used to intimidating people," Rodland said. "Some hunch."

Caleb's brow rose. "You don't think we should go north?"

"I didn't say that. I believe we should go north."

"Why?"

"Not because I have a hunch. North is the Highlands and it's rough, wild country and Jane mentioned that she's familiar with it. She'd believe she'd be harder to track."

"But I'm also familiar with it."

"She knows that in the end that wouldn't be a factor. You're the Hunter." He paused. "And there's another reason she might want to go to the Highlands."

Caleb looked at him inquiringly.

"Which I won't divulge. After all, I can't let you have all the cards." He smiled mischievously. "If you're lucky I might tell you when we get up there to Rob Roy country."

"Or I might squeeze it out of you if I get too impatient."

"That might also happen. But it might keep the trip interesting." He leaned back on the headrest and closed his eyes.

"I'm beginning to get a headache. Don't wake me unless you have an emergency. I promised you I'd get stronger, and I need my rest."

———◆———

It was sunset by the time Jane reached the foothills overlooking the twisting brook that wound down through the valley leading to the purple-shaded mountains.

Beautiful...

She reined in the stallion and gazed out at those mountains. There was no doubt this was the scene that MacClaren had painted on the wall in that railroad car. There was a small, sod building on the far ridge that she didn't remember being in the picture, but it was incredible that was the only difference. Considering the passing of time, the entire glen could have been changed. But perhaps that was why MacClaren had chosen to paint this scene in the Highlands. He might have wanted to keep the memory of this poignant beauty as long as he could, and the chances were better if it remained wild.

Was Fiona with you when you came here? She knew this country. She'd studied it when she was preparing herself for the races at the castle. Maybe she wanted you to see it.

Stop it. She shook her head impatiently. This wasn't about Fiona. She was here because it was going to be easy for her to become lost in these hills. More important, it would be difficult to be found by anyone tracking her through this wild Eden.

She also knew these Scottish Highlands from her visits to MacDuff's Run. And from the long walks she had taken here with Caleb when they had wanted to escape the castle and just be together.

She blocked the thought. Don't think about Caleb. It was going to be difficult enough when she had to confront him. Which would come very soon. She knew he was on her trail, and he wouldn't allow a temporary stop to pick up Nojer to delay him for very long.

And it was time she found a place to settle for the night and find water and grass for the stallion. Tomorrow she'd have to find food for herself. She'd helped herself to Nojer's rations before she'd left his camp, and that would suffice for the time being.

And perhaps she'd light a fire and take a look at that letter that she'd tucked away in her art case. It seemed a suitable place to try to decipher it. Providing Fiona had really brought MacClaren here to show him the true beauty of MacDuff's Run. She'd meant to take a long time to examine that letter, but perhaps this would be better. Heaven knows, she needed something to take her mind off Caleb and the tragedy of what had happened back at the castle. The memory of that burning gate would stay with her forever.

"Come on, Jocko." She turned the horse toward the trail leading up the mountain. "You've been a wonderful friend, but now it's time to rest. I know a place that will suit you. Let's see if we can find you something to eat. No oats, but you'll like the grass in these hills."

———

It was fully dark, but the moon was shining brightly when Caleb parked the Range Rover in the trees at the bottom of the foothills. "Wake up, Rodland." He put on the brakes and got out of the car. "Gather wood and build a fire. Then you can put on some coffee." He added caustically, "If it wouldn't be too much of a strain."

"No, I feel much better." Rodland smothered a yawn. "And I assume you're not going to make me hike through these hills in the dark. By morning I should be almost normal."

"I'll decide whether we go on after I check the trails to make certain this was her destination. This would be my best bet. She knows these Highlands inside out. But she might have decided to come this far and then taken another road in another direction to fool me."

"You believe she's capable of that?"

"I believe she's capable of anything when she makes up her mind," Caleb said. "And she's probably more upset now than I've ever seen her. I don't know how I can change it. But I've got to. I'll use anything I have on hand to turn this around." He turned and headed up the path toward the mountains. "I don't know how long I'll be. I'll be back as soon as I'm sure that she's somewhere near here."

"And then you'll tell me what you're going to do?"

"No." He smiled faintly. "I'll tell you what *you're* probably going to do."

———

Rodland handed Caleb a cup of coffee when he came back to the camp two hours later. "It took you long enough. You had trouble locating her?"

He shook his head. "She was on the horse. As soon as I saw the hoofprints, I knew she'd have to take care of him. I could have followed her, but that would have been dangerous for her. She would have run from me. The mountains can be lethal at night."

"Not for you."

"We're not talking about me." He took a drink of coffee. "Chasing her in daylight is still going to be a risk. I'm not going to make it harder for either one of us." He added ruefully, "And Jane might make it difficult as hell for me to capture her. It's not as if I don't have to pull my punches. She knows I'd never do anything to hurt her."

Rodland started to laugh. "My God, you're helpless. I never thought I'd see it."

"I'm glad you're amused," Caleb said through set teeth. "I'm not helpless. I just have to figure a way to do what's needed."

"Well, you're almost helpless." He was still chuckling. "I can see the problem. My sympathy."

"Another word for sympathy is pity," Caleb said softly. "I really wouldn't use either one when referring to me."

"Certainly not." Rodland's smile vanished. "I'm not that stupid. Let's talk about how I can help. You did mention that, didn't you?"

"I believe I did." He cradled his coffee cup in his two hands. "I want you to call Jane tonight and talk to her. She doesn't know what's happening and she's probably feeling alone and unhappy. She's very much on edge and I need you to make that go away."

"I beg your pardon? Shouldn't that be your job?"

"You're damn right it should," he said roughly. "But right now, I can't do it. She won't accept anything I can do for her. She might have accepted it from MacDuff, but she believes she hurt him and that blows that. But for some reason she trusts you. So it's up to you."

"What am I supposed to say?"

"I don't care. Anything. Just make her feel better. She's aching, dammit. I can *feel* it."

"Okay." He took out his phone and started to dial. "I'll do my best. But you stay out of it, Caleb."

"Whatever." He was staring into the fire. "Evidently that's what she wants anyway. Do it right and I won't cause you any trouble."

CHAPTER

10

Jane hesitated as she checked the phone ID. Rodland. She was tempted to not answer. There were probably several reasons why she should ignore it. But she wanted to know if his wound was better, and she was feeling very isolated at this moment. It wouldn't hurt to talk to him for a few moments. She had no doubt that the call was connected to Caleb but that might not be bad. She couldn't hide from him indefinitely, and going through Rodland might be less painful. Rodland's relationship with Caleb was complicated but he had always been honest about it. His relationship with her had been equally aboveboard . . . yet less complicated. Keep it that way.

Decision made.

She answered the call. "Hello, Rodland. How are you?"

"Okay. The gunshot wound was nothing. But the doctor said my head wasn't as hard as I've been told." He paused. "I was wondering if you were going to answer. You took your time."

"You probably know why. Are you with Caleb?"

"Yes, and you're on speaker, but he said that you don't have to talk to him. He can take a hint. You made it fairly clear. He assigned me to make contact." He added, "For tonight. Tomorrow all bets are off."

She stiffened. "How close are you?"

"Closer than you'd like. I believe I've never seen anything more beautiful than these Highlands. I'm eager to see these hills in the daylight." He added quickly, "But I just got a frown from Caleb. He's afraid that I'm going to send you on the run tonight. He's already warned me that these mountains could be dangerous in the dark. There's no way he'll go after you until after dawn." He chuckled. "You have him over a barrel. I admit I've been enjoying it."

"Don't enjoy it too much," she said. "It would be like baiting a panther. Though you may be an exception. He's already saved you once. He might not want to spoil his record."

"Well, tell me that you'll hold out until dawn before you take off so that I won't get on his bad side."

"I'm not about to break my neck to avoid being caught by Caleb. I know these hills as well as he does," she said. "Maybe a little better. I stayed at MacDuff's Run long before I became close to Caleb. And I'd have no compunction about using everything I know about Caleb or the Run if I had to."

"I guess that's a yes," Rodland said. "I still think you might have an edge on him. Women can be ruthless. That's why I wasn't sure I could trust you at Kilgoray."

"Which you promised me you wouldn't mention."

"And I won't. It will be up to you from now on. I'll keep my word." He went on, "But now that we've settled that, I should go on and do my duty by filling you in on what happened at the castle. Caleb said you'd want to know.

Five dead. Two guards, three MI6, damage to the gates and the stones of the courtyard and fountain. The front door was scorched and will have to be replaced. They didn't get inside the castle. No damage to the paintings in the gallery or any of the furnishings. The attack only lasted a short time and then they were gone. MacDuff notified the local police and Her Majesty's Coast Guard, but Bohdan's forces were gone before they caught up with the two yachts." He was silent for an instant. "And we know what happened with the staff resident houses outside the gates."

"Yes, we do." She shivered. "The entire attack was terrible. My fault. I should never have been there."

"Caleb doesn't agree," he said. "He'd staged an attack on one of Bohdan's prime assets in Italy to lure him into a trap. He's sure that triggered the strike on the property."

"Of course he is. He's mistaken. I could have said no. For that matter, I could have said no when he called me and told me how things had gone wrong in the Congo. I didn't do it. I could have walked away. And I should have remembered that Felicity might be vulnerable. I keep thinking about her. Have you heard anything about the investigation?"

"No, but I'm sure MacDuff is questioning Nojer. We might know something soon."

"Maybe. I made wrong choices. But I'm not the one who had to pay."

"Bullshit."

"No, you had to pay, too. You could have been killed."

"But that was my choice. You can't carry the weight of the world on your shoulders. For the most part I enjoyed being sent to the Run to fetch and carry for you."

"Even Kilgoray?"

"I admit Kilgoray was a challenge. But that was even rather interesting. And I liked doing the Fiona research. Though I preferred digging deep on Farrell MacClaren. I found I could identify with him."

"Digging deep? How deep?"

"Ah, I knew I could intrigue you. I told you that I was almost there before we left Jamie's house. But thanks to Maisie bouncing me on my noggin, I had a little more time to loll around and make more phone calls."

"It was the sniper, not Maisie to blame," she said absently. "Almost there? What about MacClaren?"

"What about him? Which would you prefer? Sit up there in the mountains feeling sorry for yourself, or have me tell you about MacClaren's adventures in America?"

"I'm not feeling sorry for myself, I'm feeling sorry that I couldn't—" She broke off. "What are you up to, Rodland?"

"Obeying instructions. Caleb doesn't like the idea of you being depressed. I'm supposed to distract. I thought this might do the trick." He paused. "He's frowning at me again, but I told him that he was to leave me alone if I was going to do this. He didn't like that."

"But I'm certain you liked saying it to him."

"You take pleasure where you find it. Do you want to hear about MacClaren or not?"

"You know I do."

He nodded. "Because you're curious. Farrell MacClaren grew up on the border. He was a town boy; his father was an alcoholic, and his mother died when he was ten. He was always a brilliant artist from the time his mother gave him a pad and pencil when he was a toddler. But he was a wild kid and he spent most of his time roaming the countryside drawing and selling his work wherever he could. That's where he met Fiona. She was the daughter of gentry and four years younger than he was. But she was as wild as MacClaren, and they found something in each other that they evidently could find nowhere else. They became friends.

"But when MacClaren was seventeen, he ran away from home and took passage on a ship to New York. When he reached there, he earned his living the way he'd earned it all his life. On the street corners and in bars sketching. He even started to paint and saw his work begin to come to life. But he couldn't afford the paints and time it took so that led him to another adventure. He started to work for the railway. First in New York and Boston, but then he realized they were building railways all over America. Sometimes the pay was better if you went out west. He found it far more interesting. Cowboys, Indians, and gold miners, and buffalo . . ."

"And Cowboy Bob catching the dangerous train robbers," she murmured.

"Yep, you got it. MacClaren started to do the illustrations for the dime novels. If you check the credits on that novel, it was written and illustrated by D. B. Ward. That was one of the first novels MacClaren wrote and illustrated. He sent a copy to Fiona as a present."

"He kept in touch with her?"

"She was both family and friend to him. Neither of them could give up that tie. MacClaren traveled all over the West and had adventures and love affairs and did everything that young men dream of doing. He made his living doing the dime novels and occasionally he painted a portrait or landscape. But principally he was involved with life and learning how to best live it." He shrugged. "And then he heard from his old friend Fiona about Jamie's plans for her. Now, how could Cowboy Bob ever let that happen to the only family he'd ever known?"

"He came back to her?"

"And because they were both clever and determined, they managed to find a way to fool Jamie into hiring MacClaren to paint Fiona's portrait. But somewhere along the way friendship became love and they had another problem to face when they realized that Jamie would never permit Fiona to break off with Graeme. He'd hunt her down no matter how long it took. What a conundrum."

"And?"

He chuckled. "That will be the next installment. But I promise you that it didn't involve Fiona being thrown down a deep well in the forest."

"I may strangle you," Jane said.

"But it did involve her bringing MacClaren to this mountain hideaway. So enjoy the anticipation, and next time I'll end the story for you."

"Maybe I'll find out on my own. I still have the letter."

"And that would provide your own distraction. I'm sure Caleb would consider that fair. That would work . . . if the letter tells you the entire story."

"You're impossible. Good night, Rodland."

"Wait. Caleb is holding out his hand for the phone. He wants to talk to you."

She tensed. "Then by all means let him talk. Hello, Caleb. I've already said what I wanted to say to you. I haven't changed my mind."

"And you won't as long as I can't corner you and keep you

from running away. You're going down the wrong path, and I have to stop you." He added harshly, "For God's sake, I'm not trying to keep you prisoner. But we can face this together."

"And you'll still try to step in front of me and keep me safe," she said fiercely. "I may not be a prisoner, but I feel like a damn captive that everybody is trying to protect no matter what the cost. Well, the cost is too damn high. Do you wonder why I've been so intrigued by Fiona lately? It's because we're alike. We've both been taken captive and we've been fighting to get free. She had everything against her, and I don't want her to have lost her battle. I'm luckier than she was, and I have no intention of losing mine. But the stakes are getting higher and higher. And you could die, like those other people have died."

"You're not listening," he said thickly. "And we *have* to talk. I'll see you in the morning."

"Maybe." She had to steady her voice. "Is that all you wanted to say to me?"

"Yes, though I knew how stubborn you'd be. It didn't matter to me." He added quietly, "I just wanted to hear your voice."

And she had desperately wanted to hear his voice. It was the only reason she hadn't refused when Rodland had turned the call over to her. She couldn't speak for a moment. "Good night, Caleb."

Rodland immediately turned to Caleb. "I think I did very well. You couldn't have done better. You have to admit she was distracted."

"You're a regular Scheherazade," Caleb said caustically. "But you did a decent job."

"Scheherazade." Rodland made a face. "I've heard she was a magnificent storyteller, but I prefer a more manly description of my own talents. Though she was supposed to be very persuasive, and I've always considered my own skill in that arena to be extraordinary."

"I'll keep it in mind." Caleb threw the rest of his coffee into the fire. "When you tell me about Kilgoray. Why did you go there?"

Rodland slowly shook his head. "You'll have to get that from Jane. That's why I warned her you were on speaker. She made me promise that I wouldn't tell anyone about our trip there." He added, "Besides, why should you be curious? She told me that you'd visited there with her before."

"The only thing that meant for either of us was a pleasant day away from the Run. But why take you there? And why at this particular time?"

"I made a promise. Ask her."

Caleb's lips tightened. "I will. Count on it. Tomorrow."

"Then am I off the hook?"

"For the time being. Go to sleep." He was looking into the fire again. "Dawn will come soon enough."

———◆———

Jane hung up the phone and sat there gazing into the darkness. That talk with Rodland had been both upsetting and oddly bracing. She had needed to know what she had to face, as well as what she had to make right. The cost of Bohdan's attack had been staggering and it must be paid. She just had to figure out how.

She wearily rubbed her temple, then spread the blanket she'd taken from Nojer's camp before the fire and curled up for the night. It had been an exhausting two days; she needed to rest and try to prepare for what waited tomorrow.

She had known she would have trouble explaining to Caleb why she had gone on the run instead of letting him talk to her. Everything had seemed to bombard her after she had witnessed the deaths caused by those drones; her guilt had seemed enormous. It had brought home to her all the depths of terror she'd been experiencing about losing Caleb. But she'd known he was so damn persuasive, and it would have been like arguing with herself if she hadn't made the choice to run. She knew he only wanted to protect her, and she desperately wanted to stay with him. But how could she allow herself to do that as long as she was the bait that might kill him? She had to rely on herself. She had to stay as far away from him as possible until one of them managed to take Bohdan down.

Caleb had said dawn, but she had to be ready for him before that. She had already started when she'd first arrived here in the hills after settling Jocko. She had taken the time to look over this section of the Highlands before dark and refreshed her memory of the time she'd spent here. Now it was only left to rise early so that she'd be ahead of the game.

Only it wasn't a game. She and Caleb had played games before in these hills. Wild, passionate games that had seemed to have no beginning and no end. This was something entirely different and she wasn't sure that she could make Caleb understand that the rules were different now.

Because God knows she didn't want to live without him.

◆

NEXT DAY
2:15 P.M.

Jane ran through the medieval cemetery, barely glancing at the long-faded markers. Normally she could spend hours at a place like this, photographing the ancient headstones and imagining the amazing lives of the people buried just a few feet below. Now, however, she had only one purpose, running from Caleb, and it was a task both challenging and exhausting. She stopped as she was about to leave the cemetery to catch her breath and glance over the terrain. No sign of him yet. Their game had begun earlier in the morning with a chase along the Fife Coastal Path, and Caleb almost caught up to her when she'd tried to take a brief rest in a docked fishing boat. At that point he'd been less than forty minutes behind her. Then shortly before noon, she'd thought she'd given him the slip by hitching a ride with a motorcycle-riding delivery person only to realize that Caleb had anticipated her move and was watching a NorthLink ferry terminal for her arrival. Another close call...

He was fast as a panther and silently relentless. She had never been stalked by Caleb before. At first, it had been a challenge that was almost enjoyable. Pure cat and mouse with no consequences. But as time passed, she could appreciate the panic Caleb must engender when that challenge was a case of life or death. Relentless, indeed.

She'd seen how Caleb could track anyone, anywhere with ease. And he often said that the better he knew his mark, the easier it was for him.

And no one knew her better than Caleb.

But she couldn't let him find her. Because there could be

consequences this time. Their relationship had already cost too many lives. She wouldn't let herself be the bait that would again bring Bohdan down on him.

Cat and mouse, Caleb. She started to run again.

She entered a dense forest near Rannoch Moor, an area she'd visited on her first trip to Scotland. This was Cira country, near the place where she and her husband, Antonio, had founded the first MacDuff family castle. Caleb was familiar with it, too. She'd shown it to him during one of their trips up to these Highlands last year. She knew he'd been everywhere, and he seemed to remember everyplace he'd been with incredible clarity. That was okay. Today she was counting on it.

She jumped over a rotting log and glanced behind her. She wasn't just running from Caleb, she realized. She was still trying to escape the horror she had witnessed at MacDuff's Run. She couldn't shake the image of those workers bleeding on the ground in front of her, and every time a strong wind blew through the trees, she swore she heard another one of those awful drones.

Stop it, she told herself.

Move forward, not back.

There was a clearing up ahead. If she remembered correctly, she would soon—

Yes. Exactly as she recalled.

Jane crouched and moved toward the clearing. Here she would be able to see for miles, and if Caleb was as close as she suspected, she'd soon know it.

Damn. There he was less than ten minutes behind. Knapsack slung over his shoulder, walking with that long, powerful stride. She knew he'd be able to track her, but it still amazed her to see him in action. He was already through the cemetery.

He paused at the clump of trees she'd just entered, looking one way, then another. After a moment, he forged ahead into the woods.

Shit.

She was in love with a damn bloodhound.

———◆———

Caleb pushed through the overgrown path. He was positive that Jane was nearby. The bent branches and freshly stepped-upon grass told him that *someone* had come through here in the last few minutes, and the farmer who had identified Jane from his phone photo indicated that she had walked in this general direction less than half an hour before. He was closer to her than he had been since he'd begun tracking her.

One thing he hadn't quite worked out: What would he say to Jane once he found her?

She refused to believe she wasn't somehow responsible for the attack on the Run. Of course, there were enough guilty feelings on that count to go around. He still had no idea how he'd ever make it up to MacDuff. Worry about that later. One crisis at a time...

Caleb followed the path up to the ridge that overlooked Kinsey Loch, a long body of water that twisted and turned for miles.

Damn. No sign of Jane. Maybe he'd been wrong about the direction she'd—

Wait!

There she was, walking along the loch's northern side. If her goal was to remain inconspicuous, her bright blue Burberry rain slicker made that impossible.

Caleb left the path and ran down the slope's side, working his way toward her. But as he drew closer, something didn't seem quite right; her walk was different than usual, and Jane never swung her arms so broadly.

He jumped in front of her, and she recoiled with a start. "Hi." Caleb pulled back the jacket's hood.

It wasn't Jane.

The woman couldn't have been older than seventeen or eighteen, and she was obviously terrified.

Caleb gripped her arm and inspected her slightly scuffed left sleeve. "This isn't your jacket. Where did you get it?"

The woman spoke with a Shetland dialect. "She's mine, sir. I promise you that."

"Stop lying. This jacket belongs to my friend."

The woman pulled away. "No, sir. She was given to me just a peerie bit ago."

Caleb cocked his head. She appeared to be too frightened to be lying. He showed her Jane's photo on his phone. "Do you recognize her?"

Her eyes widened. "That's her! She gave me this jacket."

"Why would she do that?"

"Don't know. She took it off and told me the jacket was mine. All I had to do in return was pull up the bonnet and walk this way for twenty minutes, then walk back."

Caleb cursed under his breath. Of course. Why had he even bothered to ask? For an instant he'd been afraid something might have happened to Jane. But Jane knew he was hot on her trail. Just another bit of sleight of hand. He glanced back down the path.

"How long ago? Where did you see her?"

"Mmm, not quite ten minutes ago. We were over near the old boathouse."

"Boathouse?" He looked back. Far in the distance, he spotted what appeared to be an old shack and dock at the water's edge. And at about the same place, a small motorboat was puttering out into the loch.

Jane!

Caleb sprinted down the path.

———————◆———————

Jane gripped the tiller and headed toward the loch's gentle curve. She would miss that Burberry jacket; it had been like an old friend. But it was worth it to buy her the time she needed to board the boat that MacDuff always left at the Rannoch boathouse. She gunned the outboard motor, but unfortunately the tiny boat wasn't built for speed.

It didn't matter. It was fast enough to lose Caleb.

She turned toward land and raised her binoculars. Caleb was running like hell toward the dock and boathouse, holding his phone to his right ear.

For what purpose? Coordinating with someone for an interception? It couldn't possibly happen fast enough to catch her. He pocketed his phone and ran into the rickety boathouse, practically tearing the door off its hinges.

He probably hoped to find an old rowboat in there, but she'd peered in and saw only a few old cobweb-covered life vests, melted candles, and beer cans.

Tough luck, Caleb.

A minute passed. Then another.

What in the hell was he doing in there? Still strategizing on his phone?

A strong wind blew across the water, and the boathouse's

tiny wooden frame shook. The shaking continued even after the breeze abated.

She tensed. Suddenly the old structure looked extremely fragile.

The roof gave way!

A moment after that, the entire structure collapsed.

Caleb!

She eased back on the throttle and kept her binoculars trained on the collapsed boathouse.

There was no movement.

Come on, Caleb . . .

Still nothing.

Her heart was pounding as she turned the boat around and motored back toward the dock. Still no movement in the collapsed boathouse.

Dammit, Caleb . . .

She gunned the motor until she reached the dock, which had also sustained heavy damage from the collapse. She stepped off the boat and gingerly moved toward the splintered wood and broken glass that had been the boathouse. She crouched next to a broken windowpane and peered inside, afraid of what she would see.

Caleb was lying on his side, apparently unconscious, with a large beam across his neck.

God, no!

Jane crawled frantically through the opening, grabbed a two-by-four, and turned back to wedge it under the beam.

Caleb was gone!

What the hell?

"Hello, Jane."

She whipped around so quickly that she hit her head on another fallen piece of wood. "Oww!"

Caleb had slipped out from under the beam and was now crouched next to her, steadying her. "Sorry about that," he said quietly. "But thanks for saving me."

She shoved him back. "You son of a bitch."

"I'm sure I deserve that, but I couldn't be more sincere. I'm genuinely touched. You came back for me."

"You brought this thing down on purpose?"

He shrugged. "It didn't require a great deal of effort. It was halfway there already."

And he'd made sure it had fallen the rest of the way. She was beginning to shake. She couldn't forget that moment when she'd seen him lying there beneath that beam. "You're an idiot. You could have gotten yourself killed."

"A calculated risk. I pulled one beam and lay between two floor joists. I'm no structural engineer, but I figured I'd be okay." He was looking appraisingly at the sway of the dock. "But we should really get out. I think we're tempting fate with each additional minute we spend in here."

"Oh, then *you* can stay."

He gestured toward the broken window. "After you."

They crawled onto the dock and stood up. Jane clenched her jaw. "I thought you might be dead in there."

He reached out and touched her cheek. "I'm sorry. It was the only way I could think of to bring you back. I had to get you to talk to me. You're too damn good. We've been playing this game for most of the day, and I didn't want it to go on until it started to get dark again."

"No, you'd rather pull a house down on top of you. You imbecile." The blasted deck was still shaking. Jane grabbed his arm and pulled him off the deck and onto the grassy bank. "You guessed, you couldn't be sure that beam wouldn't have crushed your skull, dammit. Some people may have told you that you're made of cast iron, but you could have been killed. Did you think about that? You would have left me alone. I couldn't have taken it." She reached out and shook him. "Why would you do something that stupid? What was I supposed to do then?"

"Probably come after me," he said quietly. "As you did just now." He gently took her hands from his shoulders. "And start crying again." He reached out and touched her damp cheek. "After you saved my life, of course. Because don't tell me that you can't take anything I throw at you. I know you better than that."

"You don't know anything." She jerked her hands away and wiped her cheeks on her fists. "You've never known. I've tried to tell you, but there's no way. I thought someday, but it's all coming too soon. And then you do something like—" Her hands clenched. "Why did you do that? I wasn't expecting it. You're the Hunter. I knew I was going to eventually be the prey. Then I was planning on just starting the hunt again. But that move you made was reckless and stupid."

"And necessary," Caleb said. "Because I couldn't stand going through this again. We have to get this straight. So I couldn't win this one, Jane. You had to win it so that I could show you that I'd never put you in a position again where you'd feel that helpless and yet totally responsible."

"So you put yourself in a position where you couldn't save yourself and had to rely on me?" she asked incredulously. "Talk about responsibility."

"I trust you," he said. "And you had to realize that from

now on in situations like this, we'll work together. I won't keep anything from you to protect you. If there's a problem, we'll figure it out."

She gazed at him dazedly. "That will be…difficult for you."

"It will damn near kill me," he said bluntly.

"That's what I meant." She was silent. "It probably won't work, you know."

"It will work. You'll be keeping an eagle eye on me, and I'll be too scared of losing you to screw up." He leaned toward her, and his voice was caressing. "We'll do it together. I promise you. Everything together. We'll start right now. Believe me."

She did believe him. How could she help it when he was sensual and coaxing and so damn wonderfully beloved? "I believe…you think it will work. I hope you're right."

He smiled crookedly. "You're not making it easy. But you've had a tough time lately, and we'll have to figure out how we can put Humpty Dumpty back together again." He brushed his lips along her cheekbone. "I'll take my time and maybe we can talk about it. We've never had trouble communicating."

"Stop treating me like a child, Caleb." She frowned. "I do want this to work out. I just believe it may take longer than either of us think. I'm not sure there are any simple solutions."

"I've never cared for simple solutions. We'll go for the complicated ones that will last a lifetime." He looked away from her. "Like the one you suggested some time ago. Marry me, Jane."

She instantly shook her head. "That wasn't why I thought we should get married. I'd seen what marriage could be with Eve and Joe. I wanted that for us. But it's not a Band-Aid, and I won't treat it as one. And you've seen the worst marriage and family life could be, and I'd be afraid you'd be waiting for it to fail."

"It wouldn't be like that. We're not Eve and Joe." He grimaced. "And thank God we have nothing in common with my honorable parents. We'd start out clean and hope for something better."

"Hope?"

"We're already halfway there. I'd have you." He added lightly, "You'd have all the heavy work. But a woman who could pull my ass back from the depths of hell would have no trouble keeping me in line."

"Don't give me bullshit." Her voice was shaking. "No one's managed that yet, Caleb."

"I told you once that I'd die for you," he said hoarsely. "That hasn't changed."

"I don't want you to die for me. I want you to *live* for me. Every day. Every way."

"We'll get there," he said gently. He lifted her hand to his lips and kissed the palm. "As long as you'll come along for the ride. Okay?"

She didn't answer for a moment. Then she shrugged. "It appears that's the direction I'm heading for the time being. Did you con me, Caleb?"

"It didn't feel like a con to me when I was balancing that beam on my neck. Did it to you?"

She shivered. "God, no."

"Then we'll have to accept that it was meant to be." He smiled. "Want to go down the hill and combine camps? I'll call Rodland and tell him that we haven't caused irreparable damage to each other. And that it may have turned out a draw."

She shook her head. "You said I won. Are you going back on it?"

"No, I was just trying to save my pride. I'll tell him that I was completely vanquished."

"Not completely. You also got what you wanted."

"It just didn't seem to be that way. I guess I'm accustomed to more complete victories." His hand tightened on her own. "Maybe I'll get used to it. Give me time. Maybe fifty years or so..."

CHAPTER
11

Rodland looked Caleb over critically as they walked into the camp an hour later. "You don't appear vanquished. But then that's such a complex word. It could mean many things." He glanced at Jane. "Is he vanquished?"

"Definitely," she said. "He told me so, and Caleb never lies to me. But you're right, too, it can mean many things." She walked over to the fire and took the cup of coffee Rodland was extending toward her. "Caleb said that he asked you to call MacDuff today and find out if he'd gotten any information from our sniper, Nojer, after they'd picked him up at his camp and taken him back to the Run."

"Not much." He grinned. "But MacDuff told me to compliment you on such a fine shot. It wasn't necessary for him to rush Nojer immediately to a hospital, so he was able to squeeze a few things out of him. Since MacDuff was furious about the damage done to the Run, he wasn't gentle or patient about getting what he needed from him. Bohdan ordered but wasn't part of the attack. It was launched from two yachts offshore, but they were planning on abandoning them and going into hiding immediately afterward." He paused. "Providing neither you nor Caleb had been killed or captured at the castle. Since Nojer could only speak for his assignment of taking you hostage, he was disappointed when you showed up at his camp."

"No location?" Caleb asked.

Rodland shook his head. "Nojer was only a sniper, and his job was to infiltrate the outlying grounds and try to kidnap Jane if the opportunity presented itself. Even that changed when Bohdan went into a rage after Caleb blew up one of his assets. He changed the kidnapping to a kill order. Nojer didn't have direct access to Bohdan or Chiswick. He did know that other units would be sent to help him if he wasn't successful. Other than that, all he knew was general gossip."

"Anything else?" Caleb asked.

He hesitated. "Kilgoray." He glanced at Jane. "A unit from the yacht was sent there on an exploratory fact-finding mission a few nights ago. As far as Nojer knew, it was unsuccessful."

Caleb stiffened and turned on Jane. "Kilgoray? I've been wondering about that. I think we need to talk about it."

So did Jane. But at the moment she was in shock. The fact that Bohdan had known that she and Rodland were at Kilgoray that night stunned her. "Perhaps, let me think about it." She reached out, grabbing for something, anything. "Nojer said it was unsuccessful anyway."

"Jane, this is Bohdan." Caleb's lips tightened. "What the hell were you—"

"I said, let me think about it," she interrupted. "I didn't say I wouldn't talk about it. Just give me a little time." She turned back to Rodland. "Anything else?"

He nodded. "He said Chiswick tortured and murdered a woman on the yacht a couple of days before that. They sank her body off the coast near the Scottish border."

"Felicia," Jane said numbly. "It had to be Felicia."

Caleb was next to her, his hand on her shoulder. "Jane. I'm sorry."

"I know. So am I. I should never have come here to the Run. I should never have told her where I was going. So many mistakes..."

"Not your mistakes." He took her face in his two hands and gazed down into her eyes. "Mine. Always mine. Remember that. Since the beginning. Always mine."

"You're doing it again. Even when no one blames you, you blame yourself." She shook her head vehemently. "You can't do it this time. I won't let you. Do you know how much that hurts me?" She broke away from him and strode off from the fire toward where the Range Rover was parked.

She opened the driver's door and slipped into the seat. She drew a deep breath as her hands clenched on the steering wheel. Just hold on. The entire day had been a disaster in one way or another. Yet she hadn't dreamed it could get worse.

Kilgoray. Who would have guessed that she would have to face that today? Along with all the pain that—

The passenger door opened, and Rodland jumped into the car. "Don't yell at me. Caleb didn't have anything to do with sending me this time. He told me to stay away from you and let you have your space. I'm just feeling guilty as hell for not taking better care of you. I thought I was handling that Kilgoray business pretty well. And you told me Bohdan didn't have anything to do with—"

"Be quiet, Rodland," she said. "I can't stand having another man taking the blame for anything I've done. Caleb is bad enough. And I told you the truth, Bohdan didn't have anything to do with me going to Kilgoray." She looked away. "Until he did."

He was silent a moment. "That doesn't compute. I'll back off, but you have to talk to Caleb. This all sounds weird as hell from the outside."

"I know that it does. I'll take care of it." She drew a deep, shaky breath. "Just not right now. I've got to plan how I'm going to do it. And I don't want to sit here and make excuses to you. Go away, Rodland."

"I'm going." He opened his door. "Can I get you something to eat? You haven't had supper."

She shook her head. "Maybe I'll grab something later."

"Want to hear the end of MacClaren's story?" His tone was coaxing. "It's much more cheerful than all this Bohdan crap."

"Not in the mood," she said. "Though I'm all for a happy ending if I can work one out. Thanks, Rodland."

"My pleasure." He got out of the car. "But I'll try to work one out for your horse, Jocko. I'll go up the hill to your camp and get him some water and then bring him down here."

"I could do that myself."

"But I have to become accustomed to horses. I've got to be ready to face Maisie when we have our great confrontation."

"Maisie's very gentle."

"Tell that to my concussion. I'll take care of Jocko for you." He slammed the car door.

And Jane leaned back in her seat and closed her eyes.

He wasn't the only one who was going have a confrontation soon, she thought wearily. But her own might shake her to her very core.

She needed this time to try and come to terms with it before she had to face Caleb again.

———◆———

Jane braced herself as she got out of the Range Rover and walked over to the fire where Caleb was sitting. "I'm sorry. I didn't mean to run away. I just had to pull myself together."

"Your friend Felicia," Caleb said quietly. "I realize that you cared about her. She was a fine woman." He reached for the coffeepot on the warming stone and poured her a cup of coffee. "But it seems there are other things we have to talk about. Are you ready to do it?"

"No, but if I don't, you'd have to go to Rodland, and he doesn't really know anything. I made sure of that when I asked him to go with me." Her lips curved in a sardonic smile. "Though 'asked' isn't really the correct word. I had to go, and I wanted to make sure that I'd be safe. I knew this time I couldn't rely only on myself. It wouldn't be fair."

"Why not? You've proved yourself dozens of times. You did it again today." He tapped his chest. "By saving my ass."

"This was different." She sipped her coffee. "I didn't have the right. I didn't know how to tell—"

Her phone was ringing. She didn't want to answer. These next few minutes were going to be difficult enough. She glanced impatiently down at the ID.

She froze. No name. Only a location.

Kilgoray!

She inhaled sharply. "Something must be wrong. I have to get this." She pushed the ACCESS button and then SPEAKER.

"Jane MacGuire?" It was a man's voice, deep, slick. "How delightful to make your acquaintance. You've been most elusive. This is the second time I've had to send men to Kilgoray to try to track you down. But I'm glad I've finally reached you. Do you know who this is?"

"I have an idea."

"Stop playing games, Bohdan," Caleb bit out. "I recognize your voice. It's me you want to talk to, isn't it?"

"Not at the moment, Caleb," Bohdan said. "I'll get to you eventually. I have great plans for your demise. But I'm more interested in your Jane's fate. You've caused me a few headaches by stashing her at that castle. I need to show you that you can't do that to me." His voice lowered. "And I believe I know exactly how to do it. Are you familiar with a T. S. Campbell, Jane?"

"I never heard of him."

"You answered too quickly. Because he remembers you. Though it took a while before he'd admit it. We had to check his records. As I said, this is the second visit we've paid to this village. The first time I gave orders not to draw attention to why we were here. But when we came back here after the attack on MacDuff's castle, I told them to tear this village apart to find out why you were here." He paused. "We found someone who recognized you as visiting at Campbell's office. And then we had to persuade him to tell the truth. I'm particularly good at that kind of persuasion."

"I'm sure you are," she said bitterly. "But I don't know him."

"Yes, you do, and I'm going to see how well you know him in the next few days. I'll call you back and let him talk to you...if he still can." His voice was almost a whisper now. "And then I'll let you beg Caleb to give himself up so that I won't cut you open as I intend to do to Campbell."

She felt sick. "You could be bluffing. How do I know that you aren't?"

"Because you can tell how much I'd enjoy it. I'd go very deep, Jane MacGuire. What would I find?"

"You son of a bitch."

"I'll talk to you soon." He cut the connection.

"Jane." Caleb took her in his arms and held her tight. "You're shaking like a leaf in a windstorm."

"He's a monster." She was clutching at him. "We can't let him do that to Campbell. He's innocent, just like all those other people Bohdan has killed. Did you hear him? I can't let him do that."

"We won't, but I have to know everything you know. I have to know about Campbell."

"I was going to tell you. I just didn't know how. There seemed to be so many things that were in the way. And I thought that no one would—"

"Jane." He gently shook her. "Stop giving me excuses and tell me now."

She drew a deep breath and then said in a rush, "I'm going to have a baby."

He blinked. "What?"

"You heard me. Why else would I leave MacDuff's property where everybody had bent over backward to keep me safe? I had an idea I was carrying something very precious. I didn't want to risk it. But I had to be sure, dammit."

"I can see how you would," he said slowly. "Would you care to tell me who T. S. Campbell is?"

"He's a doctor," she said. "He's my obstetrician. I'd been feeling edgy and depressed for the past couple of weeks. I couldn't understand why I felt as if I was caught, almost suffocated by everything around me. That night after I saw you in the stable, I thought that I noticed...changes. When I suspected I might be pregnant, I decided I had to be certain. But I didn't want anyone to know until I found out, so I decided I'd go to Kilgoray to a doctor. I thought it was better if I went to somewhere no one was familiar with me. I made the appointment and asked Rodland to go with me."

"What the hell," Caleb said. "Didn't it occur to you to talk to me?"

"No." She straightened. "I had to get used to the idea myself. It was scary...and yet magical. Besides, I didn't know if you wanted to have a child with me. There was a possibility that any child we had together would have the same blood gift you inherited. We've talked about it before, and you weren't sure that you'd want to inflict that on any child."

"But you said it wouldn't matter."

"And I still wouldn't care. I was happy when I found out I was pregnant." She moistened her lips. "I told you once that I thought you'd be a wonderful father. If for no other reason than you'd know what *not* to do with a child. But I didn't get pregnant on purpose. I was surprised. It just...happened."

"Which seems to occur frequently where we're concerned. I really didn't think you'd plotted to trap me," he said huskily. "You're too honest. It was you I was trying to protect anyway. Having a man like me around is difficult enough. You didn't deserve to have a problem child to care for, too."

"Yes, I do." She met his eyes. "I do deserve it. No one can say my brother, Michael, isn't a bit strange, and yet he's loving and wonderful and I wouldn't trade him for all the so-called normal kids on the planet. Don't you *ever* tell me I don't deserve to have him or a child of my own who may not be what's considered 'usual.'"

"No, I won't tell you that. You're clearly a woman who has a mind of her own." He reached out and touched her cheek. "But may I suggest that we don't discuss this anymore right now? We've been going since dawn, and I can tell you're exhausted. Then Bohdan pulled the rug out from under us in more ways than one. Why don't we try to get some sleep and let it sink in? We'll have decisions enough to make tomorrow."

"Are you being soothing and trying to take care of me again?" She nodded. "I think you are. I'm not insulted. I don't care. I'll take care of you, too. It's not such a bad idea. I don't want Bohdan to occupy any more of our minds tonight." She lifted her hand to cover a yawn. "You're right, I'm very tired and everything seems to be a blur. Besides, I just want to think about my baby now. I haven't let myself do that since the night I came back from Kilgoray. There seemed to be too many things getting in my way."

"Then by all means." He was laying out the sleeping bags and blankets. "You don't want to let Bohdan cheat you of anything. We'll work out how to take him down together. But right now, just let everything else go away."

"Together," she murmured as she crawled into the sleeping bag. "That's what you said before. I was hoping that you meant it."

"I meant it. Though I've been known to try to manipulate situations to suit myself, that's all in the past." He lay down beside her. "I didn't even cross my fingers when I said it."

"What a relief," she mocked. "But then I told MacDuff that you never lied to me."

"I would have been tempted this time. I could feel you edging away from me. I was afraid I was losing you." He put his arm over her body. "You're still shaking. Come closer to me."

She didn't move. "I'm fine. You can't solve everything that's wrong with me."

"I won't try. Perhaps I'm hoping that you'll try your hand at solving everything that's wrong with me. Heaven knows that would be a monumental task. It would make me feel less insecure if I could feel you close to me."

"Insecure?" She lifted her head to look at him. "You?" Then she nestled nearer to him. "On the chance that you're not joking, I wouldn't want to deny you. I've always wanted you to have whatever you wanted or needed."

"I know you have." He cradled her head to rest on his shoulder. "And there's something that I need to know." He hesitated. "How soon, Jane?"

She stiffened. "When am I due? The doctor said I'm three months' pregnant. I probably became pregnant during the weeks we were in London watching over Eve, Joe, and Michael." She looked at him. "But I want you to know that I'm keeping this child. Whether you want it or not. I'll take care of it, if you decide that you want to walk away. It will be my child and you'll—"

"Be quiet." His hand was over her mouth, silencing her. His hoarse voice was intense. "You're right, it will be *your* child. Do you think that I'd ever walk away from your child? It will be a part of you. I'd never let either one of you go. But I have to know everything about it so that I can take care of it, and you. I've never had to worry about anything like this before. But you've got to tell me things and let me help you."

"And I will." She went into his arms. "You know more than you think. You'll always know what to do. You practically raised your sister Lisa. And you did a great job. But we might have to learn together. I may have to call Eve and Joe and have another talk."

"Later," Caleb said. "I think I could handle Eve, but I don't want to deal with an angry ex-SEAL at the moment. We have too much on our plates right now. Go to sleep and we'll get everything settled in the morning." He paused. "There is one other item. Would you mind if I fill in Rodland when he comes back to camp?"

"No, why should I mind? The last thing I want is to have to repeat any of Bohdan's threats again."

"Just checking. Our arrangement is too new for me to violate any of its clauses. Your relationship with Rodland did have certain secrets."

"The only thing in the least confidential was our trip to Kilgoray. He didn't even know who I was going to see." She added suddenly, "Dr. Campbell. I'm worried about him. He was very nice to me. We've got to make certain Bohdan doesn't hurt him."

"I'm not forgetting about him. I'm going to call Palik right away and get him to send a team to explore how we can find him." Caleb kissed her forehead. "But there's nothing you can do right now. Go to sleep, Jane..."

———◆———

The first thing Jane was aware of when she woke the next morning was the scent of bacon and pancakes.

"It's about time you stirred." Rodland turned away from the fire as he picked bacon out of the skillet and put it on a plate. "You were sleeping hard, and I thought I was going to have to wake you. I hate the idea of serving cold bacon. It offends my culinary expertise. Go down to the creek and take a quick bath but be back in fifteen minutes."

She sat up and looked around. "Where's Caleb?"

"He's on the phone with MacDuff. He talked to Palik last night after I came back to camp." He saw her frown and said, "It's not as if he's getting ahead of you. He didn't want me to wake you because he thought you needed the rest." He suddenly grinned. "A baby, Jane? Not anything I expected. You could have given me a hint."

"Why should I? It wasn't your business." She made a face. "And look at the way you're behaving now. Just what I didn't want to happen. I'm very strong, and having this child shouldn't make any difference to my general good health. I remember Eve was as strong as a horse all through most of her pregnancy with Michael. I'll exercise and make sure that nothing gets in the way of my keeping my baby well."

"Yes, ma'am," Rodland said. "Caleb did warn me. I'll watch myself from now on. I only meant that Caleb wanted to put Palik and MacDuff in place right away in case he decided to bring them into going after your Dr. Campbell." He added, "Which you should be thinking about yourself. You know Caleb is unique. Take advantage of him."

"I will." She got to her feet and grabbed her clothes, towel, and soap. "But our agreement is that we take advantage of each other for the greater good. I prefer that philosophy."

"Very concise, but a little puritanical. Caleb is a loner. You might have trouble keeping him in line."

"Not if we work at it." She took off in the direction of the creek.

"Fifteen minutes," he called after her. "And don't try to keep me in line. I'm the cook."

She was chuckling as she reached the creek. But the smile faded as she waded into the cold water. She had no desire to keep Caleb in line. They had a long way to go, and she had no idea how it was going to end. She instantly rejected the thought. It had to end well because she wouldn't accept anything else. She had Caleb, and now she had a child, and she would work and do everything to make them happy.

"You have five more minutes." She turned to see Caleb speaking from the bank. "Rodland said to remind you that he was the cook." He shook out the towel and held it out to her. "I told him that I wasn't the one to send after you."

"Yes, you are. Because Rodland told me how unique you are and that I should take advantage of you." She stood there looking at him and could sense the sheer arousal enveloping him. It was electric, almost as if he were outlined in fire. Every muscle was poised and ready as his gaze ran over her naked body. How many times had she seen him like this? Yet it was always new and created an instant response. She could feel the muscles of her abdomen clench and her breasts swell. She knew what was coming, and good heavens how she *wanted* it.

She walked over to him, and he wrapped her in the towel and then slowly began rubbing her down. The sensation was excruciatingly intimate as the soft roughness of the towel left her breasts and the friction became lower, hotter. "Though I'm not sure this is what he meant. I still believe I should follow his advice. What do you think that—"

He was stripping off his clothes.

He was inside her! His hands were on her buttocks, lifting her, and her thighs went around his hips. Then she was on her back on the creek bank, and he was moving, lifting, pushing inside.

Deep.

Deeper.

Deep. Deep. Deep.

Hot. Filling. Too full...

She couldn't breathe.

She didn't want to breathe.

More. More.

Then he rolled her over and she was on top, taking all of him, his lips on her breasts, pulling at her nipples.

She gasped, moaned.

She couldn't stand the intensity.

She opened her lips to scream but it was too primal even to permit that release.

Then the explosion came with the same fiery power that he'd shown from the instant she'd seen him standing on the bank.

She collapsed on top of him.

She couldn't move for a moment.

Evidently neither could Caleb. His heart was pounding hard against her. "I think we've blown your five minutes." Then he was on his feet, picking her up and carrying her back into the creek. "I hope you believe it was unique enough to be worthwhile." He let her slide down his naked body; she experienced the coolness of the water and his every hard sinew and muscle. She began to feel another stirring. He added softly, "It was for me."

"Cook or not, I'm not letting Rodland orchestrate this particular action."

"Hallelujah. Then let's see how it feels underwater."

"I don't know if that would be—" Then he was inside her again and the chill and heat blending together was wildly erotic in both sensation and texture. The rhythm of the movement was like nothing she had ever felt.

And she forgot what she had been about to say...

———◆———

It was over an hour later that they were both dressed and heading back toward the camp.

"I was wondering if Rodland might decide to drop in," Jane said. "Sometimes his sense of humor has rather mischievous overtones."

"I would have drowned him," Caleb said flatly.

"I wouldn't have been pleased, either." She gave him a sideways glance. "Though I was surprised to see you at the creek this morning."

"But you were ready for me."

She nodded slowly. "I was ready. I'd been thinking about you. But it was still a surprise." She turned to face him. "You don't often do anything impulsively. Was this an impulse?"

"No, it didn't start out that way. But once started it was pure sexual impulse and a kind of spectacular lust." He stopped and thought about it. "Yes, 'spectacular' is the right word. I couldn't have stopped if I'd wanted to. I needed you too much." He smiled crookedly. "And you needed me. I was hoping that you would."

"Impulse," she prompted.

"I didn't sleep much last night. Most of the time I just lay there and watched you. I realized that everything was changing for us, and it was scaring me. I wasn't stupid enough to believe that I'd be able to just coast along when something this world shaking was happening to you."

"And happening to you," she said quietly. "If you meant what you said about accepting the fact that this child will always be part of our family."

"I meant it." He looked away from her. "And that's a gigantic change for me. But it's one I'm looking forward to making because I know it will be a joy to watch you with him." He suddenly frowned. "Him. But it might not be a boy. Did Campbell tell you about the sex?"

She shook her head. "Too early. Usually between eighteen and twenty weeks. Does it matter to you?"

"I just don't want to keep calling the baby 'it.' That seems...rude."

She started to laugh. "I don't think the baby would care. But if you don't want to offend, you could take turns with male or female pronouns."

"That's not efficient...or satisfactory."

She was still chuckling. "I could consult a crystal ball or maybe a Ouija board."

He grinned. "Or you could call your brother Michael and see if he has any special insights."

"We don't try to treat Michael as special." She glanced at him. "You should understand that, Caleb."

"Oh, yes." His tone was wry. "I was joking. Michael and I understand each other. I'll go for alternating the pronouns."

She was no longer smiling. "And I'd ask Campbell to rush the test, but that might be difficult unless we can get him away from Bohdan."

"Which we will." He took her hand. "Another problem to

take care of. That was why I called Palik this morning. I asked him to send out a team to Kilgoray to track down any signs of Campbell ASAP. Bohdan mentioned two trips to Kilgoray. He must have made contact with some of the villagers who might have info." He paused. "And I told him we also need to get our hands on one of Bohdan's men who can give us information about his location. That sniper you tracked down wasn't able to help much."

"Except about Felicity," Jane said bitterly. "And no one considered her of any importance."

"We did," Caleb said gently. "And we'll make them pay for her death. But first, we have to rid ourselves of Bohdan and his troop of mercenaries. Self-preservation is the name of the game right now. I can't let him near you."

"Aren't you back to square one?"

"No, the game has changed with the characters. You can't be my only focus right now." His gaze moved over her body. "You don't have the right to complain about everything I've done to protect you any longer. Our agreement has certain holes in it now. It can't be a totally fifty-fifty arrangement any longer. You're carrying my child. To protect that child, I have to protect you. I have no choice."

Her brow wrinkled. "That sounds very . . . complicated. And it appears to end exactly where you want it to. I don't like this."

"But you're very smart and you know that I'm being reasonable." He added, "Think about it. What's most important to you? What would you do? What lengths would you go to in order to protect that child?"

"Damn you." She stared with frustration into his eyes. "Everything. Anything."

"Then you realize that we might have a balance problem," he said softly. "And you realize that no matter how hard I'm going to try, there are going to be times when I have to make certain that child comes first even if you don't appreciate my methods."

"I'll think about it." She was silent for a moment. "You're turning me against myself. I'm feeling manipulated."

"I knew you would," he said. "Which is why I came down to the creek this morning. I wanted to remind you that what we have together has been worth it to both of us." He added softly, "And that was how we ended up with a child to protect."

"Oh, you demonstrated that exceptionally well," she said. "But it really wasn't necessary, we've gone way past the sexual basics."

"Nothing basic about it. It's strictly stratosphere stuff. But we might be heading for something entirely different. That's why I thought we had to go back and get our bearings."

"I don't want to go back, I want to go forward," she said. "Though you were very inventive today. However, we'll have to discuss any 'methods' you decide to put in place. You should realize that children never stand still. They tend to always go forward."

His lips quirked. "Like their mother?"

"Exactly." She tossed him a smile over her shoulder as she made the turn leading to the camp. "You must have heard the saying about mother knowing best. But you might be permitted an opinion if you don't become too rambunctious."

"Rambunctious?" he murmured. "I don't believe anyone has used that word to describe me."

"You were talking about different paths. I was trying to oblige." She waved at Rodland as the camp came into view.

"But I'll leave it to you to persuade Rodland to make me another breakfast since it's your fault that the first one was ruined."

"I warned him he shouldn't send me."

"Because you knew he would anyway. You were going to do what you wanted to do. Rodland always wants everything to go well for you. You're his hero."

"No, he just believes in payback. I understand it, I just try to avoid it. I'd resent it if I was him."

"But then few people are like you. Some of us don't mind owing someone a debt."

"Yet you'd do anything on earth to repay it. And I can't imagine anything worse than having you feeling forced to do that." He took her elbow and nudged her forward. "Which is quite a change for me. It must be your influence. There was a time that I wouldn't have given a damn, if it meant I could still keep you."

"I don't believe that."

"No? You should." His fingers tightened on her arm. "Believe it, Jane."

CHAPTER

12

After breakfast that morning Rodland didn't give Jane a chance to do more than help break camp before he told her, "Caleb told me to go saddle Jocko for him. MacDuff wants to see you and make sure you're okay so we're going back to the Run. Caleb said for me to drive you in the Range Rover, and he'll ride Jocko."

"I could ride Jocko. We're used to each other."

"Caleb said he wanted to do it. He needs to stretch out and he said it was a chance for me to tell you the rest of MacClaren's story on the trip back." He wrinkled his nose. "I've evidently been designated to keep you entertained. Not that I mind. I was a little pissed off that you left me to twiddle my thumbs earlier today. I'd far rather talk about Fiona and MacClaren. I've sort of been thinking about them as family."

She groaned. "Don't say that." Then she saw his eyes were twinkling. "Go saddle Jocko. Where's Caleb? Why didn't he do it?"

He shrugged. "He's been on the phone with MI6. I

supposed he's trying to pull something together. And I need the practice."

Jane finished packing up and was settling in the passenger seat of the Range Rover when Rodland opened the driver's door. "All finished," he said. "I turned Jocko over to Caleb, who looks as depressingly dashing as Zorro, or maybe some desert sheikh on his favorite Arab stallion. It isn't fair, you know. I never looked like that on Maisie. I guess there's something to say about horses, though." He waved as Caleb passed them on Jocko. "See what I mean?"

She did, and it was causing her to experience a sudden vivid physical memory of what had happened at the lake this morning. Dressed in jeans, with the sleeves of his black shirt rolled up to the elbow, Caleb did look lean and tough and vibrantly sensual. "I'm sure he wouldn't have looked nearly as good on Maisie, either," she told Rodland soothingly. Then she frowned. "He's going on ahead?"

"He said that he wanted to check out the woods to make sure they're safe for you."

"From snipers? He's the one who's vulnerable. He could be picked off with no problem. We have all this metal around us."

"Well, I don't think we should worry. He knows what he's doing. He'll see them before they see him. He managed to take down that general's bodyguards as well as the bastard himself before he escaped Bohdan's army."

"I don't care, I do worry. And he promised me that he would—" But he probably thought he had nullified that promise when he'd talked to her earlier today. No way. "I have to talk to him."

"I suggest that you wait until these woods start thinning out before you start in pursuit. We might get in the way," Rodland said. "Just in case I'm wrong about Caleb."

"You're probably not," Jane said. "I remember that most of the threat of attack should be over by the time we approach the road. That should be time enough for me to call him." She added grimly, "Unless he's dead."

He gave a low whistle. "There's always that possibility. You don't mind if I opt out of any discussion you have with Caleb?"

"Why should I? You're not worried. He's not worried." She leaned back in her seat. "And I'm going to try to follow your example. Until I see him. Didn't you say that Caleb wanted you to entertain me by telling me the rest of MacClaren's story? He's so good with plans that I think you should just go along with it."

"Are you certain?" he asked warily. "I don't believe you're in the mood."

"You'd be wrong. I want MacClaren's story to be happy and successful and hopefully brimful of ways to sting the bad guys." She paused. "As long as it includes Fiona in a way that has meaning and doesn't leave her to trail after MacClaren like a lost puppy dog."

"Some of it you'll have to judge for yourself. You have the letter. I can only tell you what I know about MacClaren."

"And the last thing I heard was that he'd talked Jamie into letting him paint Fiona's portrait. But the chance of Jamie letting her have anything to do with him other than that was nil. True?"

He nodded. "She was gentry. He was a penniless artist. So they had to find a way to work around it. Not easy during that period. They decided to play a waiting game. Jamie wanted that portrait, and he didn't know much about the artistic process. So MacClaren showed some of the razzmatazz he'd learned while he was in America and pretended that the portrait wouldn't be any good if he didn't take a long time to create it. That gave him and Fiona months together, and as long as they played it cool, Jamie wouldn't object. But money became a problem, and since MacClaren was doing Fiona's portrait for a pittance, he told Jamie he'd contracted to do murals for the railway to make ends meet. That gave them the opportunity to go up to the hills and stall even longer while he painted the murals. Graeme was in Europe on an extended business trip, and Jamie suspected nothing. It was a good time for them. Fiona even managed to go to the rail yards with him once when he officially turned over the murals to the owners of the company. But the good times ran out and they couldn't stall any longer. Other clients of the railway were trying to hire MacClaren to paint similar works for them." He shrugged. "And Jamie wanted his portrait. He needed money and Graeme, Fiona's fiancé, was due to come back from Paris. He planned on showing him the portrait and then making the final wedding arrangements to clinch his deal with him."

"They were in a corner," Jane murmured.

"Not yet. But they could see it coming. They were already making plans, and MacClaren had started to look for ways that they could be together. But every way was going to be danger-ous for Fiona if anyone knew that MacClaren was part of those plans. She was a woman in a man's world, and Jamie had total control of her. And he had enough power as the laird's brother to arrange for an accident to happen to anyone who got in his way if he chose. That put both of them in actual danger."

"But you can't tell me that either of them would let themselves tolerate that kind of treatment," Jane said. "They'd fight back. She'd been fighting all her life, and so had he. It might have been in different ways, even in different hemispheres, but now that they'd come together again, they'd fight together."

"It seems you've decided to write your own story," Rodland said with amusement. "You don't mind if I chime in?"

"If you can give them something to work with. I've not been happy with all this male-dominance crap."

"Well, it was more subterfuge than outright battle, but it worked for them. Not that you'll approve." He glanced slyly at her. "MacClaren finished the portrait, and it was a great success. He took the agreed fee from Jamie and then booked passage to go back to America. He was gone a week later."

"No," Jane said definitively.

"Yes. I tried to tell you that it was a different time and mind-set. He settled in Buffalo, New York. But after a few weeks he got restless and moved to Denver, Colorado. That was the last place where he could be traced. Though there were rumors he might have gone on to Sacramento, California."

"And you're saying he just left Fiona in the lurch and went back to wandering the frontier?"

"What else could the poor lad do? Fiona was betrothed the week Jamie and Graeme got together after he returned to Scotland. Everyone said she appeared perfectly contented and was charming to Graeme. The nuptials were arranged to take place six months later. Graeme was completely happy with the arrangement because he became besotted with Fiona. He couldn't believe it when she disappeared. He was the one who wouldn't give up looking for her. He was totally humiliated that she'd jilted him, and at one time he even paid a visit to

America on the wild chance that MacClaren had something to do with her disappearance."

"Wild chance? He didn't find her?"

"Not as far as anyone knew. Graeme had an unfortunate fall from a train crossing over a bridge in the northwest territory of Montana. No one knew how it happened. He never made it back to Scotland."

"And he didn't locate MacClaren?"

"Didn't I mention no one heard from him after Denver? Why would he be in Montana?"

"You tell me."

He was silent a moment. "I couldn't find any trace of Mac-Claren after Denver." He smiled. "But I did find that D. B. Ward located very happily in Seattle, where he continued to write and illustrate dime novels. He also painted several landscapes that were very well thought of by the critics of the time. He invested his profits in the local railway and did fine economically. But that might have something to do with his wife, who took over the running of the railway and evidently had a terrific head for business."

"And her name?"

"Not Fiona. They would have both been too smart to make that mistake when they couldn't be sure whether the hunt was still going on." He smiled. "Her name was Maggie. A fine Scottish name from the Borderlands." He added softly, "And one of the meanings is 'she knows.'"

"I'm glad someone appreciated her." Jane added thoughtfully, "So they decided that MacClaren was to completely leave the scene so he wouldn't be under suspicion. Then he could find a place for both of them and arrange for Fiona to disappear six months later."

"If that's what you think happened." He smiled. "I can only give you the bare facts. It's up to you to twist them to suit yourself."

"And I've already done that." She frowned. "But I wonder how she got from MacDuff's Run to America?"

"With help from MacClaren, of course. Just as he probably helped her to eliminate Graeme a few years later on that train in Montana when he was hunting her down."

She nodded. "Too coincidental. I can see a confrontation happening. But it might have been Fiona, not MacClaren. If it was as passionate a love affair as it seemed, she would have wanted to protect what they had together."

"'If'? You haven't read the letter?"

"Not yet. I meant to do it. But I've been a bit busy." She added bitterly, "That's an understatement. Bohdan managed to poison everything lately. We've got to stop him." Her lips tightened. "And not let him take over our lives. I'll read that letter, dammit. I promised MacDuff that I'd solve his Fiona mystery. It's the least I can do after what he's gone through for me. I'm dreading what I'm going to see at the castle."

He nodded. "The damage isn't a pretty sight." He glanced out the windshield. "And we're getting close to the road. You'll be seeing it soon. You said you wanted to call Caleb?"

She was already reaching for her phone. "Pull onto the road as soon as possible. I'll tell him I want to talk to him before we reach the gates."

"Good idea. You might lose your train of thought. Not much left of those gates," Rodland said. "I think I see Caleb just ahead..."

And Jane was already talking to him. "We're right behind you. Could you rein in and let me talk to you? Rodland is stopping when we reach the road."

"Any problem?"

"A misunderstanding. We'll take care of it." She ended the call.

"Brief and to the point." Rodland was already stopping on the edge of the road. "Not necessarily warm."

"I wasn't aiming for warmth. I wanted clarity." She opened the car door. "Caleb will understand. At the moment he's probably rapidly going over in his mind all the things that I might be about to say." She got out of the car. "And because he's really quite brilliant and knows me very well, no doubt he'll reach the right conclusion before I have a chance to go into it with him." She was walking toward where Caleb was sitting on Jocko a short distance away. "I don't think I'll be long."

"A misunderstanding?" Caleb was smiling faintly as she approached. "Then let's take care of it. You didn't like me doing the advance sweep to make certain we weren't going to have company in that forest."

"I told Rodland that you'd have it worked out before I had to open my lips. You probably knew it was a possibility before you told Rodland to saddle Jocko." She looked him in the eyes. "You were very persuasive about the fact that you knew I'd be reasonable about never wanting the baby to be in danger and I was the natural guardian because I'm carrying that child. All that was true. I will be careful, but I won't let you go riding off and taking chances that aren't necessary. There will be times when I'll have to make decisions, but this wasn't one of them. I won't lose this baby and I won't lose you. You went alone today, and I could have been there and helped. Don't do that again."

"Do I dare ask what you'd do if I did?"

"I'd come after you. I almost did today. I won't hesitate again." She smiled crookedly. "The solution is that you find a way to use me to help, and you won't have to worry about it."

"Oh, I'll worry." He paused. "But I'm reading you loud and clear. I don't believe we'll have to have this conversation again."

"Thank God," she said wearily. "I didn't want to face arguing with you. Because I'm going to have to get back in that car and go down to that burned-out gate and face MacDuff. It's going to hurt, Caleb."

"I know. I don't want you to be alone." He turned Jocko and gave him a kick. "Give me a five-minute start. I'll meet you at the gate."

She stood looking after him for a few moments and then turned and headed for the Range Rover.

"Everything okay?" Rodland asked as she got in the car. "He didn't give you a hard time?"

"No, everything's not okay." She might still have problems with Caleb's protective instinct, yet that wasn't all bad. That moment when he'd reached out and told her he wanted to be with her at those burned-out gates had magically soothed and eased the pain she knew was coming. "But some things are a lot better than others."

———◆———

MACDUFF'S RUN

Caleb jumped off Jocko and was opening her car door as they pulled up at the gates. "I called MacDuff and I told him we'd meet him at his library. He's busy with the local insurance adjustors down at the boat docks. There was some damage down there, too."

Jane flinched as she gazed at the broken, blackened gates. "It makes me sick to see all this senseless destruction. Sick and angry."

"Be angry, not sick," Caleb said. "Anger translates to action, and we'll have use for action very soon." He turned to Rodland, who had come to stand beside them. "I assume you've seen more than enough of Bohdan's work the last time you were here. Will you take Jocko back to the main stables and then come back and see what you can do to help MacDuff?"

"Sure, just what I had in mind," he said flippantly. "You know how I adore dealing with horses. And MacDuff has had a soft spot for me since I showed up here to meddle in his business." He waved his hand. "No problem. I'll take care of it." He went over to Jocko's saddle and took Jane's art case from the pommel. "But you might need this." He came back and handed it to her. "You said you had some reading to do." He took the horse's reins and turned away. "And now I'll see if I can find one of MacDuff's grooms who I can con into taking this fine animal to that stable for me. I'm certain Jocko would be much happier with him." A moment later she saw him strolling toward a group of workers near the fountain.

She turned back to Caleb. "Okay, I've braced myself. Take me for the grand tour." She gazed at the destruction of what had been the beautiful front door. "But you did say that none of the paintings were stolen or damaged."

He nodded. "I think you should see for yourself. You're looking at the broken tiles and the burnt doors, but MacDuff is seeing the treasures that were left behind and how he can save what's here. Even more, how he can build to make it even stronger and more beautiful." He was nudging her toward the steps leading to the front door. "MacDuff is indomitable, and it will happen. It will be exciting to stay around and watch him do it." He added softly as he pushed her through the shattered door into the grand hall, "And offer a little help now and then so that we'll have our share of the great rebirth to come." He was pulling her toward the gallery. "Now come and see that even a bastard like Bohdan couldn't destroy those paintings."

She was already in the gallery and gazing at the collection of the Old Masters and the portraits of MacDuff's family through the centuries. He was right. It was vaguely comforting to see that this gallery and the paintings were just the same as before the attack. Comforting and yet engendering a fierce protectiveness to keep that status quo at any cost. She turned to Caleb. "But he'll probably try again. We'll stop him, Caleb."

He nodded. "The drones surprised us. But Palik has guard units all over the castle and grounds now. No more surprises. They won't be able to touch the Run again. MacDuff will be able to make his repairs in peace." His lips tightened. "And we'll be able to go on the hunt and reel the son of a bitch in."

"It had better be soon," she said. "Dr. Campbell may already be dead. You haven't had a report from Palik about the unit he sent to Kilgoray yet?"

He shook his head. "But we may have time. Bohdan might not want to kill him right away. It sounded as if he wanted to use him."

She flinched. "And that's what I haven't allowed myself to think about since that damn phone call. I liked Campbell; he was kind to me. I called him out of the blue asking for an appointment. I must have sounded desperate because he was very gentle and patient with me. I was so grateful he made time for me on his schedule." She moistened her lips. "It would have been so much better if he hadn't. None of this would have happened to him."

"You would have found someone else. As you said, you were desperate. You had no idea that you were being followed."

"I'm afraid for him, Caleb," she whispered.

"I know, and it sucks," he said roughly. He made a step toward her then stopped. "You won't let me go after him and that's the only way I can take care of it. Which means I have to wait for Palik to find him. Tell me what else I can do."

She nodded quickly. "I'm not being fair. I just wish Palik would hurry." She turned and moved toward the wall where Fiona's portrait hung. She tried to change the subject. "You'll be glad to know that, as ordered, Rodland tried to keep me entertained on the way here. He almost finished the MacClaren/Fiona story."

"Almost?"

"I have to read a letter and fill in some blanks."

"Did you like the way it turned out?"

"I like her, I like him. I found myself rooting for them. But I was frustrated about how the world was treating them until they took their fates into their own hands."

"That's the way it sometimes works out. So did they live happily ever after?"

"It wasn't a fairy tale. I think it turned out to be a murder mystery. But they lived their lives the way they wanted to. I'd bet that they had a good time and a good life and tried not to hurt anyone if they could avoid it."

"Except for the murder?"

"I'm sure that wasn't their fault. He was supposed to have been a terrible man."

He laughed. "I can't wait until you fill me in on the rest of the tale. But I want you to check out the rest of the castle, so you'll know that it's in as good a shape as the gallery. Then we're supposed to meet MacDuff in the library. Who knows? He might want to hear about Fiona's murder mystery."

She shook her head. "I'm not entirely sure it's a murder mystery. It just makes sense that it might be. I won't talk to MacDuff until I can tell him more than we know right now. I have to keep my promise."

"You always do." He brushed his lips across her temple. "Now let's look around the castle at all the good things that are still here and then we'll go talk to MacDuff."

———◆———

"You've caused a hell of a lot of trouble, Jane." MacDuff was frowning as they walked into the library an hour later. "You should have come directly back here as soon as you knew the immediate danger was over. It was stupid of you to try tracking that damn sniper. Didn't you realize that I'd be worried?"

"I resent that, MacDuff. It only would have been stupid if I hadn't managed to catch the bastard. And how did I know if and when the immediate danger was over? The only immediate threat I could see was the man who had shot Rodland, and it seemed smart to take him out of the equation." She walked across the room toward him. "And yes, I'm sorry you were worried, but I was busy, and I told you as soon as I could." She reached out and grasped his hands in hers. Her voice was shaking as she looked up and met his eyes. "And I can't tell you how sorry I am for my part in what happened here. It broke my heart."

"Good God, you're ready to burst into tears. That's not like you at all." He glanced over his shoulder at Caleb. "She's embarrassing me. Can't you do something?"

Caleb shook his head. "She can be like that sometimes. I tried my best. But you'll have to deal with it."

"No, he won't." Jane gave MacDuff a quick hug. "I won't put him through it. It just had to be said." She released him and took a step back. "But you will have to deal with the fact that I won't let you go through this without me. I realize you can handle what happened here with your hands tied behind your back, but I can't. You'll have to let me help...after we take care of Bohdan."

"That sounds reasonable." His voice was gruff. "Now is all this emotional nonsense over? I wanted to tell you that you should move back into the castle. It will be repaired, and it's now even better guarded, and you won't have to worry about another attack."

"I'm not worried," she said. "There won't be another attack unless we want it to happen." Her lips tightened. "And it will never be here again. From now on we're the ones who will be going on the assault."

"We?" He glanced at Caleb again. "I'm not sure I like the way that sounds."

"You don't know the half of it," he said dryly. "But I'd advise you not to go into it in-depth. You have enough problems right now."

"When did I ever take advice from you?" MacDuff asked. "Occasionally, it's true you can be useful, but everyone knows I'm much wiser. After Jane and I have a discussion, I'm sure she'll agree with me." He smiled down at Jane. "Now, where shall we go to have our talk? Could I get you a cup of tea?"

"No." She smiled back at him. "And I have no intention of baring my soul to you. Caleb is right, I'm not giving you any more burdens." She tilted her head. "Where shall we go? I'm going to let you take me around the property to all the unhappy places and destruction that will probably make me sad and angry. Caleb carefully avoided showing me any of those because he wanted me to see your brighter vision of the MacDuff's Run to come."

"Not a bad idea," he said warily. "Better than usual for Caleb."

"Kind," she agreed. "But I have to see both sides so that I can be prepared for what's on the horizon. I've always loved the Run. I *will* help you heal what they did here. However, I have to know the damage before I can do that." She headed for the door. "Let's get it over with. You're a busy man."

MacDuff followed her; his brows rose as he passed Caleb. "Join us?"

Jane answered for him. "I don't think that would be a good idea. He's also a busy man, and he has calls to make and plans regarding what we need to do about Bohdan. I wouldn't want to take up more of his time."

"Jane," Caleb said.

"It's true." She glanced at him over her shoulder. "I've made demands you don't like. I had to do it, but you don't have to hold my hand through all the hours of the day." She paused. "Campbell. Please, Caleb. Check on Campbell."

She didn't wait for an answer but left the library.

———◆———

"Yes and no. No direct word on Campbell," Palik said when Caleb reached him. "We know he disappeared from his home one evening after his office files were rifled by two thugs that afternoon. Jane had been seen going into the office by the owner of one of the food carts in the streets outside the building. The receptionist in the office was interrogated by them and identified Jane's photo. She was beaten badly, but not killed. They must have been flashing that photo all over the village."

"It was their second visit to the village and Bohdan was impatient," Caleb said grimly. "Where does the 'yes' come into this?"

"We showed some photos ourselves, and we were just as determined as Bohdan's scum. We had several photos of Campbell that we took from his home. We covered the village and all the outlying areas, and we got lucky because Campbell is also well known around the village. He appears to be a nice guy who has delivered quite a few babies to the villagers over the years. It became clear that the pier was out. He wasn't taken anywhere by boat. But four separate people in the hill country thought they'd seen him walking with two other men toward the northern fishing lakes. One of them knew Campbell and spoke to him. He thought it strange that Campbell hadn't answered him."

"Did you follow up on it?"

"Of course. But that's a lot of territory and it's filled with small farms and those lakes where city folks come to spend weekends fishing. It will take time."

"I don't know how much time we'll have," Caleb said slowly. "I'm finding it a little odd that you were able to locate Campbell that easily."

"I haven't located him yet. Still, I see where you're going. Only two men to hold a valuable prisoner? And we managed to do the initial tracking with no problem. Add the area where Campbell is presumably being held is going to be very difficult to explore or negotiate." He paused. "Which means it could be a trap."

"Very likely. And if it is, they'll want to set the bait up in an appetizing way so that I'll be lured into the trap," Caleb said. "Which means if you send a sharp enough team down to the lake area and tell them to keep their eyes open, they should be able to spot Campbell." He smiled sardonically. "Then we can only hope that we can pluck the good doctor out of the lion's den before Bohdan lets loose the big cats."

"You know as well as I do that it all could be for nothing. What do you think our chances are?"

"I've no idea. All I know is that we've got to try. Even if Campbell isn't the good guy you tell me he is, Jane has a vested interest in keeping him alive. I won't let her down."

"Second question. Do you want me to be the one to go in and pull Campbell out?"

"No, I'll do it myself. Just set up the operators to locate the place they're hiding Campbell. You do what you do best and run the teams. You never can tell when a job is going to go to hell, and a little fine-tuning might become necessary."

Palik was frowning. "I'm not sure that I should let you go in alone."

"I beg your pardon?"

"No insult intended. But if Jane is involved, I'll never hear the end of it if anything goes wrong. You did say she had a vested—" He broke off and started to laugh. "It just hit home! The doctor, all those babies born in the village . . . Jane?"

"I'm glad you're amused."

"A little amused, mostly scared to death. Either way I look at it, I could be in trouble if I screw up."

"Then don't screw up. I've done enough of that to go around. From now on we all walk a very tight, straight line."

"Whatever you say. I'll go right to work setting up a way out of the lion's den, and I'll try to make it foolproof."

"Thank you," he said mockingly.

Palik didn't speak for a moment. "But a baby is never a screwup. I guess it can be a kind of challenge, but that's usually not the kid's fault."

"What are you talking about? That wasn't what I was referring to. Any child Jane brought into the world would be a miracle."

"Yes, she's exceptional. I'm glad you appreciate her. I just thought I'd make certain you weren't being an ass, so I decided to add my few words of wisdom."

"Very few and totally misguided. And you never told me you had kids."

"I don't. I've been too busy keeping reckless clients like you out of major trouble. Sometimes I kind of wish I did. You're lucky as hell, Caleb." He cut the connection.

Lucky? Caleb stared down at the phone for an instant before he shoved it into his jacket pocket. Lucky to have a chance to keep Jane if he could fight his way through this nightmare. Yes. But even if he managed to keep both her and the child alive and she still was willing to stay with him, how long would it last? It was true any child of Jane's would be a miracle, but that child would also be his. He'd been told from the time he was a toddler that his heritage and blood gifts would always condemn him and his children to be hunters and outsiders.

The last thing he wanted was to have Jane suffer because she had to fight a constant battle. It didn't matter that she'd told him she'd trust him and what they were together to have a family. It was still a risk he hadn't wanted to take.

But the risk was now here, and he had no choice. Not only that, but he was being forced to walk that line he'd warned Palik about. Obey his instincts and handle Bohdan the way he thought necessary. Or keep a promise and run the danger of losing Jane and her child.

No, not just her child. The risk had been taken. This was *his* child, and he was totally committed. Which meant that there was no question which direction he would go.

He was not going to lose Jane or the child. He'd handle the consequences of that decision when he had to face them.

He turned and left the library in search of Jane and MacDuff.

He found them talking to a carpenter at the front gate about rigging a temporary structure until MacDuff could arrange for an architect to plan a permanent gate resembling the original.

Jane turned eagerly toward him. "Palik?"

"I reached him. He's been very busy."

"Campbell?"

"Who else? No definite info. He said it was yes and no. Yes, he'd been sighted alive and well in Kilgoray. No, he hadn't tracked him down yet."

"Damn."

"But Palik is sharp, and he'll let me know as soon as he does. He told me it would be soon."

She made a face. "How soon? I'm scared, Caleb. Do you think we should go to Kilgoray ourselves? Maybe it would make him hurry a bit."

"Or piss him off because you're nagging him to do his job. I put a priority on it, Jane."

"And you're never impatient, are you?" MacDuff turned away from the carpenter. "Caleb knows what he's doing... sometimes. And Palik is very efficient. So why don't you resign yourself to staying here at the Run until you hear from him? You're close to Kilgoray and can take a boat over whenever he calls you. What do you say?"

She hesitated.

"Not a bad idea." Caleb stepped in. "You mentioned you had some reading to do, and you're accustomed to being here." He glanced at MacDuff. "And you don't mind if I also invite myself? I could make some calls this evening to contractors with whom I have influence. I hired a lot of work done on my house near Sky Island, and I can pull some strings for you."

"I really don't need your help."

"Sure you do. You're going to have to bring mega labor from Scotland and England rushing here to do these repairs. They have to be special craftsmen. You might be able to use snob appeal, but I've found that people seem to want to do what I ask them to."

"I wonder why," MacDuff murmured. "Charm?" He shook his head. "Terror? Ah, by George, I believe I've got it."

"Stop it," Jane said. "Thank you for inviting us, MacDuff. You know Caleb can help. Let him do it. Now let's go back and have tea and sandwiches before you return to work." She wearily brushed her hair back from her face. "I'm afraid I've had enough of seeing Bohdan's ideas of renovation. I'm going to take a shower and then curl up and read that letter to Fiona. I may join you in the library later to help out with the recruitment."

"Take a nap instead," Caleb said. "You don't need to referee." He glanced at MacDuff. "Does she? You prefer it to be no-holds-barred?"

He nodded. "Much more stimulating." He started back toward the castle. "Come along, Jane. It must have been upsetting for an artist like you to see all of this destruction. Now we can get on to the plans to change it to creation."

CHAPTER

13

After a shower and putting on her nightshirt Jane settled down propped up in bed and carefully took the Fiona document from her art case. Some of the letters were faded and almost indistinguishable but every now and then she could detect a phrase or a few words that kept her glued to the task. Finally, she had a fairly readable document.

My darling,

Everything is set. I've made the deal with Saldaron. He'll get you away in exchange for me stealing that Cira treasure Graeme's tucked away up in the foothills. Saldaron is just as big a thief as Graeme and I'd love to find a way to cheat them both, but I haven't worked out a safe way to do it yet. You're the important one and I have that plan in place. All you have to do is put on the trousers and jacket I sent you and then make your way to the Highland Railway Yard. Slip onto the mural car through the back entrance door and then lock yourself into Saldaron's private compartment. Don't answer the door if anyone knocks. When you reach the main station south of the English border, I'll be there to meet you and whisk you out of England to Ireland. We'll be on the ship out of Dublin heading for Boston the next day.

And if you change your mind, I'll understand. Though why you'd leave a fine, brilliant man like myself for Graeme, I'll never be able to figure out. Look at all I can offer you, hair-raising adventure, constant insecurity, danger. I'm obviously quite a catch. At least, that's what you've told me. At any rate, if you haven't changed your mind, I'll thank God if I see you on that mural train, my own love.

Until then,
Farrell

Farrell MacClaren was coming across as being very human, she thought, and with a nature that had hints of devilish mischief every now and then. He seemed capable of being something of a scamp, but it was clear he had loved his Fiona.

And there was that intriguing bit about the Cira treasure. He had to be referring to the legend of the lost treasure that Cira, the founder of MacDuff's family, had brought to Scotland when she had fled Herculaneum. But she knew Cira's treasure had already been discovered, because she'd been involved when MacDuff had found it. She doubted if there could be two such treasures connected to MacDuff's Run. Or could there have been? Legend or truth? And if there had been a second treasure, could it have surfaced back in Fiona's time? What would Graeme have had to do with it? Interesting...

It took more than three hours for Jane to be sure that she

had a fairly clean copy of MacClaren's letter to Fiona. She copied it over and then just sat there going over it, thinking about it. Trying to probe the Cira possibilities that had come to light with MacClaren's letter.

There was a soft knock on the door, but Caleb didn't wait before he opened it and came into her room. "I thought you'd still be up. I'm glad, you needed something to distract you. I'd volunteer, but we can go into that later." He crossed to the bed and sat down beside her. "Did you make any progress?"

"I think I did. They arranged to use the railroad to smuggle Fiona away from the property into England and from there to Dublin. And there may have been another reason that Graeme was so eager to find Fiona and MacClaren he'd even risk getting killed hunting them down. It might have had to do with the MacDuff family treasure. Remember that the MacDuff fortune was founded on a treasure brought from Herculaneum by the original founders of the MacDuff family. That was an actress, Cira, and her husband Antonio, and we thought we'd discovered all the treasure she'd hidden to protect it from thieves and robber barons. But there were always those rumors that Cira had divided the treasure and only the major part was hidden in that cave. That she was too smart not to have stashed a second treasure somewhere else to protect herself in case the first treasure trove was found. It was reasonable since she—" She broke off. She knew that expression and she wasn't sure he was listening. She took a good look at him. "Your hair is damp; you've showered and changed. I thought you'd just come from working with MacDuff."

"About thirty minutes ago." He was grinning. "I did him several favors tonight and he very kindly gave me my own chamber as a reward. I ducked inside it to shower, but I had no intention of using it tonight. He does know we sleep together, so I assume that it was only wishful thinking that you might change your mind about me considering the hell I've put you through this time."

She shook her head. "We've already discussed your work. I could have said no."

"But you didn't. Very generous. But I'm afraid MacDuff will have to be disappointed again. Because, with your permission, I don't want to let you go tonight. There are a few things I want to say to you."

"You don't want to hear about Fiona and MacClaren?"

"I'll be fascinated to hear about them, and the treasure, but not at the moment." He bent his head and pressed his lips to the hollow of her throat. "And I love this little hollow, but I can wait for that, too. Palik said something when I was talking to him this afternoon and it made me uneasy. I have to get this out."

"Then you'd better do it quickly," she said. "Because you're not getting your point across very clearly. I'm going in the other direction."

"In most cases that's to be applauded." He turned out the lamp and lay down beside her. "It will be better for me if I can't see you." He put his arms around her and held her close. "And this is good, too." He said softly, "You know why I've been hesitant to bring a child into the world who might be like me. It can be...painful. I didn't want to hurt it. And God knows I don't want to hurt you."

"And you wouldn't," she said fiercely. "I know it. I know *you*. You wouldn't let it happen."

"Hush. I don't want you to try to convince me. Because I am already convinced. I will never let harm of any sort to come to either of you. Palik thought I didn't want this baby. I wondered if perhaps you believed that, too. I couldn't let you continue to believe it. Nothing is further from the truth. *Yes,* I do want our child. I was almost afraid to want it this much." His voice was hoarse, almost guttural in the darkness. "I know what it is to be different, special. It's like that even if there's no threat involved. The fear can make the people around you see a threat even if it doesn't exist. But I won't let being special hurt our child. I'll find a way out of it."

"I know you will." Her arms tightened around him. Thank heavens he had come and told her how he felt. This was a miracle in itself. She was filled with a profound joy and almost heady with relief. She could handle anything else that came their way. "But you might not have to. We don't know what's going to happen down the road. We have to believe that this is going to be a gift." She had a sudden thought. "And I was lying here after I finished reading Fiona's letter and I was thinking that sometimes things come together when you least believe they will. MacClaren was able to arrange to get Fiona away when he painted the train mural and got to know the owner of that railroad. One thing led to another and maybe that's how things are meant to be. Something pops up out of the blue to let you know that there's something else good on the way. Then, if you reach out and grab it, you've got a chance to get what you want." She suddenly sat upright in bed. "That's when I remembered the sketch."

"Sketch?"

"I didn't show you the sketch." She turned on the lamp and jumped out of bed. "I think you should see it."

"I have no idea what you're talking about. But you're certainly excited about it." He smiled. "I bared my soul to you, and I thought it might be a little too heavy and melodramatic. But look at you. Your cheeks are flushed, your eyes are shining, and you're talking philosophy. I like it."

"I *loved* when you bared your soul to me." She was opening her art case and taking out her sketchbook. "It's one of the highlights of my life. Feel free to do it anytime. I just want you to look on the bright side." She flipped through the sketchbook. "Because you brightened up my life considerably tonight." She turned the sketchbook so that he could see the sketch. "I drew this sketch that misty morning you called to give me all that depressing news about Bohdan. I had no subject, I just started drawing freehand and she came to life out of nowhere. I couldn't let it go. It might be one of the best things that I've ever done. MacDuff calls it *Mist Child*. He wanted to buy it."

"I think I remember him mentioning it. It's wonderful. It looks a little like Fiona."

"That's what MacDuff said, I couldn't see it."

"And also like you," he said softly. "MacDuff can't have this sketch, Jane."

"That's not why I showed it to you. You can argue about it later. I wanted to point out that when I drew this little girl, I had no idea that I was pregnant." She made a face. "At least I didn't believe that I did. That came later and hit me like a ton of bricks. But I still drew this enchanting child that anyone would want to claim as their own. Wishful thinking? Or was it a sign that something good was coming and we had to be ready for it?"

"I'll vote for the latter," he said gently. "But I do have to mention that this cynical world would not agree with me. However, I refuse to be cynical about it. It's what you want it

236

to be, or I'll know the reason why." He gazed back down at the sketch. "So does that mean we'll be expecting a girl?"

"No, I wouldn't go that far. Accept the idea, not the factual conception."

"Hmm," he said. "I don't think I can. She looks like you. So until I see bona fide proof to the contrary, I'll have to assume that I'm right. It will also simplify the pronoun problem that we had. That's good."

"Really? I've heard most men want a son."

"Propaganda. I'm good either way, but there's something about your mist child." He glanced back at the sketch and repeated, "And she looks like you." He handed her the sketch. "But you'll have to do the portrait. Then you can give MacDuff the sketch."

"Thank you," she said curtly. "I choose, Caleb."

"You chose to give me a beautiful child," he said quietly. "Now can we go back to bed so I can hold you? Maybe we can discuss a name for our daughter."

She looked at him incredulously. "We will not. There's no way you can be sure. You're being completely ridiculous, and I won't—" She broke off as she saw his mischievous grin. He was standing there, sensual, complex, handsome, and intriguing, the complete package. Everything she wanted, everything she could ever want. "Damn you." She slipped the sketch back in the case and dropped it on the floor. "I was thinking about Hepzibah." She turned out the lamp. "As for the other, put up or shut up, Caleb."

"By all means." He shed his clothes with lightning speed as he spoke. He picked her up and then they were on the bed, his arms encircling her from behind. He pulled her sleep shirt over her head and threw it on the floor beside the bed. "But right now, I just want to touch you here." His hands were on her belly, rubbing, stroking, with a magically gentle caress. He added, "And I want to touch *her*. I need to welcome her, don't I?"

"Whatever you want." It was such a beautiful moment that she was having trouble keeping back the tears. "Crazy man."

"That goes without saying. It took me long enough to get you to let me stick around." His hand stroking her belly paused for an instant. "I just want you to know that it will be worth it. I won't always do the things you want me to do. We won't agree all the time. But there won't be a time I won't love you and keep you and our family safe. Will you remember that?"

"I think it's possible." She turned over in his arms. "If you'll stop talking and make love to me."

"It's a deal." He was over her, then coming closer still. "As long as you promise not to call my daughter Hepzibah..."

1:35 A.M.

Caleb silently let himself out the front door of the castle and then moved swiftly down the steps and headed for the court-yard stable. He reached for his phone to call Palik as he was going down the curving staircase leading to the boat dock.

"You must have gotten my text," Palik said. "You could have answered."

"No, I couldn't. I was busy. You said that you'd located where they took Campbell. Still only two guards?"

"At the house where they're keeping him. And we haven't run across any other of Bohdan's men in the vicinity. That doesn't mean he hasn't arranged to turn loose his hounds and surprise us when he gets the chance." He concluded, "I don't like this, Caleb. It stinks of a trap. Don't go in alone. Let me send in a unit."

"And if it's a trap, the first thing they'll do is kill Campbell the minute they see a unit that poses a threat. I have a better chance of getting him out by myself if there are only the two guards. When was the last time your men caught sight of Campbell?"

"About four hours ago they took him outside the shack to pee. He was a little beat up, but he seemed okay."

"Just so he can walk and move once I get him out." He'd reached the boat dock and headed for the speedboat he'd put there in readiness for departure before he'd gone to help MacDuff. "And you do your job to get me an escape hatch when everything goes south."

"When, not if?" Palik asked mockingly. "You don't like the odds, either. I'll get your ass out. When can you get here?"

"I'm on my way. I'll meet you on the south beach at Kilgoray, and make sure you're ready to give me maps of the entire area." He jumped down into the speedboat. "I've only one more thing to do and that's to call Rodland."

"You're bringing Rodland?"

"Hell, no. I just have to assign him to do something for me." He cast off and started the engine. "You might say he's the escape hatch I set up for this end of the job." The water was spraying on either side as the boat tore through the water. "Not that it will probably do me any good..."

5:15 A.M.

Wrong.

Something was *wrong*.

Jane's eyes flew open in stark terror.

Her bedroom was still dim, only the faintest blur of light filtering through the window.

But that wasn't what was wrong.

"Hey, don't panic." Rodland got up from the easy chair across the room. "It's only me. I'm one of the good guys, remember? I didn't mean to scare you. But Caleb didn't want you to wake up alone and asked me to sit here with you until you woke."

Caleb.

She looked at the empty pillow next to her. The panic was coming back. Her heart started to beat harder.

Wrong. *Very* wrong. "At the moment I'm not certain you are one of the good guys."

"That's okay," Rodland said quietly as he walked over to the bed and turned on the lamp. He handed her the terry-cloth robe lying at the bottom of the bed. "Natural reaction. Believe me, I didn't want to do this. I told him you'd be pissed off. I see you have a coffeemaker over there on the cabinet. Can I make you coffee while you slip on that robe and go wash your face and do all the other things women do?" He was already moving toward the cabinet. "I'd appreciate it if you didn't call for MacDuff and tell him that I spent half the night here without you knowing it. He can be difficult, since he thinks you're family."

"You haven't even seen how difficult *I* can be." She threw on the robe and headed for the bathroom. "I have one question and I want it answered now." She looked over her shoulder at him. "Where is he?"

He was silent. "Kilgoray."

"Alone?"

Another hesitation. "Mostly. Not entirely."

Jane had barely slammed the bathroom door before she wilted back against it. Kilgoray. Bohdan. She could scarcely breathe for a moment. Sick. Then she staggered over to the commode and threw up.

Anger. Fear. Panic, again.

"Jane?" It was Rodland at the door.

"Leave me alone." She drew a deep, shaky breath. "I'll be out in a minute."

"I'll give you ten, but I'm worried."

She didn't answer.

Control. Get control.

She took the entire ten minutes. She showered and brushed her teeth and had a few minutes to try to put together what Caleb must have done. "I'm ready," she said as she came back into the bedroom. "Tell me everything he's done." She sat down on the easy chair. "Though I think I probably have it figured out. He's not hurt or dead or he wouldn't have sent you to hold my hand."

"God, no." His gaze was searching her face. "Are you all right? I heard you—"

"Throw up," she finished for him. "I'm pregnant. It happens."

"Not when it's my fault. Not to me. I'm the one who made you do it."

"It was most definitely not your fault. If we're assigning blame, it was the fault of Caleb who is in Kilgoray at the moment." She gave him a tight smile. "On several different levels. And also my fault, but I won't take the blame for sending him alone to Kilgoray. That was his own idea. I would have gone with him to help. I'm sure Palik and MI6 would have, too."

"He knew you were worried about Campbell. He's used to extracting prisoners and diplomats and decided it would be safer if he did it alone. Neither Palik nor MI6 would have argued with him. They would have trusted his judgment."

"Because he's the Hunter," she said bitterly. "That doesn't mean that he can't be killed. Is there anything I can do? If he's not quite alone, I assume Palik is with him. Will you take me to Kilgoray so that I can see Palik? He might listen to me."

He shook his head. "It's too late. It's been hours since Caleb arrived at Kilgoray. Even if you could manage to involve yourself in the action, you'd endanger him." He paused. "And maybe yourself. You wouldn't want to do that."

"No." She felt that terrible sensation of helplessness. Not only couldn't she help save Caleb, she might kill her baby if she tried. "How long before we know if he's successfully extracted Campbell from those sons of bitches?"

He gave a half shrug. "Caleb told me he'd tell Palik to let us know as soon as Campbell's safe." He added, "You know that if anyone can pull this off, it's Caleb. And he doesn't make mistakes, Jane. No one would know that better than me."

"I realize you're his biggest fan. But accidents can happen. And we don't know that this wasn't a trap."

He didn't speak for a moment. "He'd take that in consideration. He'd just work to get around it."

Rodland had hesitated too long, she realized. "Dammit, he *told* you that he thought that he could be walking into a trap, didn't he?"

He didn't answer directly. "We discussed several possibilities. You picked up on that one right away yourself."

"Because Bohdan isn't stupid, and he's already managed to attack this castle and kill people. I'm not going to let him kill Caleb." Her hands clenched as she experienced that wave of helplessness again. "But if I get the opportunity, I might kill him myself. Why would Caleb *do* this?"

"You know why," Rodland said bluntly. "I don't have to spell it out for you. The same reason he made me come here and make sure that you'd have someone with you so you wouldn't have to face this alone. Dr. Campbell is a good man, and he helped you. Caleb thought he deserved a chance to make it out of there alive. He decided to give it to him."

At what cost? Jane thought. But she mustn't think of that right now. "You're right, of course." She got to her feet. "And since Caleb gave you the job of seeing that I didn't fall apart, I'll let you continue. I don't seem to have been doing too well. I'm going to dress and then I want to get out of here. Come with me."

Rodland was immediately wary. "You can't go to Kilgoray. It's not safe for you."

"Do you think I don't know that? That entire area may be crawling with Bohdan's men. If I was seen, Bohdan might try to kill or take me captive. I'd be much more tempting bait for him than Campbell." Her hand touched her midriff. "So would my baby. I can't run that risk. I just want to go for a walk along the seawall. I need to get out of this room. I have to have you with me because Caleb may call you instead of me." She was taking her clothes from the wardrobe. "I hope that's not true, because that would make me even more upset, but I can't be sure, can I?"

"You can be sure that he only wants to do whatever is best for you," he said quietly. "He didn't want to handle it this way. Give him a break, Jane."

"I can't promise." She slammed the wardrobe door shut. *Strength. Maintain control. Don't let the tears come.* "How can I be sure I'll even get the chance?"

"Because he's Caleb," he said gently. "And I'll be glad to go for that walk with you. You didn't do yourself justice, Jane. I think you're doing very well, indeed."

KILGORAY

Caleb reached the top of the hill and glanced at the sky to the north. It was turning the faintest pink and soon it would be dawn. He imagined that Jane would be awake and probably furious at him by now.

Which meant if Bohdan's men didn't kill him, Jane certainly would.

Their viewpoints were so radically different that he didn't know if she'd ever agree his action was for the best. It would be a lie if he told himself anything else. Everything was different now and it always would be. Even at this potentially lethal moment, he felt a deep tug inside him that hadn't existed before. She wasn't the only one who was changing.

Stop thinking about what he'd left behind him at MacDuff's Run, he thought impatiently. He put away his phone as he ran across the northern edge of the moor. If the GPS was correct, the shack was only a few minutes ahead. Right now, the only thing he should be thinking about was finding Dr. Campbell and getting him safely away.

In less than two minutes, he spotted the shack. It was on a remote plot of land that had clearly once been a farm. The shack was a two-story structure that didn't look much stronger than the rickety boathouse he'd brought down the other day.

He raised his binoculars and surveyed the scene. There were no vehicles nearby and no movement in the area. A few fresh tire tracks pressed into the soft earth in front of him.

He activated the binoculars' thermal imaging component. No body heat detected on the ground floor. But on the upper floor, there was . . . something. The heat signature was lower than he might have expected, but he'd seen cool temperatures in drafty environments wreak havoc on heat sensors before. There appeared to be someone in the back of the house.

He circled around the structure. No sign of booby traps or an ambush.

He pulled out his gun and approached the shack's back entrance. He looked down at the door. No lock or even a knob.

He pushed it open a crack. No trip wires.

He slid inside. The sparse furnishings were from another era, now covered with dust. Wind whistled through cracks in the walls. Floorboards creaked as Caleb made his way to the stairs.

He climbed to the second level. It was a standard three-bedrooms-and-a-bath layout, with the open bathroom at the end of the hall. Next to it was the room where he'd seen the heat signature.

He moved toward the closed door and pushed it open.

The room was empty except for a single chair facing

away from the door, toward a broken window. Tattered white curtains blew in the breeze. There was a man in the chair, Caleb realized.

"Dr. Campbell?"

No reply.

Caleb raised his gun and stepped around the front of the room. "Dr. Campbell?"

He stopped. It was Campbell in the chair, but his face was so bruised and swollen that he was almost unrecognizable.

He was dead.

Shit!

Caleb touched his neck to be sure. No pulse. He was still somewhat warm, meaning he'd probably been murdered in the past few hours.

A message from Bohdan.

A creak from the hallway. More than a message. A trap!

He raised his gun, but in the next instant a knife whistled across the room and buried itself in his shoulder. The force knocked him backward to the floor and his gun went flying.

A bearded man stepped into the room. Caleb recognized him from the international watch lists. Gabriel Dopple, international killer for hire. Just the type of high-priced thug Bohdan would employ. A heavyset man stepped in the room behind him. No one Caleb recognized, but he assumed it was just another murderous sleazebag. Both men were wearing black NEMESIS suits that hid them from thermal sensor scans.

Dopple turned toward his partner. "Take his gun, Vito."

Vito picked up the gun.

Caleb nodded toward the knife in his shoulder. "Don't you want your knife back?"

Dopple smiled. "I'll leave it for now. It looks good where it is."

Caleb glanced up at Campbell's corpse. "This man was no threat to you. You didn't have to kill him."

"Orders. You know something about that, don't you, Mr. Caleb? When you're paid to do a job, the whys cease to matter."

"Maybe to you, Dopple."

Dopple raised his eyebrows. "Ah, I'm famous. You flatter me."

Caleb pulled himself up to face Dopple. "We both know every criminal gets his picture up in the post office. It makes you common, not special. Nothing to be proud of, believe me."

Dopple's face flushed with anger. "You're alone. I was disappointed when I found that out. I'm sorry your friend Jane MacGuire didn't choose to accompany you."

"She wouldn't bother. She has nothing to do with this."

"My employer begs to differ."

Caleb said softly, "Leave her out of it."

"Not possible. We've been offered just as much to take care of her as you. An example must be made." Dopple smiled. "Now we know that she's with child, perhaps he'll give us a bonus."

Caleb bared his teeth. "Enough."

Dopple crouched beside him and turned the knife in his wound.

Caleb gritted his teeth but never broke eye contact with Dopple.

"I'll decide when it's enough," Dopple said. "You fucking son of a bitch. You're nothing. I've no idea why they warned me to be careful around you."

"No." Caleb's voice was almost indifferent. "You're finished. You shouldn't have gotten this close to me."

Dopple's eyes suddenly began to water, and a moment later the tears turned to blood. He stood and staggered backward. He wiped his eyes and looked in horror at the blood on his hands. "What the hell?"

"I believe you have something in your eye," Caleb said.

Blood from Dopple's eyes was now dripping down his cheeks. "I can't see. I can't see!"

Caleb smiled. "I know."

Vito recoiled in horror. "What's happening?"

Caleb turned to face him. "You tell me."

Blood suddenly spurted from Vito's nose and mouth. He dropped to his knees as he gagged.

Caleb stood up and pulled the knife from his shoulder. "Don't worry. You won't suffer for long."

Still blind from the blood in his eyes, Dopple fumbled for the gun in his shoulder holster. Caleb quickly took it from him. Blood began to gush from Dopple's left ear. He gasped, "You're a demon!"

"Hmm, I'll try not to take offense," Caleb said. "But I assure you it's about science, not superstition."

Dopple screamed in pain and held his head in his hands. He fell and began writhing on the floor.

Caleb watched the two screaming men for a moment longer. "Why were you warned to be careful around me, Dopple? Perhaps because it's been discovered that some animals secrete odors from their glands or emit vibrations that provoke all kinds of harmful physical reactions in their prey? There are also rare cases when that ability appears to occur in humans and can occasionally be inherited. And what may begin as an instinctive, involuntary ability sometimes can be controlled. As you gentlemen are finding out. I can't tell you how pleased and fascinated MI6 was when I demonstrated that skill to them."

Vito coughed up a mouthful of blood.

"Whatever pain you're now enduring, I'm sure it's no worse than what you two put this poor man through," Caleb said. "Perhaps you'll think about that in these last moments of yours."

An electronic chime sounded from Dopple's jacket pocket. Caleb bent down and pulled the phone from his pocket. A text message flashed on the screen: ONE MINUTE OUT. SUBJECT NEUTRALIZED? It was clear he'd signaled for Bohdan's soldiers to come out of hiding the instant Caleb had shown.

Caleb heard the sound of vehicles outside. He went to the window and saw half a dozen SUVs bearing down on the shack. "That's my cue. Goodbye, gentlemen." He turned back and saw that Vito was dead. Dopple, still choking and gagging on his own blood, wasn't far behind.

Caleb ran from the room and bolted down the stairs. He could hear Bohdan's men taking positions outside. The front and back doors were probably already covered, so he needed to find another way out before he was totally surrounded.

Caleb ran to the shack's far side, away from the road. His first instinct was to go for a window, but he needed a less conspicuous option.

He looked down at the creaky floor. Of course.

He stomped on the floorboards until they finally gave way. He dropped into the crawl space below and scrambled for the shack's edge.

He peered outside. From there, he had a straight shot to the forest, but he'd have to cover thirty unprotected yards first.

He heard more vehicles arriving at the front of the house.

Shit. The situation certainly wasn't going to get any better for him.

Caleb kicked out the crawl space panel and rolled outside. He jumped to his feet and ran for the forest.

So far, so good.

He'd almost made it to the trees when someone cried out behind him.

More shouts, then gunshots.

He sprinted into the forest. Great. Now he had fifteen or twenty armed killers on his tail. Just another day in the life.

He tried to find a path that would offer him the most cover, but he could already hear Bohdan's men fanning out behind him. And did he just hear a dog back there?

No, two dogs.

Awesome.

Time to signal for the escape hatch he'd told Palik to have ready.

He pressed the power button on his phone so that he could be tracked. Then he was running hard and fast through the forest. For the next ten minutes, Caleb bobbed and weaved through the brush, wondering where the next bullet would land or when the order would come to release the hounds. Either way, not a great position to be in.

Uh-oh.

Up ahead, he could see that the forest was ending. No more cover, no more protection from the trees. He appeared to be at the edge of a tall ridge.

He turned back. Bohdan's men were closer than ever.

His options were dwindling. It appeared his only choice might be to—

An engine roared in front of him. Ah, Palik to the rescue. *A Bell LongRanger helicopter rose over the ridge!*

But it wasn't Palik piloting. He'd tapped Henry Galdon, an expert pilot he used in touchy situations. This certainly qualified, Caleb thought grimly. Henry frantically motioned back toward the open side panel door.

Yes. Caleb leaped from the ridge and landed hard inside the copter.

"Hang on!" Henry shouted.

Caleb gripped a support bar with one hand as the helicopter banked hard right and roared over the valley.

Bohdan's men—and a pair of barking German shepherds—appeared from the clearing, then stood there stunned as they saw the helicopter. A few of the men fired at the copter, but most of them just stared openmouthed as it flew away.

CHAPTER

14

The helicopter was coming over the horizon.

Jane stiffened and then started down the courtyard steps as the blue-and-silver copter began its descent. MacDuff came to stand beside her as the whirring propellers created a tornado of wind. "What's the word?" MacDuff asked. "Rodland just came and told me that Palik had asked permission for a pilot to land here. Why?"

"I don't know. We just heard that a copter had left Kilgoray fifteen minutes ago. Rodland hasn't found out anything else since then. I'm hoping it's only because they got Caleb and Campbell safely out of Kilgoray." She swallowed hard. "But it may mean medical attention is needed, and they wanted to land somewhere they could give them fast emergency treatment."

"Don't borrow trouble," MacDuff frowned. "We'll know soon enough. Caleb could have told me what he had on his plate last night. Did you know then?"

She shook her head. "He didn't see fit to confide in me,

253

either. Rodland was the only one who knew." She was barely paying attention. Her eyes were straining to see into the cockpit, which was almost overhead now. The only figure she could make out was the pilot at the controls. It wasn't Caleb or Palik, and that frightened her. What had happened in Kilgoray?

But then the helicopter was on the ground, and she was running toward it.

"No." MacDuff was right behind her. "Wait until—" He was cursing as he saw her reach the passenger door. "The damn propellers. Stay out of the way..."

But the door was opening, and she saw Caleb getting out. She stopped short as the waves of relief and terror almost overcame her. Blood. His shirt was ripped, and blood was soaking the front of it. There was another bloody patch on his left shoulder. His face was sweat-stained and his eyes looked red and swollen. She took another step forward. "You're hurt. How bad? Let me help—" Then she was in his arms, but she was fighting to get him to release her. "No, don't do that. I have to look at that shoulder and your chest. That second wound looks worse than—"

"It's Bohdan's goons' blood," he said bitterly. "And the shoulder wound is nothing. I'm okay, Jane. Aren't I always okay?" He looked over her head at MacDuff. "Look, I'm a mess in a couple ways. I'm going to have to go take care of it. But she's going to need someone, so you'll have to do it. Where the hell is Rodland?"

"I sent him to alert my marine forces camped on the hill to be on guard when he told me that the helicopter was coming."

"Oh, damn, that's really great. Then over to you." He drew a deep breath as he turned back to Jane. "I'm sorry, I failed. I tried to save Campbell, but I couldn't do it." His hands gripped her shoulders. "It was a trap. He was dead before I even got near that shack."

"Dead," she repeated numbly. "I don't understand why they'd do that. He was bait. What would they get out of it?"

"Bohdan would know he was hurting you even if he didn't get his hands on me this time. He'd consider it a win."

"It can't be a win." She tried to make him understand. "He was such a good man. He helped so many people. I was going to see if I could stay near Kilgoray so that I could have him as my doctor."

"It won't be a win for Bohdan. We won't let it." He looked down into her eyes. "I know this won't help, but Bohdan didn't get everything he wanted. It could have been worse. He has a passion for exotic tortures, but he didn't have time with Campbell. He'd obviously been tortured, but not as Bohdan would have done it. No marks except for the bruises on his face."

"No, it doesn't help much," she said dully. "I need more. Bohdan has hurt so many people. And I almost lost you, didn't I? You look like you've gone through hell."

"I'll look better after I have a shower and get rid of this blood. I only wanted to get to you as quickly as possible. I knew what you were probably going through worrying about Campbell." He glanced at MacDuff. "I'm going to use that bedchamber you offered me last night to clean up and take a look at the shoulder wound. Get her a cup of tea and find Rodland and tell him to watch out for her until she can look at me without flinching."

"I'm not flinching," Jane said. "And you used Rodland once, don't do it again."

"I had to do what I could," he said wearily as he headed for the front door. "I'll see you later. I did everything I was able to do. If I could have saved Campbell, I would have."

"Do you think I don't realize that?" But she didn't believe he heard her. He was already climbing the steps. She turned to MacDuff. "You heard him, I've been thrown once more into your capable hands to shelter and cosset again. I promise it will only be for a little while. I have to go after him, I can't let him walk away hurt and bleeding."

"It sounds as if you're the last person he wants to have tending him at the moment. I'll send Fergus to check on him and report back to me."

He was probably right, she thought. After what Caleb had evidently been through, he didn't need her to be around him in this emotional state asking questions. "Then I'll take that cup of tea and you can get back to work."

He shook his head. "I don't think so. Caleb has already relegated me to second rank, and I resent it. He has an uncanny ability to show up as some kind of Marvel hero on occasion and I need to spend this time with you to erase it." He put his arm around her and led her toward the castle. "You're family and I have the right to give you comfort, as is my duty as head of our household." He smiled as he saw her open her lips. "No complaints, like it or not you know you've been heading in that direction. It's only a matter of time. Now, I want you to tell me everything about Campbell."

———————

3:40 P.M.

"I hear you made quite a splash when you arrived at the court-yard," Rodland said when Caleb answered his phone. "But you can hardly blame me for not hanging around waiting for your grand entrance. I had to do what MacDuff ordered since Palik wasn't exactly explicit about when you were going to arrive. I'd already had a rough time with Jane, and I didn't want any other problems."

"Problems?"

"You don't want to hear about it." He paused. "How are you? I hear you showed up covered in blood and scared Jane. Not good, Caleb."

"I hardly had a choice. I wanted to get back and tell Jane about Campbell myself before she heard it from some-one else."

"How did she take it?"

"The way you'd think she would. I've let her have it with both barrels during the last twenty-four hours. I *hated* it."

"Well, the last I heard MacDuff was being amazingly char-ismatic and kind to her. Just what you wanted. He hardly even let me talk to her."

"That could be bad or good."

"I agree. But I'm opting out of sessions like the one you put me through last night. It was too damn rough." He continued accusingly, "She threw up. And it was your fault."

"I don't doubt it." His hand clenched on the phone. "And I'm sure I'll hear from her later. Don't worry, I'll never make you go through that again. I just didn't want her to be alone." He added, "I've got to hang up. MacDuff sent one of his marines with EMT training to stitch up that knife wound in my shoulder. I'll talk to you when I get a plan together to go after Bohdan."

"Do that. It's only Jane I'd have trouble with. She was holding it together, but she was hurting. I can't take that." He added mockingly, "I'm glad you came out of Kilgoray without losing any vital organs. But then what's a knife wound to a guy like you?"

"Fairly painful. Good night, Rodland."

He cut the connection.

She was hurting. I can't take that.

Well, neither could Caleb. But he knew that he was going to have to very soon.

———

Four hours later Jane knocked on his door. When he opened it, she asked, "May I come in? I've ordered you dinner. They told me you haven't had anything to eat since that helicopter dropped you off."

"I've been busy." He stood aside to let her enter. "I had to talk to Palik several times. I assure you that I've not been wasting away."

"You look much better." She moistened her lips. "I'm glad, it frightened me. Though that EMT MacDuff sent to check you out told him the wound was minor." Her gaze went to his shoulder. "Minor doesn't necessarily mean pain-free. If you'd prefer not to talk to me until tomorrow that will be fine, but you did lose blood and you need to eat something."

"Jane." He smiled faintly as he shook his head. "I don't have to remind you that probably no one knows better than I do about how the blood flow through the body can affect the organs. Don't try to tutor me."

"Okay, I won't. I've had enough." She slammed the door behind her. "But knowledge doesn't mean that you won't be careless. You're not perfect, and you certainly haven't demonstrated lately that you take proper care of yourself."

Caleb gave a low whistle. "That's better. You were being so polite and concerned that I was afraid I was going to have to be worried about you."

"I'll watch it," she said curtly. "I've been a little upset lately. And I don't really care what you prefer. Since you're clearly in tolerable shape, we need to talk now. This can't go on. A good man was killed today. You could have died, too. Later, I fully intend to go into the way you treated me and didn't consult me. I even know why you did it. But it sucked. It *hurt*. What went before was beautiful and I'll treasure it. That's why I'm trying to ignore that you manipulated me and didn't give me a choice. That's why I have to give us a chance to go on to what's important."

"I tried to tell you," he said quietly. "I can't even promise it won't happen again. I have to keep both of you safe."

"We won't talk about it right now. I'm still raw." She needed to change the subject. She'd thought she was ready, but she was being bombarded by emotion. She quickly glanced around the huge bedroom. "MacDuff gave you one of the grand chambers. But I like my own room better."

"So do I." He smiled. "It's much better furnished and equipped."

"I hope Rodland thought it was comfortable," she said dryly. "Being there made him very uneasy. You owe him, Caleb."

"I think so, too." His smile faded. "But I couldn't stand the thought of you waking and believing I'd just left you alone. I knew you'd guess I'd gotten the call from Palik." There was a knock on the door. "Dinner? Did you order enough for two?"

She shook her head. "I wasn't hungry. MacDuff had them bring me sandwiches with tea. He was being very laird of the castle." While he answered the door she went over to the window and looked out at the sea. "Why did you talk to Palik so many times today?"

"I'd given him orders and I wanted to make sure if he'd been able to follow through with it." Then he was speaking to the housekeeper. "That will be fine, Mrs. Gordon. I'm sure it will be excellent as usual."

Jane turned to see him walk with the housekeeper to the door and give her that warm smile before he shut the door. "Nice woman." He turned back to Jane. "Salad and steak. And if you won't change your mind about dinner, she brought a thermos with enough tea to last us for a few hours while we talk about Palik's search for the perfect Judas."

She went still. "Judas?"

"Well, that sniper, Nojer, wasn't close enough to Bohdan to be useful to us. Bohdan evidently has a fondness for traps like the one he tried to set for me today. I can't tell you how pissed off I was when his men showed up after I found poor Campbell's body." His lips twisted. "So I thought we'd work out a trap of our own to turn the tables on him. I told Palik to find someone under Bohdan's command who might be close enough to manipulate him. And who would be smart and crooked enough to do it right."

She was fascinated. "How?"

"That's what we'll have to figure out. It will no doubt start with a con. From there the stakes are wide open."

"A con." She tilted her head. "That's not usually your thing, is it?"

"It depends. I've done a few with MI6. I have certain capabilities that make me believable."

She nodded ruefully. "I imagine you have. But will your Judas have them?"

"If we choose correctly. A dash of pure chicanery, a tempting story that will intrigue Bohdan, and a trap with very sharp teeth."

She was studying his expression. "It's not only the trap that has sharp teeth. You're very angry."

"You bet I am," he said softly. "I've debts to pay. MacDuff and his people. Those MI6 agents." His eyes were glittering in his taut face. "Your friend Felicity. Dr. Campbell." There was a touch of recklessness in his voice as he added, "And you. Maybe you most of all. Because it's all tied up with you and I couldn't seem to do anything about it. I might be to blame for some of it, but in the end I'll be glad to hang most of it on Bohdan and strangle him with it."

"Quite a list," she said grimly. "You're wrong, in the end all of it is Bohdan. That being true I think we should get to work on finding that Judas. How do we go about it?"

"It's in the works. Palik has been assessing Bohdan's men's military personnel records. He'll choose the ones he thinks we'll be interested in and text us the files to examine."

"When?"

He smiled. "Is tonight too soon?"

"No." She glanced at his shoulder. "Not for me. But maybe for you. I could go through them by myself."

He shook his head. "Debts to pay," he repeated.

"We'll talk about it." She went over to the desk where Mrs.

Gordon had set the tray. "Sit down and eat your dinner. I'll get a cup of tea and maybe give Palik a call."

"I'm sure he'll be delighted to hear from you. He's been concerned about you ever since he found out I was worried about Bohdan targeting you."

"He might not be all that delighted," Jane said. "I want results and I've been known to be persistent on occasion."

"What? You?" Caleb asked teasingly. "I would never have guessed." He sat down at the desk and picked up his napkin. "Palik won't be surprised. I've told him how you felt about Campbell. He knows what a good man he was."

"Yes, he was." She looked down into the depths of the amber tea in her cup. "I've got to call his wife and tell her how sorry I am that—" She drew a shaky breath. "No, not yet. She doesn't even know me. I have to be able to tell her that the man who did this won't be able to hurt anyone else ever again." She turned and sat down in the easy chair at the desk. "So that means it has to be soon." She took out her phone. "I won't be able to think of anything else until I get it done. Oh, yes, I'll be persistent. To everyone and in every way, to try to make it up to all those people on your list." She started to punch in Palik's number. "Because I have debts to pay, too."

"My list," Caleb said. "Not yours, Jane."

"Bullshit." She smiled recklessly. "Wrong answer. That's why you've been so blind about what we could be together. I have very specific requirements in that regard. Catch up or I might leave you behind, Caleb."

His lips tightened as he met her gaze. "Never."

"We'll see." Palik had answered and she spoke into the phone. "Palik, Jane." She was still holding Caleb's gaze as she continued, "Since Caleb seems to be under the weather, I thought that perhaps you and I should be talking about the Judas you're going to supply us..."

———◆———

COURTYARD
MACDUFF'S RUN
11:40 P.M.

"What are we doing out here?" Rodland asked Caleb as he strolled toward him from the direction of the burnt-out gate. "Jane's not going to like it. Aren't you supposed to be an invalid?"

"No, don't be ridiculous. I took a nap earlier in the evening. I'm okay." His lips curved sardonically. "And there's not much that Jane does like about me at the moment. She couldn't wait to leave my room after Palik texted her those military records we were waiting for earlier tonight. I hardly think she'd object if I took a midnight stroll around the property." He glanced up at the window on the second floor. "And her lights are still on. She's evidently very busy."

"My question is why aren't you busy?" Rodland asked. "And why did you let her walk out on you?"

"I'm trying to give her space," Caleb said. "She's the one who needs healing time. The one way I'd be sure to make her leave is if I insisted on her staying with me." He added, "You should have learned that since you've spent so much time with her."

"You hurt her," Rodland said. "But that doesn't mean she'd leave you."

"It doesn't mean she wouldn't. Talk to MacDuff. He's been

trying to persuade her that she could do much better." He smiled bitterly. "And he's right. But if I do lose her, it won't be because he manages to convince her. It will be because she makes the choice. That gives me an edge. I'll keep coming back and changing and adjusting until I find a way to keep her."

"MacDuff can be a difficult bastard, but I still think he likes you."

"We appreciate each other, but he's never given up the idea that Jane could be family. That puts me squarely behind the eight ball. He has the idea he has a duty to vet any and all possible suitors who might be bad for her." He made an impatient gesture. "But I didn't ask you to come down here to meet me because I wanted to discuss Jane or MacDuff. I might have an assignment for you, but I didn't want to go through Palik to ask you to do it. This is between you and me, and you should feel free to tell me to go to hell."

"Then it definitely doesn't have anything to do with acting as bodyguard for Jane any longer," Rodland said wryly. "That will be a relief. Jane wasn't pleased with me, and she wasn't shy about telling me."

Caleb shook his head. "Nor me. But as I told you on the phone, we're going to hit Bohdan with everything we have. We're going to need a contact to handle the snitch that we bribe to lure Bohdan. Palik will do the initial bargaining, but after that he'll be too busy to keep tabs on him. There will have to be someone else to make certain he doesn't turn double agent and get us killed."

"And I'm to do that?"

"If you choose. I trust you. But you'll have to decide for yourself. It will be dangerous as hell. We'll try to select someone who won't be able to sell you down the river to Bohdan. But we're dealing with weasels and backstabbers. It's bound to be a crapshoot. You might have to give us a warning and then get out fast. Either way you'll get the same fee we give to the Judas."

"And then be tarred by the same brush?" Rodland grinned. "I'd prefer to have you eternally grateful to me. Which I'm sure would annoy the hell out of you. I'll magnanimously take just the fee Palik would pay me and perform with my usual brilliance. Suck it up, Caleb."

"I may change my mind," Caleb said.

"Too late. You said I could choose. Now you're stuck. Serves you right for making me watch Jane go through all those hellish hours." He turned and walked back toward the gate. "But at least you're giving me something interesting to do. Keeping a Judas tricked and lassoed could be a challenge. I thought I was going to have to go back to digging into Fiona and MacClaren history for Jane. There was only so much more I could find out about them..."

Caleb shook his head as he watched him walk away. Though he was sure Rodland was the best man for the job, he wasn't sure that he wanted him to do it. That's what was wrong about forming an attachment to a person. There were always second thoughts and sometimes regrets. Jane accepted the concept without thinking because people were so important to her and therefore worth the risk. But he hadn't learned to do that yet. She'd even become involved with the story of Fiona and was still searching for the truth that—

He stiffened and gave a low whistle. "Fiona." He was suddenly once more gazing up at the lights in Jane's room. Then he reached for his phone and dialed her. Her voice was tentative when she answered. "Caleb? Are you all right? Did that wound—"

"I'm fine. I realize you're not in the mood to talk to me right now. You've been closing me out because that's what I did to you. But I was sitting down here by the fountain, and I had a thought. I'm going to hang up, but after I do, I want you to think about Fiona."

"Fiona? Why?"

"Just think about her. This has always been her story. If you decide you want to talk about her, call me back."

He cut the connection.

He waited.

She called him back in seven minutes. "What are you doing sitting down there on that damn fountain? Get up here."

"You're sure?"

"I wouldn't have called you back if I wasn't sure." Her voice was crackling with energy. "Get up here. We've got work to do!"

Caleb was grinning when she opened the door. "What work?"

"You know what work." She turned and went back into the bedroom. "You spelled it out to me. Judas to furnish the chicanery, an intriguing story to lure Bohdan." She glanced at him over her shoulder. "And very sharp teeth." She gestured to the files scattered on her bed. "I've been working all evening on finding a Judas. I've narrowed it down to two, though I have a preference. But I haven't thought about the intriguing lure for Bohdan yet."

"Neither did I, until Rodland mentioned he might have to go back to digging for more Fiona stories to entertain you. It reminded me of the Cira treasure that MacDuff discovered all those years ago." He added softly, "And what is more alluring than an ancient treasure? Particularly to a crook who thinks he deserves to get something for nothing. A portion of which has already made MacDuff an incredibly rich man? All we'd have to do is build the story and set it up."

Jane nodded. "And we already have the letter that MacClaren wrote Fiona about a second Cira treasure that had been hidden in the Highlands and was supposedly stolen by Fiona's fiancé, Graeme."

"It didn't sound as if there was any 'supposed' about it," Caleb said. "I don't believe MacClaren would have lied to Fiona even if he might have been less than honest on occasion with someone else. She was his guiding star."

She frowned, puzzled. "How do you know?"

"Oh, I'm very familiar with guiding stars. I can recognize the signs. Though I'll have to have you and Rodland go over their in-depth history with me so that I can get with the general program. But you also have to consider that she looked like you and he was an artist. He would have known he could trust her. And by that time, they'd spent months together and become lovers." He added thoughtfully, "He was telling her the truth as he knew it. Since he was supposed to steal the treasure from Graeme as payment to that rail baron, it could have been the truth. It wouldn't make sense that Saldaron would lie to MacClaren."

She tilted her head. "You're talking as if you believe there *was* a second treasure."

He shrugged. "There might have been. There might not have been. It might still be out there. It might have disappeared into some fat cat's bank account over two hundred years ago. It shouldn't matter to us. The only thing that should matter is that we're convincing enough to make Bohdan believe it's still out there and he can get his hands on it."

"Or that the Judas is convincing enough."

He nodded. "He's the important one. You're right, our job is to distract and keep Bohdan off guard until we can close the trap."

"And plan how we can do that," Jane said. "It won't be easy." She suddenly stiffened. "Though it may not be that hard." Her eyes were suddenly glittering with excitement. "Not if we continue what we've started and follow what we've been doing with Fiona and MacClaren. You were right when you told me it was Fiona's story, Caleb. But it was also MacClaren's and maybe we haven't paid as much attention as we should have to his parts of it." She was reaching for her phone. "But that can be remedied." She punched in Rodland's number and hit SPEAKER. "The Judas might even be able to use it when he's trying to con Bohdan." Rodland answered and she said, "I need to know more about MacClaren, Rodland. And I have to know both facts and hearsay as soon as possible."

"You might not have heard, but Caleb has given me a new assignment," he said caustically. "Talk to him."

"I will. He's here now. But he agrees with me that you should split up your duties." She added, "And this might be even more important. When you were doing the research on MacClaren, you were doing it from Fiona's point of view up to the very end when she received the letter. But we need to know everything that he was doing from the moment he came back into Fiona's life after she told him she was being forced into that marriage with Alastair Graeme. Particularly his relationship with that railroad magnate who hired him to do the mural."

"From his point of view? You don't want much, Jane."

"I want *everything*. And I know you can give it to me."

"After a couple hundred years? Why not?" He paused. "Caleb's there with you?"

"Do you want to talk to him?"

"No, he'd enjoy it too much." He sighed. "I'll get on it right away. Is there anything else?"

"Actually, yes. We were discussing lures to attract Bohdan, and the Cira treasures came up. Do you remember that chapter in the MacDuff historical record that featured those bizarre stories about all the myths and scams concerning the Cira treasure hunts? You laughed about some of them."

"How could I help it? Talk about cons."

"But it might be something to build on. Which one did you think had the most substance?"

He thought about it. "The Johnston Drakeman scam had the most research behind it. Some of the details were amazing."

"That's what I thought, too."

"Cira?" Caleb asked. "Am I missing something?"

"Not really." She reached over on the bed, picked up her tablet computer, and typed in a keyword. "Or maybe you are. When we were looking through the history books from Mac-Duff's library, we found a story in which this Drakeman swore that a part of Cira's treasure was hidden in the area. There was even a map with instructions. It included landmarks. A waterfall, limestone cliffs, an ancient cemetery. Several others I can't remember." Jane swiped her screen until she pulled up a hand-drawn image. "Here. The instructions are very detailed, with the starting point at the end of the railroad branch line."

Caleb looked at the drawing. "Interesting."

"But that's all it is. The archivist checked it out, and none

269

of the landmarks on the map match up with what's actually in the area. It's a total fabrication. He did some further research and found that this map was offered up by a local laborer to his landlord as payment for his back rent. He was probably buying time so that he wouldn't get evicted." She looked speculatively at Caleb. "But what if Bohdan believed we were on the verge of finding this?"

Caleb nodded. "If we could make him believe it, it would definitely be a good lure."

"Back off," Rodland said flatly. "Let me do more research and see if I can find someone who would be a better fit for our purpose. And it's going to depend on who you choose as Judas whether he can sell a specific story."

"Sorry, Rodland," Jane said. "By all means, research."

"Thank you. May I go back to sleep now?"

"If you insist."

"I insist. Good night, Jane."

"Good night, Rodland." After she pressed DISCONNECT, she turned to Caleb. "He's really amazing with computers and research. I've never seen anyone who could do as well, even among some of the heads of tech companies I've worked with. He may get us answers."

"He learned from Palik." He was staring thoughtfully at her. "But you gave him something to work with." He grinned. "Along with a little sting of the whip to goad him along."

"I wasn't doing that, I was just being persistent. He understands that." She gestured at the files scattered on the bed. "Do you want to read those two files that I chose? We should really make a selection right away so that Palik can get to work on bringing them over to the dark side."

"Only it's just the opposite." He smiled. "He's on the dark side now and we're trying to save his soul."

"Whatever. Do you want to read them?"

"I'm interested in your choices." He leaned back in his chair. "But it's been a tiring day. I'd prefer that you read both of them to me, if you don't mind. Then we can discuss why you're set on one above the other."

"Are you putting me on the spot?"

"Perish the thought. As I said, it's not been a good day. I wanted to bring Campbell back to you. I like the sound of your voice and it would be good to hear it for a little while longer until you kick me out."

And he'd been wounded, and he could be feeling it more than he'd allowed her to see. "Have it your way." She pulled the first text in front of her. "But it's pretty boring details. This guy is the one I think might be best. Burton Adams. Born in London but he's a world traveler, he's been involved in some very shady deals involving banks and mortgage companies with Bohdan. Most of them took place in Africa and Greece and seem to entail the use of the almighty con. He must be smart because Bohdan requests him for quite a few jobs. He doesn't have anything to do with any other of his dirty military slaughters. He's slick and crooked but he seems to stay away from that kind of wholesale nastiness." She tapped another file. "I can't say the same for William Hanks. Bohdan uses him to do white-collar thievery, too. But he also gives him occasional jobs with his armies that are beyond the pale."

"Faint praise," Caleb said. "It seems you're going to hire Mr. Adams?"

"I am? You're leaving it up to me?"

"Why not? I've always trusted your judgment. I'll get on

it right away. I've already told Palik that he'll hear from us tonight. I'll give him a call after I leave here. The only caveat would depend on whether Palik discovers anything that would cause us to doubt his con abilities when dealing with Bohdan. Agreed?"

She nodded slowly. "Agreed." Her brow arched. "Giving me this responsibility wouldn't be a ploy to keep me from what you might deem interference? It won't work."

"I'm not naive enough to believe it would," he said quietly. "You know me well enough to realize I'd never have gone to Kilgoray if I'd seen any other way out. I'm trying to find a path to get us through this, Jane."

He was telling her the truth. He was always so strong and contained. Yet he was sitting there in that chair across the room, and she was suddenly aware of a weariness, perhaps even discouragement, that he rarely let her see. She couldn't *stand* it. "Then stop working so hard at it," she said jerkily. "Do you think I'm blaming you because Campbell died? I know that you did everything you could to save him. What happened wasn't even your fault. Bohdan is a monster." The words were spilling out. "But as usual, you think that you should have been able to perform some kind of magic and everything would have been fine. Well, it didn't happen, and the reason I'm so upset is that you didn't give me the opportunity to be there to help. How many times do I have to tell you that?"

"Evidently too many to count."

"Then don't do it again. We're a family now. I won't have either you or my child dying. Figure out a way that we can work safely together. I don't care if you don't like it or that it damages the ego of the Hunter."

"It appears you're already on your way to taking care of that for me." He was smiling faintly. "But maybe if I study your technique, I'll be able to follow in your footsteps."

"It's possible." She drew a deep breath. "But not if you pull anything like this again." She tried to joke. "I'm not about to let you go after I've taken so much time training you, but you'd definitely have to return to square one."

"Heaven forbid." He got to his feet and moved across the room toward her. He saw her slight withdrawal and shook his head. "I'm not in a hurry. I just wanted to make sure that the square-one rule wasn't in force yet." His finger pressing her cheek should have been rough and callused but the touch itself was gossamer soft. "What are you going to do tomorrow?"

"Research. I set Rodland to doing it, and it doesn't seem fair if I don't pitch in. There are probably some things I can do that he wouldn't be able to."

"I don't doubt it." He leaned forward and gently kissed her. "You're the one who performs the magic. I'll see you tomorrow, Jane."

Then he was gone.

MACDUFF'S RUN
NEXT DAY

"I don't have time to talk to you, Caleb." MacDuff looked impatiently over his shoulder as Caleb strolled into his office. "I have to approve the architect's plans for the replacement houses for my staff that were destroyed. They're having to live in the village right now."

"I can wait." Caleb sat down. "I wouldn't think of

inconveniencing you. Particularly since I'm going to have to beg you to lend me an exorbitant amount of cash when you get around to paying attention to me."

"Beg?" He smiled. "I like the sound of that."

"You always do. That's why I thought I'd drop in and make your day."

"You have your own money. Why are you trying to borrow from me?" His smile had a catlike malice. "Or have you been foolish and blown all that inheritance? I'd have to disapprove, I'm afraid. Perhaps I should have a talk with Jane since I wouldn't want her to become a virtual pauper. After all, I'm head of the family."

"Debatable. And Jane wouldn't give a damn, as you know."

"I'm afraid you're right. But I can always hope. Proceed with your begging."

"You're sure you have time for it?"

"I'm curious."

"I still have plenty of cash, but the problem is with quality, not quantity," Caleb said. "I need you to pay a visit to the bank where you deposited your treasure and take out enough of it so that it would not only look substantial but be able to convince anyone that it was actually part of *another* Cira treasure."

MacDuff gave a low whistle and then started to laugh. "What are you up to? Of course, I've heard the stories that there might be another Cira chest hidden somewhere in the hills. I even searched for it at one time. But I didn't find it, and I decided that Cira had given me enough and I shouldn't be greedy. Have you heard something?"

"No, just rumors. But Jane and I thought perhaps Cira might want to have any treasure she still has out there to be used to punish the people who had caused her family to suffer. What do you think?"

"Bohdan," he murmured. "You're going after the son of a bitch. You have a plan? You should really leave it in my hands. I'm much better able to handle it."

"I don't believe you can. You're being greedy again."

"You're the one who is begging me. Do you realize what a risk I'd be taking? Just the insurance alone is going to cost me a fortune."

"Now, I do believe you can handle that better than I can. Look, the treasure might not be used at all. Its prime value will be as a lure. We'll take photos of it, and a few incriminating ones of me in the same photos with the treasure. Most of the time it will be in a safe in a railway car." He paused. "Though I admit that it's possible we'll have to use it for other purposes if everything goes to hell." Caleb got to his feet. "I'll need the treasure no later than the day after tomorrow."

"I didn't say you'd get it."

"You didn't say I wouldn't."

MacDuff was swearing below his breath. "You'd better not leave me out of this. You saw what they did to the Run."

"I saw it." Caleb was heading for the door. "Look, MI6 doesn't work well with others, and you have enough to do with protecting and keeping the repair work going on MacDuff's Run. That doesn't mean I won't keep you in mind if I can find a way to do it." He gave him a glance over his shoulder. "It wouldn't be a bad idea to keep your marines handy in case you need them..."

CHAPTER

15

STABLE STORAGE ROOM
MACDUFF'S RUN
TWO DAYS LATER

I'd forgotten how dusty these rooms are," Rodland said as he came down the curving staircase. "You don't know how lucky you were that I put up with them. It was a great sacrifice."

"Well, you haven't had to put up with them for the last couple of days," Jane said dryly. "I haven't seen anything of you since I called. You didn't even phone me."

"I was busy. You couldn't expect me to be at your beck and call. Caleb got to me first, so I had other fish to fry." He squatted down on the step beside her, his gaze narrowed on her face. "You're looking good...glowing. I always thought that was bullshit about pregnant women." He frowned. "But should you be down here? Is the dust bad for you?"

"No, I take breaks down on the boat dock. But it is bad for me to not know what the hell is going on with you. I gave you an assignment."

"I had to strike a balance." He took out his phone and dialed photos. "Want to see your competition? This is Burton Adams.

But so far, I've only been meeting him at the dark of night outside his apartment or in the men's rooms of restaurants." He showed her the photo of a slim, thirtyish man with a receding hairline. He was wearing an elegant white jacket over a navy silk shirt. "Bohdan and Chiswick are stashed in safe houses in a small town in Wales and they move almost every day. Adams has his own apartment nearby, but he doesn't hang out with them." He shrugged. "He's a bit on the nervous side, but he took Palik's money, and I don't think he likes Bohdan or Chiswick. We'll have to see if it works out for us. He's very slick, but he can sometimes come off as sincere and enthusiastic. He's got a meeting with Bohdan tomorrow and we've got to hope he can convince him. I'm going to make him wear a wire so that I can hear if he's going to be okay. I had him spin his story for me once before and he was very believable."

"If he's not, he may end up dead." She shivered. "And I chose him." She gave Rodland back the phone. "And what story did you give Adams to spin for Bohdan? Did you get any hints from tracing MacClaren?"

"Actually, I did. MacClaren had a life completely different from the one he lived when he was with Fiona. He rented a two-room shack near the main railway station at the border. He got to know all the engineers and people who ran the trains. He spent most of the evenings he wasn't with Fiona in a bar sketching them. He loved the life. He liked the people. That's where he got to know Kevin Saldaron.

"And that's where Saldaron hired him to paint his murals for the train car. MacClaren thought he was going to be working up in the foothills, but Saldaron sent him up to a branch of the main line located in the Highlands. It had been paid for by a rich stockholder in the company, a procedure that wasn't

CAPTIVE

that unusual. Money was everything in getting a new railway started. Saldaron transferred the railcar up to the Highland rail yard so the measurements would be correct. He said it was quiet up there and MacClaren would be able to concentrate. That was fine with MacClaren. All he knew was that he'd be close to Fiona and be able to work. Life was good."

"But the branch was bought and paid for by Graeme," Jane guessed. "And he had a reason that he wanted that diversion off the main track."

"If he knew the treasure was hidden somewhere in that general direction, it would be very convenient," Rodland said. "He would have time and leisure to grab this particular Cira treasure and not have to share it with Colin, the current laird of the Run. And he'd made arrangements to marry Fiona, one of the MacDuff women, and no one would question if he suddenly got an additional influx of cash."

"Only his plans fell apart?" Jane was taking it step by step. "Fiona disappeared and at first he wouldn't have suspected she had anything to do with stealing his treasure because MacClaren had left for America months before." She added, "And Fiona had made certain Graeme believed she was reconciled to the marriage."

"Then who was the culprit?" Rodland asked in a mock-hushed voice.

"Saldaron. He would have been on the suspect list, because he agreed to the spur arrangement and Graeme wouldn't trust him not to have snooped." She tilted her head. "Right?"

Rodland nodded. "That would be reasonable. Particularly since Saldaron's home was ransacked two weeks later. The police found a few pieces of clothing belonging to Fiona when they searched the house. Saldaron knew better than to try to vindicate himself when it came to the laird's niece. He packed up and left the next day." He met Jane's gaze. "Was it just in time to avoid getting killed by Graeme who thought he'd stolen his treasure? Or was he framed by MacClaren to draw the heat away from Fiona? It could have gone either way."

"You mean you didn't find out?"

"I only had a few days," he protested. "But I'd bet the treasure was stolen from Graeme or he wouldn't have shown up later in America looking for MacClaren and Fiona. MacClaren could have stolen the treasure himself to have a nest egg for his Fiona."

"Or not."

"Or not," he agreed. "I know you prefer to believe in love's young dream. But at any rate, I'm sure that Adams will embroider the story to suit himself and his audience. I guarantee that Bohdan doesn't give a damn for love's young dream. Adams will go for capturing you and Caleb and forcing you to tell him with whom or where that treasure can be found in the most painful way possible."

"You always know how to cheer me up."

"You don't need anyone to do that. You'll be floating on air if you and Caleb can bring Bohdan down." He grinned. "And at least Adams can use that rail yard in the Highlands to make his story more authentic." He winked at her. "And if you're extremely lucky, I might free myself to help you a bit. I've been feeling quite like a second father lately toward that child you're going to produce."

"I'm touched. But it might be better if you just work at keeping Adams alive and let me take care of her."

"Whatever you say." He got to his feet. "It's a girl?"

"I have no idea. Caleb appears to think so. It's easier not to argue."

"I've found that to be true." He added, "But I'm glad that you don't seem to be angry with him any longer." He gazed at her curiously. "Or are you?"

"I might be. I haven't had a chance to test the waters lately. We've both been busy for the past couple of days." She was no longer smiling. "Be careful. I'm grateful that you're doing this for us. But I don't want it blowing up in your face. I'd much rather you come back and help me find a happy ending to Fiona's story."

"I've already given you that."

"No, you haven't. Not yet. You gave me too many question marks."

"Then I'll have to work on answering them." He was grinning. "Did I tell you that I stopped in at the stable to say hello to Maisie?"

"No. That's a surprise. I thought you were too busy to waste your time."

"That wasn't a waste. It was an investment. I can't let her forget me. Face it, that horse and I have a history together. When all this is over, we have to come to terms with each other."

"I can't wait."

"I can." He laughed as he started back up the steps. "But not too long. I'll call you after Adams has his meeting tomorrow. Don't worry. It will be fine."

Then he was gone. But she heard him talking to someone as he reached the stable level.

Caleb.

She tensed and then forced herself to relax. It wasn't as if she was nervous about seeing him again. But she'd expected that he'd contact her sooner. No, admit it, she'd wanted to see him. It hurt her when things weren't right with them. Even if she'd been the one who had taken the step back.

"Find anything interesting?" Caleb was coming down the steps toward her. "I ran into Rodland on the way down and he seems to have accomplished what you wanted."

She nodded. "If that meeting tomorrow works out." She looked down at the book in her hands. "Not exactly interesting. I've gone through most of these books several times and there's nothing new for me. I'm just verifying everything in case I've missed something."

"That's valuable, too." He paused. "I just came down to tell you that MacDuff has temporarily turned over a fairly impressive coffer of the Cira treasure to me. I'm taking a photo of some of the gems and having Rodland turn it over to Adams to impress Bohdan at his meeting."

"The lure..." Jane murmured.

He nodded. "We're on our way. After that meeting, we'll have an idea about Bohdan's numbers and personnel. But I think we should check out locations so there won't be any surprises."

"Locations?"

"Rodland didn't mention that the branch in the Highlands still exists? I think the rail yard does, too. If Bohdan goes for the story, then he'll be heading up there."

"And expecting us to be there, too." She grinned. "Counting our ill-gotten loot?"

"Presumably. We'll probably still be safe in that area tomorrow. But once Bohdan makes a decision then he'll be pouring men and weapons into the Highlands."

"Then we'd better go tomorrow." She closed the book and put it back on the shelf. "What time, Caleb?"

"Seven? I've got to talk to MI6 about a few emergency plans." He held up his hand as he saw her frown. "Of which I'll inform you when they come to fruition. Fair?"

"Fair." She was beginning to get excited. "It's coming together, isn't it? And I'm eager to actually see the branch and see where it goes. Do you think that MacClaren's mural train car will be there, too? That clerk said it was somewhere in the Highlands."

"I wouldn't be surprised. But this isn't actually the Highland yard, only a branch." He was smiling. "But we can go hunting. I've been told I'm good at that."

"I've heard rumors." She took his hand as he helped her to her feet. "But be prepared, I might be the expert. I've got most of these Fiona facts memorized."

"I'll be prepared." His hand tightened on hers. "Want to go and look at Cira's treasures? Everything connected to Cira has always been special to you. Those jewels have been stuffed in that bank almost since the day MacDuff discovered where they were hidden. It must have been a long time since you've seen them."

"Yes, it has. I remember how thrilled I was at the time." The memories were flooding back to her. "It felt as if Cira was actually with us that day." She suddenly turned and brushed a kiss on his cheek. "But we've seen so many things together, and most of them have been wonderful. And we have a chance to have a life that keeps on being just as wonderful." She had turned and was running up the stairs. "I *want* that life, Caleb!"

The wire was in place.

Rodland carefully rechecked it. So far, so good. Then he leaned back in his chair and tried to listen critically. He was in the apartment across the street from the restaurant where the meeting was taking place. Adams had gone over the treasure story, shown Bohdan and Chiswick the photo of the jewels in the coffer, told them how he'd actually seen the safe in the train car where Caleb and Jane had placed it. He'd been amazingly persuasive for the last twenty minutes. But now he was going for the big guns. His voice was eager as he went in for the kill. "Why did I do it?" He repeated Bohdan's question. "You've put a bounty on Caleb. I'm tired of everyone getting fat bonuses all around me. I want my share."

"You haven't complained before," Bohdan said. "And this time you came to me. I find that...odd."

"We've worked together in the past," Adams said. "You've been pleased with the money I've poured into your pockets. I just got fed up with watching those stupid thugs you keep on call get all that cash when I knew that I deserved it more. So I set about figuring out how I could get you what you wanted." He added silkily, "So you could pay me what I wanted."

"And what did you decide to do?" Chiswick asked. "Don't waste our time, Adams."

"I used my brains instead of my muscles." Adams's voice was suddenly eager. "I asked myself why Caleb had stashed his woman at MacDuff's castle, so I researched MacDuff and the fact that Caleb and the woman were frequent guests there. And then I found out about the treasure MacDuff had discovered several years ago and the fact that there were rumors of another treasure that was still out there in the hills just waiting to be found."

"Go on."

"You saw that photo of the treasure. The woman must have found it and was waiting for Caleb to come back to her. Then after you attacked the castle, he joined her at a deserted train station up in the hills. I followed them and located a train in the yard. I took the photo of the treasure. Yesterday I even had it verified by the same professor who examined the original treasure MacDuff found." His voice became tense. "Don't you understand? We can have it all. Caleb's not going to leave that treasure. He's going to stay there in that train yard until he can arrange to move it away from the castle. But you can come into those hills from the lakes to the north. Bring your men and go after what you want. Take the treasure and then do what you want with Caleb and the woman. All I want is the bonus you offered for catching Caleb, and a small portion of the treasure. That's not too much to ask."

"It sounds like a lot to me," Bohdan said sarcastically. "You arrogant asshole." He was silent. "But I might be persuaded to give you the bonus. Forget the percentage of the treasure. If I decide to take a chance that you're not the stupid nerd I always thought you."

"You'll take the chance," Adams said. "I can see how hungry you are. I'm hungry, too. Let me give you what we both need."

Another silence. "He's right, we could go to the Highlands by the northern route," Chiswick finally said. "It would be fairly safe."

Bohdan was cursing. "Send a man up to the Highlands and

see if there's any sign of Caleb. If he's there, we'll go after the treasure, too." His voice was harsh. "We'll head for the north tonight. It will probably take us all day to make our way down to MacDuff's land from the lake country. And you'd better be right, Adams. Or you won't live another day once we reach there."

"I'm right." Adams's voice was a little high-pitched. "Do you think I'd take a chance if I wasn't sure? You can trust me, Bohdan."

"Yes, I can." Bohdan's tone was malicious. "Because you're going with us."

"I don't do well on the trail. I thought I'd meet you when you reached——"

"Shut up. I'm tired of hearing your voice, Adams. Now get out of here."

Rodland heard Adams's breathing come sharp and shallow as he ran out of the office.

Rodland was already out of the apartment and in the car by the time Adams made it out of the restaurant and was running down the alley.

Adams jumped into the passenger seat. "Let's get out of here. Did you hear him?" His voice was shaking. "This was a mistake. He's going to kill me."

"Not if you handle it right. You did a good job in there." He was driving out of the alley and down a side street. "You'll get the rest of your money, and you'll never have to deal with Bohdan again."

"He wants me to go with him and those butchers. I've seen what he lets them do to anyone he gets angry with. Sometimes I get nervous." He moistened his lips. "He'd know if I was lying."

"Just stay away from everyone when you're on the road." He was shaking his head vehemently and Rodland could see where this was going. "Take a chance. The cash is worth it."

"I won't do it," Adams said. "Unless you're able to find a way to go with me. You've said that you've done a lot of tracking. I want you nearby if I need you."

And hold the son of a bitch's hand all the way to the Highlands? Rodland thought in frustration.

"Do you hear me? I'm not going to risk my life. You have to do what I want."

"I don't have to do anything," Rodland said through set teeth. "I just have to step aside and let Bohdan find out you might have betrayed him."

"You wouldn't do that." Adams's voice was panicky. "We have a deal."

Yes, he did, but the deal was with Caleb. Yet he couldn't let that deal go down the drain. Too much depended on taking Bohdan down. "I'll think about it," he said sourly. "Just keep your damn mouth shut."

———◆———

HIGHLANDS
NEXT DAY
12:15 P.M.

"You've been very quiet," Jane said as Caleb made the turn that led to the upper Highlands. "Correction. Quiet toward me." She glanced at him speculatively. "You've been talking to MI6 and Rodland almost nonstop. Do we have a problem?"

"Maybe. But it's more Rodland's problem than ours. I've

just been trying to ease his way in case it develops into a gigantic mess."

"But he called and told me that Adams had convinced Bohdan." She frowned. "A half-truth?"

"Total truth, he just didn't mention that he was going to be chaperoning Adams on the trail to keep Bohdan from massa-cring him en route to the trap." He shrugged as he glanced at her. "What can I say? I'm not the only one who didn't want to disturb you in your delicate condition."

"Delicate? That's bullshit. What's he going to do?"

"He'll just be on watch and take care if Adams causes an upset." He smiled. "And you don't have to go to his rescue because it's already been set up."

"MI6?"

"Only if needed." He saw the way she was looking at him and said, "You want to know the complete plan? Okay, no problem. I told you that Bohdan and his forces were coming in from the lake country to the north. He's going to bring a substantial force with him, but I've arranged for MI6 to be camped out along the route with enough agents to counter it. Bohdan is expected to attack the railway yard because they'll know we're there and Bohdan wants us very badly. We're the bait that's drawing him into the trap. Unless I can talk you out of it?" She shook her head and he continued. "Plus the fact that he thinks we've found the treasure that Adams used as a lure to get him here and are keeping it in a safe in one of the railway cars." He added grimly, "But I've told the MI6 chief that they've *got* to wipe Bohdan out before he tries to launch an attack on the rail yard. They've said there shouldn't be a problem since Bohdan's reported numbers are seventy percent less than what MI6 has brought in. They'll stage the attack about three miles from the gates of the rail yard."

"But what about Rodland?"

"Rodland will be with MI6 for the entire trip unless Adams sends a message that he needs him. Then he'll find a way to go after him." He paused. "Rodland can handle almost anything on his own. He's very innovative. And he'll call if he wants me to make any special arrangements. Nothing is going to happen to him, Jane. Trust me."

She nodded slowly. "But what he's doing is something we didn't expect, and it's not only the surprise that's making me uneasy. I think it's a sign that we'd better check this place out thoroughly in case we need to be innovative, too." They had turned a bend in the hill and Jane suddenly saw what lay below them. "And right now, I'm going to forget everything but doing that. Do you see that railroad yard? There must be eight or ten cars down there. I didn't expect it to be that big. I love it! How old do you think those cars are? I can imagine Fiona putting on those boy's clothes MacClaren sent her and running down to board her train to go to meet her lover."

"You *are* getting excited." Caleb was amused. "But we're not sure that the mural train is one of those cars. You told me that it wasn't discarded but kept renovated because it was considered an antique. This is obviously a supplemental yard used for storage. I see a couple of engines and three fairly modern-looking cars. One of them even appears to be a refrigeration car. No antiques."

"It wouldn't necessarily look like an antique if it was well maintained. Stop raining on my parade."

"I wouldn't think of it. If it's not down there, I promise

I'll search every rail yard in the United Kingdom and find it for you."

"You think I'm being foolish." She made a face. "You're probably right. But lately I've been feeling very close to Fiona. I want to share what she must have felt like on that day when she was rolling the dice and giving up everything she knew to go away with her Farrell MacClaren. It's strange, when I've been fighting all these years to keep her at a distance. Now I feel like I need to protect her."

"Not so strange," he said gently. "You've been protecting friends, family, everyone in your circle ever since I've known you. And through the years you've been drawn to Cira, the founder of the MacDuff family, in the same way. Maybe it's time to admit that you're seeing a connection between Fiona and Cira and instinctively protecting family."

"And you say that's not strange?"

"No." He took her hand and brought it to his lips. "That's Jane."

She was incredibly touched. "Then it's good that you manage to put up with me. Eve would approve."

"It's my pleasure. I look forward to doing it for the rest of my days." He released her hand. "Not the right time. We'll go into this later." He parked the car outside the wire gate. "Let's go see if there's anyone minding the store or if we have to break into this place."

It took them thirty minutes to locate a weathered, gray-haired man who was eating his lunch under an oak tree a short distance from the gate. He identified himself as Tim Fraser, the caretaker of the property, and seemed friendly enough. When they told him they were tourists who had seen the rail yard and wondered if they could get a tour, he was almost enthusiastic. After checking their IDs, he invited them to come inside the gates for tea and scones. "I'm glad to see you. There's not much to see here, but I'll be happy to show you around."

"Are you alone here?" Caleb asked. "Aren't you bored?"

"Sometimes." Fraser shrugged. "But it's an easy job and they send me help when they want me to transfer any of the equipment back to the main border station."

"Do you have an index of the cars and equipment on hand?"

"Sure." Fraser pointed to the outer wall of the office building at the center of the complex. "I have to change it all the time when they send me new cars and equipment to repair or exchange. What do you want to see first?"

Jane was striding toward the wall. "There might be one that I've heard about..." She ran her gaze down the lists. Then she saw it! "*Yes.*" She whirled on Caleb. "The Reiver." She turned back to Fraser. "I've heard about an antique railcar with fancy murals. Could I see that one? I was afraid that it might not be here."

"Why?" Fraser asked. "I'm surprised you've heard about it. It's just an old car they have me send out of this yard once or twice a year when they want to publicize the railway." Fraser shook his head. "Nothing really fancy about it except those paintings."

"They're fancy to me," Jane said. "Because I'm an artist, too. I wonder if I could take my sketchbook and make a copy?"

"I don't see why not." Fraser was frowning. "I'm sure there are all kind of copyrights and legal restrictions, but as long as it's for personal use."

"Very personal." Her smile was dazzling. "I'll just run to the car and get my sketchbook."

Caleb nodded. "And while you're busy, I'll take up Fraser's valuable time by asking if he'll give me a tour of the rest of the cars and equipment. I'm afraid I'm more interested in the engines than pretty pictures."

Fraser nodded eagerly. "Me, too. Ever since I was a kid, I always wanted to be an engineer. But I've never had much schooling, so I joined the army and I did pretty well there. Medals and other stuff. Maybe that's how I ended up here after I retired."

"I'm sure that the railroad company was happy to have you come to work for them," Jane said. "Those medals should make you proud." She could see that Caleb was going to use her request as an excuse to take care of examining every important aspect of the facility. Mission accomplished. She took off running and reached the gates a few minutes later. Another couple of minutes and she was back with her sketch pad. "Where is it?"

Fraser was smiling indulgently. "Two rows over. It's even got its own REIVER plaque on the steps." He turned to Caleb. "And the engine that pulls the Reiver train is in tip-top shape. Everything in this yard is kept in good repair, and they sent to London for all the computer upgrades that let me practically run this entire railway station all by myself. We can check out the Reiver engine as soon as we let her into the car." He chuckled. "No fancy plaques on that engine. It's just sheer power. You'll be impressed."

And Caleb had already done a good deal of impressing on his own, she thought. She headed for the row of cars Fraser had indicated. "After I do the sketches of the murals, I might want to do a few of the engines, if that's okay?"

Fraser was nodding. "Just let me unlock the Reiver car and then we'll leave you to your art."

"Thank you." She opened the door of the train car. "I'll see you later, Caleb. I'll try to get some sketches that even you might appreciate."

He nodded. "Peasant though I am? I can't wait. Come on, Fraser. Let's go see those engines."

Jane noticed it was dim in the car even though it was still early afternoon. The upholstery of the chairs appeared to be a dark green velvet, and that only seemed to add to the dimness. But she was able to see the star attraction at the far end of the long car. She could count seven exquisite chandeliers on the car's ceiling leading toward the splendid murals. She was tempted to go and examine the paintings immediately, but she knew she'd want to spend more time on them than on the remainder of the car. So she stopped just inside the entry door and opened the rich walnut door to the left of the aisle. It was a small bathroom with marble antique commode and vanity and a small crystal chandelier that glittered from the ceiling. She took pictures with her camera. Then she opened the carved walnut door to the right of the aisle. It revealed a much larger room with a red leather divan and chair and the richness of a faded Persian carpet. Another crystal chandelier . . . This must have been the room in which MacClaren had told Fiona to hide herself until she reached the main station. It gave Jane a warm, expectant feeling, as if she was waiting for old friends to come in at any moment to say hello. Crazy? Yes, but it didn't change the sensation. She gave the room a last lingering glance and then took some more photos and closed the door.

Time for the murals. They were as much a part of Fiona and MacClaren's story as what had happened on this train when they had escaped from Jamie and Graeme and fled to another life. Farrell and Fiona had been together in these hills while he had done those paintings. She had probably taken him to her favorite places so that they would come to belong to both of them.

Is that how it was, Fiona?

She was walking down the aisle now beneath the seven crystal chandeliers that led to the paintings. Then she was standing in front of them. They were not only breathtakingly beautiful in color and artistry, but seemed to be a part of the Highlands they portrayed. Even part of the people who had lived and loved in these hills since Cira had come here from her volcano-torn land over two thousand years ago. The woman with the blue parasol sitting by the lake watching her child playing nearby. The young shepherd boy and his brown dog climbing a hill. An old, white-haired man sitting on a bench in front of a chapel.

You did good, MacClaren. It was too bad you couldn't have taken these paintings with you. They're almost all still perfect except for a ding here and there. But maybe there was a reason why you felt they should stay here. Or maybe we'll have to think about a way to fix that.

But there was no question that she would take more than photos of these murals. She wanted to feel as if she belonged to the paintings and these Highlands in a special way. Perhaps in the same way as Fiona, MacClaren, and even Cira and her husband, Antonio. She spent thirty minutes taking the photos with painstaking care. Then she opened her sketchbook and sat down in front of the paintings.

Do you mind if I join you? I promise I'll behave with all due respect.

No, that wasn't...quite right. Jane went through the

sketchbook and found the *Mist Child* and propped it on the seat next to her. *That seems right. MacDuff said she looks like Fiona. She'll be good company.*

Then she started to sketch.

———◆———

It was after dark, and Jane had already turned on the chandeliers when Caleb squatted down beside her chair. "How's it going? Get a little carried away?"

She nodded. "But I expected that. I wasn't trying to copy the paintings. I only wanted to add my part of the story so that it showed I was here for them, too. It seemed important, somehow. I think I've done enough that I can transfer it to canvas."

He gave a low whistle as he gazed at the sketches. "I know you have. It's going to be spectacular."

"No, it's not. It's just me saying, *Here's how things have changed and yet stayed the same. Like all life.*"

"That's fairly profound."

"Not really." She was carefully putting the sketches away. "I believe it was what MacClaren might have been trying to tell all the people who had been here in the Highlands before him. I just added my bit."

"A spectacular bit. It's a little like MacClaren's and yet completely different." He picked up the sketch in the seat next to her and handed it to her. "The *Mist Child*." He was smiling. "Did she have something to say about the murals?"

"No, she was just good company." She tucked the sketch back into the sketchbook. "Very quiet. How did your exploratory trip with Fraser go?"

"Fine. I probably know as much as he does now about the equipment and engines here at the Highlands yard."

"I don't doubt it. That's good. Now, do you have any other questions? Because I'm starving. I didn't realize it before, but I'm very empty. Can we do something about that?"

"That's why I came to get you. I shared our rations with Fraser and he's making supper." He took her arm as she started back up the aisle. "Why was *Mist Child* good company? Did she remind you of our daughter?"

"I didn't say that."

"But you called her she."

"Because I drew a little girl, which has nothing to do with the child I'm carrying." She stared at him in exasperation. "And you know it."

"But it would be a gift if I did. Do you believe it's a girl?"

"Caleb."

"It would be a gift. The minute we go out that door, there will be no more ancient magic Highlands and we'll have to concentrate on death and vengeance and survival." His tone was wheedling. "What does instinct tell you? What do you believe?"

He was almost boyishly appealing. So different from the Caleb she knew. In this tension-fraught moment, she desperately wanted to keep that Caleb. Oh, what the hell. "It's a girl."

He tilted his head. "That's what you believe?"

She stared him directly in the eyes. "It's a girl. But I'm not going to tell you her name. Now leave me alone."

For an instant he looked a little uncertain. Then he started to laugh. "That's impossible." He kissed her, hard. "Thank you for my gift." He opened the outside door. "And now I'll give you food and wine as a reward."

CHAPTER

16

Supper that night was filled with laughter, and an excellent stew, though Jane had to refuse the even more excellent wine that Caleb had offered her. Life was already being dictated by that little girl who had appeared in their lives, she thought ruefully.

It wasn't until after supper that Jane was brought abruptly down to earth. Fraser received an emergency call from his supervisor at the border station recalling him from the Highlands to return to the city. He was obviously upset but, after he went for a short walk with Caleb, he came back resigned and even cheerful. Caleb had offered to take Fraser's place and stay the night at the facility until he could arrange to have a substitute come to the Highlands the following day. He did it with an offhandedness that made it seem ultra-casual. He even asked Fraser to tour the yard with him to make sure the area was safe. He listened patiently to Fraser's advice and admonishments and then helped him load his van.

Fraser's last words were to Jane. He stuck his head out the

window as he was backing out. "Sorry about this. But you'll be fine. You've got a good man here. If there's anything I can do for you just give me a call."

"I'll do that," Jane said. "Don't worry about us. We'll be fine. Thanks for giving us such a good day."

Then Jane watched as Fraser waved and then drove off down the road. She immediately turned to Caleb. "How did you manage to get him away from here?"

"I called MacDuff and told him to contact the president of the railway and tell him to get Fraser out of here before midnight. All business executives are eager to do favors for MacDuff." He glanced at his watch. "Right on time. He only had another fifteen minutes."

"Midnight? Are we running that close?"

He shook his head. "I figure we've got at least until dawn. As a last resort, I told Rodland to give me twenty minutes' notice when Bohdan was near enough to be a threat. But I didn't want to cut it any closer where Fraser was concerned. He was an innocent, and you'd just lost Campbell. It would have torn you apart if something had gone wrong." He looked at Fraser's taillights disappearing around the curve. "Do you know how much I wanted to push you into that van and get you out of here?"

"Fraser would have understood." She wrinkled her nose. "You heard him tell me what a fine man I had to take care of me."

"And you were very polite. So instead of doing what I want to do, we'll spend a good portion of the night checking out the north trails and the forest." He took her elbow and turned her back toward the camp. "And then I'll open the trunk of the Range Rover and go over the three semiautomatic pistols and two rifles that I stashed there for you. I'm not sure about the handguns, but I've already got a plan for the rifle. I approve of long-range weapons for you."

"I've no objection. Just so it's effective."

"But before we go into hunting and any other skills Joe Quinn might have taught you, I suggest we go lie down and you let me hold you for a while."

"That's a fine suggestion." Jane's voice was trembling as she reached out and took his hand. "I can see why Fraser was so impressed by you."

"I hoped you'd feel that way." He slipped his arm around her waist and was leading her into the rail yard. "Because I really want to hold you and my little girl tonight."

2:40 A.M.

Jane's eyes snapped open.

"There's more!" she said aloud.

Caleb woke and turned over. "What?"

Jane quickly reached for her tablet computer and scrolled through the hundreds of photos she'd taken the day before. "I've been dreaming about the mural."

Caleb sat up and rubbed his eyes. "Of course you have."

"I'm serious." She was still scrolling through the photos. "I've been going through every inch of that mural in my mind ever since we first saw it. The right side looks...different." She pinched her screen to zoom in on one of the mural shots. "See what I mean?"

Caleb squinted at it. "I'm afraid I don't."

"The style and colors are the same, but the brushstrokes have a slightly different quality to them." She zoomed in on the lower right-hand corner, where there was a slight discoloration. "And look at this."

"An imperfection?"

"It's more than that. It's a chip." She pointed at the spot. "Maybe something was bumped against this painting at some point. In any case, it shows that there's something underneath this section of the painting. It's been painted over."

Caleb nodded. "Don't artists do this all the time when they're creating their works? Including you?"

"Of course. But coupled with the difference in brushstrokes in this entire side of the painting, this looks like a drastic revision, possibly by someone else. There has to be a reason for it."

"Interesting."

She stared at the photo a moment longer. "I want to see what's underneath."

He nodded. "Museum researchers have equipment that can do that, don't they?"

"Yes. They use infrared reflectography scanners."

"I know some people at the Louvre who can—"

"I want to see it now."

He smiled. "Well, unless you happen to have an infrared reflectography scanner with you..."

"I do, kind of."

His smile faded. "What?"

She reached for her bag and pulled out her camera. "Most digital cameras can be modified for infrared photography. If you know what you're doing, it only takes a few minutes."

"And you know what you're doing?"

She nodded. "I've done some IR work myself for a mixed-media piece I did a few years ago. It's not at the level of a full-bore museum scanner, but depending on the paints used, it could work. You just have to try different focus points to find the layer underneath. I want to go over to the Reiver train now and check it out."

"Now?"

"Why not?"

"Well, perhaps because we're waiting for people to arrive who want to kill us?"

"You told me there's an entire squad of MI6 agents out there making sure that won't happen."

"It won't happen."

"So if we're stuck here, why not make use of our time? We're here, the mural's here, let's do this."

He leaned his jaw on his fist, his lips curving with amusement. "It's still early. We have plenty of time to do anything we feel like doing."

"No, we don't." She sat up. "We're on borrowed time just as Farrell and Fiona were. Only this is our decision. I was just lying here and wondering if they were struggling to find a way out, too, when Farrell was painting that wonderful mural."

"Maybe. We don't know."

"But maybe we could if we tried." She smiled at him. "I think I want to try, Caleb."

He suddenly laughed out loud. "I know that glint in your eye. You're not going to take no for an answer."

She leaned down and gave him a kiss before she tossed the blanket aside. "I'm glad you realize that. It'll save us both a lot of time and aggravation."

REIVER CAR

"It looks different, doesn't it?" Jane walked slowly down the aisle toward the painting, her gaze intent. "Earlier I thought it gave off an aura of eternal power, but that's not what I see now."

"What are you doing?" Caleb asked as Jane bent over to get a closer look at the mural. "May I help?"

"No." Jane crouched in front of the mural. "It's strange..."

"What's strange?" Caleb asked. "I don't know what you're talking about. It's the same mural we saw yesterday."

"Yes, but the light's different now. It's amazing the difference it makes. In my exhibitions, I always specify the type and color temperature of the lightbulbs they use. Yesterday this looked warm and welcoming. Now it looks a little... menacing."

Caleb studied the mural and then nodded. "I think I see it. Or could it be just a warning?"

"Either way, it's a powerful piece of work." Jane set her tripod on the floor and rooted through her bag for the camera. She pulled it out and inspected it.

"How did the modification go?"

"Well, I think. It may not be as effective as a museum infrared camera, but it may show us what's on the layer beneath this one."

"You're certain there's another painting underneath this one?"

"I won't be certain until I can verify. But I'd swear I'm right about this, Caleb." Her eyes were glittering with eagerness and excitement as she stared at him. "And why would anyone want

302

to do that unless they had a very good reason? Don't you want to know if MacClaren had one?"

He chuckled. "Oh, yes. And if you're ready to swear, that's certainly enough for me." Caleb checked his phone. "Okay, but I'm afraid you'll need to work fast. The last time Rodland texted he said there are some signs that Bohdan's already on our trail. But we should be safe here until the MI6 strike team can take them into custody."

"Good." Jane turned her attention back to the camera. There was no guarantee this would work, however effective she thought her camera's infrared capabilities might be. Lead-based paints could reflect the IR radiation, obliterating any opportunity to see the layers beneath. Alternatively, certain paints and materials absorbed IR, making them visible with astonishing clarity. It could go either way.

She set up her camera and adjusted the lens. She had already programmed dozens of focus points since any of them could be the one to best reveal the painting underneath. There were no shortcuts, at least not with her makeshift rig. She just needed to keep trying different focus points until one would hopefully reveal this mural's secrets.

Focus point one . . .

———◆———

MULBERRY ACCESS ROAD

Rodland didn't like this development at all.

He crouched in the shrubbery half a mile from the rail yard, his gaze on the dense brush in front of him. He should be able to hear someone, something, in that wall of trees and shrubs that bordered the tall wire fence enclosing the yard.

He wasn't hearing anything, dammit. Which could be a silent threat. The MI6 strike team commander had lost contact with his outer-perimeter sentries shortly after they reported that Bohdan's men were on the move.

Those sentries were twenty highly trained agents on the roads surrounding the rail yard, surely more than enough to rout the small but lethal team that Chiswick had sent to capture Caleb and Jane.

Unless the report of the size of that unit was false. It was entirely possible. Bohdan was known to be a crafty snake in the grass, and he might have brought in an extra-strong unit to guarantee that he'd be able to take Caleb down at last.

He looked down at the one-word text from Caleb: STATUS?

He wished he had an answer. Caleb and Jane had agreed to use themselves as bait, and now—

RAT-AT-AT-AT-AT-AT!

Automatic weapon fire shattered the early-morning silence. It had come from behind him.

RAT-AT-AT-AT-AT!

Another burst came from ahead.

Suddenly there was gunfire all around him!

He hit the ground and started to crawl through the shallow creek deeper into the forest.

The MI6 commander's voice blasted over the radio. "Speak up! What's going on out there?"

The only replies were screams and more gunfire.

Dammit!

Finally, one of the team members shouted through the shared frequency. "Bohdan's brought in a bloody auxiliary unit to take us down. I've already lost two men. Watch your backs! They're coming from all—"

RAT-AT-AT-AT-AT-AT!

The agent was silenced.

Rodland kept on crawling. What was the status? If he didn't find a way to take down those bastards, it could well be terminal.

———◆———

Jane joined Caleb at the train car window as the shots continued. "What the hell's going on out there?"

"I don't know." Caleb looked down at his phone. "Rodland isn't answering. I need to get you out of here."

"To where?"

"I'm working on it. Presumably anywhere they won't be looking for us."

There was a sound at the rear of the train car. Someone was tampering with the locked door!

Caleb pulled out his gun and crept toward the door. The knob jiggered.

Caleb's phone vibrated.

It was a message from Rodland: IT'S ME. LET ME IN.

Still keeping the gun trained in front of him, Caleb unlocked the door and flung it open.

It was Rodland, and he was covered in mud and blood.

"Oh, God." Jane rushed toward him.

Rodland stepped inside and closed the door behind him. "Don't worry. I'm okay. The blood isn't mine."

"Then whose is it?"

Rodland walked over and peered out the window. "Two

gunmen who tried to ambush me on the access road after I'd jerked Adams away from Bohdan's troop and sent him into the forest to hide out. Bohdan had sent word to stagger the number of his military forces to keep MI6 from knowing the exact number; he wanted to keep them off guard until he was ready to strike. It turned out to be a massacre. I may be the only survivor."

"What?" Jane said.

"I saw eight dead MI6 agents on the way over here. Bohdan's mercenaries are swarming all over the roads." His gaze was searching the darkness outside the window. "He really wants you, Caleb."

"Then we need to get out of here," Jane said.

"It may be too late for that," Rodland said. "They've surrounded the railway station, and they have all the roads covered. I phoned MI6 for backup, but it could be hours before we get any help. I barely made it here."

"So what's the plan?" Jane asked. "Hole up here until the cavalry arrives?"

"You've got a better one?"

Caleb slowly nodded. "I just might." He reached for his phone and started dialing. "We know someone who's a lot closer." When MacDuff picked up, Caleb's words were clipped. "It appears we have a problem. Would you care to have your marines join us at the Highland Railway Yard and attempt to save the day?"

"I never attempt," MacDuff said. "I always accomplish, unlike some people. Is Jane all right?"

"At the moment. Get the hell up here." He cut the connection and then turned back to Jane and Rodland. "His marines are a formidable fighting force and they're spoiling for a fight after what happened at the castle. They may keep some of Bohdan's men at bay, but Bohdan himself will probably be knocking down that fence and trying to blow up this car to get at us within minutes." He glanced at Rodland. "I'm the main target. Is there any way you can get Jane out that fence and into the forest if I distract them?"

"Only a marginal chance," Rodland said. "There are too many. And they're like hungry crocodiles smelling blood."

"Then maybe a trade if I can contact—"

"You're doing it again." Jane stepped in front of Caleb and said fiercely, "I *won't* lose you. I won't go anywhere without you. Think of something else that will get us out of here together. You're supposed to be damn brilliant, now figure it out. You always have triple plans in mind before you go into any assignment. It's instinctive with you. I don't believe you'd do anything less to save your daughter and me. What was your first thought when you sized up the situation?"

"The train."

Her eyes blazed into his. "Then find a way to use the damn train to keep us safe."

"Talk about marginal," he said hoarsely. Then he whirled again on Rodland. "Before he left, I had Fraser set up the engine computer programing on my laptop. It's comparatively simple since Fraser was anything but a genius when it came to computers. That simplicity might be a help. But you're definitely a whiz at them, so go get my computer out of my backpack and see if you can make it sit up and do tricks."

"Ah, computers..." Rodland was already moving toward the seat where Caleb had thrown his backpack. "I already like this plan better."

"I'm not sure I do," Caleb said. "But we'll make it work. Though, as Jane ordered, I'll just have to figure out how."

Jane was gazing speculatively all around the train car. "You know, there are all kinds of places to hide in these cars. The passengers were afraid of the reivers and the owners of the trains made certain adjustments to keep them riding the trains. But you're right, those marines might not be here for another hour or so. We can't defend ourselves for that long."

"No way," Caleb agreed thoughtfully. "We'll have to leave."

Rodland shook his head. "We can't do that. I was just out there, remember? Bohdan's men have the place surrounded. If we go out on foot, it would be a massacre."

"Not on foot."

"Even if we managed to get to a car, the roads are covered."

"We won't be using the roads."

"Then how do you suggest that we..." His eyes widened as the realization hit him. "You can't be serious."

Jane took a step closer. "Are you suggesting...that we actually *take* the train?"

"You asked what I thought of first," he said simply.

"I didn't think you meant to steal it. I didn't think you could. I thought maybe you'd find a way to use it to hide us from Bohdan."

He shook his head. "Not efficient enough. Why not just take it? This car is already connected to a two-hundred-ton locomotive engine. And there are five other cars connected as well. We'll pulverize anything that gets in our way." He smiled at her. "Let's take it for a spin."

"Just like that?" Rodland said. "It's not that simple. Modern rail lines use a central control system."

"You would know," Caleb said. "As I remember, you were

fairly well versed on the PRAM software package that MI6 was trying out before the London Olympics. As I understand it, it enabled the operator to hack into any of the U.K. rail systems."

"It was buggy as hell."

Caleb shrugged. "Any port in a storm. Can you access it?"

Rodland thought about it for a moment. "Maybe."

Caleb nodded at his computer. "Use this."

Rodland produced his key ring, where a tiny USB stick was attached. He inserted it into Caleb's laptop and booted the computer into his own operating system. As his fingers flew across the keyboard, Jane turned to Caleb. He took her hand into his. It was meant as a gesture of reassurance, though she was anything but reassured.

After a couple of minutes, Rodland leaned back. "I have it. The PRAM was still on the MI6 training server. But we'll still need to go to the forward car and manually power up the engine. Once it's online, I'll be able to control it and the local track switches from this laptop."

"Good," Caleb said. "You and I will make our way up there and see if the engine is as efficient as Fraser told me it was."

"What am I supposed to do?" Jane asked quietly. "How can I help?"

"Keep yourself and the baby safe so I won't regret doing this. I'll tell you if there's anything else for you to do as it comes along."

"That's not enough. I've got to *do* something." She glanced back at the paintings. "Maybe MacClaren will help to keep me busy so I won't go crazy. I'll finish the job I started."

"Only you," Caleb murmured.

"Don't worry, I have my priorities straight. I'll keep our

daughter safe." She was opening the weapons box and removing a 9mm Luger pistol. "I won't let those assholes touch her."

"I can see you won't." Caleb gestured toward the two long guns on the floor beside the box. "Why don't you take one of those?"

She shrugged. "I will." She ignored the AR-15. "I prefer the carbine. It handles better if you have to use it short range." She took the M4 carbine. "I remember you said you liked the idea of me with a long gun."

"I definitely do. And if anyone but the two of us tries to come in here, don't hesitate to use one of those." He added grimly, "Like Rodland said, Bohdan really wants us."

———◆———

"Why the hell haven't I heard something?" Bohdan stood up in the rear of his mobile command center, an old Russian war-surplus vehicle he found much more robust than the newer and shinier units he'd owned. "Chiswick has his orders. He knows what I want." He'd ordered the vehicle parked five miles north of the train yard, but it still wasn't close enough to make him feel part of the action. He whirled on Lasoff, the young tech who was communicating with his attack team via a headset. "Well?"

Lasoff moistened his lips nervously. "We have them, sir."

"They're alive?"

"As far as we can tell."

"What's that supposed to mean?"

"We have them cornered. They're trapped in a railcar."

"You *fool*." Bohdan's face flushed with anger. "Then we don't really have them, do we?"

The tech was almost stuttering. "According to the unit commander, it's a simple matter of—"

"The commander is an idiot." He reached for his cell phone. "And that's what I'll tell Chiswick. I'm not going to lose Caleb or the MacGuire woman because you're all being clumsy. I've waited too long." He'd make that clear to Chiswick. Bohdan wasn't sure if he was being impatient or if he just wanted to get his own hands on that son of a bitch, Caleb. It didn't matter. The result would be the same. He put down the cell phone. "No, I'll tell Chiswick in person. I'm going there myself. Tell the driver."

———

Caleb and Rodland dropped to the ground between the train cars and froze. When the movement wasn't met with a hail of gunfire, Caleb took that as a win. He nodded toward Rodland, and they crawled toward the engine car. The darkness offered them cover, but he was sure that at least some of Bohdan's soldiers were equipped with night-vision goggles.

They hoisted themselves up onto the engine car platform and Rodland smashed the side pilot window with the butt of his gun. The sound of breaking glass was startling. If their attackers hadn't been aware that they were out here, surely they were now, Caleb thought. They waited a moment to see if there was a response. But there was so much shouting and talking among Bohdan's men surrounding the train that they'd lucked out. The glass breakage hadn't been noticed. Rodland reached inside and slid open the door.

The two men crouched behind the main console.

"What now?" Caleb whispered.

Rodland was ready. He pulled the laptop from his pack and flipped up the lid to reveal a screen filled with a photo of the exact same console in front of them. The screen was filled with handwritten annotations that described the engine start-up routine.

"Another MI6 resource?" Caleb said.

Rodland shook his head. "Even better. A railway enthusiast website." He flipped a dizzying array of switches, some of which were hidden behind safety panels below the console.

The lights on the panel switched from red to green. "Good," Rodland said. "Sometimes you have to wait for the oil and water to warm up in the prime mover. But this is equipped with a Smartstart system to keep them ready."

"So how long will it take?"

Rodland took a deep breath and pushed the power lever up. The engine roared to life. "Here we go!"

The five-car train lurched forward and moved sluggishly across the rail yard.

———◆———

Jane peered out the window as she felt that first lurch.

Caleb and Rodland had done it!

She could see some panicked movement from the shadows, then the flashes of gun muzzles as shots rang out! She ducked down and then hit the floor as the train picked up speed. Bullets rained against both sides of the car, but the assault seemed to dwindle as they left the rail yard. But the train was picking up more and more speed as it zoomed down the track.

They'd bought some time, but no telling how much. Bohdan's forces would be in hot pursuit.

Don't think about it, Jane told herself. Her job right now was to stay out of the range of those bullets and hope that Caleb and Rodland could do the same. Then find a way to keep them all alive.

Distraction. Keep moving. Keep thinking about something else. *Help me, MacClaren.*

She turned back toward her camera, which had been automatically snapping pictures of the mural at various focus points until she'd felt the train move. She suddenly froze. Something was different from when she'd been crouching on the floor as the train had started barreling down the track. The first several dozen photos had revealed nothing, but the electronic viewfinder screen now showed something else entirely.

It showed the painting *beneath* the painting.

Jane felt her breath leave her as she watched. With each focus point, the image grew richer and more detailed. Finally, when it started to fade, Jane grabbed the camera and stepped back through the photos until she found the clearest one.

The hidden image was similar to the one she was accustomed to seeing with the shepherd boy with the brown dog, playing children, and the lady with the blue parasol. But there was one major difference: This mural included a train and a station with a sign reading BENTLEY IND. Only details relating to the train and station had been erased in the final mural.

BENTLEY IND? Jane pulled out her phone for a quick search.

She found what she was looking for in seconds.

She gasped.

The phone rang in her hands. It was Caleb. She punched the TALK button.

"Are you okay?" He was worried. "We took some gunfire back there."

"Tell me about it. But I'm fine. Are you both all right?"

"For the time being. But we threw Bohdan's men back at the railway station into an uproar. Lots of activity going on. They're bound to be after us any minute. We're trying to figure out the next move. There might be more bullets flying so don't be moving around the car. Keep down!"

"I will. Because there's no reason for me not to any longer." She drew a deep breath. Then her words came as fast as she could get them out. "Listen, Caleb. This has to be quick. I found what I was looking for in the mural. I know why no one could ever find the treasure."

"What?"

"You heard me. MacClaren decided to hide it. It's because the instructions' starting point was the end of the first branch line past the McNaughton Branch. Anyone who would go looking for the treasure wouldn't find the landmarks referenced in the instructions. No big rock, no forked stream. No waterfall or ancient cemetery."

"That's right. It's why the treasure map was bogus."

"But what if there used to be another branch line? A temporary one built to serve a single construction project? Companies used to pay for them all the time. They're called spur lines. There was once a factory that belonged to Bentley Industries in the area, but it went out of business before World War One. This mural showed a rail line for Bentley, but as far as I can tell, one never existed, at least not officially."

"What are you saying?"

"I ran across this kind of thing in my research. Occasionally local railroad administrators would accept huge amounts of money from companies to build temporary spur lines for their projects, then just pocket the cash and not inform their home office hundreds or even thousands of miles away. When the project was completed, the administrators would strike the spur line and erase all evidence it even existed. That's why no records exist of this one. And I think it's why MacClaren painted over this part of the mural. He made a deal with the administrators before he and his Fiona left for their new life. He probably got a fat fee, and still had the option of going back and searching for the treasure himself if he chose to do it."

"It makes sense."

"It gets better. This line would have been the first branch line past McNaughton. And I know there's a forked stream and a waterfall near there, and an ancient cemetery. I'm willing to bet there's a big rock. *This* is where we look for the treasure."

"Holy shit!" Caleb murmured. "MacDuff is going to love this. I can't wait to—"

A sudden crash shook the train!

"What's that?" Jane said. "It came from behind!"

"Rodland is trying to see what—"

"Never mind." Jane looked up as she heard a series of thumps on the roof of the car. "Caleb, I think we have company. Footsteps on the roof, heading your way."

"I'm on it. Stay down!"

CHAPTER

17

Caleb pocketed the phone and pulled out his semi-automatic. "We're about to get some company."

Rodland's eyes were still glued to his laptop screen. "I'm afraid I can't be much help to you there. I need to switch to the main line, and if this software doesn't cooperate, it's going to be an extremely short trip."

"Understood. I'll handle it."

Caleb ducked outside and moved along the side platform. He looked up as cold winds whipped against his face. If Jane was right, someone would be appearing above him at any—

BLAM-BLAM-BLAM!

Caleb fired at the two figures that appeared on the roof of the railcar above. One tried to fire back, but Caleb fired twice more to finish him off. One of the men fell from the train, the other onto the platform next to Caleb.

Caleb kicked him over the side.

The train lurched as they switched tracks and headed north on the main line. They picked up speed.

Caleb ducked back into the engineering compartment. "Did *you* do that?"

Rodland nodded. "Yes. With this software, I can control the switch tracks, traffic lights, and pretty much everything else we run across."

"Excellent."

"Shit," Rodland said in disgust.

"What is it?"

Rodland nodded toward one of three monitors mounted above the main console. It showed a rear-camera view of the train, where an open-bed truck was speeding alongside. One by one, half a dozen men in paramilitary fatigues jumped from the truck to the rear train car.

Caleb cursed. "Bohdan's mercenaries."

"Who else?" Rodland increased the train speed again. "I'll do what I can to make things uncomfortable for them."

Caleb replaced his gun's ammo clip. "So will I."

———◆———

Jane backed away from the rear door. She could hear men's voices, shouting and talking just outside that door. She had no idea how many there were or where they were located. One of them sounded as if he was talking to someone on the roof. Then someone was pounding against the door, splintering the mahogany frame.

Shit!

She had to get out of here. But she couldn't go out that door. And she knew that someone had been on the roof heading toward Caleb only a little while ago. They could still be there. Think. Where else could she go?

The reivers! She'd even mentioned to Caleb that there had been hiding places built in these cars because of the reivers. She looked up at the ornate paneled ceiling. She tried to remember the sketches of the remodel when the chandeliers were added in the late nineteenth century. If she remembered correctly, there was a sizable gap between the drop ceiling and the train car's roof. At the time she'd studied them she'd wondered if this gap was used by passengers as hiding places from the reivers.

BAM. BAM. BAM.

They were almost through the door.

Jane stood on a chair and pressed against a square ceiling panel. It didn't budge.

BAM. BAM. BAM.

She tried another. No dice.

BAM. BAM. BAM.

Bohdan's men were almost inside. She pushed up yet another ceiling panel.

It moved.

Hurry. Not much time. They'd be breaking in any second.

She gripped the sides of the opening and hoisted herself up into the ceiling. She replaced the panel just as the door finally gave way!

She heard a single set of footsteps in the train car below. Only one man. She could hear him shouting and laughing to someone still outside the door. Carefully, quietly, she moved toward the clump of wires that fed one of the ornate lighting fixtures. She looked through the fixture opening and saw one of Bohdan's men alone in the compartment, standing where she'd been just moments before.

Now he was speaking to someone through his headset, and

she heard him identify himself as Chiswick. She'd heard that name before. Not good.

One of Bohdan's top lieutenants.

She slid across the ceiling structure, making her way to the far side of the car. Every time she reached a lighting fixture, she paused to see what he was doing.

At one point, he crouched behind her camera and looked at the mural. Chiswick had no idea what he was seeing, she was sure.

Jane turned. It was difficult to see, but there appeared to be a small door on the car's far side. Could she use it to get to the roof? From there, she might be able to reach Caleb and Rodland in the front engine car.

She slid toward the door panel, hoping the clattering of wheels on the tracks would mask the sounds of her movements.

Just a few feet more...

SMASH!

The ceiling panels erupted in front of her, and Chiswick's face was only three feet from hers! He was standing on a table and had broken through the ceiling with the butt of his rifle. He turned his gun barrel toward her and smiled.

"Going somewhere?"

She inhaled sharply and couldn't speak for a moment.

He smiled. "Jane MacGuire. Poor woman, afraid and cowering in the ceiling. It seems I've come up with a prize. Bohdan warned me I'd better come back with you or Caleb today. He has great plans for you. If I help him, he might just forgive me. This must be fate; I ran into a friend of yours at your gallery in London. She was most cooperative."

Felicia. This must be the man who had killed Felicia.

"You're right, she was a friend of mine," she said hoarsely. "And I think 'fate' is a very good word for it."

Only when it was too late did Chiswick notice that she was holding a half-hidden gun in her right hand.

BLAMMM!

She shot him in the face.

———◆———

Rodland glanced back at the rear camera monitor. "Dammit."

"What?" Caleb said.

"It looks like we have eight more troops climbing aboard the train from another truck. And I'll bet there could be another couple of trucks on the road behind this one."

Caleb stepped closer to the monitor and watched Bohdan's men climb aboard from their truck. "This isn't going to get easier."

Rodland looked back at the laptop. "I might be able to do something about the trucks coming up behind them."

"Do what?"

The train shook as it switched off the main line and crossed the river Thurso.

"Well done," Caleb said.

Jane suddenly appeared at the side door. "Yes, well done."

"What are you doing here?" Caleb stepped toward her. "I thought I asked you to—"

"Bohdan's right-hand man Chiswick paid me a visit and changed my mind." She slung her carbine on her shoulder as she entered the engineer's compartment. "I suddenly didn't have a back door any longer and there were other soldiers climbing on the Reiver car."

"What?"

"Don't worry, I took care of Chiswick. But I thought I'd be safer up here."

"I can't argue with that," he said bitterly. "So much for trying to keep you secure."

Rodland studied the map on the laptop screen. "I have an idea. But I'm about to do something that may get us all into a great deal of trouble."

"I doubt if it can get any worse than it is for us right now," Caleb said.

"Don't say that. It *is* worse," Jane said. She pointed at the rear camera monitor where a dozen men were running toward them across the train car roofs. Two of them had already drawn their guns and were firing in their direction. "I believe those were the mercenaries Chiswick brought aboard the Reiver car. If you can do anything to get rid of them, to hell with the trouble."

Rodland increased the speed. "Hang on, I need to get going for this maneuver to work."

"*What* maneuver?" Caleb asked.

"There's a drawbridge on the trestle up ahead. I just opened it."

"And...?" Jane said.

"And I'm about to uncouple the last three cars of this train."

"And...?" Caleb said.

"Don't talk to me. I need to time this just right..." Rodland concentrated and then punched a key. There was a jarring ripple as the last three cars uncoupled from their train. Bohdan's men tried desperately to steady themselves on the train car roofs. A few seconds later, Rodland activated a switch command for the track behind him.

The three cars with Bohdan's men coasted through the switch and toward the open drawbridge.

Jane's jaw dropped. "No way."

In the next instant, the three cars hurtled over the drawbridge. The men screamed as their train tumbled to the river hundreds of feet below!

Jane and Caleb watched in stunned silence. The train cars with the men had simply vanished in the darkness.

"How far down was that?" Jane said.

"At least a couple hundred feet," Caleb said.

"Three hundred and twenty-seven," Rodland said. "Big trouble if they hadn't been scum of the earth. But I'm getting a little tired of playing with this train, Caleb. Time for you to figure how to get us out of this mess."

"I'm working on it. But it may not be necessary." Caleb had grabbed a pair of infrared binoculars hanging from the console and was looking behind him. "I believe I just heard something that sounded very familiar on the road heading toward the railway station." He focused carefully and then gave a low whistle. "How the hell did he manage to get them here this fast? Wouldn't you know that MacDuff would pull a stunt like this?" He started to laugh. "I believe the marines have landed. Just in time to reap the glory and cheers from all and sundry. I almost expect a ticker-tape parade."

"What?" Jane took the binoculars and looked for herself. It was true. Trucks, armored cars, motorcycles all being operated by the marines they'd become so familiar with. All of them were engaged in the attack on Bohdan's forces. MacDuff himself was at the forefront; she could hear the sound of explosions and saw Bohdan's camouflage-clad soldiers scattering before them. "Thank God." She breathed a sigh of relief. "Don't you say one thing against MacDuff, Caleb. I think he looks absolutely fantastic at this moment."

Caleb grinned. "Hey, so do I." He took the binoculars and handed them to Rodland. "Take a look and admire the laird, a man who has even greater timing than I do. Then do you think you can get this train back to the yard double quick so that we can help them out a little?"

"I don't think they're going to need it," Rodland said as he gazed through the binoculars. "They've got Bohdan's guys on the run and most of them are disappearing into the forest." He handed the binoculars back to Caleb. "Even Bohdan himself. But I'll get you back to help do a final cleanup." He started punching the buttons on his computer. "I don't know about double quick, but it will be—"

Caleb stiffened. "Even Bohdan himself?" he repeated. "You saw Bohdan at the rail yard just now?" He raised the binoculars to his eyes again. "It *is* him." He began to curse softly.

Rodland nodded. "I thought it was him. He was on the run heading for the forest with his entourage. I know he got out of that mobile command center he always uses. That old Russian-made Ranzhir is hard to miss."

"Yes, it is," Caleb said. "Which means you should put on some speed getting us back to that station so I can see if he's still there, or if I have to chase him down."

"Chiswick didn't mention to me Bohdan was on-site," Jane said quickly. "Only that he had orders from him to get the two of us." She felt a chill as she gazed at that expression she knew so well. Caleb was in hunt mode. "Why not let MacDuff and his marines go after him?"

"Because it's my job. I should have gotten him when I took down the general." He was staring straight ahead. "And

324

I won't let anyone else be butchered by him when I've got a chance to stop it from happening. And you know he'll never stop now that he's zeroed in on us."

Of course she knew it. Nothing could be plainer after what they'd gone through tonight. "That doesn't mean you have to do it alone. I told you I wouldn't let you do that again."

Just then a helicopter roared overhead. Then another. On the road behind them another half a dozen military vehicles suddenly appeared. "More firepower," Jane said. "Call them and let them go with you, dammit."

"No time. He's on the run. He's slipped through MI6's fingers half a dozen times before this. He'll disappear as he's done before," Caleb said. "And he could do it. The bastard has contacts all over the world. Stop here, Rodland."

"That'll take a while," Rodland said. "But I've slowed down enough for you to be able to jump off. Just give me another couple of minutes."

"Good enough." Caleb crouched, preparing for the leap.

"I'm coming with you," Jane said desperately.

"No, you're not. For every reason we've discussed. And we both know there's no way you're going to jump from a moving train right now."

"Don't you dare do this."

"I can't *not* do it. He's hurt too many people. Not this time, Jane. It will be okay. I promise." Caleb's face was sober as he leaped from the train. He rolled as he hit the ground.

Jane's hands clenched at her sides. "Caleb!"

Caleb ran back toward the forest trying to duplicate the path he'd seen Bohdan and his men taking.

Move fast.

Be silent.

But it was almost dawn. Careful. Darkness would have been his friend. But there were no friends in this forest. He had to worry about not only Bohdan but also any of the other mercenaries in Bohdan's army trying desperately to get away from those marines.

Track swiftly, accurately, just as he'd always done.

If he'd seen correctly, Bohdan had run in a cluster with two of his men. They had scattered in panic as MacDuff's marines had attacked. His men had likely been wearing the boots that all of his soldiers wore; Bohdan favored black athletic shoes. Easy enough to track.

Move faster.

Keep a sharp eye out.

It didn't take long for him to find Bohdan's footprints in the woods. The two other sets of prints had peeled away from their dear leader's after only a few hundred yards, indicating a possible lack of physical conditioning on Bohdan's part. His men obviously had no intention of giving Bohdan backup in this dire situation.

Forget them. Bohdan was the only one of importance.

And he was close. He could hear him, *sense* him, *feel* the flow of the blood in his veins.

Perhaps only a few yards ahead of him.

But Bohdan had stopped running.

What are you up to? A trap? I'm tired of dealing with you, too. Let's see if we can play that game and get this over with.

Listen . . .

Footsteps in the brush.

He was moving back toward Caleb.

No doubt he had a gun, but would he use it?

Not right away. His hatred of Caleb was too intense. He'd want to let loose some of that poison before he put him down.

And Caleb was feeling some of that same hatred after what Bohdan had done these past days. All the agony he'd put Jane and MacDuff and all the other people who lived here in these Highlands through. He wanted to *hurt* the son of a bitch.

Come on. Start it. Come a little closer.

Come on!

And here he was. He sensed him even before he saw him.

"Stop there, Caleb." Bohdan stepped from the shadows, holding a gun in front of him. "I really want to savor this moment."

Caleb froze. "Enjoy it. You've obviously got me. I'm clearly helpless."

"Are you? I can't take the chance. I've been hearing wild stories about you. Throw aside your gun."

Caleb had already decided he wasn't going to need the weapon. "Sure." He tossed aside the Glock. "I know when I'm beaten. What do you want from me? Can we make a deal?"

"A deal? After how you've humiliated me?" Bohdan was almost hissing. "Do you know what I'm going to do to you when I get you out of this forest?"

"No, but I'm sure you'll tell me." He took another step forward, and now he was in range to do anything he wanted with the bastard. "Do you want me to beg and plead?"

"It wouldn't do you any good," he snarled. He motioned with the gun. "Your tracking skills are supposed to be legendary, yet

I managed to take you down, didn't I? I knew I couldn't outrun you. So I came out here and waited. You didn't disappoint."

"Make the deal. It's over," Caleb said. "A detachment of Royal Marines will be swarming all over these woods no matter what you do to me."

Bohdan smiled. "You think I'm not ready for every contingency? I didn't get where I am by being ill prepared. I will walk out of these woods, trust me. And when I do there will be a helicopter to pick me up. So get in front of me because I'm going to take you with me. I'm going to need something to amuse me once I'm away from here."

"I guess I don't have a choice." Caleb took another step forward. "You're obviously the better man."

"Don't come any closer." Bohdan was suddenly tense. "You're saying the right words, but I don't think I like the way you're saying them." He was raising his gun. "Maybe I'll have to give up my plans to—"

BLAMM!

The shot rang out from behind Caleb, the bullet tearing through Bohdan's upper arm! He howled in pain as the gun flew from his hand.

Caleb whirled to see where the shot had come from.

It was Jane, and she was standing there, panting, out of breath, her eyes glittering wildly in her pale face. But she was still holding her long carbine gun absolutely steady. "Stop this, Caleb. I know what you intended to do, but I've had enough of it."

"Bitch!" Bohdan scrambled to pick up the gun he'd dropped. "Do you think I won't kill you? I'll get you, too."

Caleb had no time to do anything but remove the immediate problem. He dove for Bohdan's gun and was there only a second before Bohdan's hand closed on it. "Never again, bastard." Caleb pointed the gun directly at Bohdan's chest and pulled the trigger. He stopped him with a single shot in the heart.

"Is he dead?" Jane asked.

"Absolutely." Caleb was on his feet and running toward her. "Are you okay? What the hell are you doing here? I told you that—"

"You told me a lot of things. But there was no reason for me to listen to you." She turned and headed out of the forest. "And I refuse to do it right now. Did you think I wouldn't find a way to follow you?"

"I was hoping to God that you wouldn't. How did you do it?"

"I waited until the train turned the curve to go into the rail yard; that slowed it down even more. It had almost stopped, but I decided the little girl might need a cushion."

"A cushion? There were no cushions."

"I improvised. She had to be protected. So I pointed my gun at Rodland and told him to jump off the train and cushion me as I made the jump myself. It worked very well. Practically no jarring."

He blinked. "You used Rodland as a cushion?"

"Why are you surprised? He wasn't about to argue with me. He knew I was dead serious."

"I imagine he did. You had a gun in your hand."

She shrugged. "We both knew I probably wouldn't use it, but it gave him an excuse when he realized he'd have to face you for helping me."

He shook his head. "'Probably' was the key word in that sentence."

"Yes, it was." She looked directly into his eyes. "Because he also knew I had to keep my daughter safe, and there was no question in my mind that I had to get to you."

He was suddenly jarred out of his stunned incredulity. He started to laugh. "I would have liked to have seen Rodland scrambling to get back on that train to stop it after you were safely on the ground."

"He made it. I looked back just before I entered the forest. Besides, that was his problem. He had his computer to help him, and I had other things to do. I've spent the last quarter of an hour running through this blasted forest worrying about what you might do when you caught up with Bohdan." She was looking straight ahead now, and her pace increased. "I'm out of breath, and upset, and I have my baby to take care of. So I'm getting out of here, away from all the monsters. You can come with me if you like."

"I like." His concerned gaze was on her face. "You didn't have to worry about me. I knew what I was doing."

"I know you did. You always do. But there was too much ugliness and bitterness this time. You *wanted* to hurt him." She still wasn't looking at him. "Some of it was because of me. Would he have deserved it? Of course. But I'm never sure what using that blood talent might do to you. I couldn't bear it if destroying him hurt you, too." The sun was beginning to rise as they came out of the woods and her gaze was once more searching his face for answers as she turned toward him. "I knew I couldn't let it happen this time. It didn't matter how you felt about it. I can't let it matter if you're angry or not. I have to take care of you."

"Do you?" He reached out and touched her lips. "I believe I said something of that nature to you recently."

"That was different."

"It always is, but it just means adjustments and understanding. But then *I'm* different and you're probably right."

"I was right this time." She was looking around the forest. "I don't hear gunfire any longer. I want to rest. Do you think we're safe here?"

"Considering all the men and weaponry MacDuff showed up with, those mercenaries would be crazy not to be on the run. But I've been keeping an eye out just in case."

"Good. Nothing gets past you. Then keep on doing it." She gave a sigh and dropped down on the ground to sit beneath the trees. "I thought you'd be more angry. Are you giving in too easily about all this?"

He shook his head. "Not if it means I can keep you away from the monsters, or thinking I'm one. It's worth it to me to have you ordering me about occasionally. Now can we discuss something besides Bohdan or me?"

"Such as?"

"Are you really all right?" Caleb fell to his knees beside her. "I didn't like how short of breath you were."

"It happens when you're chasing two idiots through a damn forest." She took a deep breath as she threw the carbine gun aside and then launched herself into his arms. "Now be quiet and just hold me. I'm fine, but I don't believe our daughter approved of that last few yards I bolted when I went after you."

"Or maybe she didn't think that cushion you used was to her liking." He pushed her back to look down into her face. "I repeat, are you all right? Should I get you to a doctor?"

"Don't be ridiculous. I felt fine after that jump. Yes, of course I fully intend to have a checkup after we get out of here. That's the responsible thing to do. It's time I'm under a doctor's care. I would have done it even if nothing had happened during the last twenty-four hours. But it's not because I think anything is wrong." She paused. "I just felt a . . . flutter. She might have moved a tiny bit. It's a little unusual this early, but she evidently has her own set of rules, and I must have violated one of them." She touched her abdomen. "I like it that she has a mind of her own."

"And I like the idea of you taking it easy until you know what those rules are." He stood up and pulled her to her feet. "That means embracing civilization. Let's head back to the Run so that I can return this treasure chest I borrowed from MacDuff before he sends Scotland Yard after me."

"He wouldn't do that. He'll be grateful that you took down Bohdan." She glanced at MacDuff; he was a little distance away giving orders to his marines, who were still rounding up the last of the soldiers streaming out of the forest. "Besides, he appears to be having too good a time to let it bother him." She paused. "It's over, isn't it? We don't have to worry about them any longer. No one is going to come after you?"

"Not anyone from the Congo at least."

"That's enough for right now. We can discuss anything else later." She began walking toward the Range Rover. "There's still so much to do for MacDuff and his people. I'll have to see how I can help."

"Later," Caleb said quietly. "I can see you're revving up to mount a vigorous campaign to save the world, but that's not first on our agenda."

"Of course it is. We owe MacDuff for all the damage done to his property. We not only need to help with the repairs, but I told you what I'd discovered about what lies beneath that MacClaren painting. There's a good chance that if we follow *those* instructions, we'll be able to give MacDuff the real treasure that would pay for those castle repairs a hundred times over."

"Later," Caleb repeated. "I see where you're going and that was my first reaction, too. But I decided it's the wrong time."

"What are you talking about?"

"We've just blown Bohdan and his soldiers to hell and back. To do it, we've spun that tall tale about the fake treasure, and that story is going to not only be told but retold by every crook and con man in the business. Plus on the other side, it will be bragged about by MI6 agents who helped take down Bohdan's forces. It might have been the big lie, but it will be absolutely notorious for months. Which means that these Highlands are going to get plenty of visitors who want to see if that bogus story might actually be true. At least until word finally gets around that it's completely bullshit. We need to wait to go looking in the correct direction for the treasure until we're not stumbling over all the treasure hunter wannabes."

She could understand the logic of what he was saying, but she was disappointed. "And when will that be?"

He shrugged. "If we're lucky, a few months. It will start when MacDuff returns the treasure he lent me to the bank. Which will be today. Then we wait and see."

"I want to tell MacDuff right away."

"I know you do. But you know MacDuff will be curious and want to go hunting for it. That's his nature. And it's not as if he doesn't have money to burn to keep on with the repairs." His voice lowered persuasively. "Look, I'll send Rodland to take care of MacDuff's Run for the next few weeks or months. Whichever you prefer. He'll do a superb job and keep us informed about all of MacDuff's decisions."

"Maybe. But that's not what I want to do. And you're being entirely too controlling."

"On the contrary. I'm not being controlling at all. This is exactly what you want to do." He added coaxingly, "You told me you wanted to go home. It's what I promised you. I offered you a trip on Bezos's spaceship, but you said the lake cottage would be fine." He added gently, "You wanted to go home to Eve and Joe. I believe you still have a need for family. Perhaps more than ever now. You've not even told Eve that you're going to have a child. You should do that, Jane. It will give her the opportunity to anticipate and think about what's to come."

"Yes, it would." And the idea of being together with Eve and sharing that news was bringing that same wonderful anticipation to Jane. "You'd come with me?"

"I wouldn't miss it." He smiled. "It will be an experience."

"Better than that. You'll be able to test the waters of how it feels to be a member of a real family. I *want* that for you, Caleb."

"Then I want it, too." He opened the door of the Range Rover and watched her get in the passenger seat. "Why don't you call her now on the way to the Run? It seems like a good time."

Jane looked out the window as he started the car. A good time? Smoke. Small fires burning in the forest. Soldiers being taken into custody by MI6. Violence and terror.

But they had overcome all this and soon it would go away. Just a little longer... It was time for life and laughter and the love that could heal all pain.

She punched in Eve's number. "Hi, Eve. Do you feel like having visitors? I need to see you. I'm so excited. Because I have very special news..."

EPILOGUE

I'm big as a house." Jane frowned as she looked down at her belly. "I don't remember you looking like this when you were pregnant with Michael."

"I did. You just don't recall because I always wore my loose chambray shirts all the time when I was working on the reconstructions." Eve brought Jane a cup of tea and sat down on the couch beside her. "You look beautiful. And you're not as big as a house."

"At least a small house," Jane said. "And I can't stand not being able to keep up with Michael when he does his morning runs."

"And you haven't seen Caleb since he and Joe headed to Montana two weeks ago." She gave a mock sigh. "Poor Jane. I guess you've been deserted."

Jane wrinkled her nose. "Okay, I'm behaving like a brat. I guess I don't have enough to do. I finished transferring all the sketches to canvas this week and I've been envying Caleb being busy ever since. Selfish, since I was the one who suggested that he go track down the descendants of Fiona and Farrell MacClaren so that I could determine if MacDuff was right about my really being a relation."

"Actually, I talked you into that," Eve said serenely. "I wanted it settled to put MacDuff out of his misery. And you needed some research to occupy you when you weren't painting. You've always had to be almost feverishly busy to be happy."

"Not feverishly." Jane smiled. "And you can't say I haven't been happy during these last months. I'm always happy with you, Joe, and Michael."

"And we've been happy to have you here," Eve said. "But it's time you stopped marking time and started living again."

Jane's brows rose in surprise. "I beg your pardon?"

"You've been on the phone with MacDuff and Rodland several times every week. It's clear you're worried about the damage done to the castle. If you're that concerned, you need to be there to take care of it yourself."

"Anything else?"

Eve nodded. "And you need to go right away. Most doctors don't like women to travel during late pregnancy."

Jane started to chuckle. "Does Caleb know you're kicking us out? I've been very careful not to even hint that he'd not be welcome in our family."

"And he's aware of that. He's very intelligent and he wants you to be happy. He'll make his own way in our family to assure that ending." She tilted her head. "And naturally I decided I'd have to go through Caleb first to make everything turn out right. I gave him a call last night and we had a nice discussion."

"And?"

"He has that Gulfstream that's super comfortable and I suggested that it would be best for you. He agreed, of course."

"Of course." Her eyes were twinkling as she gazed at Eve. "And he thought you were as wonderful as I do. You're an amazing woman, Eve."

"That goes without saying. We're both amazing. And that's why we can be honest with each other—because we know it's all about love."

Jane got to her feet and gave Eve a hug. "Ever since the beginning," she said huskily as she headed for the porch. "And now I'd better call Caleb and tell him that everything you've planned is great with me. Any other instructions?"

"Call me every other day. Take care of yourself. And tell MacDuff to get a room ready for me, because I'm going to show up when it's time for that little girl to appear on the scene and be with you for the birth."

"All will be as you command." Jane was grinning. "She's already making her every desire known. I can hardly wait to see the two of you together."

———

MACDUFF'S RUN
THREE WEEKS LATER

Jane smothered the scream, her fingernails digging into Caleb's hand. "Did you call Eve?"

"Right after you told me. She said she'd be on her way as soon as she could pack a bag." His gaze was on her face. "I don't like this. Why don't we call an air ambulance and get you to a hospital?"

"By the time we got there, the baby would probably have already been born and be howling her lungs out. You know she marches to her own drummer or she wouldn't have been in such a hurry to send me into labor. It happened in the blink of an eye."

"We should still try to—"

"No!" She tried to keep from screaming at him. "MacDuff said there's a midwife in the village and he's already sent Rodland there to bring her here. It will be fine, Caleb."

"Son of a *bitch*. You're in pain," he said harshly. "I can't take it. There's nothing fine about that."

"But there's nothing that weird about it, either. It's happened to women for thousands of years. Do I like it? Hell, no. But I can put up with it since she seems determined to immediately join the human race." She was feeling dizzy, and she shook her head to clear it. "Maybe she thinks she has something to...say." She tried to keep from slurring. "Or maybe she's an artist like her mom or...even...Rembrandt." She giggled. "Rembrandt. Wouldn't that be cool?"

"Absolutely," he said hoarsely. "Can I go get some whiskey for you?"

"No, I don't know what the rules are. I suppose I should have read up about it."

"You didn't realize she was going to be this impatient. She should give you a break."

"We'll work...it out. I can see you...in her."

"Heaven help you."

"It already did. She's going to be...like Eve. Special...or maybe not...She reminds me of someone...else. Tough, so tough, and ready to take on...the whole world."

"Like you." His grasp on her hand was almost painful. "Where the *hell* is Rodland?"

"No, not me either. Don't be so upset. I told you...this kind of thing happens all the time. It...happened to her..."

"Who?"

"Here I am." Rodland suddenly burst into the room, dragging a plump dark-haired woman behind him. "And this is Eileen Cameron. She's going to help you, Jane."

"Thank God," Caleb said. "*Do* something."

The woman had already lifted the covers and was appraising the situation. "It appears that it's already been done," she said. "All we can do is help her along." She patted Jane's knee. "The babe's in a bit of a hurry. I told the laird that I thought she would be when I saw you walking in the courtyard the other day. Sometimes I can tell. Relax now."

"She's in pain," Caleb said between set teeth. "Make it stop."

"Happens all the time," the midwife said cheerfully.

"I'm getting tired of hearing that."

"I've got a potion I can give her," Eileen said.

"Do it," Caleb said.

Jane was vaguely aware that his tone was very sharp. "Rodland, get him . . . out of here."

Caleb shook his head. "I want to see what she's going to give you."

"Rodland . . ."

Rodland whisked Caleb out of the room and Jane relaxed. She smiled at Eileen. "You're right, she's . . . in a hurry. Let's help her along. And maybe someday she'll do the same for us."

"Wouldn't surprise me, ma'am. Now take a little of this potion . . ."

"Bitter . . ."

"The little girl doesn't mind. She just wants you to relax and then help her come out. All right, here she comes . . ."

———◆———

Jane screamed!

And the baby was howling with indignation.

Caleb was instantly in the room. "I told you not to hurt her. What kind of—"

"The mother's doing fine. Couldn't be healthier." Eileen was beaming. "Neither could the baby."

"Take her, Caleb," Jane gasped. "It's you she wants now." She watched Eileen wrap the baby in a blanket. "I think she could tell how upset you were." She turned to Rodland. "Get MacDuff in here. I want to talk to him. Now! I'm so tired I'm afraid I'm going to drift off..." She turned to the midwife. "Eileen, make certain that doesn't happen." She looked at Caleb, who was now holding the baby, gazing down at her face with wonder. The baby had stopped crying and was staring intently back at him. Then she closed her eyes with a contented whimper and turned her cheek into his arm.

"What...do I do with...her," he murmured.

"You know," Jane whispered. "You'll always know. I told you that, Caleb."

"You did, didn't you?" He was smiling down at her. "Maybe the first thing I should do is give her to Eileen to clean up so that you can take her back. It appears I'm no longer needed at the moment."

"You'll always be needed...by both of us. But you might be wise to go with Eileen or the baby might start to howl again. She didn't want to let you go. I think she was afraid she might not get you back."

He shook his head. "She's got me, hook, line, and sinker."

"She might not have known that. She's very smart, but after all, she just met you a couple of minutes ago."

"I'll make certain to reinforce it twenty-four hours a day."

He handed the baby to Eileen and bent down and kissed Jane. "She's as beautiful as you are," he whispered. "But maybe one child could be enough? I don't know if I can go through another day like today."

"Yes, you can." She kissed him back. "Stop being a wimp. We did this great. Now get out of here. MacDuff is going to be here any minute."

"I wondered why you sent Rodland to get him. It seemed a peculiar time to demand to see the laird. You intend to tell him about the spur?"

She nodded. "We've waited long enough. I thought I'd give MacDuff a special birthday present." She grinned. "It will keep him busy plotting and planning how to find where that other treasure is located while I'm recovering. That way we'll be ready to go on another treasure hunt by the time I'm totally well and functioning again." She frowned. "Though it might not be as quick or efficient as we'd like. Remember? It took us all a while to find the other treasure trove in that cave." She chuckled. "Our tiny baby daughter might be big enough to resemble the *Mist Child* before we discover where this other treasure is hidden. But that might be fun. We could take her along and she'd probably love it."

"You have it all planned." He smiled. "How do you know that she won't be a wonderful, ladylike little princess who won't want to go after hidden treasure?"

"Because she's our daughter. I just have a feeling that she'll do what comes naturally to her." She paused. "And MacDuff won't let her totally leave these Highlands any more than he let me. But she'll love MacDuff's Run just as I do. It won't be the prison that Fiona thought it because our child will make it her own, just as she'll do with the lake cottage. She'll have the personality and the guts to take what she wants from the world and make it her own."

"Yes, she will," he said gently.

"And that's what I was thinking when I was sketching in that train that day. That things change, but they can remain the same if we have the strength to take the right steps." She rubbed her temple. "I'm getting tired. Go see if you can hurry MacDuff in here before I fade away."

"You'll never fade away. You'll always blaze your own path." He was whisking Eileen out the door. "I'll bring the baby back to you right away."

"That's what I want for our little girl," Jane called after him. "That she'll never fade away... That every move she makes will be bold and brave."

"So be it." He glanced over his shoulder. "But we've been talking in pronouns again. Isn't it time you told me what name you've chosen? Eve?"

Jane smiled. "No, Eve is a supreme individualist. She wouldn't thank me for naming our daughter after her. She will love her and take care of her, but she'll want her to be on her own and independent." She added, "But I did think it was time that we did honor someone who was totally independent, who started life as a slave but was strong enough to have made her mark on life and all the people who came after her." She smiled. "And that mark has never faded away for the last two thousand years."

"Ah, Cira?"

Her smile became brilliant. "You've got it. And we can only hope our child will blaze her own path just as boldly. We're going to call our daughter Cira!"

ABOUT THE AUTHOR

Iris Johansen is the #1 *New York Times* bestselling author of more than fifty consecutive bestsellers. Her series featuring forensic sculptor Eve Duncan has sold over twenty million copies and counting and was the subject of the acclaimed Lifetime movie *The Killing Game*. Along with her son, Roy, Iris has also co-authored the *New York Times* bestselling series featuring investigator Kendra Michaels. Johansen lives near Atlanta, Georgia.

Learn more at:

IrisJohansen.com
Twitter @Iris_Johansen
Facebook.com/OfficialIrisJohansen